The Nostradamus Traitor

By the same author

THE BOYSIE OAKES BOOKS

THE LIQUIDATOR
UNDERSTRIKE
AMBER NINE
MADRIGAL
FOUNDER MEMBER
TRAITOR'S EXIT
THE AIRLINE PIRATES
A KILLER FOR A SONG

DEREK TORRY NOVELS

A COMPLETE STATE OF DEATH
THE CORNER MEN

NOVELS

THE CENSOR
EVERY NIGHT'S A BULLFIGHT
TO RUN A LITTLE FASTER
THE WEREWOLF TRACE
THE DANCING DODO

THE MORIARTY JOURNALS

THE RETURN OF MORIARTY
THE REVENGE OF MORIARTY

AUTOBIOGRAPHY

SPIN THE BOTTLE

COLLECTIONS OF SHORT STORIES

HIDEAWAY
THE ASSASSINATION FILE

The Nostradamus Traitor

by

John Gardner

BOOK CLUB ASSOCIATES LONDON

This edition published 1979 by
Book Club Associates
by arrangement with Hodder & Stoughton Ltd.

Printed in Great Britain by
Richard Clay (The Chaucer Press) Ltd.,
Bungay, Suffolk

In Memory of S.W.'s Father
GEORGE THOMAS

Killed over Germany 1945
R.I.P.

Who was the first agent from the operations branch of F Section to reach French soil? The question is straightforward; the answer is not. The war diary for March 1941 includes a laconic remark under a French section heading: 'After a second failure to land the Brittany Agent, the operation was successfully carried out on the night of 27th'. An undated postwar note of Thackthwaite's in an honours and awards file mentions that the agent was a gaullist one. Nothing else seems to be recorded about him, not even his name or field name; and for lack of evidence about him we must assume that he fell straight into enemy hands or that he joined some other service on arrival.

M. R. D. Foot: *The S.O.E. In France 1940–44* pp. 161–2

I

She was dressed in a severe grey suit: stylish, but cut by a tailor who lacked flair. No overcoat, in spite of the chill overcast afternoon.

Yeoman Warder Kemp watched her approach with some apprehension. Though he had been with the elite band of pensioned NCOs and Warrant Officers who make up the Yeoman Warders of the Tower of London for less than six months, Kemp had learned to smell out the questioners before they reached him. This one had questioner stamped all over her plumping figure.

It still amazed Kemp that, whatever the season or weather, tourists flooded the Tower in droves. The magic of its horrors and associations was an historic magnet which defeated snow, ice, rain, fog or heat. Even now, early on this unpleasant spring afternoon, the place was full, and the usual long queue snaked from the Wakefield Tower to view the Crown Jewels.

He turned and walked two paces down the path, his back to the rising stone of the White Tower, as though to meet the woman half way.

She would be late fifties, early sixties, he judged; the hips filling out and breasts starting to sag heavily: hair, once golden now almost silver. Flecked with gold—Kemp imagined that he had a poetic bent. Good looking piece at one time. The face had the bone structure for it; the high cheek bones and good jaw line, yet even that was starting to flesh out. Her eyes, however, were remarkably clear—grey, like the colour of the suit she wore and the day itself. Shrewd eyes, taking in everything and already holding Kemp steadily as she drew near.

She was foreign, he was pretty certain of that; but, the school outings apart, most visitors were foreign—Yanks, Arabs, Pakis, Nips. They all came to have a sniff at Britain's past. The English who came were in the minority; though, to Kemp's delight, the Tower seemed to be on most Scottish people's visiting lists.

9

'Excuse me.'

He had been right. Middle European accent. Kraut probably.
'Ma'am?'

'I am trying to find someone in authority.'

'Perhaps I can help. What is it exactly that you're ... ?'

'No, I think not. I need someone in authority.'

'If you could tell me, Ma'am. Difficult to get to see any of the office people here without an appointment. Or do you, perhaps, have an appointment with somebody?'

'No. No. There is a Governor of the Tower of London, yes?'

'Yes. The Major of the Tower. He acts as Governor in Residence. Not an easy man to see.'

'He would have records?'

'That depends what it was you wanted to know. Now the guide book...'

She smiled, as though out of pity for him. 'No, it will not be in any guide book.'

'Ah, well, I'm not sure. If you could give me some inkling ...'

'Inkling?' Her brow furrowed.

'Some hint.'

'Ah.' The woman paused, her eyes leaving Kemp's face for the flutter of a moment. Then back again. An intake of breath; controlled, but like someone about to take a plunge into icy water. 'Very well. Your name first though, please. You are a Beefeater, yes?'

'Yeoman Warder, Ma'am. Beefeater's a kind of nickname.'

'So.'

'Yeoman Warder Arthur Kemp.'

'Kemp,' she repeated so that it came out 'Camp.'

He nodded.

'I am Hildegarde Fenderman. Frau Fenderman. I come from Germany. The West. The Federal Republic; though for a long time I lived in the East. This is my first opportunity to visit England. I came from the East, with permission, a year ago, and have been made a citizen of the Federal Republic. I came to nurse my sister who is now dead, leaving me a little money. This is how I make this visit. It is a pilgrimage here to the Tower of London.' She hesitated, as though uncertain whether she should continue.

'Yes?' Kemp prodded.

'I come, because I wish to see where my husband died and where he is buried.'

'Your husband?'

'Claus Fenderman. He was a spy, Mr. Kemp. A spy for the Nazis. Your people caught him, I understand. I am told he was executed here, in the Tower of London. May 16th, 1941. It is not in your guide book.'

When telling the story long afterwards, Kemp could not resist a touch of the dramatic. He would say that he went cold. Looking over Frau Fenderman's shoulder he could see across one corner of Tower Green to the Chapel Royal of St. Peter ad Vincula. On the Green, many people had gone to their deaths and some of them—including Anne Boleyn, Catherine Howard, Lady Jane Grey, Monmouth and Essex—lay at rest within the Chapel. Yeoman Warder Kemp was one hundred per cent certain that Frau Fenderman's husband, Claus, was not among them.

2

Before retirement to the Yeoman Warders, Arthur Kemp had served with the same Scottish regiment for the best part of thirty years. Roughly a decade of that time had been spent as Warrant Officer to the Regimental Intelligence Officer. He had, in fact, seen off three IOs who, in their time, had been promoted laterally, in the perpendicular, and, in one sad case, horizontally. But Warrant Officer Kemp had always remained. The reasons for this were simple. He was dedicated and cunning; a double-triple-checking bastard, with a highly developed sense of suspicion.

It had been said of Kemp that, on the Day of Judgement, he would step forward and demand to see the Archangel Gabriel's authority in writing, his ID, and a certificate from the Celestial School of Music before one note could be blown on the Last Trump.

Kemp was highly sceptical now, about Frau Fenderman and her unlamented ex-agent husband; yet he retained a correct and courteous attitude towards her, giving the impression that he would do all within his meagre power to help in her quest: making it plain that it might take a day or two. Did she have that kind of time? She did. She would be in London for at least ten days.

From under his tunic, Kemp drew out a small, four-ringed plastic covered notebook into which he carefully recorded details in a smart, legible, hand. Full name; place of birth (Dresden); nationality ('You did say they'd granted you a Federal Republic passport?'); passport number; address during her stay in London. The latter turned out to be a small private hotel in Bayswater.

'Know it well, Frau Fenderman, know it well. Now, someone will be in touch once I've passed these details on. You'll get an interview here no doubt. Just leave it to me.'

She thanked him, nodding slowly several times—a woman well-used to answering questions and filling in forms.

Kemp watched her walk away towards the Bloody Tower and through the gate which would take her out, past the café and souvenir shop to the modern main entrance. Returning his notebook, he glanced at his watch and made a mental note of the time. There were a little over twenty minutes of his duty left to run before the relief would arrive.

By rights he should report the incident to the senior Yeoman Warder, but ex-Warrant Officer Kemp's experience in these matters told him that if he followed that course of action nothing would be done.

Less than an hour later, notebook held like a weapon, Kemp stood outside the Major of the Tower's office, having cut aside all possible red tape and asked for an appointment, *on a matter of utmost urgency*: Kemp's dramatic phraseology.

Within two hours of Frau Fenderman's conversation with the Yeoman Warder, the Major of the Tower was on the telephone making two short calls—one to a Home Office contact, the other to an old school friend at the Foreign Office. The Foreign Office won hands down.

Nobody really imagined that there was anything desperately important attached to this odd request, from a German national wishing to see where her husband had been executed and buried, but the Foreign Office man was sharp and knew all about intelligence straw gathering. At least he could place the report.

Kemp was recalled to the Major of the Tower's office where he repeated his statement which was then typed up for him to read and sign.

At about eight that evening, a nondescript youth on a motorcycle picked up the document from the Tower.

3

Herbie Kruger got the job. Big Herbie as the older and more knowledgeable called him to his face. Juniors copied their elders in this, but had a tendency to be unkind. They said Herbie was burned out. It happens to legends in all walks of life. Herbie was a Cold War legend. For part of the Fifties and Sixties he ran a straggling, widely spread network within the Deutsche Demo-kratische Republik; on the ground itself, with plain local cover as an engineer—and no help from the diplomats. His was the last group of cells to get rolled up in the mid-1960s purge, and Herbie only got out by his fingernails.

Since then, having once been a German national, they'd given him trade cover in Bonn, but that began to get threadbare so London brought him home, gave him what the wags called a grace and favour flat in St. John's Wood, and an office in the Annexe off Whitehall where he looked after some of the Eastern Bloc paperwork and went out on vetting jobs when the Trade Delegations came to town.

Where it really mattered they had few doubts about Herbie Kruger. They certainly did not think of him as being over the hill. At forty-eight he was at the height of his powers and it was even suggested that if the Federal Government in Bonn had left him alone they might well have been spared a great deal of the embarrassment over the long-term filching of NATO documents which came to light towards the end of '77. Herbie always main-tained that the pundits were wrong and that modern intelligence gathering was not merely a question of satellites, computers, and electronic hardware.

When the Bonn NATO secrets disaster first became known in Whitehall, Herbie smiled, shrugged and said it was inevitable: there were not enough human bodies on the ground. Those who mattered did not shrug; they cursed the Treasury for its short-sighted niggardliness and nodded wisely to Herbie, for they agreed. They agreed to such an extent that Herbie Kruger's desk in the Annexe was, in fact, cover for a recruiting drive.

What Herbie Kruger was really doing among the Eastern Bloc paperwork and the Trade Delegations was quietly putting together a new team to be manipulated in Germany—a pair of watchers in Bonn and a brand-new cell in the East. All this he would run from London. Hence the current job landing on Herbie's desk on the morning after Yeoman Warder Kemp's conversation with Frau Fenderman.

Herbie had massive hands to scale with the rest of him : hands which put the fear of God into friends and enemies alike. Particularly when their owner was drunk. Now the hands caressed the flimsy document with that characteristic gentleness of which big men are so often capable.

This gentle manner had given Herbie Kruger another nickname among the lowest echelon juniors who, behind his back, called him Moose Malloy—after the character in Raymond Chandler's *Farewell My Lovely*.

Young Worboys and his crony Hablin went as far as a bad impersonation of Herbie uttering Malloy's immortal line, 'Cute as lace pants', following which they would collapse in giggles like a pair of schoolboys.

When this second nickname came to the attention of the Director, he nodded and smiled, for it was apt. Big Herbie could not hide, nondescript, in a crowd like the perfect covert operator, but he had other assets. He looked as thick as lumpy porridge and had a slow and decidedly stupid smile which had been the undoing of many people.

He was smiling now as he read Yeoman Warder Kemp's statement for the third time, though the smile was directed at the line of writing, in the Director's green ink, scrawled at the foot of the page. *Thought you would be interested. Suggest you check out and keep happy, warm or on ice!!*

For all the outward display of lumbering good humour, drunkenness (well-attested by any of the juniors who had been invited for an evening out with Herbie), and sentimentality (again verbally documented and often taking the form of floods of tears while both stoned and conducting Mahler on the stereo), Herbie Kruger was as methodical as they came.

After reading the document for a fourth time, he leaned back, large fingers laced behind his dome of a head, and considered the correct line of approach. After ten minutes he picked up the telephone and put in a call to the Bayswater private hotel and discovered that Frau Fenderman was registered there but out at the moment.

He then called Pix and asked them to send up a bright boy whom he instructed to go out into the wilds of W.2 and get what he described as 'A set of sneak previews'.

Next he rang Registry and asked about the status of their files on German espionage agents (1934 through '45), arrested, tried and executed in the United Kingdom. They did not hold the files, he was told. Special Branch had them in the archives at the Yard so he filled in a *Most Urgent* requisition and boosted it along to the Director for action. To underline the urgent part he called Tubby Fincher who was food taster and whipping boy for the Chief and let him know that he wanted the files last week. Tubby sighed and pointed out that they would be restricted and that the SB would try to heel tap. To which Herbie promised that he would personally heel tap—on people's asses—if he didn't have what he wanted by the morning.

That left two more calls. One to Grosvenor Square, the other to the West German Embassy in Belgrave Square.

'No sweat,' his CIA contact in Grosvenor Square said. If they had any details on Frau Hildegarde Fenderman they'd be passed on. He'd go rake over a few files right away.

The representative from the BND, the Bundesrepublik Deutschland's equivalent security service, did not give a direct yes or no until Herbie hinted that he would share any resultant information. It was always a question of horse trading with the West German boys—especially with their recent record of security failures.

During the afternoon, Herbie got Tubby to come over to the Annexe—Tubby being privy to almost everything the Old Man did or thought.

Herbie half-rose when Tubby—so-called because of his emaciated build—arrived. He also gave his Moose Malloy smile.

'Ah, the Chief's ear. Frau Fenderman.'

Tubby dropped into a chair as though exhausted, nodding before his skeletal rump hit the seat.

'It's okay, Herbie. I've talked to the SB personally. Restricted, of course, but they're supposed to be pulling the stuff you want today. In turn they want it back pronto.'

'Copy the lot. I would in your shoes. Stuff like that could produce results. I've been thinking ...'

Herbie went on to slowly expand his theory that surviving members of Nazi agents' families should be checked as a matter of routine. It was a vague and somewhat pointless theory, but Tubby knew Herbie Kruger well enough to detect this was mere chat, vocal deflection before he came in with his real request.

'What you want, Herbie?'

'Ah. Well, I thought, maybe, it would be a good idea if you called Frau Fenderman at her hotel to fix the appointment. If she gets a thick accent like mine over the telephone ...' The thought drifted off like smoke.

'If she's got a conscience.' Tubby nodded. 'Anything to hide from East or West she might scarper.'

'A good Anglo-Saxon voice, I think. That would be best.'

So the call was made, the appointment fixed. No names. Just that a Civil Servant would like to give her tea the following afternoon to discuss the matter of her request made at the Tower. Five o'clock. She would arrange the tea at her hotel.

Herbie hoped that by then the files would have arrived and that his security contacts at the American and West German Embassies would have given him negatives or positives. He went back to St. John's Wood alone that night, ate a hearty dinner, drank almost a whole bottle of gin, watched a mediocre TV play and then listened to the Mahler Ninth with all its forebodings of death.

He did not cry—as he often did with certain visitors present. Instead he allowed the music to let his mind range over the network he was setting up, wondering from time to time if Frau Fenderman would turn out to be a likely recruit.

On the table, laid out in a neat row, were the six matt prints he had selected from the Pix man's sneak previews. He thought how good looking Frau Fenderman must have been twenty or thirty years ago. At least her husband, Claus, probably went to his death with fond memories of her.

4

Grosvenor Square turned in a blank, but, with all its usual Teutonic thoroughness, Herbie's contact at the West German Embassy produced a small folder of documents with bare, though essential, details regarding Frau Hildegarde Fenderman.

It was known that she was born in Dresden on January 25th, 1922, which, Herbie thought, made her younger than she appeared in her photograph. Fifty-six looking sixty-three or four.

Widow. He knew that. If her story tallied she had been widowed at the age of nineteen.

No details of her life before the end of the war. In 1948 she was working in East Berlin. Secretarial work, it said, for the Department of Labour. In 1958 she was in charge of an office connected with the Ministry of Culture. Until the clamps came down, in 1961, she made infrequent visits to her sister, Fräulein Gretchen Weiss, who worked for the American Secretariat and was four years Hildegarde's junior.

Once the East put the screws on, Gretchen had tried to make yearly visits to her sister in the East. Three out of four came off.

Then, in '73 Fräulein Weiss was taken ill. Diagnosis: cancer of the right lung. The Americans operated, and there was partial recovery, but inevitably she eventually started going downhill. There was record that, on June 15th, 1975, Gretchen Weiss asked for assistance in getting her sister permanently into the West. Reading between the lines, Herbie Kruger could see that some kind of low-grade diplomatic efforts were made on her behalf. In the following year the DDR relented and allowed Frau Fenderman a permanent exit visa.

By the autumn of '76 she was nursing her sister through the final stages of illness, and had been granted a Bundesrepublik passport. Fräulein Gretchen Weiss died on September 3rd, 1977, leaving her small apartment and the equivalent of some £15,000 in Deutschmarks to her sister—a tidy sum for a national who had worked for the American Secretariat.

The appended intelligence report was a simple, *Nothing known or suspect*. That covered a multitude of sins, omissions and possibilities, particularly in the light of the American negative response.

Herbie Kruger thought it smelled. Not strongly, but a hint of something carried on the breeze from Berlin. True, there had been a slackening of the rigidity between East and West in 1976. But Herbie had a lot of suspicion going when it came to relatives being given permanent exit visas. Family pressures often brought with them temptations—particularly when applied to the split and divided country that was once the Third Reich.

Strange, he thought, that the Americans did not offer a report on the sister of one who had worked for them. Particularly one who had so obviously worked hard and effectively. He made a mental note: what did Hildegarde Fenderman's sister actually do for the US Secretariat?

He had just turned from the problem of Frau Fenderman to his daily paperwork when the files from the Yard Archives arrived.

The year 1941 was not particularly good. Twenty-five arrests had been made, but nineteen were simply on questions of nationality. Ten of those were held under the Detention of Aliens Act. The other nine were either errors or pliable material. According to the records they had been returned undamaged.

Six were unfortunate. Tried. Found guilty of espionage. Executed. None, according to the records, on May 16th; or at the Tower of London. None bore the name Claus Fenderman, but Herbie was not over worried about that. In the secret world, names—true names—were often lost for ever.

He sent the six dossiers down for copying, with a request that they lift the photographs and let him have a batch of ten-by-eights.

The name Fenderman did not appear in any of the files, from 1934 right through to '45.

It was after two o'clock in the afternoon when he got back to the day's normal paperwork, and the first thing confronting him was a memo that the Director would be away on the Washington trip for the best part of a month. All queries and new files were to go through the Deputy Director.

Herbie Kruger was not keen on Sir Willis Maitland-Wood, the

DD. Better the devil you know, he thought.

At four, Tubby called down with the suggestion that one of the juniors got in some practice on the ground and kept an eye on him from afar during the teatime meeting in Bayswater. They sent up Worboys, and Herbie gave him a rundown without telling him anything.

Worboys left at four-twenty which gave Big Herbie enough time to sign out of the building and get to a pay 'phone, where he called one of his already selected new team. If Herbie had to have someone playing ass-watcher, he preferred one who knew the ropes.

It started to rain just as he hailed a cab and asked for the next street to that in which Frau Fenderman's hotel was located.

5

Bayswater lies to the north of Kensington Gardens. To those who have a sensibility about these matters, Bayswater is on the wrong side of Kensington Gardens. There are one or two moderate three star hotels in the area. There are also some pretty dreadful pensions intermingled with many which try to be refined. Some are good, but to the point of anonymity. Such is the Devonshire Hotel with its twenty bedrooms, small dining room and residents' lounge. The staff are few, mainly European, but try to please.

Hildegarde Fenderman had done her best to persuade the staff to serve what she felt was a typical English afternoon tea in the residents' lounge.

When Herbie Kruger arrived, he found himself expected, and Frau Fenderman already seated next to a table which carried cups, heavy tea, and hot water, pots, a plate of triangular sandwiches and another with little cakes, each in a crinkled paper container.

Herbie, who carried an official-looking briefcase full of buff forms and yellow paper, did his best to look awkward and out of place: not hard for one who has spent most of his life doing that kind of job.

Though Frau Fenderman was alone in the lounge, Herbie stared around foolishly, as though this lady could not be the one he expected to see. He opened the batting in German, taking in her face and, particularly, the eyes, searching for signs of momentary panic. He detected something. Surprise possibly. Close up, Hildegarde Fenderman indeed did look a good five or six years older than her true age.

'It was thought that someone who spoke your native tongue ...' He flapped his arms and almost knocked over the tea tray with his briefcase. 'In a delicate situation like this ... A painful situation for you ...'

She shook her head slowly and motioned him to put his briefcase down and take a seat. The circumstances were not painful to her any more, she said, speaking softly as though the room was full of other residents. He started to take off his coat and she stood up, putting out her hands to assist, but he waved her away in the same clumsy motion he was using to free the raincoat from his body. He reminded her of a large snake making heavy weather of shedding its skin. Finally she took the garment from him and put it over the back of a spare chair.

'It is raining, Herr ... ?' as she felt the dampness on the collar.

'Nothing. A fine drizzle. Kruger. Mr. Kruger. Eberhardt Kruger.'

He patted his pockets, going through each in turn until, with a grin of triumph, he produced a card which was proof that he was indeed Eberhardt Kruger Esq., Assistant to the Chief Archivist, Public Records Office. With a self-effacing motion of the hands, he said that he was really only one of many assistants.

'You are German?' She had him organised now, sitting down, though still fiddling with the briefcase, first holding it on his knees, then trying to make up his mind whether it would be better at his feet, or by the side of the chair.

'I am nationalised British. Second generation. Born in Hanover, but our father brought us here in the Thirties—soon after I was born. Funny, though, we spoke nothing but German at home. I still have the accent when I speak English, but it does not seem to trouble the Civil Service.' He gave his slow foolish smile and she lowered her eyes, asking if he would take tea.

No sugar, and the milk in last. Just like my father, she told him. 'My father liked his milk in last: that was when he drank tea.'

'In Dresden?' Herbie queried. 'Yes,' she nodded, cocking her head in what was obviously a characteristic mannerism, then pouring the tea which gave Herbie a chance to fiddle with the briefcase and watch her at the same time. She seemed poised, calm. No shake of the hand. Good bone structure, as Kemp had said, but the face starting to go flabby. Too many pastries, he diagnosed. Her hair was striking: soft and full with a twinkle of the original gold flecking the grey.

He managed to plunge his hand into the briefcase just as she passed him the cup of tea.

'I have to establish certain things,' he began once they were properly settled, knowing that he must present a ridiculous picture, seated on the edge of the chair with a minute cress and cream-cheese sandwich in his great paw.

'Naturally.'

The papers were out now, he went into the business of her identity; age; status. Then—

'Two days ago you made a statement to one of the Yeoman Warders of the Tower of London. You claimed that your husband, er . . .' he referred to his notes before naming Claus Fenderman and repeating her claim that he had been executed at the Tower on May 16th, 1941.

'That is so. Out of respect I wished to see where my husband died. It is not morbid, you understand.'

Herbie waved his big hand as if to say that he would swat anyone who even suggested such a thing. Then he tried his first deflection shots and asked where she had been on that day—on May 16th, 1941.

She answered immediately. She had been in the Reich Ministry of Propaganda. She worked there. Herbie said that she must have been very young. Hildegarde Fenderman looked at him steadily, right in the eyes—or directly between them, Herbie thought— and said she was nineteen at the time. She worked at the Ministry from 1939 until just before the end.

'And you were married to Claus Fenderman?'

'On April 30th, 1941.'

My God, less than a month. Aloud he said they should have been on their honeymoon. She said they were, but Claus was recalled.

'What exactly was he? You say he was a spy. Arrested and executed by May 16th, 1941—two weeks after you married. I'm afraid I do not understand this, Frau Fenderman.'

She told him, simply, with no drama. Not even a hint of sadness. 'My husband was with the SS. With the Ausland SD. You know . . . ?'

Herbie nodded and said he knew the Ausland SD was the Foreign Intelligence Service. 'Rank?' he snapped, sounding like a Hollywood SS man.

'Hauptsturmführer,' she snapped back, as if they were playing a game. A Captain in the SS Foreign Intelligence Service. Married and dead, in two different countries, in just over two weeks. He asked her how long she had known her Captain. Not long. A matter of weeks. A whirlwind romance. They were given per-

23

mission to marry. He had three weeks' leave—he was stationed in Berlin. About the 11th or 12th of May he was ordered to return to Berlin (they were honeymooning in the Black Forest). She saw him last on the 13th. He was on a special mission.

'Three days later he was supposed to be executed in the Tower of London. How can that be?' Herbie smiled and spread his hands. 'Who told you all this?'

'That he was dead? Fräulein Hildebrandt, the Reischminister's secretary. I would run messages for her sometimes. She sent for me—it would be a week or so later—and told me. She was very good, like a mother. Very good.'

'What did she actually tell you?'

'Just that he had been killed.'

'No details?'

'No. Later I had the details. Excuse.' She picked up her handbag and drew from it two letters.

They were worn, stuck together with sellotape, faded, but had the look of the real thing. One was an official notification letter— *It is my painful duty to tell you that your husband ... died on active service for the Fatherland and the Führer ...* It was signed by Himmler as Reichsführer of the SS.

The other was from Fenderman's boss: SS-Brigadeführer Walter Schellenberg himself. Big Herbie scanned it quickly. For the Chief of Foreign Intelligence, Schellenberg had been uncharacteristically indiscreet.

You must be aware that your husband was on a mission of great importance to the Reich and, particularly, to the Führer. The mission was on enemy territory and your husband was arrested and died bravely as a soldier on May 16th, 1941.

Herbie pointed out that there was no mention of execution in the Tower of London.

'I went to see Schellenberg.'

'Yes?'

'I only saw his adjutant.' She gave a little smile. 'He said he really should say nothing, but Claus was on a secret mission in England. He was arrested and shot almost immediately. In the Tower. He said that. He said that all officers arrested for spying in England were taken to the Tower and shot. No trial. Nothing.'

Gently, Herbie leaned forward and told her that it was not true. Things were not done like that in England. Not even during

24

the war. She said she knew now that it was not likely. But . . .

The 'but' had a tail to it, trailing something else, as though she had been hiding vital facts. For a moment he wondered if she had falsified the dates, but they were plain enough on the letters from Himmler and Schellenberg. She looked away, as though caught in some act of deceit, then sighed.

'There is something else. He wrote to me. It was, what do you call it? A strict breach of security?'

Herbie nodded, asking if she had that letter.

Silently she reached for her handbag again, retrieved the official letters from Herbie and handed him another, complete in its faded envelope. It was addressed to Frau Fenderman. He did not recognise the name of the street. Berlin. There was no stamp or frank, only a *By Hand, Confidential* scrawl.

Inside were two sheets of plain paper. No letterhead. The date was May 13th, 1941, and a quick glance told him that the first page, at least, was full of written endearments. He held the pages uneasily, sliding his eyes over the love talk and turning quickly to the second page, and the part that mattered—

You are not to worry if you do not hear from me for some time. I should not say this, but I go on a mission of great secrecy to England. Burn this. It would not be good if anyone discovered it. Think of me, my dearest . . . and so into the intimacies again.

Big Herbie shook his head. No wonder Claus Fenderman got himself lifted if he wrote letters like this to his wife. But, then it was all so full of holes. The cold, educated, SS Intelligence whizz-kid, Schellenberg, writing a letter of condolence like the one he had just read. The dates. The absurdity.

After the scribbled signature, at the bottom of the page, there were four extra lines and a notation. No explanation, simply—

> The kingdom stripped of its forces by fraud.
> The fleet blockaded, passages for the spy:
> Two false friends will come to rally
> To awaken hatred a long time dormant.
> *Nostradamus, VII: 33.*

God in heaven. A quotation from the prophecies of Michel de Nostradame: doctor, seer, astrologer to the court of Catherine de'Medici. A small signal triggered itself in Herbie Kruger's mind, but he couldn't finger it. Instead, he asked Frau Fenderman why she had not burned the letter as her husband instructed. She was vague. You know how it is when you are in love?

'This quotation ... ?' he began.

'Nostradamus,' a small nod, as though acknowledging the obvious.

'A code? Something which interested you both?'

She said, no. Claus had spoken about astrology a couple of times and she had seen him with copies of *Zenit*—the officially sponsored astrological magazine. But she had no interest.

'Why? I mean why this quotation here in the letter you should have destroyed?'

She had no idea. It had puzzled her for years, and could only presume that this was some clue to what he was to do in England.

It all seemed highly improbable to Herbie—particularly the insecurity of the whole business, not to mention the timing.

He let silence fall between them, sipping his tea and helping himself to one of the sticky cakes. It was sickly and not really to his taste. The silence stretched out to breaking point as he looked at her with a vacant expression, as if he had nothing to say, no facility for small talk or anything outside his daily round.

Eventually, he spoke—'We will do all that is possible, Frau Fenderman. Anything we can do. You are here for some days?'

He left the photographs until last, as he was gathering his things together. 'Ah, yes. One more thing.' Delving into the briefcase to extract the six pictures of the men who had actually been executed for espionage in Britain during 1941.

He handed them to her, one at a time, asking her to study each one with care.

She took them in turn, spending a long while, like somebody uncertain, whose word might identify a murderer.

'You see anyone you recognise?'

Slowly she shook her head. 'No. I am supposed to know one of these people?'

6

Herbie Kruger walked down to the Bayswater Road, hailed a cab and asked for St. John's Wood underground station. The drizzle was turning to heavy rain now and he had been lucky to get a cab easily. The evening traffic hell was starting to build up to its crescendo.

At the station he paid off the cab, bought a *Standard*, and walked slowly up Finchley Road until the blue Rover pulled out of the traffic and halted long enough for him to get in—a feat he performed with amazing speed for one of such a size.

Worboys ignored the illegal trumpet voluntary of irate horns and pulled back into the traffic. 'You're clean as a whistle,' he said.

'Nothing?' Herbie sounded disgruntled.

'I did the whole road before you arrived. Checked the windows. The lot. Clean as a whistle,' he repeated.

Herbie said that was good, and that Worboys could now drive him home. 'Take your time. Do a few of the back-doubles,' pulling down the mirror on the passenger side and watching their own back, occasionally giving directions—'Left here, then a quick right ... Now pull over and reverse into that road ... Wait one minute then we'll go back the way we came.' Like giving someone a driving test—which, in fact, he was doing: that and more.

Worboys was less than gracious, being one of those young juniors who think they know it all from the word go. At last Herbie took them to his block, told him to check the car back in (*No joyriding with your girls tonight*), and walked the hundred yards or so that brought him to his own apartment building.

Inside, he built himself a large gin and tonic, then carefully settled down to wait, first selecting the Mahler Fourth because he knew there would not be long to wait.

In the cab he had switched off the trigger which had been activated by the Nostradamus quotation. Frau Fenderman had

27

worked for the Reich Ministry of Propaganda. Sly Goebbels had used some of those odd and pliant prophecies as propaganda during World War II. He had no exact memory of details, but they were mentioned in several books. Hadn't he used the famous one?—the one occultists claimed mentioned Hitler—to help soften up the French. Certainly the Psychological Warfare people had used them, or versions of them, for retaliation. Playing them back. Might be worth looking up a file or two.

Then he thought of the whole ludicrous business of Frau Fenderman and her Claus. Maybe she was worth examining at close quarters. Maybe she could be used. Certainly he'd have to talk with the Americans who could only be withholding. As for the matter of her husband, the executed spy, it was all so vague and unlikely. Maybe she was working some kind of come-on. Yes, see the boys in Grosvenor Square and ask what they were playing at; what Gretchen Weiss had done for them. How they'd sweet-talked the East into letting Hildegarde Fenderman out for life.

Had there indeed been a Claus Fenderman? Certainly there had been a Gretchen Weiss. For a second he wondered if Hildegarde Fenderman was the original Hildegarde Weiss from Dresden.

The bell buzzed from downstairs. 'Yes?' he asked the Entryphone grille.

'Schnabeln,' said the voice from below.

Big Herbie pressed the electronic lock that would admit his visitor to the elevator. A minute later he was ushering him in—a small man, neat with cheeks like Red Delicious apples. He was one of Herbie Kruger's new team—the one who was doing the real ass-watching.

'There were two of them.' He took the proffered gin with a nod, then put it down to remove his soggy raincoat. 'Two of them, apart from your boy wonder.' He spoke without a trace of an accent.

'So.' Herbie looked interested.

Mahler came to an end.

'I went in and asked about availability of rooms next month. She was the one in the grey suit?'

'Yes.'

'Running to fat?'

Herbie nodded.

'Pity I didn't have a camera. One was with her. Just leaving as I got there. Tall, mouse hair, thinning, small moustache. Dark blue raincoat. Had DDR written all over him. Thanked her in English and left.'

Herbie nodded again and began to rebuild his shattered drink.

'They had a Mini Clubman parked up the street. No cameras from what I could see. You threw them off in the traffic.'

'When I made the Rover?'

Schnabeln laughed. 'When you made the taxi. They weren't very good.'

Herbie smiled, looking extremely stupid. 'You were good. I couldn't throw you and *I* was giving the instructions to the *wunderkind*.'

They sat in silence for a while, then Herbie gave Schnabeln his orders. He was to watch the Fenderman woman full-time. He'd get a replacement in the morning so that they could do the job turn and turn about.

'Go and draw a camera,' scribbling a requisition. 'They'll turn up again and I'd like IDs. They couldn't possibly be our own? Home Office? SB?'

'Could. They were clumsy enough. But I think not.'

None of it makes any sense, Herbie considered. Yet it was interesting. Tomorrow the Americans; and something else—have a look-see in the Registry files. Nostradamus, the sixteenth-century prophet of doom and destruction. See if there's anything there. File under what? P for Prophecy or Psychological Warfare Executive? A for Astrology? N for Absurd Nonsense.

7

Ambrose Hill held the exalted title, Head of Registry. As keeper of the Archives his charges were all paper: files, cases, ops in progress, right back to the long forgotten, but still restricted, material of over fifty years.

Ambrose Hill was probably one of the few men in the West who had access to more blackmail material than anyone else living; and he took the job seriously.

Registry was in the basement: vast and vault-like, but always full of activity which seemed at odds with the sombre aesthetic Hill.

'Just a riffle through the books, Ambrose.' Herbie looked huge even in the cathedral-like surroundings of Registry.

'Something special?' Hill had the manner of a shopkeeper which did not go with the donnish appearance.

'Just wondered if we had a case file under Nostradamus. Cropped up yesterday. Field name probably.'

Hill smiled. A rare event. 'No, the field name was Caspar. My God that's going back a long time.' He opened one of his card index drawers and walked his first and second fingers through the indexes to withdraw a red card, which he flicked, with the elegance of a card sharp, across his desk to Herbie.

The card gave a File and Restricted number and was headed: NOSTRADAMUS. Then a whole list of cross-reference files: STELLAR NETWORK 1941. PWE 2659862/41. CASPAR. MELCHIOR. BALTHAZAR. MICHEL. DOWNAY, M.; THOMAS, G.; ...

'That our Thomas?' Herbie looked up and Hill nodded.

'Yes, old George Thomas. His big one. That and the other you'll find there. All restricted until the year 2025, then the war historians'll have a field day.'

Herbie went back to the card and saw that George Thomas's personal file was cross-reffed. George. Coming up for retirement soon, he supposed. Angular and balding George. He shook his head and went on reading: LEADERER, S.; SOLDATENSENDER CALAIS: WERMUT (Op. Amp VI).

'Jesus Christ,' Herbie breathed, for there it was, further down the list. One name, there under his nose all the time: FENDER-MAN, CLAUS.

'Can I pull the lot?' He felt short of breath, for his eye had gone racing ahead.

'Take me a day. Lot of reading, Herbie. Lot of good stuff there. You'll have to get the Director's okay to take 'em upstairs.'

'The Deputy Director,' Herbie Kruger said, sadly. 'Good. Pull them. Assemble them. I fix.'

'Nostradamus, eh?' muttered Hill. 'A long time ago. Old George'll ...' But Big Herbie was already half-way out of the vault, fan-tailing his fat rear between the filing cabinets and desks.

To himself, Hill muttered, 'George'll have a ball going over that little story. Come to think of it, Willis was working with Ramilies at the time.' A nostalgic sadness overtook Ambrose Hill, for when the Nostradamus thing broke he was under training at the Abbey. He shook it off quickly. Nostalgia was phoney and dangerous. You were selective with nostalgia, and the kind of war they had all been through was not the sort of thing any of them would really want to repeat.

At that moment, Herbie Kruger was speaking to Tubby Fincher and requesting an urgent meeting with Sir Willis Maitland-Wood.

8

If big Herbie Kruger prayed at all, he prayed that time would not wreak revenge on him as it had done upon Sir Willis Maitland-Wood, the Deputy Director. Willis had turned to fat with the years, but it was that sleek plumpness often seen in senior Civil Servants. He was a smooth man with perfect grey hair, thick and rarely out of place, immaculate of dress and manner.

None of this bothered Herbie. He had some knowledge of Maitland-Wood's past—who hadn't in the Department? A war record which could not have been bettered, followed by the steady climb up the ladder—a climb which led him out of field work and into that coldest of areas: stalking the corridors of power.

It was the veneer of pomposity, the clubland manner and outrageous sense of his own importance which, for Herbie's money, were Maitland-Wood's besetting sins. He was ruthless, sure, you had to be ruthless to survive in the Whitehall jungle. What Herbie mourned was the passing of a personality which had once been vibrant and adaptable, clear and concise. The personality had now taken on a rigid shape in tedious matters, a profound schoolmasterish attention to trivia, and an almost obsessional lack of foresight. The havoc of time had brought bureaucratic conformity.

Herbie slumped into the armchair in front of Maitland-Wood's desk while the Deputy Director completed a protracted, ingratiating, telephone conversation with a senior member of the Treasury.

Yes, old boy, they must have lunch sometime to talk the whole thing over. Of course. Oh, and how was lovely Helen and the children? Oh dear.

While the conversation rolled on, Herbie realised that he disliked the Deputy Director even more than he had imagined. Disliked him from the pelt of grey hair to the dark and beautifully cut pinstripe suit, the stiff white collar and perfect pearl silk tie.

'Herbie. Sorry. Very difficult with the Chief away. Got to keep the wheels of politics turning. Oil. Most of my time's taken up with oil. Pouring it. All over our lords and masters.' Maitland-Wood leaned back in the padded chair and fixed Herbie with a look which fell half-way between the friendly and the suspicious. 'Now, what can I do for you?'

Herbie told him.

'My God, that's an awful lot of paperwork. Must run into a hefty batch of files: and so long ago. Really worth while?'

'You've seen the Chief's memo to me?' Big Herbie was not inclined to argue.

'Mmmm.' Maitland-Wood nodded, and started to talk about the necessity of spending so much time researching the past because of some tiny hint coming from an untried and unknown source.

Herbie cut in, telling him that he really was anxious to recruit the Fenderman woman if she was clean. 'Sometimes the burrowing is worth it.'

The DD rose and paced around the desk, tapping lightly at his smooth cheek, as though checking that this morning's shave was holding.

Then, as though to himself, he began to talk. 'It started off as one of those operations run by the people who finally formed the nucleus of PWE—Psychological Warfare Executive. I was around. Helping various people and running a network from over here. Knew a lot about it. It was George's big show. George Thomas. Recruited and trained specially.' He ran on like someone thinking aloud. Hadn't talked about it in years. Didn't suppose George had either. Rum show the whole thing. Ramilies constructed it. (*You wouldn't remember him. Died in '47, or was it '48?*) Did all the running; and it went wrong. Wrong for George that is. Nobody knows if the idea behind the Op paid off. But, Christ, it put George in a pickle. Hard to believe what George went through. But then, it helped as well. One door closed and another opened, that kind of thing. Crazy though, the whole idea, to push phoney occult predictions into the Nazi mind and set the SS at odds with the Wehrmacht. Nostradamus, bloody sixteenth-century seer who wrote a book of prophecies.

33

Herbie said that he knew about Nostradamus and his historical context. What with the leaning towards the occult these days, people were still reading the famous quatrains and making them fit the facts.

'Odd those prophecies.' The Deputy Director leaned back against the edge of his desk. 'Some of them are uncanny. Mentions Hitler, you know.'

Herbie knew.

'Old Goebbels used them. Think that's what gave Ramilies the idea.' He paused, looking at Herbie—hard, the eyes like gunmetal. 'You'll have to talk to George as well. Odd story. My God, it'll shake up the historians when they finally get to see the files. Himmler and all that; and the other fellow.'

Herbie quietly asked if he could have the DD's okay.

There was one more moment of hesitation, then Maitland-Wood nodded.

As he was about to leave, clutching the signed requisition form, Herbie received another admonition. The Deputy Director did not actually wag his finger, but his tone of voice said it all.

'You'll get some surprises, Herbie. Reports on file don't tell you everything. Talk to people like George when you've read the stuff, and remember that even he'll only recall that which he wants to be retained.'

Herbie nodded and was mildly shaken when Maitland-Wood wished him luck with the Fenderman woman.

He flashed the requisition down to Ambrose Hill who said the paperwork would be ready tomorrow, and did the requisition allow him to take any of the stuff out of the building?—by which he meant was Herbie's apartment clean and regarded by the upper security echelons as a safe place for highly restricted documents? It was. There was more than just wit in calling it a grace and favour flat.

Herbie glanced through his 'in' tray. Made sure that he was up to date, checked that Schnabeln had not called in, and rang his man in Grosvenor Square. They made a date for lunch on the following day. 'You come over here, Herbie, old buddy. Our cantina does better steaks than yours.' There was no hint of the subject for conversation from either end.

A few cryptic notes went into Herbie's private notebook, ready for the Grosvenor Square dance, as he thought of it. Now for George; leafing through the internal directory. George Thomas whose name appeared on the same cross-reference file as Claus Fenderman.

George was Head of Forward Planning (Europe), a heavy desk assignment with a great deal of responsibility. That meant his Income Tax returns would show him as a very high grade Civil Servant. Top bracket and ranking almost with an Ambassador in the Foreign Service.

Herbie dialled the number, got past a silken-voiced watch-bitch and asked George if he could see him.

9

It started off as one of those odd operations run by people who finally formed the nucleus of PWE. The Deputy Director's words did a slow and continuous elipse around Big Herbie's mind. Then, later—*It went wrong ... But even then it helped as well.*

The problem really was why Registry still carried such a bulk of files on a PWE Op thirty-six years old. It was way out of their field, particularly files which would remain restricted until the year two thousand and dot. You would expect cross-refs from things like George Thomas' personal file. But they had the lot here in the building. Most of the restricted SOE and kindred Orgs stuff was kept at the Public Records Office. Even the Yard, as he knew, still held the files on executed Nazi agents, going back to the start of World War II.

So Herbie pondered as he took the lift up the main building to the warren that was the fourth floor, George Thomas' domain.

As he ruminated over the strange anomaly of the long-kept files, he regarded his feet and thought how large and clumsy they were. He couldn't even disguise them with elegant shoes. The years spent slogging around East Germany in heavy badly made boots had not helped: there was a legacy of fallen arches, hard skin, corns and bunions. Herbie's feet were part of his personal cross.

Suddenly, as the lift slid up past the third floor, he felt very much alone and would have given a lot to go back immediately to St. John's Wood, a large gin and the Mahler Fifth—that reconciliation of opposing worlds of grief and frenzy, as someone had written.

Grief and frenzy he knew. Just as he knew the desire to escape, and the sense of being alone among hostility. Certainly he knew its source: a nexus with the past; for there had been so many times in the field when things got bad, and all he wanted was a drink and Mahler.

As the lift hissed to a halt, Big Herbie was in another of his own many worlds—dangerous nights waiting in the open, or making a house call in daylight when watchers could pick him off like a monkey nips fleas from its mate. He thought of the deaths.

The fourth floor was alive. Telephones rang from behind doors; at the end of the long corridor a teleprinter ticked urgently. Young women moved patiently from office to office. An occasional whizz-kid slid out of one door and disappeared through another. George at least made them look busy.

The watch-bitch in George Thomas' ante-room turned out to be a lady nudging her late fifties and doing her best to make mutton look like young sheep. She did not seem pleased to see Herbie, but she knew who he was without asking, and buzzed George straight away.

Unlike Maitland-Wood, George Thomas had run neither to fat nor pomposity. Herbie always thought of him as bald and angular—typed him, in fact, and was always surprised when they were together to find out he was wrong.

George Thomas was a tall man, even beside Big Herbie, but his natural build, being slim, occasionally gave the impression of angles. It was deceptive at a distance; for, apart from the nose, there was nothing angular about him. Nor was he bald. His lank fair hair had thinned out and left a small tonsure of baldness, but his hairdresser was skilful enough to give him the appearance of having more, and thicker, hair than was really the case.

How old? flashed through Herbie's mind. Check his file. Fifty-eight? Yet the face still retained a youthful quality. On a good day he might be taken for forty: few lines, a firm mouth, and alive, young, and alert warm brown eyes, which now smiled out as Herbie entered the room.

The smile, which started in the eyes, went immediately to the mouth as George Thomas rose from behind a beleaguered desk and stretched out his hand.

'Herbie. Haven't seen you in weeks.' He made sitting motions, after the firm handclasp was unlocked, pouring out words all the time, saying how good it was to see him, and what on earth did he want in this neck of the woods?

'Well, I don't get much chance these days . . .' Herbie sat.

'Of course you don't, Herr Doktor. (The Herr Doktor was

another little executive joke. Nicknames followed Herbie like kids after a Mr. Whippy van.) You're as busy as we are, but if the Section could be of any help?'

Herbie would never shake off the habit of watching other people's body talk, or trying to read the runes behind what was actually being said. He liked George: had always liked him, though they'd rarely worked together. For a moment the stream of chat seemed like a smokescreen. Then the cloud dropped as George got back behind his desk, leaned forward, lacing his long fingers, and waited for Herbie to speak.

That was good. George had never cultivated the superior, or too busy, attitude, sought by so many when they reached the senior grades. Nor did he bother with the Whitehall uniform. George invariably wore nondescript old jackets and odd trousers. Suits and ties only appeared when absolutely necessary. The cuffs on the check jacket he wore now were frayed.

'You must be busy.' Herbie cocked his head towards the large-scale map of Europe which covered almost the whole area of one wall.

George nodded. They both knew how much reorganisation was needed since the NATO secrets leak from the Bonn Ministry of Defence. The whole fuel supply pipeline would have to be rejigged for a start. It was in these kind of things that people like George Thomas excelled.

George made no direct comment. He just waited.

'Courtesy really,' Herbie opened up at last, his big stupid smile filling the face, while the eyes took on a vacant look. Watch, but never allow others to watch you, close up. Even here. Home, dry, safe and with a friend who shared as many secrets as you did. 'The DD thought I should let you know that he's authorised me to read your book.' For book read Personal File. Watch the eyes and the hands. Nothing.

'Christ, you're not trying to get me to sing in your new choir, are you, Herbie?'

The smile broadened and a chuckle began, deep in the belly. 'It's an idea. At least you're experienced.'

'Why?' A hint of coldness.

'Your book? Not just yours. Courtesy visit, George, as I said. I do not like it; any more than you. But, well, I'm trying to pull some birds, of both sexes you understand. But you know that.'

George nodded.

'Just a hint; but I have one in the net. Untried. Might possibly be a tasty piece of bait.'

'So why my book?' Not edgy, but something there, as though the full impact that his file was to be read by a controller had only just started to sink in.

'Because this particular bird claims to have associations with something you were on.'

'Recent? I've been out of the field for a long time, but— Fifties?'

'Rather not say, George. Just courtesy. You should know. Questions to our esteemed Sir Willis ...'

'And he won't tell me.' The coldness conquered: replaced by a smile.

'You are so right.'

'Hint?'

'George, if I could ...'

'You would. I understand.' He gave a small laugh. 'I don't think there's anything to hide. If there is, perhaps you'd be good enough to bury it.'

'Anything for you, George.'

'Good of you to let me know. Will anyone tell me? When you've sussed him, I mean.'

Herbie did not correct the assumption that he was after a male. 'I shall see to it personally. In fact, that was the other thing. I want to go through the documents and then, if we could have a session or two.'

George said he would be delighted.

'Just see what your memory can dredge up, George. Quite painless, I promise.'

It would be good for his soul, George laughed. It was a sour in-joke.

Back in his office, clearing the desk of current paperwork, Herbie thought about that fleeting moment of coldness. Worry? Conscience? Leave it alone and see what the papers said.

Around ten that night, Schnabeln called into the flat. The two heavies were still on Frau Fenderman's heels and he had some good snaps. He would run them through the computers tomorrow.

'Another odd thing. Small, but maybe ...'

'Yes?' Herbie shifted his body in the padded chair, telephone pressed to his ear.

'She knows London. Knows it like the back of her hand. Knew where she was going and how to get there; and she didn't learn it from a guide book. Didn't stop to check landmarks, or street names. I can smell it. She's either lived here or worked close. Interesting?'

Herbie said to put it all in writing and give a complete rundown on her movements. Inside it was not just interesting, but unnerving. Hildegarde Fenderman had lived in the East, and only a relatively short time in the West. It was supposed to be her first visit, a pilgrimage, to London.

Wait for the files. Don't jump to conclusions. Time enough. Tomorrow the Grosvenor Square Dance.

IO

The Square Dance turned out to be more of a minuet.

The American Embassy contact was mid-echelon CIA and spent the first half of their excellent, if bland, lunch bemoaning the current state of the market. By which he meant the general shake-up at present taking place within the Agency. There were guys, he said, with a lifetime of experience being thrown into the street overnight. At Langley, Virginia—the headquarters complex of the CIA—they were calling it the Hallowe'en Massacre, because the termination of employment notices had gone out the previous October 31st.

Some joker had even written a Gilbert and Sullivan parody and pinned it to the bulletin board, slashing at the Admiral who had been appointed Director and carried out the massacre—

> For many a year I served at sea,
> Living on grog and kedgeree.
> I paced the deck and never went ashore,
> I set the ship's course and I pleased the Commodore.
> CHORUS: He pleased the Commodore
> So mightily,
> That now he is Director
> Of the Agency.

'Who knew,' groaned Hank, the Embassy man, 'Those guys today. Me tomorrow. It's changing fast and who wants a spook when he's forty, let alone fifty?'

Who indeed. Herbie was not prepared to console. Hallowe'en was quite a time ago and his contact was still twitchy. He fired point blank at the target.

'That why you didn't loosen up about Frau Hildegarde Fenderman and her poor little sister Gretchen Weiss, Hank?'

Jesus, Hank said. Jesus, he was sorry, but he wanted to clear it. He would have got back to Herbie. No doubt about that.

'No possible doubt whatever?' Herbie allowed a sly grin which quickly became the broad and absurd smile.

Gretchen Weiss did things for them, yes. Of course she did. Even before the cancer struck, she had pleaded with them to get sister Hildegarde out of the East. It was okay, they checked her out.

'Thoroughly?'

'Like she was a plague carrier.'

So Herbie asked why they had taken so long in bringing her into the West, and doing a deal with Bonn for a passport.

Gretchen Weiss did things. In plain language while her sister was in the East, Gretchen was pliable. Okay, so she screwed visiting firemen, and leafed through their briefcases. Everyone did it in those days. Dirty tricks wasn't anything new.

Herbie left the Embassy feeling slightly sick, and it had nothing to do with the food. He shouldn't be shocked. The trade taught you to use people. He had done it. Was about to do it again. It was this last thought which made him sick.

The nausea turned to worry when he saw the total bulk of the files which arrived in his office ten minutes after he got back. It was a small paper mountain.

He began, there and then, in his office, and with George Thomas' file which he read backwards, checking quickly through the recent stuff and the last field jobs, few and far between in the early Sixties, heavy and based in Western Europe during the height of the Cold War.

He was still in the office at seven that evening and had worked back to the Nineteen-Forties, the period which most concerned him.

Flicking through to the first entries, Herbie Kruger made a notation of what seemed to be the most important cross-reference files, sorted them out, dumped the lot in his briefcase and put the balance in his office safe.

Then he went home and read through the night. He read about George Thomas and his recruitment; about the Stellar network in France during 1941, and what became of those involved. Then he read on—about a German covert operation called *Wermut*, in which both George Thomas and Claus Fenderman were deeply involved.

Though the notes and reports gave only the bare bones of the story, Herbie Kruger's hair tingled at the back of his neck. George had been through all this?—the George he had been speaking to, casually on the main block fourth floor, that afternoon?

He also realised that the Deputy Director had been right. Historians would have a field day when these files were released: and they gave no hint of the detail.

The prose was flat—authorised version—yet it gripped.

When Herbie finally laid it aside, around four in the morning, he wanted more. His head buzzed with the enormous hunk of history in which George Thomas had been involved. He wanted flesh on the bones. What George thought and felt at the time; what people actually said and looked like (for so many were now dead). He would spend the next day going through the remaining urgent cross-references, and fix his first long session with George. Already there were glimmerings about Frau Fenderman's husband, little lights at the end of the tunnel, though they did not explain the pair of East German leeches, or her familiarity with London.

Read. Read. Read. Then flesh it out with George. Clean him of every emotion he had felt during those days in 1941.

Just before he prepared for sleep, Herbie took the files into his living room and locked them in his private safe. As he did so, George Thomas' Personal File fell open. Among the notes on the first page were the words: *Recruited, Ministry of Defence, by Brigadier Harold Ramilies DSO.*

Yes, Big Herbie would like to hear all about that as well. The recruitment was dated August 1940, the year of the Blitzkrieg, the fall of Europe, Dunkirk, Battle of Britain and the London Blitz. The file showed that George Thomas was coming up to fifty-nine years of age. In 1940 he would be a child. Twenty: twenty-one.

Herbie went to sleep thinking about how the memory gets warped by the years, unless there is some particular and constant present reminder. How would George's memory stand up?

It would be a few days before he could get to grips with George's memory. Everything did not stop because he was interested in Frau Fenderman.

On the following morning there was a mass of routine paperwork, and Herbie had to get over to Camberwell at lunch-time where he spent two hours in a seedy café doing an initial vetting on another possible—a German who had been naturalised British for twenty years, but still had contacts in the East through the remnants of his family.

It was late afternoon before the big man got down to reading the files again, mainly looking for reference passages he had made notes about during the previous night.

The story that unwound was just as fascinating, intriguing, and full of built-in questions which remained unanswered.

Around six he telephoned George, who was out at some conference, so he asked, if it was possible, could he call, either tomorrow, or at the St. John's Wood number that evening.

The 'phone was ringing as he entered the flat.

Not George. Schnabeln wanting an urgent meeting.

'I have two walking computers who are willing to go on record.' Schnabeln sipped a strong gin and looked pleased with himself.

'You going to give them an exclusive recording contract?'

'*You* might. They've looked at the photographs and I've shown them the product—from a safe distance. They have also run their thoughts through the electronic machines.' Schnabeln looked smug. 'They are willing to swear that Frau Fenderman, Hildegarde Fenderman, spent two months in England last autumn. At that time her passport said she was a Fräulein Gretchen Weiss.'

'Get it in writing,' was all Herbie said as Schnabeln left. Then, as an afterthought, at the door, '*Hals und Beinbruch.*'—Break your neck and leg: good luck.

He went back to the files with greatly enhanced interest; but lack of sleep, the warmth of the room, and the gin made him dozy. He nodded over the paperwork and was roused suddenly by the telephone. The instrument intruded to the point of causing him to drop his glass which shattered on the carpet.

A sign of good luck in the old country, he thought, lumbering across the room.

This time it *was* George.

'I would be most grateful,' Herbie shook his head to clear the fog, 'if we could have our first session soon.'

George said tomorrow afternoon was fairly clear. He could spare a couple of hours then, but Herbie wanted more. He was sorry, but it was important—and interesting. He wondered if,

44

perhaps, George could spare an evening away from his lovely wife. Possibly have dinner here, in St. John's Wood? Yes, a whole evening, just to start with. Saturday was clear. Six o'clock on Saturday then. Good.

That would give Big Herbie Kruger time to finish going through the files, and also a chance to bone up on Nostradamus, the sixteenth-century prophet who appeared to have been the cause of all the trouble in the first place.

II

He read a couple of books on the Nazi party and its love-hate relationship with the occult—rubbish mainly; one autobiography of a leading light in PWE; James Laver's book on Nostradamus, published in 1942, therefore angled from the events which submerged Europe at that time; and browsed through a paperback edition of *The Prophecies of Nostradamus*, with a commentary by Erika Cheetham.

Herbie also finished the main work on the files, and conducted three interviews. All this in forty-eight hours. More, he whistled up some equipment from Audio and refused their proffered help with installation. Herbie was a great one for DIY.

Very late on the Friday night he had another meeting with Schnabeln, who was sharing his constant watch with a young Westphalian called Girren.

Herbie smiled his daft smile at the juxtaposition of the names Schnabeln and Girren. In direct translation they meant Billing and Cooing, though there was not much of the love bird about either of them. Girren would eventually go into the East under Herbie's London control. During the last three years he had become a specialist in the security services of both German Republics.

'He says he's pretty sure,' Schnabeln reported.

Why then, Herbie asked, did Girren not come personally? Because he wants a little more time to make certain and go over his sources.

It upset Herbie, because if Girren was right, his own BND contact at the German Embassy was playing him very false. Girren thought he had recognised, and marked, one of Frau Fenderman's leeches. He was, said Girren, a good all-rounder. A career man in the BND. A Federal Republic spook.

'Shit!' Herbie remarked loudly when Schnabeln took his leave. He said some other uncomplimentary things which had a lot to do with breaking necks and legs, but not in any sense of good luck.

On Saturday morning he set up the sound. A big reel-to-reel tape machine at the bottom of his kitchen cupboard was linked to a tuner/amplifier set to a pre-selected clear channel. He then scattered radio bugs throughout the main room, choosing particularly places where his visitor was most likely to sit.

The tape machine was set to sound-activate, and in the afternoon—between preparing the main course for dinner—he did a lengthy test run. There was a clean sound picture from almost every part of the flat.

Not that he had any reason to suspect George of even the slightest indiscretion, but Herbie had one set of stories on file and he wanted the skin, flesh, muscles and sinews on tape.

He had prepared a good meal. Then chose the music, switching from his passion for Mahler to Mozart. Mahler might have a disturbing effect on George, and at least he wanted him to make his entrance to music.

Shortly before six he cued the tape machine, and put on one of the later Piano Concertos. (No. 21 in C Major as it happened: Herbie Kruger tended to select Mozart at random—*There's so much of it. With Mahler I know where I am; with Mozart it's a barrel of apples.*)

The music went off a couple of minutes after George arrived, and they got down to business over dinner.

'Memory test tonight?' George Thomas crumbled a bread roll. He wore a smarter jacket, black velvet, and a white rollneck. Why? Herbie asked himself, as if it was important.

'A little journey back, I think. I am interested, George. I been reading about you. Christ, you should be Alastair Maclean. Adventures.'

'You've had plenty yourself, Herbie. They're only adventures a long time afterwards. Good soup.'

Herbie thanked him and said it came from a tin. Then out of the blue he said, 'Nineteen Forty-One. Nostradamus. Stellar.'

'Jesus, Herbie. It's old and tired.'

Herbie said that it was neither old nor tired to him, and that some history would have to be rewritten when the files came out of the bag.

'History? A footnote to history, maybe.' George suddenly

looked shocked. 'Christ. Funny the way things come back. After all these years. That's what I called Nostradamus—a footnote to history. That's what I called him to old Ramilies when he put the whole thing to me.'

'A funny way to run a war, eh? Fighting with the words of a sixteenth-century astrologer.'

Herbie cleared away the plates and brought on the main course. He was assured in the kitchen, and did a respectable Sauerbraten, a pot roast using silverside, complete with potato dumplings and a dish of red cabbage.

'It seemed crazy at the time. But one learns in the trade, Herbie. Misdirection is one of the blackest arts.' Then, rather proudly, 'I was the first one in, you know. Whatever the books say, and despite the dreadful weather that winter, I was the first.'

'February '41? Yes?'

George nodded and said something about being so young and cocky.

'As I understand it, George, the job was to make contact with a French source we did not know, and did not even trust completely. You were Caspar. He was Melchior.'

'Real name, Michel Downay. Put himself on offer through what channels were left after Dunkirk. A Professor at the Sorbonne. Wrote a book about old Michel de Nostradame: published in 1939. Goebbels thought he could use him. We thought we could use him also, and we cooked up a story for me. They tried to get into Brittany by boat but we got ourselves bounced by an E-boat and had to run away. Finally I got in by Lysander. First one,' he repeated proudly.

'I want the story, George. As you remember it; as it happened. Not just the dry words, but what you thought, what you did, what you said.'

'Tall order after so long. Why?'

'I've told you. I'm interested in someone who reckons they were there for part of it.'

'Caspar, Melchior and Balthazar,' George said to himself.

'We can always get a doctor.' Herbie's smile made him look like a Hallowe'en pumpkin. 'Give you a shot of memory juice.'

No comment from George. Then, very slowly, he agreed, but said the whole thing would take more than one evening. If he made errors...

'Don't worry about those.' Herbie had him now. They could spend as much time as they wanted. All the time in the world. 'Just try and think yourself back to being a boy of, what? Twenty? Twenty-one?'

About that, George was uncertain. 'Was I that young? Can one remember what it felt like? I'll try. Start with going in?'

Fine; Herbie thought it was fine to start there, even though he would have preferred to begin at the beginning, the recruiting and briefing. The great thing was that you couldn't hurry a thing like this.

George took a mouthful of food and chewed gently, then swallowed.

'The pilot's name was Bartholomew. I hadn't remembered that in years. Bartholomew.'

So he began the story of the Nostradamus Operation and the Stellar network.

When going through the paperwork Big Herbie had come across many photographs: some were of George taken in the Forties. So as the story started to be retold, Herbie tried to see the man opposite him as he was then, fresh, young, inexperienced, brash, a different shape even.

It had been a hard winter, George said. Snow, ice, sleet, fog, rain and frost across most of Europe. On the night of February 26/27 it was clear and frosty. There was still a lot of snow, and the slight winds were bitterly cold.

Even with the central heating on after a reasonably mild spring day, George made Herbie shiver.

They had been told that the area for which they headed was free of snow. But Bartholomew, the Lysander pilot, was concerned because of the rock-hard frozen earth which would not be level by any means.

There was a moon though.

12

'A prophet is not without honour,' said the shadow emerging from behind the poplar tree. George knew it was a poplar because they had told him to make for the row of poplars on the south side of the field. That was where the road was, and everybody knew that the roads of northern France were lined with poplar trees. There were pictures in all the best guide books.

'Save in his own country.' George completed the Biblical quotation, breathless and chilled to the bone, even after running over the field as Fenice had instructed him. He spoke French, his Maman's native tongue, which now had to be his own. For that he privately blessed Maman and thought of her. Would he see her in Paris?

English rattled inside his head: the questions, last minute, to people like Ramilies. (*What if he doesn't show his hand? What if he cons me and I don't see him? If I suspect that one of them is unhappy, what's the best lubricant?*) Their answers were of no consolation now, near dawn in the freezing cold—over the top. Blue funk they'd called it at school, and down the shabby little terraced street where George had been brought up, they were less restrained. Shit scared, they would have said.

On the far side of the field, the Lysander pilot gunned his engine. George turned, feeling a gust of wind tearing icy at his cheek like Arctic spray, watching as the machine trundled forward. He imagined the smell of oil and aeroplane he had just left: the last odour of England.

Little jets of flame licked from the exhaust pipe along the radial cowling. She bounced once, crazily, before grabbing her thin, though natural, element, becoming a silhouette against the pearl sky, the gull wing tipping as Bartholomew banked and set a course for home.

George felt sick.

'Caspar?' asked the shadow, advancing. He clasped George's

hand, the palm sweating, in spite of the cold, inside the rough woollen glove. George asked if the shadow was Melchior, knowing that it couldn't be, but observing the ritual which the dispatchers had drummed into him.

No, he would see Melchior in Paris. Tomorrow. A faint breath of relief because that was how it had been planned.

Other shapes were bearing down on them now, from where the Lizzie had taken off; probably the light-carriers who had formed the triangular flare path.

Hands touched his back and shoulders in greeting, but he still wanted to vomit.

The shadow said his name was Marc as he patted George, guiding the party through the trees. It *was* a road on the other side: flat and straight, crossed by weak bars of light—for the moon was low now—and edged with frosted grass.

Marc said it was two kilometres to the village, and that they would have to move quickly. *You'll be out of bounds. It's probably the most dangerous part*, Ramilies cautioned in the cottage near the airfield. *The curfew*, he repeated at the farm, just before the off.

'The nearest military are over five kilometres away, and they don't bother us much, but ...' Marc left the whispered words dangling, trailing like ribbons on a child's kite.

George thanked God—or the Devil, or whoever took care of moonlight riders—that they had provided him with only a small suitcase. There had been talk of a suitcase radio, a piano, but that sorted itself out. *Got a pianist all set, centre stage, ready to give you a concert. Good as Myra Hess any day*. Thus Ramilies.

He couldn't see much of the village: just the outlines of the walls which looked grey, but appeared to change colour and texture as they got deeper into the single, short main street, the pavement narrow. Somewhere nearby, a dog barked and they stopped for a second or two. Then, into the square, unlit: a bar-tabac, shuttered against the night or the occupying forces; on the wall a metal advertisement—Byrrh or Dubonnet.

At last, a door leading directly off the street. A series of knocks and a shaft of light as it opened to let them in. Just George and Marc. The others had faded outside the village.

The kitchen was warm. A single place set at a bare table, and two women standing near the stove. One old, like something by

Brueghel the Elder, all black folds, small, like a bent tub; the other younger and skinny with a face that betokened a sharp temper.

They wished George welcome, without smiling, and he was made to sit down and eat. He still felt sick, but the bread was better than he expected, while the soup, mainly potatoes, could only have been concocted in France. Marc brought out a bottle of passable rough *rouge* and they drank together, glancing slyly at each other across the table.

Eventually, Marc explained the situation, haltingly, as though the women did not know it all. A rendezvous was arranged with Melchior tomorrow in Paris. They did not want to know any of the details. Their job was simply to pass George on to Melchior. (Only he called George, Caspar, of course.) The thin girl was his wife, Thérèse Abbo, and George was to be her brother-in-law. She would take him to Paris on the train, if the trains were running, and point him in the right direction. That was their job. No more, no less.

He presumed that George's papers were in order, and George assured him they were, privately praying that they'd got it right at the other end. Somewhere, he thought, Epictetus had asked, 'What is it to be a philosopher? Is it not to be prepared against events?' He hoped that Ramilies and company were philosophers.

They made up a bed in the corner of the kitchen and left him alone. Though he was warmer now it was too late for sleep. Maybe he dozed. Probably, but hardly any time seemed to pass before the place was alive again.

They left around six o'clock after mugs of foul coffee, during the drinking of which, Marc gave out some pertinent warnings. The trick, he said, was to behave normally. George felt sick again, knowing that it had nothing to do with the coffee and a lot to do with fear.

It's the first few days that count, Ramilies had said. *That's the vulnerable period, when you're acclimatising yourself and settling in.* What did they know? They were all improvising anyway. Trying to get in by boat had been just as much an improvisation as the Lysander landing. Even his contact Melchior was an improvisation—Michel Downay of the Sorbonne, noted lecturer on social psychology, authority on superstition and the occult, not to mention Nostradamus.

Marc explained that there were spot checks on papers, particularly in the large towns and cities, but they were nothing to worry about. The Boche were too busy looking after their own. Sometimes you got landed with a pig of an NCO who had his eye on promotion, but on the whole they were okay, as long as you knew your place. George said he knew his place.

The old woman clattered around her stove muttering incantations. The newts' eyes and ragwort were not visible, but George reckoned they were not far away. Just before they left she stumbled over with glasses of amber liquid for George and the girl. It tasted like raw spirit into which someone had dropped phosphorus.

As George came up for air, Marc was saying that the police were worse than the Boche, because, being French, their arses were always at risk. They had to work hand in glove with the bastards and uphold the new law and the new order. They upheld the new law: rigorously. If they didn't, the Boche unscrewed their ears and their arses fell off. He spat. The old woman spat also. George wondered if it was into her cooking pot.

Outside, the drizzle came down like soaking woodsmoke, and Thérèse walked as though following a plough, eyes set firmly towards a fixed point on the horizon.

'How far?' George asked.

'Not far.' She inspired neither confidence nor desire. He was an unwanted incident in her life.

She stayed silent when they reached the station, and throughout the journey, during which they shared a carriage with three young German soldiers, carrying regulation suitcases. There was also a well-dressed French couple. Everyone was very polite, and the soldiers, thinking, like all foreigners abroad at that time, that they could not be understood, talked of the leave they would have in Paris and the girls they would screw.

They steamed into the Nord a little after ten, and even the soldiers went out of their way to be pleasant, saying goodbye and nodding with touristy smiles.

George had always had a thing about arriving in Paris. Since the first time his Maman had taken him there he equated it with sin. The particular smell of the city's railway stations brought out the old Adam in him faster than the scent of a beautiful woman.

The smell was just the same; and the noise and bustle. Steam rose from under the carriages, and smoke from the engines hung in the air. The same old bubble of Gallic volubility was everywhere, even French laughter, which seldom comes cheap.

The porters looked older than ever, and probably were, decked out in their *bleus de travail*. If he had expected to find a drab and cowed situation, then George would have been confounded, for it was all very familiar : like coming home.

Only when they got to the main concourse did things change. There were the usual crowds; the women seemed to be dressed as they always were, some even modishly turned out, though these were mainly the ones clinging to the arms of uniforms : German field grey. There were a lot of those. There were also a lot of posters : black, blaring headings calling *Attention!* There were flags as well, great red banners with white circles around the swastikas. But the smell of Paris was the same as ever.

At the barrier, a big peasant-faced lumpish boy in Wehrmacht uniform, rifle slung over the right shoulder, watched faces as the collector took tickets. The soldier wore a puzzled expression, as though his job was to read faces whose alphabets he had not yet mastered.

They came out on to the concourse, and Thérèse caught at George's arm, turning him. He felt the movement was like that of some movie gunman's Moll setting someone up for a bullet in the back. For the first time, she showed emotion. She was not a bad little actress, for a peasant.

'This is where I leave you, Georges,' she said, and he wondered about her knowledge of his name. Marc had called him Caspar all the time, but his papers showed him as Georges Thomas. The addition of one small *s* to the Christian name made him fully French.

Thérèse pulled him close. 'I shall kiss you as my brother-in-law and leave. You wave to me and then turn around. Melchior is right behind you, walking towards us now. He has a stick because of the limp. Good luck. God bless you.'

The limp he knew about. An accident in 1936 : motor-cycle up in Nostradamus country. Provence.

George watched her walk away, stopping, turning to wave, then vanishing into the crowd, side-stepping a small detachment of German troops being led towards one of the platforms by a sergeant who looked as though he had been boiled and flayed.

George waited a moment and then turned, prepared to look as if he was searching the crowd. He knew Melchior, Michel Downay, immediately, in spite of his height and age, for which he was not prepared. Fenice, who had known Downay before the Fall of France, had not mentioned age, imagining that the photographs were enough. In the photographs he had looked older. George was expecting a man in his late fifties. Instead he was gazing into the same face from the photographs, though it appeared to have shed years. He could have been forty at the most: handsome, beard neat and trimmed, unflecked by grey; eyes bright and hard, mouth large, with lips which looked like good news for women.

George had also imagined him to be around five feet in height; he was just over six, maybe taller, for the limp looked painful and pulled him down a shade.

He was immaculately turned out, though possibly dated by a decade. Certainly the wide-brimmed hat was from another time, and George was uncertain about the cut of the dark waisted topcoat with the velvet collar. He felt very shabby, in the badly fitting clothes they had provided in England, when placed next to this dandy of a Frenchman.

Even with the bad leg, Michel Downay moved fast and straight; no crabbing, just a painful pegging at speed, using a heavy black cane as an extra leg.

Turn him inside out, Ramilies had said. *He'll know you*, Fenice added. *He'll pick you up. It'll be very public at the Gare du Nord, so you must follow his lead.*

George did just that, hearing the words of his instructors all the time. At a distance of twelve paces or so, Michel Downay began speaking: shouting almost, 'Georges, you're here at last. Good ... good ...' and with the last 'good', on a rising cadence, he was grasping hands and muttering close that a prophet was not without honour.

The hand-grip was bone crushing. George winced as he completed the greeting. Downay went on talking, fast.

'You must not worry. Don't be afraid or act frightened. It's all right.' We have company, he said: which meant a lift by automobile—a luxury.

The 'company' stood out in front of the station. Two officers.

55

A major and a captain. An SS-Sturmbannführer and an SS-Ober-sturmführer, complete in the slick smart blue uniforms with the gold-threaded lightning flashes on the lapels. Young, crisp, sharp as knives and full of confidence.

George recognised the type. They both had that same brand of ruthless charm he had seen in public schoolboys from England : the same arrogance, from the high gloss on their boots, to the raffish angle they wore their caps. They even clicked their heels, behaving towards Downay with measured deference.

Downay did the honours. George, he called, 'My old and valued colleague, Georges Thomas.' The two SS men were SS-Sturmbann-führer Heinrich Kuche and SS-Obersturmführer Joseph Wald.

13

'Jesus. I get coffee?' Herbie Kruger rose from the table, hauling himself into the present. George sat looking at the wall, as if he was seeing it all over again. An Englishman arriving in occupied France to meet an unknown quantity contact who turned out to have chums in the SS.

Herbie indicated one of the other chairs and began to clear away the dishes. Coffee in a minute, he told George.

'At the station?' Herbie stood, his frame filling the doorway, half in and out of the kitchen, the coffee pot in his right hand. 'The SS met you at the station?' With a series of clucking noises he went back.

When he came out into the main room with the tray, he found George settled in one of his padded chairs, smoking a small cigar.

Herbie said this was what he really wanted: the story from the horse's mouth. Kuche and Wald were, naturally, in the files, but details like this, the landing, the weather, meeting Michel Downay at the Gare du Nord with the SS in tow : these were the things he wanted to hear.

They settled with coffee.

'George, forgive me. Your parents. Apart from your mother being French—she's in the files, of course—there's not much about your parents.'

George gave a laugh, head thrown back, the noise coming from his throat. His dreadful secret, he said. Nowadays it was nothing. In the Thirties, with his kind of ambition, you kept your parentage quiet.

'Herbie, I was the son of a railway engine driver and a French whore. It's as simple as that. She was ahead of her time. A drop out. Good family. Came from near Paris. Good education. Big bust-up with her parents when she was about seventeen. Came to England. Went on the game. The old man met her on some beano. He worked for the GWR, lived in Didcot. Met her and

57

married her. We lived in a little terrace on the wrong side of the tracks, as the Americans say, and I was brought up to be bilingual. That's how I got into the local Grammar School. Scholarship. I don't suppose many sons of railway engine drivers got scholarships to good Grammar Schools in the 1930s, but I did it on my French. Maman did it for me.'

He made a joke about her being the original tarte avec le coeur. 'Though I reckon her poor old coeur cracked a bit when the old man died through driving his 4-6-4 into the back of a slow goods just outside Swindon.'

That was in 1937 and the little terraced house—Lockhill Terrace—was only just down the line. But by then George had won another scholarship: the one to Oxford; to the University.

'Maman had great ambition for me.' George blew out a cloud of smoke and looked through it, his eyes softening, far away, thinking of the past. 'And I denied her so much. Very touchy, Herbie, the good old English class system. Nowadays it's fashionable to have come from my kind of background. Then? Well, I ran a mile from it.'

'Deep cover.' Herbie poured more coffee.

George agreed. Adding, that was what Ramilies had said of him. He'd spent most of his life in deep cover.

'At the University?'

George gave his throaty laugh again. 'Especially at the University. Within a week of going up, I'd established a fictitious background. Maman was a French aristo and the old man was something mysterious in steel, which, when you consider the circumstances of his death, wasn't stretching it so far.'

Herbie growled and made a comment about George doing well at Oxford. Brilliant. A First in History with sixteenth-century France as his special subject. 'And old Ramilies was your tutor.'

George nodded.

'And later, Ramilies recruited you. Can you tell me about that, George? Tell me how they yanked you into the Nostradamus thing. If I read the files correctly, they pulled you for that purpose alone.'

George asked if Herbie had talked to the Deputy Director about it—'He was fiddling about at the Abbey when they finally got me there'—as though dodging the question.

Herbie said that he needed it from George. 'I want to scour

your mind, not dear old Willis' devious brain. You been to see him, George?' As Head of Forward Planning (Europe), George was privy to the basics of Herbie's assignment. It would be natural for him to run to the Director or his Deputy.

There was a long silence during which George crushed his little cigar into the big glass ashtray in front of him. Yes, he had been to Willis. What did Herbie expect? Nobody liked to be told someone was raking through his restricted past without knowing exactly why. Particularly someone of George's seniority.

'He told you, not to worry, eh?'

Willis Maitland-Wood had said something like that, and George had been blunt with him : asked if he was being vetted for sinister reasons.

'You got something on your conscience, George?'

No, but a lot of strange things went on during that time. Then, and later. He wasn't worried. Curious though.

Like hell he wasn't worried. Herbie refilled the coffee cups. Anyone who had spent time in the field was a fool if he wasn't worried about the past. It was something none of them could out-live. There were shadows on all their shoulders. Big Herbie sometimes had nightmares about them. The double deals, the promises never kept, the devious workings within the labyrinth, the deaths. Bosch's paintings of hell were nothing compared with the souls of those who had worked among the secret alleys of Europe over the last four decades.

There was no suspicion, nothing on George : Herbie used his most gentle voice. Just a link. Nothing to fear.

George nodded again and shrugged. It wasn't personal, going to the DD. Herbie must understand that. No lack of trust. Herbie understood and asked again about his recruitment.

'Old Ramilies—the Rammer, we used to call him—was a keeper of secrets. As my tutor he knew where I'd come from; parents; everything. I kept up this veneer of coming from a better class; of having a moneyed past. Christ, the snobbery of those days. I really thought it was necessary.' He made a motion with his right hand, throwing the arm forward and twirling the hand from the wrist. Herbie thought it was meant to convey that he had already spoken about all that. Then the laugh, more hollow this time. 'I had a real conscience in those days. Found the pretence a strain. Went to Ramilies about it. He was very kind and said he understood and that my secret was safe with him.'

Nothing wrong with trying to better yourself, he had told the young, raw, Thomas. *Don't know if I approve of your view concerning parents though. Some'd be proud of that background. But if that's the way you want to do it, who am I to pull the rug from under your feet?*

Aloud, George said, 'Christ, Herbie, what an insufferable little inverted snob I was in those days.'

Herbie gently pulled on the reins and brought him back to the business of recruitment.

George stared at the wall. It happened after Dunkirk, he said. Then he began a long, sometimes painfully nostalgic, journey back as far as 1939.

What did you do with a First Class degree in History and a specialised knowledge of sixteenth-century France? That had been his problem in '39. A problem solved by the war. He had French and German as well. Elementary German, maybe, but enough. He suspected that Ramilies had a hand in putting him up for a commission. The Army. France early 1940. Then the rout. Fallbacks. Retreat. In training they had been taught things like platoon in defence and attack. The manuals and exercises said nothing of platoon in rout. That was real warfare. May 1940, when General Guderian's Panzers began to segment Europe and divide it into neat parcels for the Third Reich.

This they did in a little over two weeks. Blitzkrieg. Lightning war. George and his men stayed a little ahead of them all the way.

He talked about the heat and the clogged roads; the eyes of the terrified, fleeing refugees heading for nowhere; the dust; boiling radiators; women pushing prams and dragging children; old men being pulled on handcarts, and the Stukas which came every day, blasting anything that moved as they played the war game of leapfrog with the tanks.

For George, it ended with a shoulder full of shrapnel and three broken ribs from mortar fire at a chalky crossroads some ten miles south of Dunkirk.

He did not remember the beach, or how they got him off. He recalled only a view from the small ship.

'From the stern it looked as though all France was on fire. The oily smoke blotted out the sun. Next thing I knew was a hospital on the safe side of Guildford.'

They kept him there for a month and then sent him to convalesce near Oxford.

'We had to wear shapeless blue trousers and jackets to show that we were wounded. Let us go into the city. People stared at us without pity, as though we were freaks. I kept dreaming about Maman. She'd gone back to France in '39 and married well. He was in scent. Rich. I saw her once on a three day pass to Paris before Jerry started.'

They kept him on at the hospital for longer than necessary, and when he left it was with speed and in disgrace.

'My feet didn't touch the ground,' George grinned. 'A spot of trouble concerning the Duty Medical Officer, myself and a nurse called Gwyneth. The Duty MO walked into my room late one night: 'nough said?'

Herbie chuckled, but George was gone again, out of chronology, thinking back to France and the retreat. 'It was bloody awful. I'm one for tags, Herbie, and I remember thinking again and again about what Tacitus said. I was nearer to the school-room in those days.'

'What did Tacitus say?'

'They make a desert and call it peace.'

He expected some punishment posting. Instead, the orders were to report to Room 444 at the War Office. George got into London early one morning—into the debris of the previous night's raid. The Blitz was in full swing.

'Ramilies was the last person I expected to see. Particularly Ramilies in battledress. A ranking brigadier peering out from behind a WD desk landscaped with books and papers as though it was a model of the New York skyline.'

Ah, young Thomas. Glad you could come. That was the greeting.

The recruitment had begun. Only George Thomas did not know what it was, or how, or why.

14

Ramilies kept fussing. 'Asked for you especially, dear boy,' brushing back a lock of hair. 'Sit down. Sit ye down.'

George moved some books and sat down, thinking about the trim ATS sergeant who'd announced him. When he'd entered the ante-room she'd been looking bored, dripping what looked like blood on to nails of unregulation length.

'You've got all the qualifications, you see.' Ramilies went on patting at his hair. 'French like a native. Ruthless ambition. We know about that, don't we? Probably got the killer instinct as well. Hear you copped it in France. Better now?' He did not wait for a reply.

'French like a native. How's your mother, George?'

George said that she was fine when he'd last seen her in Paris. God knew, now.

Ramilies reminded him of a python, though he could never quite work out why. Maybe it was the smile, and that habit of licking his lips; or, perhaps the belly, bulging and out of place on his slim body, as though he had swallowed something live.

Ramilies went on. 'Good actor, as well. Know about that too, George, don't we? Good actor. Deep cover. Foxy.'

George felt disturbed. Foxy? Is that what his old tutor thought of him? He asked why he had been called to the War Office.

'Bit of research to start with.' Ramilies tipped his chair back and smiled again, setting it permanently, secretly, across the thin lips. 'All in a good cause. Been having a spot of the naughties, I'm told. Think you were here for a wigging? Wartime, George. You don't get gated or sent down these days. Don't you want to be posted to me? I rather thought you would.'

'Depends.'

'Michel de Nostradame,' he replied cryptically. 'You, being an expert on sixteenth-century France, should know all about Michel de Nostradame.'

George knew a little: that he had lived in Provence; was a good medical doctor and had become astrologer to Catherine de'Medici. That was about all, apart from the vague knowledge that his astrological prophecies were much quoted among the idiots who believed in that kind of thing.

'Ah.' Ramilies pushed back his chair again. 'The strange prophecies of old Nostradamus are much in demand at the moment. I would like you to study them for me.'

'You can't be serious. There's a war on ...'

'Yes, I know. This *is* war effort stuff. Method in madness, I do assure you. Here ...' He plunged his hands into the litter on his desk and fished out two books. It reminded George of a man tickling trout.

One was a copy of *Les Prophéties de Me. Michel Nostradamus* which looked as though it was possibly a rare collectors' item. The other was a modern work. The fly-leaf gave the date as 1939: published in Paris under some academic imprint and titled *Le Prophète de Salon*.

Nostradamus had lived in the town of Salon, so George did not have to be a genius to work out the nature of the book. Its author was a Michel Downay.

'Downay,' Ramilies spoke softly as though reading George's thoughts. 'He's something at the Sorbonne.'

'Or was. They've had a spot of trouble in France.'

'Still at the Sorbonne, dear boy. We know about him. At the Institut de Psychologie. We've been in touch.'

'Lately?' George thought he was being sarcastic, but Ramilies took it as a perfectly normal question and said, yes, in fact only last week.

'Interesting book,' he continued; rather diffident, like he was discussing some work by an enemy academic. 'Want you to read it and go over the prophecies again. You have read them, I suppose?'

'Not avidly.' During his studies of sixteenth-century France, it had never struck George that it was par for the course to wade through the thousand-odd verses, quatrains as the pedants called them, which made up the prophetic work of Nostradamus. Like most people doing a specialist study of that period in France, he had taken the odd squint at them, but reckoned they were such a jumble you could make them say anything you wanted to hear.

'You're an unbeliever. You don't think he was an important influence on Catherine de'Medici?' Ramilies' tongue was licking away like mad.

'I don't know enough about him. After all, he's really only a footnote to history.'

'Good. I like that. Still, we'll have to turn you into a believer. Propaganda stuff, this. Old Goebbels has been using the prophecies. Nostradamus does mention Hitler by name, you know? Odd bit of accuracy. Out to fight fire with fire. That's the job. Want you to read him; learn and inwardly digest him: and the Downay book as well. Probably some astrology. Your future in the stars.'

George knew he looked disgruntled. It was to be an academic chore.

'National importance, this,' piped Ramilies. 'Young George Thomas, you'll read him for king and country.' The last delivered like a coy slap on the wrist.

George sighed.

'Asked for you specially. You're the man for the job. All the talents. I'm on a recruiting drive, George. What d'you think of that? From don to press gang in one move, eh?'

George felt more depressed, and asked where all this reading was to be done.

'You're really supposed to call me "sir", you know.' Ramilies had become almost playful.

'Where do I do the reading, *sir*?'

'Got a nice little place all fitted out for you.' He flashed his teeth and rose to reveal the pot belly. 'Take you there myself,' flicking a switch on the big wood and metal intercom on his desk. 'Get the motor round, would you please, Cynthia.' He spoke into the instrument as though it might strike back.

15

LONDON 1978

'Painless recruiting, George. More coffee?' Herbie moved to the pot as they came to a natural break in the narrative.

'You never met the old Rammer, did you?' George nodded for a refill. It was time to move on to the brandy, and Herbie was already lumbering across the room. Unfortunately he had never met Ramilies who was a legend from an earlier time.

'Jocular, devious old queen. Had me hooked, as you say, without pain.'

Herbie asked when they finally gave him the bad news, and George said it took a long time. They put him in purdah; in what would now be called a safe house ('May still be on the books.') near the Aldwych. Work at those bloody quatrains all day; read Michel Downay's book; 'phone calls from Ramilies, and occasional comfort visits from the ATS sergeant called Cynthia. At night, the bombs.

Herbie asked if he became a believer in the prophecies.

No, but he took them more seriously. Downay's book helped.

They talked for a long time about George's period of study, in the heart of London, with the nightmare of the bombing going on until the small hours. Herbie listened carefully, for he detected that this was a crucial period: the time when George Thomas was, unknown to himself, taking on the role of an academic occultist: learning his deep cover.

George expanded on theories which he could still trot out, thirty years after. He could even quote from the prophecies, and paraphrase Michel Downay's book. Remarkable, Herbie thought.

Then the telephone rang. Schnabeln seeking an interview for Girren. Wouldn't tomorrow do? Not in your interest, Schnabeln made it clear. Okay, Herbie told him. Give it one hour and check the main window. (One curtain would be pulled back if all was clear. It was a house sign they had already used during exercises. Herbie was a great one for putting his people through their paces.)

George cocked a querying eye.

65

'One of *my* recruits.' Herbie sat down again, heavily. 'Making them work for a living and they don't like it.'

'None of them ever do. Did you like your controller?'

'I didn't take much notice of him. Correction: couldn't stand him. Always a love-hate thing. When did they lay the news on you, George?'

'About Stellar and the operation? Not until January '41.'

After the concentrated study in the flat, they took him out to the Abbey. (The Abbey: country seat of one of the great old English families, had been used, during the war, as both a training ground and think-tank for Special Operations Executive. Herbie had to remind himself that the time George was talking about pre-dated S.O.E.-proper by a few months.)

'I met Fenice, the Frenchman who had been giving the Foreign Office a lot of material from Paris before '39 until the Fall of France. He knew Downay. Also old Sandy Leaderer who was setting up a transmitter near Dover, all ready to beam phoney messages. They talked a lot about psychological warfare and confusing the enemy.'

George gave a wry smile. 'Should have known it wasn't that easy when they sent me up to Scotland.' It was a toughening-up course at a Strength Through Joy Camp. All the fun of the fair. Survival. Living off the land. Weapons. Maps.

'I'd been brought up tough in childhood. When you walked into Lockhill Terrace wearing the poncy Grammar School uniform you learned to fight back. In Scotland we had a leathery little instructor who had pioneered death all over the Empire: judo, karate and all their variants. I became teacher's pet. Hear him now—*You're a dirty fighter, sir. Take note of him, gentlemen, he's a dirty fighter. Just what we're after.*'

'Then back to the Abbey?' Herbie asked.

George gave an affirmative. Back to the Abbey and the news. The scope of the op. Herbie wanted all that in detail. The days with Fenice and Leaderer. The nights with Ramilies. The whole thing. All that he could remember.

George talked for a long time, and Herbie was nearing his deadline with Girren. Reluctantly he brought it to a close. 'Enough for one night, George. It's fascinating. Just what I need.' Patiently he let it be known that he needed a couple of really long sessions to fill in all that had happened on the operation and after. 'Take a couple of days. Lot of concentration. But ... If you can spare the time ...'

Of course, George agreed. It was interesting to go back over it. Good mental exercise.

Two days. Two full days and they'd do it. George begged off Monday morning, but said he'd book himself out of the office from the afternoon until Thursday morning. 'I presume you want it here and not in the hallowed halls?'

Herbie thought his flat best, thanked George profusely, and saw him to the lift. 'You can't imagine what a help this has been, George. You know how careful I must be ...'

'As long as I get the final result.'

Returning, Herbie pulled back one of his living room curtains, went through to the kitchen, turned off the tape machine. In the living room he started the Mozart from the beginning again.

With a very large brandy in his hand, he sat down to await Girren, his mind going over the latter part of the conversation with George. Tomorrow he would listen to the tape, just to get the details in his head. A George-eye view of the prophecies, and the full scope of the operation which had led to occupied Paris, face to face with both his contact and a pair of SS officers.

Girren arrived looking sour and worried. He was a small, thin, earnest man in his late twenties: ideal background for the new team and, as Herbie had already discovered, a minor authority on the West German security organisations and their personalities.

He talked very fast and did not even notice when Herbie offered him a chair or a drink. To start with, the woman. Schnabeln had told him that there was evidence she had been in England before under the name Gretchen Weiss? Yes. The Weiss woman was dead. This was not Weiss.

Herbie remained patient. He knew that. This was the Weiss woman's sister.

'I knew Gretchen Weiss.' The tone suggested that Girren had not liked her but would not speak ill of the dead. 'She worked for the Americans. She was also hand in glove with the BfV.' Federal Office for the Protection of the Constitution: the mailed fist of the BND.

Schnabeln, Herbie prompted him, had suggested that he had marked one of the heavies leeching the Fenderman woman.

Indeed he had. Both of them now. They were a good team. Inactive for a while. Probably a sabbatical. Had not been seen around the German haunts for some time. Nachent, that was the name of the senior one. A watcher; a minder : general-purpose operative. Hans Nachent. Thirty-six years old and bloody good. His team mate was a man called Billstein. Markus Billstein. Thirty-one. Same trade as his partner in crime. Both highly qualified BND field men of the more unpleasant and subversive kind.

There was no doubt in Girren's mind that they were minding the woman, Fenderman : and she knew it. Whatever the object, the whole thing was a Federal Intelligence Service ploy.

Herbie thanked him with great courtesy, checked that Schnabeln was working, and said he would be in touch.

When Girren departed, head poked forward and in an eternal hurry, Herbie poured himself another huge brandy, put on the Mahler Second Symphony, The Resurrection, and tried to concentrate his mind. Towards the end of the work he became both greatly moved and worried. Enough to warrant another brandy, which he drank quickly. It would help to bring sleep. Tomorrow, George Thomas on tape. Limited appearance only.

Herbie's sleep was deep and comforting. No nightmares until the telephone started ringing and, as he grabbed for the instrument, he saw that it was ten-thirty on the Sunday morning.

Girren spoke urgently into his ear. 'The police and Special Branch are here. Think you should come over. Some idiot took a shot at the Fenderman woman as she was leaving the hotel.'

'When?'

'Fifteen, twenty minutes ago.'

'Our friends?'

'Gave chase, but they're back. Not making contact with the authorities. The place crawls with Press and police.'

Herbie said he would be right over.

16

Big Herbie was not a man given to taking precipitate action. Later, he decided this was a classic case of double-think combined with brandy.

He was actually in a cab, heading for the Devonshire Hotel in Bayswater when he realised the error of judgement. Girren—and by now maybe Schnabeln—was watching out. So were the pair of BND men.

As far as Frau Fenderman was concerned, Herbie Kruger was a Civil Servant working with the Public Records Office. He carried ID which would get him through any police cordon, but recognition was inevitable, if not by the aforementioned Nachent and Billstein, certainly by Frau Fenderman. There would be much explaining to do, and he was not yet ready to blow cover on this one.

He redirected the cab driver to drop him in the Bayswater Road, and walked to the nearest telephone kiosk. The instrument had been vandalised which added another ten minutes' walk to find a machine which worked. Consulting his small pocket directory, he dialled Worboys' home number.

The young man was unhappy. 'I'm not on duty ...' he began, and would have continued if Herbie Kruger had not cut him short, pointing out that you didn't have to be on duty to be called out, and that refusal would mean a short and sharp interview with both Tubby Fincher and Sir Willis at the first opportunity.

Worboys turned up twenty minutes later, looking sleepy and unshaven. Herbie gave his instructions fast. 'Flash your card at any coppers, see whoever's in charge, find out who is handling it from the SB, get the story and leave. Come straight back. Oh, and find out Frau Hildegarde Fenderman's story and condition.'

While waiting for Worboys, Herbie had made a second call. Schnabeln and Girren were invigilating from the first-floor front room of a guest house on the seedy side of the road, almost directly opposite the Devonshire Hotel. Their cover was modest and satisfactory, which meant the opposition—if there was opposition—could blow them in an hour flat with both hands tied. Mid-European immigrants doing shift work as porters at Heathrow. In emergency they could be reached at the guest house call box, open and insecure, in the main hall.

Herbie rang and talked to Schnabeln who had come back on the trot as soon as Girren flashed him directly after the incident.

The conversation was double-talk, but Herbie had the gist of the affair before Worboys even arrived.

The law was having a field day in Deveron Road, in which the Devonshire Private Hotel was situated. There were Special Patrol Group landrovers parked at either end. All cars had been checked, and nobody was being allowed near until the investigating team from the local nick, plus the SPG boys and, within fifteen minutes, the Special Branch, had made heroes of themselves. No, Schnabeln did not recognise the SB Super who'd arrived in a flurry with a souped-up Rover.

As for Frau Fenderman's minders, they had been using a Mini Clubman, also souped-up by the look of what happened. They had given chase and returned to find the road sealed. They were now on foot, mingling with the inevitable crowd at the western end of Deveron Road. Yes, Girren had taken pictures. No, they hadn't made the driver who'd taken the pot at the lady, nor the number of his Cortina, except that it had a J registration. Maybe it would show on the pix when processed. They were watching and listening out. Herbie apologised for not bringing a walkie-talkie with him. It had all been a bit quick.

By noon, Worboys was back, and they sat in his car as he went through the tale.

Shortly after ten, Frau Fenderman had come down into the hotel lobby. On the previous evening she had mentioned that she would be going to church. She left the hotel at around ten past ten and walked west. She had gone less than ten yards when a yellow Cortina pulled out from parked traffic on the far side of the road (which put the driver on her side). He slowed slightly, did not lean out of the window, but fired at her four times.

There were two eye-witnesses who heard her scream, and watched as she dodged up the steps of a private house. The police had the car registration, and already knew that it had been stolen from the street, either in the night or early morning, in the West End, from outside some luxury flats off Park Lane.

Frau Fenderman was in shock, but unhurt, and could throw no light on why anyone would want to kill her. *It must be some dreadful mistake*, was the quote of the day.

Two of the bullets had been recovered, and were on their way to forensics, though one of the SB men would stake his reputation on them being old stock nine mill.

The SB officer in charge was a Superintendent Vernon-Smith. 'Public School and very how's-your-father,'' said Worboys.

Herbie grinned the stupid grin, and began to extricate himself from Worboys' little VW, telling him to hold it. Worboys could give him a lift home and, if he behaved himself, he might even get a coffee.

The sun, which had been shining coldly from the moment Herbie left the St. John's Wood flat, went behind heavy cloud as he entered the 'phone box yet again. By mid-afternoon there would be more rain, but that wouldn't matter because by then he'd be snug and listening to George Thomas on tape.

He dialled the Devonshire Hotel and asked for the Super. 'Rachet,' he said when Vernon-Smith's fruity voice came on the line.

'Christ,' said the Special Branch man, 'one of your leash-hounds has been sniffing around already.'

'Rachet Soap.' Herbie identified himself personally. *Rachet*, being the Department ID; *Soap* being his own ID contact word for the SB. It was a small joke perpetrated by the Director who remembered his father, or grandfather, reciting a piece of Boer War doggerel which went—

> Poor old Kruger's dead;
> He died last night in bed.
> He cut his throat with a bar of soap;
> Poor old Kruger's dead.

There was irony also, for Herbie was conscious that his work and life was concerned with truth, and often, its distortion. Soap was also the in-house argot for hyped up sodium pentathol: SO-PE.

'Cute as lace pants,' chortled Vernon-Smith, who was well up on all the Departmental gossip, but not so hot on classified stuff. If truth was known, as a policeman, 'Vermin' Vernon-Smith (schoolboy nicknames often follow us to the grave), did not like the 'Friends'. 'I suppose you want hands off?' He pronounced it like the composer—Orff.

'Be obliged.'

'Pleasure, as long as I don't have to carry the can.'

'We have been looking after her for a while.'

'Didn't do a very good job this morning, did you?'

'Most unexpected. Be grateful if you could leave one man in view to scare the crows and rabbits.'

'Done.'

'You going to make the shootist?'

'Nobody saw the face. Might make the weapon if you'd care to call tonight or tomorrow.'

'I'll be in touch tonight. Copy of your report to me. Oh, and how is she?'

'Shock. Even sounds real. As though she can't think why anyone would do such a thing.'

'Let you into a secret.' Herbie was not smiling now. 'Neither can I think why, and I know more about her than you do. Thank you for the help.'

'For this relief much thanks.'

'You're not that cold, or sick of heart. I will call.'

Rachet Soap closed the line and went back to Worboys' VW, which sagged visibly as he bent himself into the passenger seat. The young man asked if it was straight home and Herbie nodded, distracted.

He didn't like any of it. A German national comes to London with a tale about her husband of two weeks having been executed as a spy at the Tower of London in 1941. His name shows up on files connected with a PW operation which blew up in France and Germany. She could be of help in the future. Routine riffle through the files, and up pops a senior officer of high calibre. The Yanks are cagey, and she now seems to be hand in glove with the West Germans—very cape and shiv. Then here, on a sunny spring morning, she sets off to church and some cretin in a stolen motor tries to blow her head off with four nine-millimetre bullets.

Herbie gave Worboys a coffee and hardly spoke to him, making the young man both puzzled and uneasy. If he had known Herbie better, he would have identified distraction as the cause, for the big man hardly noticed him leave.

Where was the connection? Here and now, with the past only a coincidence? Or was Hildegarde Fenderman's current visit linked strangely to the past, to the Stellar network, Nostradamus, and what happened afterwards? She had lied to him, that was for sure; but so had his BND contact at the German Embassy. Among other things he would need a word with that gentleman. Tomorrow. Also fix a meeting with Frau Fenderman soon. Today. Fix it today for Thursday evening. Make sure she couldn't fly. By Thursday night he should have heard all of George Thomas' story in detail.

The rain had set in, heavy and hard, with a light wind splattering it against the windows, by the time Big Herbie had eaten, lugged the reel-to-reel tape deck through to the living room and linked it with his own stereo. Then, provided with a large jug of coffee and a spiral notepad, he ran through the tape to find the long section in which George had spoken about his studies of Nostradamus and the prophecies, back in late 1940 when every night the Luftwaffe sent out its Heinkel 111s and Dornier 17s to bomb London.

17

Michel de Nostradame. Born, Provence 1503. Died 1566. Another
legend in his own lifetime. A seer. A man who could predict—to
all accounts *did* predict—things which occurred during his own
era. A man who claimed to have foretold the major events which
would take place from his time until the ending of the world.

'Six weeks, I think,' George coughed on the tape. 'Six weeks
the Rammer had me holed up in that flat in a side street between
Covent Garden and the Aldwych. The Rammer. He certainly
rammed me, crammed me: Downay's book, the bloody prophecies, horoscopes. But mainly those endless prophecies of Nostradamus.'

The welter of predictions which flew from the old doctor's
pen claimed to cover a vast period. Yet, being essentially a survivor, Michel de Nostradame took great care to cover his tracks.

He knew as well as anyone else, said George, that bearers of
evil tidings are not always the most popular people. Often they
fall victim of their own news. So he wrote the predictions in
four-line pieces which often seem unintelligible; then he shuffled
them.

Each snippet of precognition was coded into a quatrain and
then arranged on the rough basis of one hundred quatrains to a
century. Ten centuries: approximately one thousand quatrains,
and the whole shooting match muddled and dealt without order
or thought of chronology.

'You probably know it all, but there were not, in fact, a full
thousand quatrains, because one of the centuries had a heavy
short-fall. That was very useful later.'

George maintained that, when he began the fevered journey
into this unknown territory, he had great scepticism. Only later,
on reflection, did he come to realise that Nostradamus and his
prophetic verses began, even then, to spin a strange web of
fascination.

'Ramilies had already mentioned the Hitler reference.' At first it seemed to George the only relevant thing. Nostradamus had called him Hifter, if you used the old spelling. Hifter. Hister. Hitler—

> Beasts wild with hunger will cross the rivers,
> The greater part of the battlefield will be against Hifter.
> He will drag the leader in a cage of iron,
> When the child of Germany observes no law.

For an obscure doctor in the sixteenth century it wasn't a bad guess. 'Give a monkey a Leica and one thousand frames of film and he should, by the law of averages, get a couple of good pictures. Yet even there, in the claustrophobic, chi-chi atmosphere of that flat, I think I glimpsed that Nostradamus was no monkey.'

At first sight, the verses appeared to be almost gibberish, particularly when some read like—

> More than eleven times the Moon will not want the Sun.
> Both raised and lowered in one degree;
> Put so low that one will sew little gold,
> After famine and plague the secret will be discovered.

George had committed those which seemed of greatest interest to memory. A long train of strange verses to be heaped into his skull.

(Listening to him talk all those years later, Herbie wondered at the fact that George could still quote the quatrains verbatim.)

'I spent a whole afternoon, for instance, thinking about the quatrain with which the old boy hit the jackpot. The one about the death of Henri II of France, late lamented husband of Catherine de'Medici herself.'

> The young lion shall overcome the old,
> In warlike field in single fight;
> In a cage of gold he will pierce his eyes
> Two wounds in one, then die a cruel death.

Nostradamus was already a favourite with the royal court

when he wrote that one. The king even took greater care because of it. But it happened—came to pass, in Biblical language—on a summer day in 1559. A day of celebration. There had been peace treaties between England, France and Spain, plus a couple of good marriages in the offing for two of the princesses.

Part of the regal cavortings included some dangerous jousting in the lists, and the king, who liked his sport, took on Montgomery—captain of his Scottish Guard.

They splintered lances, but Montgomery was unable to lower his lance in time. The broken pieces shattered the king's gilded visor (the cage of gold), putting out an eye and wounding him in the throat. He lingered, and certainly died a 'cruel death'. Soon after that, Catherine de'Medici appointed Nostradamus astrologer royal, and he was a made man. He predicted a rotten death for Montgomery as well. That happened.

Interspersed with his knowledgeable talk about the proprecies, George had a lot to say about Michel Downay's book, *The Prophet of Salon*. 'Brilliant,' he called it. 'Particularly in the original French.' He was, according to George, one of those writers whose words you could pull over your head. He knew about life in the outposts, and at the royal courts, of France during the 1550s and '60s, and was able to convey the feeling that he had actually been there.

It was like going on a journey along a route already travelled, but with a companion who had a new eye which gave him the ability to point out all that you had missed before.

An earnest note crept into George's voice, 'The old ruling house of Valois had never seemed so close; the politics, the banditry and murder so tangible; the poverty and superstition so dangerous.'

By any standard, *The Prophet of Salon* was a dazzling display: detailed, crisp and clear with the personality and background of Michel de Nostradame most sharply focused.

'He teased him into life,' claimed George. 'Followed his career, step by step.'

In particular, Downay was at his best when describing Nostradamus's early career in medicine. The doctor had a way with the plague, which lingered in pockets of France, especially in Provence. Though the author hinted that it may well not have been the true plague which helped the good doctor make his medical reputation. A hint of the charlatan? Maybe.

George even quoted a passage from the book. Downay had written—*At this time, Medicine and Magic walked hand in hand through Europe, interwoven like twin roots. In the end, it was the occult and magic root which became dominant in the work of the Prophet of Salon.*

'Yes, Michel Downay baited the hook and I bit hard. Maybe that was wrong, psychologically, but I became involved with the work of Nostradamus like you become involved and obsessed with a woman. Didn't mean I believed it all. But ...'

The involvement had side effects. During the time he spent in the flat, alone, George admitted he did not sleep well. The work became absorbing, and the Blitz put paid to part of each night. When he did manage to sleep, George dreamed a great deal—and vividly.

'One certain dream came more than once. I was back in the little terraced house near Didcot, a child with Maman, playing my favourite game of acting out plays written by myself, with me taking all the parts. I always woke with one of those long-forgotten plays in my head. Christ, I could even smell the inside of that house: smell it in my head.'

He also remembered how some of the prophecies seemed to have direct links with the present. 'Which was, I suppose, what the Rammer wanted.'

One night, the Blitz had been especially bad. Two landmines fell near Trafalgar Square, and a stick of incendiaries started a blaze in the next street. George recalled it with great accuracy—

'When the immediate fury died down, I pulled back the curtains and looked out. The road below was bright as a summer's evening from the fires. They seemed to flow, tangible as water, dancing and moving wherever one looked. The sky had turned to blood, and another of the Prophet's quatrains came singing, wailing, through my mind:

> There will be let loose living fire and hidden death,
> Fearful inside dreadful globes.
> By night the city will be reduced to rubble by the fleet,
> The city on fire, helpful to the enemy.

'Herbie, if I'd been the sombre doctor living in Salon all those years ago, this vision would have driven me out of my skull. Perhaps it did for a while. Perhaps that was the moment I started to establish the link with the old boy.'

There were other quotes:

The French nation will be in great grief,
Vain and light-hearted, they will believe rash things.
No bread, salt, wine or water, venom nor ale,
The greater one captured, hunger, cold and want.

'That made me remember the thick oily cloud of smoke I'd seen from the boat at Dunkirk. It also made me think about Maman and that smart husband of hers. I used to wonder how they were getting on. It was worrying. The wireless was giving us a lot of the "under the heel of the jackboot" stuff at the time.'

What did he, George Thomas, really believe about the prophecies at that time? 'Difficult. Knowing what I know now. I suppose I was at odds with myself: the doubting George Thomas slowly being dragged into a psychological relationship with the writings. In his book, Downay had a theory that time ran like two trains on parallel tracks. Certain people had the ability to view the countryside ahead of schedule.'

Then, before he knew it, the time was up, and Ramilies ordered him to pack his kit and be prepared for a move. The Rammer arrived in a dung-painted Humber.

'Where we going?' asked George, seated in the back.

'Trunky trouble, my old nannie used to call that.' Ramilies did his python lick. 'Nosey Parker. Have a butterscotch, they're not easy to come by these days.'

They were, of course, going to the Abbey for George to learn what he later called 'the algebra of the operation'. From a London flat to the Gare du Nord and the SS, with much more to follow. It was a long jump.

18

It was an even longer jump from George's arrival in France, 1941, to Frau Fenderman's arrival in London, 1978, and these present repercussions. Herbie thought that as he switched off the tape and looked at his notes.

As he studied them, it again surprised him that George could still quote Nostradamus with accuracy. He had his own copy, the paperback, beside him. Checking showed that George had it pat, almost word for word.

Could he remember the quotation scrawled on the bottom of Hildegarde Fenderman's letter? The one from her husband, written just before he left on that last mission. Something about passages for spies.

He leafed through the book and finally found it in Nostradamus's Seventh Century: Quatrain number thirty-three:

> The kingdom stripped of its forces by fraud,
> The fleet blockaded, passages for the spy;
> Two false friends will come to rally
> To awaken hatred for a long time dormant.

The interpreter had referred the prophecy to the occupation of France in 1940. Line three, she said, described the Germans and the Russians.

Not gin tonight, thought Herbie. Too much gin in the past weeks; too much brandy with George on the previous night. A quick bolt of Schnapps. He poured and selected some music, so that he could think. The Second Symphony again, The Resurrection? Apt, a musical commentary of life's transitory nature, but ending with faith and hope. Faith that could move mountains. Herbie wanted to move the mountain of mystery which surrounded the transitory link between George Thomas and the 1941 operation, and the German woman Fenderman.

He was about to settle himself when he realised that there were other matters to be completed first. Maybe, he considered, reaching for the telephone, that he was, after all, over the hill.

The switchboard at Scotland Yard put him through to the Special Branch offices. Vernon-Smith was in. Forensics had come up with a quick report. Old ammunition, fired, possibly through something like the good and ancient Luger. (Only pedantic Vernon-Smith called it by its correct name, the *Pistole o8.*) 'Always a thorn in our flesh. So many of the bloody things still around. Bet you've got one.'

'A good weapon.' Silent, Herbie, about what you had or had not got in your private armoury.

'Find us the weapon and we'll match it.' Vernon-Smith sounded boisterous. 'See the TV news tonight?'

Herbie's heart sank as he mumbled a negative in German, changing quickly to English.

'It's okay. No names. Nice little piece though. Had me on making a comment. Our line's that it was an isolated drunken discharge of a firearm; something like that. Your bird wasn't mentioned and we've got the watch dogs on.'

Herbie said, good, and could they please make sure she did not leave.

The hotel? queried the police officer.

The country, Herbie told him quietly.

Tomorrow he would arrange for dinner with Hildegarde Fenderman on Thursday night, and pray that by then he would have pieced together some of the skeins. Always the optimist, he thought that he might even be able to sound her out for employment. Then he thought of the BND minders. The optimism turned to irritation. Rachendorf at the German Embassy would have to be seriously compromised. That would be tomorrow as well.

He dialled again. This time to the pay 'phone for Schnabeln and a short conversation which, reading between the lines, meant that Frau Fenderman was not to be let out of their sight for a moment. He wanted none of this business of the woman suddenly disappearing without trace. What he actually said, in his strange mixture of English and German, was 'I do not want her to pull a *Nacht und Nebel* on us.'

Thus satisfied, Big Herbie Kruger went back to his Mahler and Schnapps, but his mind weaved and danced, getting nowhere.

Continually he was drawn back to the terse reports about the incident outside the Devonshire Hotel that morning.

She was still really quite attractive. If she'd only dress less severely. Possibly do something about her hair. Clearly in his mind he saw Hildegarde Fenderman come down the four steps from the hotel door and begin to walk up the street.

Then the yellow Cortina and the shots. A scream and the woman, like a chicken with its head cut off, uncertain which way to go, knowing the bullets were for her.

It was always afterwards that you were frightened. At the time, surprise, sudden and unexpected near-catastrophe, produced numbness, freezing you to the ground; panic.

Big Herbie knew all about those things. He tossed back a large Schnapps and drew comfort from it. The nightmares chased each other around his head: a man on uncarpeted stairs screaming and clutching at his throat; the smell of cordite; a dark street near the Wall and the shots echoing; the smack of death on stone. The shadows.

Mahler echoed his funeral oratory and Herbie closed his eyes. Again the Cortina. He could see the driver clearly now, the skull face and cloak. He felt Frau Fenderman's fear, as he had felt it many times in his many lives. Death, with perhaps an old Luger, driving a stolen Cortina in Bayswater.

19

George, thank Heaven, was in early. Herbie got him on the internal line and asked if they could cry off the afternoon session. If he had cleared Tuesday and Wednesday that would give them enough time. They always had Thursday morning as a back up.

George seemed pleased about it. Better to have started today, but Herbie wanted to get the whole reasoning behind the operation into his head before they began the forward journey from the Gare du Nord.

*   *   *

Frau Fenderman was at breakfast when he telephoned the Devonshire. Big Herbie was at his most obsequious. He was terribly sorry to bother her, but he really thought he might have some news. It would take a couple of days. To be safe, say Thursday. Would she dine with him on Thursday evening? She would be delighted. What sort of news? Until then. Not yet. Except one thing. Yes? Her husband did not die at the Tower of London. Only one Nazi agent was shot there during the Second World War. Only one, and he couldn't have been her husband. Till Thursday evening, then. About eight? Good.

*   *   *

Wolfgang Alberich Rachendorf, his BND contact at the West German Embassy, would love to lunch with him and was free today. 'Monday's always a slack day,' he said, which seemed strange, because in Herbie's experience all the dramas occurred over the weekend, and Monday was hell on earth.

He could never make up his mind about Rachendorf. Had his father been a devotee of Mozart who had lost his nerve about giving his boy Amadeus as a middle name? Or was it a sinister baptism? Was the father really a Wagnerian who hated the child so much that he named him for the ugly Nibelung? Herbie's shoulders shook with silent laughter.

He had brought the files from his flat. Now he arranged them with those left in the office over the weekend. Carefully he selected five photographs of five people who had been engaged in the murky events of 1941. After clearing the action with Tubby Fincher, he called up Pix who came and collected the photographs to copy and enlarge. Maybe he could use them on Thursday when dinner was finished and he had Frau Fenderman in a pliable mood.

On the dot of twelve-thirty, he met his BND contact outside an Indian vegetarian restaurant near the British Museum. What, Herbie thought, could be more logical than a German national and a former national, both in the trade, meeting at a place like that. Besides, he knew the restaurant and Rachendorf did not. He would be off-guard and not at ease.

The meal came on large circular, segmented, dishes into which you probed and chose. Rachendorf was not happy with this. Good-looking, in an old Prussian kind of way, he was a bit of a dandy who thought the best cover in London would be a well cut dark suit, bowler and rolled umbrella. He was seldom seen without a copy of *The Times*—in the street that was.

The BND man was about to take the plunge, gastronomically, when Herbie whispered Hildegarde Fenderman's name.

'So?' Rachendorf hesitated. The puzzled look could be almost genuine.

Herbie repeated the name, like a question.

'So, you have asked before. I have given you her whole file. The lot, including the intelligence report. As I remember it, *Nothing known or suspect.*'

'Come off it, Wolfie. You gave me stuff the Americans didn't give me. But if you've no interest, why the sharks?'

Rachendorf looked positively shocked, though Herbie thought that might be due to his first mouthful of food. Sharks?

Gently, with his big hands showing, almost ominously, Herbie pointed out that since her arrival on the scene, Frau Fenderman had been minded and watched—'Seemingly with her own knowledge,'—by a pair of BND thugs.

'We have no thugs.'

'What do you call Hans Nachent and Markus Billstein, then?'

'Billstein? ... Nachent? ...' The brow creased horribly.

Herbie told him to come on and talk. 'Me? I'm so old-fashioned I still think of your lot as the BND. All my colleagues talk about you as the FIA. Federal Intelligence Agency. I'm still German at heart, Wolf. Billstein and Nachent.'

Rachendorf floundered. 'They went private.' He flapped a hand as though waving goodbye.

Herbie's stomach contracted for he smelled truth here. Truth and something unpleasant.

Rachendorf shook his head. Billstein and Nachent never worked England. Both came a cropper last December. He shrugged and looked sheepish. 'The Bonn Ministry of Defence thing. They got pensioned off. True, my friend. God's truth. Other people would have been very harsh. I heard they went private.'

'Then,' Herbie was leaning over the table. Rachendorf looked frightened. 'Then you wouldn't mind if I had them snatched?'

He would be most grateful. He would show his gratitude. It would please him much. He did not like the idea of these two boys swimming around London. Come to think of it, he didn't like the idea of them being mixed up with Frau Fenderman.

Neither did Herbie. Back in the office he almost called Vernon-Smith, but thought better of it. What difference would a couple of days make?

About four in the afternoon he sent a flash to Girren, who was on duty again, warning him to watch out for the leeches. Then back to St. John's Wood for another session with George on tape.

This time, he listened on the headphones, with the spiral note-pad on his thigh. He listened to the whole of that first session, ears strained particularly for repeats, long pauses, uncertainties, hesitations. He made a lot of notes and then went back to listen again to George's version of his briefing for the Stellar network and the scope of the operation which took him by Lysander to occupied France in February 1941.

20

The old Humber took George and Ramilies straight to the Abbey, the natural country seat of an ancient and noble family, just saved from going to seed when the crisis of 1939 blew.

Parts were Tudor, particularly the main building, though large hunks of the East and West wings were early Victorian Gothic. The vast parkland in which it stood was by God.

Some said it was a relief to the family, handing the Abbey over to the War Office, but they had got their good furniture and carpets out before the military moved in. Now it was stripped for action: bare, functional, makeshift and smelling of floor polish.

The occupants, George quickly discovered, treated each other warily, and there was no shop talk in what was called the mess: once a large drawing room. They were a strange mixture—civilians, and uniforms of all kinds: a lot of French, a few Poles and Czechs. Men and women. Most of the women wore the uniform of the First Aid Nursing Yeomanry. The FANY.

There was also a sprinkling of older men. Grey-haired, or bald: distracted people with sombre faces who would gather in small huddles away from the main herd.

George was also kept away from the crowd. They gave him a room to himself, and Ramilies instructed him to go on working at Nostradamus. He also provided more books—astrology, the casting of horoscopes, general volumes on the occult. George felt unsure and strange. 'A bit of an outcast.' The books were to be kept in his room all the time and he was not allowed to take them beyond the door. Even a trip to the bathroom, just down the corridor, meant locking them in a cupboard and carrying the key with him. He was to speak to nobody about his subject.

Not that anyone else spoke about their subjects. They all seemed to be busy, and he got an almost rude rebuff when trying to make the most innocent of passes at one of the pretty FANYs.

In some ways it was even more claustrophobic than the flat.

For two days nothing happened. Then, after dinner on the third evening, George was asked to attend a meeting in one of the bare conference halls which the others called schoolrooms.

Ramilies was there; and two others: a rabbity little man wearing old-fashioned pince-nez on a black ribbon, who went by the name of Fenice; and a giant, florid of complexion, called Leaderer.

Fenice had got out of Paris three hours before the Wehrmacht moved in, and for some years before had been a Peeping Tom on behalf of HMG. In short, spying on his own successive governments and their diabolically subversive handling of the military.

Leaderer was to become a legend. Strange how, in a world of secrets, so many people become legends. Flamboyant of manner and dress (he favoured ginger tweeds which matched what little of his hair remained), Leaderer was already well-known in the capitals of Europe, where he had served out most of the Thirties as a foreign correspondent for one of London's major newspapers.

Ramilies introduced George as, 'Our Nostradamus expert.'

'Speaks French like a native, you say? That's what I'm interested in.' Leaderer grinned and patted the pockets of his vast jacket.

'Yes, you come well recommended in my language.' Fenice had the unnerving manner of looking at your left ear as he spoke. George remained nervous of Fenice for the whole time he was at the Abbey. Now the Frenchman was rattling off questions in his own tongue. It was easier than George expected. Maman again, he thought.

Then Leaderer shot him some remarks in immaculate German —immaculate in that he spoke with a perfect Berlin accent. George just about kept up.

This went on for about fifteen minutes. Everyone appeared happy. Fenice even repeated, 'Bon ... bon ... bon ...' a number of times.

'Let's get on with it then.' Leaderer lit a pipe of immense size, to match his personality. 'The Rammer here has a tale to tell, young John Thomas.'

'*George*.' George had never been one for bluff and hearty men.

'All Thomases're John to me, sonny.' 'Sandy Leaderer disappeared behind a smoke cloud.

The story—which Ramilies told with that same air of

authority, George remembered from his lectures at Oxford—began in the first few weeks of the war. It also started, if not in the Third Reich's corridors of power, at least in one of their master bedrooms.

The club-footed Reichminister of Propaganda, Paul Joseph Goebbels, was peacefully asleep in his bed. His wife, the Frau Doktor Magda Goebbels, was awake and reading a book titled *Mysteries of the Sun and the Soul*, by Dr. H. H. Kritzinger. The book included a chapter on the interpretation of the Nostradamus quatrains, and one of Kritzinger's interpretations made direct reference to events which would bring about the final noteworthy change of dynasty in Britain. The quatrain in question seemed to fit the tenor of these very days.

Magda was so startled by what Nostradamus had written that she woke her husband. Goebbels, being the shrewd man he was, decided that Nostradamus could be of value to the war effort on the propaganda front.

'Can you guess the quatrain, dear boy?' Ramilies gave George the fish-eye he knew well from Oxford days. It meant George was the star pupil and should now show off. Woe betide him if he screwed it up.

George was delighted. He didn't even have to think. The hours of memorising and study paid off. Downay had a lot to say about quatrain number fifty-three in the Third Century. Who could tell, thought George, if he had cribbed it from Kritzinger, or vice versa.

He trotted it out and elaborated by saying that it implied Britain would face a great crisis in the late 1930s; the crisis would be with Germany, at the same time as a similar crisis concerning Poland.

> Seven times you will see the British nation change.
> Dyed in blood for two hundred and ninety years.
> Not at all free through German support,
> Aries fears for the protectorate of Poland.

The astrological mathematics were not easy, but it all made sense. Ramilies looked pleased; Fenice raised an eyebrow; Leaderer inhaled, spluttered and then looked round for his gin.

Goebbels had immediately set about using Nostradamus for

the greater glory of the Third Reich.

'Astrology,' observed Ramilies, still playing the lecturer, 'is very much a going concern in Nazi quarters these days. I am given to understand that even the beloved Führer is an apostle—though who knows what we should really believe?'

Astrologers and followers of the occult had not always had it easy under the Party. Many of its main exponents in Germany had been put in the bag at one time or another. Recently though, if Ramilies' information was correct, most of those left alive had been sprung. There was word that Goebbels had some tame star-gazers in his employ.

It was indisputable, however, that, before the Blitzkrieg, the Luftwaffe had dropped both genuine and bastardised copies of selected quatrains on France to discourage the defences. The prophecies claimed that France was doomed and had no hope of beating back the invader : that Hitler would inevitably be the new, and greatest, world leader.

Astrology was also being used on the home market. A Party-inspired magazine called *Zenit* published propaganda under the guise of scientific astrological predictions, pointing to the final supremacy of the Master Race. Hitler's destiny was foretold in the stars.

The occupied countries were getting the same medicine. It would seem that the success of the war, the Party and its leaders, was clearly there—in the heavens for all to see; and already these stellar signposts had been outlined by the greatest prophet of history : Michel de Nostradame.

George latched on. 'So our job's to fight fire with fire?'

Leaderer gave Ramilies a quick look, asking if he could take over. The Rammer nodded. 'Winston,' Leaderer spoke as though he was on drinking terms with the Prime Minister, 'has given the order : Set Europe Ablaze. Lots of people getting ready to do that. Give 'em a spot of the terrorism. Organise an underground. We have a different task. We have to have a go at their minds.'

They were not concerned with what he called 'the straight, clandestine graft'. They were to dabble in the arts which were already being called Black Propaganda ('Not off the ground yet, but Winston feels we're on the right tack.')

Leaderer revealed that he had some warlock working for him, perched on the cliffs near Dover running a radio coven. Even now they were beaming broadcasts into France, the purpose of which was to spread alarm and despondency, discontent and uneasiness, among the occupying forces.

The wireless warlock had, like Leaderer, been active on the foreign desk of a daily: Germany, Austria and other points. He was causing mischief by giving peculiar English lessons to the Wehrmacht: teaching them to say, *The invasion barges are burning well*, and *The SS-Sturmbannführer is nicely on fire*. Not subtle, but effective.

There was more subtle stuff in the pipeline. A wireless station, near the one already operating, would purport to come directly from somewhere near Calais. Leaderer said that it would pose as a regular station catering for the Wehrmacht in France. It would broadcast genuine news items ('We're getting the stuff from Berlin as quickly as their own newspapers. Silly buggers; the Nazi foreign correspondents. Left their ticker machine behind in London.'), very good music—the best and most up-to-date in Europe—and the occasional tit-bits with an edge to them.

'Like putting razor blades in cream buns.' Ramilies sounded most unpleasant.

Leaderer nodded. They were getting the ideas together. Things which, if fed through as disguised news asides, would cause malicious discomfort. Tales about the Gauleiters back home getting more rations than the civilians; stories of bribes; reports of the Führer awarding decorations to gallant doctors and nurses fighting cholera epidemics in Berlin, or the 'safe' areas.

The station was to be called *Soldatensender Calais*. They hoped it would have an operational life of at least a year.

For a moment it was a charmed circle, while the three magi sat and looked at George. Ramilies broke the spell with a clearing of his throat: characteristic: two notes, one rising, the other a thump. 'One of the things we have in mind for *Soldatensender Calais* . . .' He let it hang for a moment. 'A rumour, tittle-tattle, backed up with some of Nostradamus' famous quotes. A rumour that Himmler is out to give Hitler the order of the boot.'

George admitted later that he should have known then, because, at Oxford, Ramilies always coughed and weighed his words like that when he was about to spread fertiliser all over you.

'Putting the SS in the ascendant,' Fenice mused. He appeared to be lost in admiration for his own feet.

George tried, vainly searching for a better tag. 'Set dog against dog.' He knew it was lame and that Ramilies would cap him.

He did. *'Take but degree away, untune that string, and hark what discord follows.'* Shakespeare had said it all.

It would, they claimed, make the Wehrmacht twitchy. The Wehrmacht were twitchy about the SS at the best of times. If they played it right, the idea might even sow dissent into the heart of the Nazi Party, right where the power was.

'And most of it will be done from long range.' Fenice fiddled with his pince-nez.

'This astrological rubbish.' Leaderer appeared embarrassed about even touching on the subject.

Ramilies stepped in hastily. 'We feel that the whole thing could be backed up.' Once more the sinister pause. 'It could benefit with some planted astrology.'

'Astrology being the popular science of the Party,' Fenice added.

Ramilies went on, fast. 'Such as Nostradamus having already prophesied the fall of Hifter and the rise of Himmler.' He repeated the name *Hifter* to make sure George followed him.

George felt suddenly at ease and confident. He had seen enough of battle. Now, the idea of sitting here in the Abbey, or at Leaderer's warlock's coven near Dover, concocting phoney quatrains and horoscopes appealed to him. 'You want me to make some adjustments,' he said.

'Sort of.' Ramilies did not look at him.

Later, George confessed that he should have known then, but they were all so full of the idea—of broadcasting the stuff on the fake wireless station—that it did not enter his mind.

He should have known then. He should have known that something was up when Ramilies said he was looking peaky. Too much study. Need to clear your head, Leaderer added. Fenice said something about getting the body muscles prepared for the brain work.

He should have known when they sent him off to the Strength Through Joy Camp in Scotland with its exercises, dirty fighting, and even radio procedures.

* * *

Big Herbie ran the tape on. George had a lot of anecdotes about his time in Scotland and there was nothing of value there, except one reference to the fact that Maitland-Wood had visited him for a day. They were doing silent kills that day. Silent kills and evasion techniques.

Maitland-Wood suggested that Ramilies might want him to get some time in on simple ciphers: encoding and decoding.

Herbie ran the tape on to the point where they really laid the news on him, back at the Abbey.

* * *

George spent his Christmas leave in London. A sombre and austere festival in many ways, lightened by the fact that he stayed with an old girl friend from Oxford. She was called Heather Dare and was, therefore, subject to all the permutations of jokes concerning her name. Happily, she lived up to them.

He reported back to the Abbey on January 2nd, 1941, and was plunged straight into the cipher course. Basics only, together with some work on the Mark I portable transmitter, which packed into a suitcase and had been quickly developed for clandestine use within Hitler's Fortress Europe.

He had his same old room, and the pile of books was re-delivered. Procedure was just as strict: no talking about his work; no leaving the books unattended. But now there were some subtle pressures.

For instance, Ramilies took out at least one hour of each day, just talking to him. Slowly, the time spent talking with Ramilies lengthened. Mainly they spoke about the techniques of carrying out psychological upsets within occupied Europe and Germany. But, slowly the scope of discussions widened.

Ramilies occupied a small, bleak room high up in the West wing. It was there, seated in aged armchairs—originally from the servants' quarters—that the news was finally broken.

The only thing that was in any way new in the room was a small gas fire, recently fitted; two bars only, therefore not really warming unless you sat hunched over it.

'The adjusted prophecies,' the Rammer began one evening, when the wind rattled hard at his window and the cold seemed to blast its way through the casement. 'Dear boy, you do realise that if they're to take effect, it's no good letting them come out just from our one source—the wireless: *Soldatensender Calais*. To give real credence they've got to come from the inside as well. Pincer movement; don't you see? It would be preferable if they seemed to emanate originally from one of the poison-dwarf Goebbels' tame star-gazers.'

'Asking a lot.' George was interested in the theory. 'But how on earth could you do that?'

Ramilies leaned further forward, hand to his hair, patting. A nervous gesture? It was certainly some kind of body signal which George had yet to divine. 'Ah,' he sounded as though it was all very painful; as if someone should have already wised-up George. 'Ah, well. I have a taker over there, dear heart. Comfortably settled in. But we have our reservations about him. Nobody's been able to test him out. Untried. Foreigner, of course, and that's ... well ... We need someone with good cover: someone with him, working over there. In the lion's cage. We—well I, actually —thought you might be the other one. Our taker's the fellow at the Sorbonne: wrote the book, *Prophet of Salon*. Michel Downay. We'd like you to be his assistant. On the ground. In the field.'

21

The dream about acting his own plays, single-handed in Lockhill Terrace during childhood, now became almost a nightly occurrence for George.

After putting the boot in, Ramilies left him in no doubt that this was the end product of the training. There was a period of deep depression, after which, George just did not have the time to worry about what might, or might not, happen to him.

Fenice ran through Michel Downay's background and physical characteristics. Leaderer was over at the Abbey for long periods and, on one occasion, even drove George down to Dover to meet the warlock at the radio coven which was to become *Soldaten-sender Calais*. George thought most of the people there were like resting actors. There was an air of unreality about it all.

But that was probably his own safety mechanism. Already he was starting to remove himself from the person of George Thomas, Oxford graduate, young officer, to the new one—Georges Thomas, scholar, historian, student of the occult who had assisted Michel Downay at the Sorbonne in 1937/8 while he was working on *The Prophet of Salon*.

Fenice claimed to have known him well—Downay that is—and felt that he was probably clean. 'He spoke to me many times about how he could help France. Because of his leg he could not fight.' Fenice had only just got out in time. Downay had sent messages with him. He would help in any way. He would even infiltrate the enemy if he could.

There had been more messages, via the Swiss route and, mainly, the Breton fishing boats. Though the latter was dicey. As Ramilies said, 'If they picked up one message, Downay was blown. They could have turned him around.' As the messages were usually long and detailed letters, only one going astray would have been necessary.

Downay's last contact had asked for assistance, and details

had been sent in, via a pianist in Austria. For pianist read radio operator. Downay claimed to have been approached by Goebbels and the SS. ('Double top,' said Leaderer.) Ramilies had told him to expect the arrival of his old colleague Georges Thomas. Georges would send him a telegram to say he had decided to come and help. Downay would have to stall both Goebbels' people and the SS, who, he said, were asking him to go to Berlin.

'Told him to say he'd written to you in your hidey hole of a village near Compiègne. We'll see to the telegram and we've already installed a pianist for you in Paris.'

The network, if that is what it was, had been coded Stellar. There was Caspar and Melchior. The pianist was Balthazar. Object of the exercise—to place subversive horoscopes and phoney Nostradamus quatrains into the mouths of senior officers. Split the leaders; set the SS more at loggerheads with the Wehrmacht than it was already.

Ramilies worked daily on the quatrains with George. Once they had been placed, Balthazar would signal back and the same bits of astrological garbage would be mentioned by *Soldatensender Calais*.

That was all straightforward enough. What worried George was the fact that he was a guinea pig. 'If we're being set up, they'll put me in a dungeon, bleed me dry about what covert assistance we're organising, then bury me.'

'Quite possible, dear boy. But you don't know anything, do you?' Ramilies licked his lips and gave a thin smile. 'Yes, it's possible that Downay is neither Snow White nor any one of the seven dwarfs. On the other hand, we must act as though he is absolutely honest. Honourable intentions and all that. It's unlikely they'll clobber you fast. They'll play you out to start with. So you, George—or may I call you Georges?—must play him.'

'I'm a bloody tethered goat.'

'Something of the sort, dear heart.' It was their operation : something of a means test. George realised that this was part of the job. He was to test the temperature; be a water diviner who might get lost down the well if it turned out to be poisoned. It was part of the game.

In the second week of February, they told him it was time for the off. There was little more they could do to help him now.

Except for Ramilies.

On the night before the first attempted landing, Ramilies locked George in with him, in the monastic bedsitter perched among the eaves of the West wing. There, he began to deal out a whole new set of intriguing rules which took into account the definite possibility of Michel Downay being a plant, ready to sell them down the river.

'You're not as alone out there as we've led you to imagine, George.' They sat hunched, once more, over the gas fire. 'My job is to initiate you into some of the really black arts. I'm out to tie a double knot which will leave you as the only person in the world who can untie it. Because, while you are not alone, your friend may belong to another even longer-standing enemy.'

He examined the various ways in which Downay might well be used. How would they, the enemy, use him? How would George be used through him?

There were variants so complex that Ramilies had to lead George very gently through tortuous mental caverns. The twists and turns of the man's mind were an eye-opener to young Thomas. The astuteness, deviousness and cunning of the Rammer were to remain object lessons for what George described as 'the rest of my active life in this godforsaken profession'.

Ramilies' will was undoubtedly to drive a deep wedge into the very heart of the Nazi Party: between Hitler himself and his most trusted hatchet-man, Heinrich Himmler, Reichsführer-SS and Chief of the German Police. He was determined to do it, long range, from the Abbey; and, like it or not, George was to be the mallet in his hand.

As dawn broke, Ramilies, priest of the dark sciences, exacted one final toll as a safeguard. Like some witch he required from George Thomas a personal name, known to both of them and to be kept by Ramilies alone. Later, if Downay was proved hygienic, this token would be given to him: and, lastly, to one other person whom George would know only through the revelation of this secret within a secret. The name George gave to Ramilies would be played back to him by the chosen one.

George speaking. 'It was like a childish game, and the choice was mine. I'd been having this recurring dream of childhood, where I was acting out all the parts in my home-made plays for Maman. There was a character, buried deep inside me from this theatre of infancy, which fitted the bill perfectly. I gave Ramilies the name and he had the decency to laugh at the irony.'

On the next night they set off in a converted Breton fishing boat. Luckily the Navy had installed a pair of high-powered engines in her, because the E-boat bounced them in fog a couple of miles from the coast.

They turned tail and fled back to England.

It wasn't until the night of February 26/27th that they finally put him in by Lysander.

Herbie left the tape running: right up to the point where George met Downay at the Gare du Nord and found himself being introduced to SS-Sturmbannführer Kuche and SS-Hauptsturmführer Wald.

22

February 1941. Herbie was barely eleven years old. A lifetime. Another of many lives. The bombing had started and his father was already dead, killed by a British fighter pilot over the English Channel. He remembered the solemnity. The citation for bravery. *He died for the Führer and the Fatherland*. The awe with which his mother had held the personal letter from Goering.

He was, himself, with the *Jugend*. But the death of his father was the first moment that iron entered his soul. The first time that he felt guilty. The Führer had taken his father from him. For Führer and Fatherland. That was, for Herbie Kruger, the start of the divorce, the first crack. He was not quite fourteen when he finally ran from the ruins and his dead mother, making his way to the Americans and offering to help them. That was in 1944.

The guilt at having sinned against the Führer and the Fatherland in thought, was expunged by the sins he committed in word and deed. He had cause to hate the Party. Not just for his father, but for friends. Abraham Schultz; David Steinberg; Arnold Klein. Their parents as well; and the old couple who used to give him sweets. Taken. In the night, taken. Claimed by the chambers and the ovens. As an adolescent he knew what happened to them. They all knew—well, maybe not those who buried their heads in the sand. Some even saw, or carried back stories.

He knew fear as a boy; and hatred. He had known fear ever since, though the hatred mellowed. The enemy then wore many heads. It had grown a few more since then.

Big Herbie built himself an extra large brandy. A horse's neck. Ginger ale. He brought it over to his 'thinking-and-listening' chair, trailing the telephone with him, and putting it on the floor as he took a tentative sip of the drink.

Seven o'clock. Time for food later. He needed another look at the files to refresh his memory on what he would hear, in its minutiae, from George tomorrow. In the meantime there were

97

some telephone calls to make. Much later he would listen to the Eighth Symphony: the Symphony of a Thousand. The Solti recording.

The 'phone rang, like it had ESP, just as he was about to reach for it.

Bob Perry, Head of Photography Section—better known as Pix. He was glad to have caught Herbie because their man had taken the prints up to his office and wanted a word with him.

Which prints? Of course, the ones he had pulled from the files. Five different photographs. All vintage. Early Forties. Copies and enlargements. For use with Frau Fenderman on Thursday.

It wasn't important, Herbie told him. He would pick them up. maybe tomorrow, or Thursday morning most likely.

Apparently, that wasn't the point. The blow-ups showed hanky-panky. Old prints, Bob. Historical. No, he couldn't ask what or where they'd come from. What hanky-panky?

Only two of them, Bob Perry told him. Two had been done against phoney backgrounds.

Wartime. Hush-hush. Sort of back-projection jobs? Herbie asked.

No: scissors and paste: and there was more. They were well done. Almost departmental standard, though the techniques weren't as perfect as modern fakes.

Herbie thought for a few seconds. 'Put them under lock and key, Bob. I'll come over tomorrow if I've got the time. But they're to go out to nobody but me. Not even God gets them. Right?'

'Right.'

Doped-up photographs. It appealed to one theory Herbie had in the back of his mind. Not really a theory. More of a half-cooked idea—and that without hearing all the detail. The files told one story; but who knew? Wait and see. A larger gulp of the brandy.

He dialled the Yard. Special Branch. 'Vermin' Vernon-Smith. They went through the Rachet and Soap routine, then Herbie gave him a rundown on Nachent and Billstein. Descriptions, and their vehicle, the Mini Clubman, together with registration.

'Sound like amateurs. Using the same car all the time. You've just caught me, dinner with the wife's brother.'

'May have to wait. I'd like you to snatch those monsters.'

'On what?'

'Loitering. Whatever. Keep them for a while. Turn them over.'

'And what nefarious outfit do they represent?'

'Freelance.'

'How long you known?'

'Not long. Thought they were FIA.' He was careful not to say BND so that the Special Branch man would not be confused. Federal Intelligence Agency would be more amenable to 'Vermin' than *Bundesnachrichtendienst*.

'You're sure they're not?'

'Spoke to the Embassy man this morning. Ex-FIA the pair of them. Sacked and went private. You'll probably get them on an arms charge. Who knows? Like them out of the way until Thursday or Friday, Friday would be good.'

'So would dinner with the wife's brother.'

'Well, do it after dinner. Late. Later the better. They won't go away, not if the bird's still at the hotel.'

Vernon-Smith said he would do his best. He sounded disgruntled. Worried.

Herbie called Schnabeln and asked to be notified when the leeches were snatched. 'Are they there now?'

'Sitting there as conspicuous as foxes in a hen-house.'

Time for food. Herbie felt a great lethargy. He sipped the drink again, then tossed it back in one, his eyes half on his notes. The masochist in him wanted to call Worboys and give him a job. That young man needed some ginger up his backside and there was something he could get on with tomorrow.

His hand hovered over the telephone, as though he expected it to ring. It didn't and he changed his mind. Get him later, as well.

Big Herbie Kruger spends a quiet night at home, he thought, and treated himself to another massive drink. To consume while cooking an omelette.

As his huge hands gently shook the pan over the gas flame; as the butter melted, Herbie sang softly: bitterly—

For the last time the rifle is loaded ...
... Soon Hitler banners will wave over the barricades ...

He sang in German. The Horst Wessel song. Then he laughed. The laugh mocked his childhood and seemed to come from long ago.

It was nearly nine-thirty when the Entryphone buzzed. Maitland-Wood was there and would like a word.

He came, like Agag, treading delicately, as if he craved a boon. This Fenderman woman? Herbie was diffident. Was it worth all the work? Herbie asked all what work? Maitland-Wood had been given to understand that people were being given odd jobs, that there had been a shooting incident yesterday. Was she a subversive or were the small paragraphs in the papers more or less accurate? More or less, Herbie told him, adding that he was the one doing most of the work, and the Fenderman woman had been passed on to him by the Director himself.

Yes, the Deputy Director knew that. He understood, but George Thomas was having to give up two days' work, or so he was told. Did Herbie really have to do all this background stuff?

'George complaining?' Herbie had offered the Deputy Director a drink, but he had refused, just as he refused to take off his coat, as if he was trying to make it plain he was on business. He also made some remark about not being able to get Herbie in his office and having to trail out to St. John's Wood.

'You could have called. The telephone ...'

'Is an insecure instrument.' Frosty.

Herbie grinned. Stupid. Dunderhead. 'Not this one. This one is special. Delousing gear included at no extra cost.'

About what Herbie was doing. Did he think the Fenderman woman would be of use? Herbie couldn't say. 'Not until I've been through all the background.'

Again, back to George. 'He's a busy man, you know.'

'Aren't we all? What's the matter, Willis? George been complaining?'

The negative was exceptionally hesitant. Herbie read it like banner headlines. George had not complained, but had asked Maitland-Wood if this particular dog could be whistled home. He could almost hear the conversation.

No fuss, Willis. But if it could be circumvented.

Do what I can, George. Do what I can. No promises. It's the Director's pigeon and I've okayed the files. No option.

'Look,' Herbie's hands spread wide, terrifyingly huge. 'I'm putting a team together. This woman has an interesting background. It crosses vaguely with something George was on during the war. I'd like to take her on, or at least drop something her way. But I need to be certain that she's clean and starched.'

Maitland-Wood went away looking unhappy. Herbie was far from certain about Hildegarde Fenderman. He was uncertain about a lot of things. Soap. Truth.

Eventually he got around to Worboys and asked him to start checking first thing in the morning. German Federal Passport. Did not know the number. Woman : Gretchen Weiss. Number of visits and their duration to the UK during the previous year. Herbie was a great one for independent checks. Schnabeln had said Hildegarde Fenderman had been in for two months last autumn under the name Weiss. Unlink it, and let Worboys have fun with the records.

'I want it by Thursday morning latest.' He rang off, aware of the irritation he had left at the other end of the line.

At last Mahler's Eighth Symphony, the choral masterpiece.

Veni, Veni, Creator Spiritus, the chorus of the Vienna State Opera began. Then the telephone rang. Girren to say the leeches had just been lifted, with a lot of noise and complaint, by some rather ferocious policemen including Vernon-Smith.

'Good,' Herbie said and put down the instrument.

Mentes tuorum visita; continued the Choir.

* * *

George Thomas arrived on the dot of nine-thirty the next morning. In the kitchen the big reel-to-reel tape machine was switched on. The bugs nestled at the ready. Herbie poured the coffee.

'Forgotten where we left off,' George began.

Herbie gave his idiot smile. 'Gare du Nord. Arrival. You've just met Downay and the SS duet. I am sitting most comfortably, George. So let us go on. I like stories with plenty of adventure.'

George closed his eyes, passed a hand over his brow, and started afresh.

23

'We are relieved you have arrived safely, Herr Thomas.' Kuche, the SS-Sturmbannführer, the Major, spoke in clipped French. Too perfect to be natural. He was slightly shorter than Wald. That was all Thomas noticed at the time. 'The Herr Doktor Downay had been making us wait especially for you. You have been most coy : not wanting to come to Paris.' It sounded strange, the French with the German *Herr*, and *Herr Doktor*.

George opened his mouth, but Downay closed it swiftly by taking over. 'You know what these academics are like.' He shrugged charm at them with deadly accuracy. 'Georges here wishes to write in solitude. I disturbed him. That's all. He's here now.'

They were leading, shepherding George across the concourse to the main façade of the station.

'The General will be pleased. We can expect some results soon ? Yes ?' Wald's French was not quite as perfect as Kuche's, but it served well enough. He stepped forward and opened the car door. It was a big black Opel, and the driver, a tubby corporal, jumped forward, bouncing to help. Wald fended him off as though he was not really a fit person to assist passengers of their calibre.

George got into the back with Downay and Kuche : Downay shifting close, lightly touching his thigh in a gesture meant to convey calm. Wald sat next to the driver.

George lamely said something about the car being an unexpected luxury.

Downay smiled. 'Paris is not like the country, you know. There, you are used to walking and riding the bicycle. It's hard for me.' He waved a hand towards Wald and then back to Kuche. 'These two gentlemen are our liaison with the General. They are very kind over matters of transport.'

George nodded and turned his head away from the window. The eyes of a passing cyclist had closed with him, and he did not like the look of contempt he saw.

They pulled out into the stream of bicycles which appeared to be the main form of transport. Any motorised vehicles were military, except for the odd official French car, or van. For the rest it was two feet, either on pavements or pedals.

Kuche leaned forward. 'We expect great things from this collaboration.'

George said they would do their best, and Downay once more came to his rescue. He had already told them, and the General, what he could accomplish with Georges' help. Having told them, he hoped they would be good enough to leave him and his colleague in peace for a while.

They slid through the streets at speed, moving cyclists with horn blasts like grenades. George was able to take in only a montage of the city he knew so well. It was a painful sight to one who was half French. Uniforms everywhere, many of them slung about with cameras, the eternal rubbernecks on the tourist run. There was an impression of queues, reminiscent of home, mainly around bread shops: and of old men perusing newspapers and posters stuck to otherwise empty stretches of wall. Many of the posters displayed garish paintings of Marshal Pétain.

From the car, it looked as though the troops outunmbered the civilian population by two to one. George was unprepared, though, for the number of young women who strolled with officers and other ranks alike. That kind of collaboration was only to be expected, but it had gone unmentioned at the Abbey.

They crossed the Pont Neuf, clipping the corner of the Ile de la Cité. The Germans had not moved any of the buildings. A sharp turn off the Rue Dauphin, and the car pulled up gently in front of one of those inscrutable buildings with a big door, part-panelled by glass, and a grille of metal bars behind.

The two SS men saluted as Downay pointed George towards the door. They would be calling in a day or so. You couldn't tell if that was a threat or a promise.

Inside the door, a withered and bent concierge poked her head from a cubbyhole and gave Downay a venomous glance; then eyed George up and down, smiled sadly and disappeared.

'I'm on the sixth floor.' Downay seemed relieved that they were alone. George knew the feeling.

L'Ascenseur ne marche pas. French elevators are as bad as

those in other parts of the world. At that time they were even worse.

George tried to ask about the pair of SS brigands, as they toiled up the curving stairs, but Downay shushed him, sharply : suggesting that he should guard his tongue until they got into the apartment.

There was no way that he could have given George a warning, he said when they were inside his front door. The SS officers were his direct liaison with General Frühling who, in turn, was being controlled by the Propaganda Ministry. He'd played them along, but in the end it was impossible for him to keep Georges' arrival date a secret. He hoped to God they hadn't checked out the other end. George was lost, and said so.

They were well inside now, through the small vestibule with its rack for coats, and what looked like a piece of old drainpipe which was the depository for two or three walking sticks and an umbrella. The vestibule led to the main room, large and uninviting, almost spartan : books lining one wall, the furniture big and heavy. A desk, table, several chairs, two of them deep and padded, pulled up in front of a metal stove.

There were three water-colours, insipid landscapes, on the walls. The place looked unlived-in; the only sign of reality being the desk with its piled jumble of papers and books. That reminded George of Ramilies.

Downay had his coat off, calling out a name. Twice. Loudly. 'Angelle. Angelle.' He shouted in the way a farmer calls to cows.

There were three high windows spaced along the far wall. (In fact they looked down into the street.) To left and right, in the adjacent walls, were two doors. The one on the right opened—it was the kitchen door—and the girl came in, smiling, wiping her hands on the big apron she wore over a plain grey dress.

'This is Georges.' Downay went on to introduce her. 'Angelle lives here. She is safe : our head cook and bottle washer as you say in England. Just as Kuche and Wald are our way to the hearts of the Boche, Angelle is our way to the heart of France.'

She was tall. As tall as Downay. It was the first thing George noticed about her. The second, though far from being her finest quality, was her hair, a reddish-gold, indescribable as one definite colour. George doubted if she helped it over-much from a bottle. In some lights it looked red, in others it was more like that soft thick silky gold which so many Scandinavian women seem to possess. On other days, and in other lights, it took on every possible variation in between.

(Later, George said, 'I particularly remember a heavy afternoon, when the sky over Paris seemed to reach down on to the rooftops, heavy with leaden rain, when her hair was transformed into that dark beech-red of autumn. But that was much later, and in the open air, and so many things were by then distorted by what I learned to think of as tricks of light.')

She came towards him, holding out her hand like royalty. As their fingers touched and he looked into her face, George first saw the most essential and embracing virtue of Angelle Tours: humour. It was as if some pent-up geyser of comedy was always about to burst from that tall and elegant body. You saw it on the mouth and in her eyes: in the way she moved her face. Later, he was to find that the effervescence within was not always comedy. Tragedy was there also, and, while nine times out of ten it was humour that came out, the tenth time was nearly always tears.

But, at the moment of meeting it was sheer bubble, and he could read it all in her face and in the way she fluttered her hands, pale, butterfly hands, the long fingers of which ran riot as she spoke. Angelle illustrated conversation with her fingers, as illuminating as the way some continentals illustrate words with the whole of their hands or their arms and shoulders.

'How did you take to Castor and Pollux?' She had a laugh that was more of an epidemic than an infection.

Downay caught the laugh, chuckling to himself. 'It's her name for Kuche and Wald. Apt in the circumstances.'

George said that it was as apt as the codename for their own network—Stellar.

Downay nodded. Would George care to eat now; or coffee, even a little brandy? George opted for the brandy and was motioned towards one of the chairs in front of the stove. He would be shown his bed later.

Angelle, still laughing, disappeared into the kitchen and Downay's face went grave. '*Stellar* is good. What instructions have you brought?'

Let him come to you, Fenice and Ramilies had both said. *Before you commit us to anything, make him spill the lot. Remem-*

ber he's a psychologist and knows more about Nostradamus than we do. Your cover may be as his curate in prophecy, but your real job is to protect our interests and see that what has to be done, is done.

On the last night, Ramilies had said, *Keep the distance; hear him out and then hear him again. After that, keep listening until you're certain. When it's time, feed him gently.*

The brandy arrived. Raw spirit.

'The SS seem to treat you like an oracle,' George began. 'What's the deal?'

Of course, Downay said, you will want to know the whole thing.

It was a good story and he told it straight out, as though it was well rehearsed, without pausing long enough for George to ask questions. In the kitchen, Angelle clattered around. *Hear him out and then hear him again.*

24

Michel Downay said that if things had been different he might have gone to England. Friends and colleagues urged him constantly during the week before the fall of Paris. 'I thought about it. Who wouldn't?'

If his politics had been wishy-washy. If he'd had any faith in the government; in Reynaud, Daladier, Laval—any of them—he might have gone. Like a lot of other people in France he had seen it coming. (Like a lot of other people in England also, George thought.)

We had a brave army, Downay sighed. Sons of the thousands who died with courage on the Somme. They didn't let their fathers down. They were, themselves,, betrayed: by ineffective politicians and old, revered, Generals who learned nothing from progress.

It was the same at the Sorbonne: or so he believed. The establishment was, on the whole, past its prime, living on former academic glories. Old men most of them, and, though men full of years were supposed to be wise sages, the larger portion had closed minds. Their wisdom held no truth for the present.

'There were a few of us, teachers and students—intellectuals if you like—who were liberal and progressive in our thinking.'

For liberal and progressive, read Communist, thought George. At the Abbey they nagged—*if you're cut off, go to the Communists or the Church. Preferably the Communists.*

Three days before the Wehrmacht entered Paris, Michel made up his mind. It was now or never. People poured out. Others shrugged. He would stay.

'I know enough people. I have people here in Paris and I know others—all over—who made the same decision. Carry on. Go about your work, but organise. Organise resistance. Some have, as the American Western films say, taken to the hills. Maquis.'

He breathed the word in a tone reserved for the most brave and the most foolhardy.

The right way was to go out and meet the enemy on their own terms. Play collaborator if need be. But organise all the time. He thumped his black cane into the carpet, asking, rhetorically, when help would come. 'We need people over here. You've promised to help, but they have not come. We need organisers; communications; arms and explosives.'

The Nazis wanted collaboration; they wanted the country intact—labour, police, judiciary, agriculture and industry. God knew, they made it plain enough. They wished to work in harness. In a common cause. Some bastards had even fallen for it.

They were thorough, the Boche. That was a fact. We knew they would have lists, Downay thumped the floor again. But we also knew the only ones who needed to fear were the Jews and subversives, and, perhaps, the old and infirm.

It had taken the Boche only three weeks to arrive at Michel Downay's door. Then not the Boche but the French. Two of them. Very polite. Plainclothes men. *Les flics.* A few details. Just simple facts. Name. Birth date. The things already on the *carte d'identité.* Verification.

Two days later, Kuche and Wald came around. 'Living Wagnerians,' Downay called them. Nordic gods of destiny. *Merde.* Wald even had a scar on his chin—you noticed it?—imagined that it was a duelling scar? Wrong. It was a fall, but Downay only found that out later. Wald got drunk and fell down some steps.

However, there they were, full of courtesy, and charm, and Herr Doktor, acknowledged expert of psychology, learned scholar of Astrology and the Modern Mind. ('They had got that : the title of my new treatise, and it's not yet written : not finished anyway.') Maestro—he scoffed as though this was what they had called him, playing with languages—Maestro of the Nostradamus Prophecies.

If he had set out to bait a trap in 1937, when he began to write *The Prophet of Salon,* Downay could not have expected more. There were gentlemen from Berlin, Kuche and Wald said, who would like to talk to him about a project. Would he come? Quite informal.

They drove to the Crillon. Downay did not care for that. He

knew just how informal the Crillon was these days with the High Command using it as their Headquarters. Still, it was better than the house on the Avenue Foch where the Gestapo held court.

Downay went into an almost sentimental reverie. 'It's a little easier now, not the Crillon, but Paris. Or, perhaps it's because I'm working for them.' He rose and started to limp across the room, painfully leaning on the cane. 'This was last year, don't forget. Now it's *this* year, and soon it will be Paris in the spring again. A lot of people are trying to forget who the monsters are walking among us, drinking our wine, fucking our girls, eating our food and running our lives into hell knows what. Then. Last year. Then, the streets were empty and the curfew very strictly enforced: one hour before dusk. They roamed the streets. Sometimes the bars and cafés did not open at all. Paris seemed ...' He hesitated as though emotionally full. 'Empty. Streets. Bars. Shops. Boulevards. Like a woman whose doctor has told her that she is barren. That was Paris. It's different now. The woman has adjusted and lives with her grief, or is having a good time because of what the doctor has told her. She has accepted the illusion of safety.'

At the Hotel Crillon there were three men, in civilian clothes. They stood up when Kuche and Wald brought him in. Stood, and treated him with great respect: hoped the unfortunate, but necessary, activities of the military had not disturbed him too much. The war was a sad business and they had not asked for it. Hadn't Frenchmen said, in 1939, that the British would fight to the last drop of French blood? The Führer had not wanted this. But, did not Downay agree, there was a common enemy now? Negotiations were going on at top level with the Americans. England would have to capitulate sooner or later. All they wanted was to save more bloodshed. As a good and loyal Frenchman: as a scholar, a thinking man, it would be wrong for him not to assist in bringing that day closer: sooner rather than later.

They were proud of the fact that they had come with a direct request from the Reichsminister of Propaganda: Doktor Goebbels himself. Did he know that the Reichsminister was a great admirer of his work on Nostradamus? Did he know the Führer, himself, was a devotee? Astrology was the new science. Had not Nostradamus already prophesied Hitler's greatness and destiny?

Downay had neither agreed, nor disagreed.

Don't give him a hint, Ramilies whispered in George's ear. *Until you have all the proofs of the existence of God cut and dried, with a personal signed statement from the Holy Trinity— in triplicate and authenticated by the College of Cardinals. Until then, don't let him know you think it's all a load of old balls.*

Downay responded to his hosts by saying that the Reichsminister was very kind. If there was anything he could do ... Well, if it was within his capabilities.

Who better? They smiled warmly at him. Gave him a drink. The Reichsminister already had astrologers working for him. There was one particular man from Switzerland. Herr Doktor Downay, though, was the most qualified man in Europe regarding the prophecies of Nostradamus. The messages of the great prophet had to be reinterpreted now that the Third Reich had won the bulk of Europe. Surely that was a challenge the Herr Doktor could not resist?

The Reichsminister was convinced, and they understood the Führer agreed, that Nostradamus was the great prophet of the Nazi Party. Its destiny could be found in the quatrains. It was essential, to bring the present troubles to a quick and conclusive end, for someone with the brilliance of the Herr Doktor to set forth in plain terms—terms which could be understood by even the most ignorant—that the future was safe in the keeping of the Party and those who led it.

They needed to have chapter and verse to prove to the dissidents within the already occupied countries, to Britain, and to the rest of the world, that further conflict was useless. Could the Herr Doktor? Would the Herr Doktor, take on this momentous task?

Smooth as butter; Downay said he would have to think about it. They drove him home and he got a message off in double quick time. ('I believe it came to London through a fisherman. They're still getting some messages over on the boats, yes?')

They left him alone for three days. Then Kuche and Wald once more. Still very polite, but this time they took him to their commanding officer, General Frühling. The General—Downay puffed his cheeks and laid a hand to his belly—had also been charming, but came out straight away with the statement that he understood the Herr Doktor was working for Reichsminister Goebbels. If he could be of any help. It had been suggested that the Herr

Doktor be removed to Berlin where he could be closer to the Ministry of Propaganda. 'They were not asking me any more. They were telling me.'

Downay stalled. Got the messages through to London. Saw the pianist they sent in from Austria, and played the game of waiting for his brilliant young colleague Georges Thomas.

It had been difficult, but the fiction kept the ball rolling until now. Only just. They were pressing for results. Talking about Berlin.

'Balthazar arrived yesterday, thank God,' Downay suddenly volunteered.

George was twitchy. At the Abbey they had told him the pianist, Balthazar, had gone in from Switzerland long before this. *Unbreakable cover. Safe as houses and very experienced.* Fenice speaking. *Myra Hess.*

'He's here?' George meant in Downay's apartment.

'My God, no. I'm not having him sitting on my doorstep.' Downay made Gallic noises and explained that Balthazar was holed up with some girl in a garret near St. Sulpice. He didn't actually say that the girl was one of his students. He did say that George had a rendezvous with Balthazar that night in a bar on the Boul. Mich. which did nothing for the fear-flies in his gut. It would mean flying solo in Paris.

Downay laughed. 'It is not so bad, my friend. Each time it will get easier. You are one of us, and must move like one of us now.'

George preferred to be an ostrich for the time being. He turned the subject, asking if Downay had given any thought to the prophecies—Nostradamus and the Nazi Party.

For a second he thought Downay had gone coy on him, then realised that Angelle had come into the room and was fussing about laying the table for their meal.

'A good deal of thought.' He raised his eyebrows. 'Perhaps we could discuss it later.' Like, not in front of the children, or the servants, or his mistress if that was what she was.

George started acting ('Foxy was what Ramilies called me.') and put on a troubled look, saying that he was uncertain about the ethics involved, unless they could prove, beyond doubt, that Nostradamus had indeed made predictions concerning this particular era, and the part which the Party had to play in it.

Downay laughed again. Then looked puzzled, as though he had

just understood what George meant.

Play him as if you're a one hundred per cent believing virgin that we've dug up from the occult community. So Ramilies, on the night of the labyrinthine cunning.

Throughout lunch, Downay continued to look at George with the same unsure puzzled expression, but said nothing about the prophecies until they had finished eating.

The meal was simple. They spoke of Paris and the general situation, Downay being subtle and trying to feed George information that would be of use once he got on to the streets.

They touched politics, and Angelle, who had bubbled and taken nothing very seriously throughout the meal, raised her eyes to heaven declaring that politics was the worst subject ever; food and clothes were the things she liked best. Food, clothes and literature. Was George a literary man? Did he like Jane Austen?

Afterwards, Downay said he had to go over to the Sorbonne. 'To keep up the fiction.' Angelle would show George his room. She left them for a moment, and, as he walked to the door, Downay swivelled on his stick—

'Think hard about what we are doing, Georges. Nostradamus may be your Bible, but we have to play with him, misquote him and tamper with him if we are to do the thing properly.' He said they would talk again later, and stumped out.

Angelle came back as the door closed, then turned away when George looked at her, as though she did not want him to see her face: hiding some private sorrow.

The room they had prepared for him was small and functional, and by the time she had finished giving George a quick guided tour of the apartment, Angelle was her effervescent self again. There were things she had to do in the kitchen.

'Like washing up?'

'Yes.'

'I'll help.'

*   *   *

'You like some coffee, George?' Big Herbie sensed it was a strain.

'Could I?' Brow creased. 'It's not easy. When you know the whole story, who was really who, and doing what. It's difficult. I've tried to clear the mind and give you the impression I got in

112

those first hours. Are you sure it's what you need?'

Herbie said it was perfect. All that he could remember. The more the better. Think himself back. He got the coffee and had just poured when the telephone burred.

'They've gone private like you said.' Vernon-Smith.

'I told you.'

'Tried your office. They said you were at home.'

'They said I was at home and didn't wish to be disturbed.'

'I had to disturb you. I've got them on carrying illegal weapons. Could manage a holding charge, but I doubt the magistrate will wear it. Out in a trice. Easy bail.'

'Try. Try to keep them until Thursday night at the earliest. Oh, and clean them out.'

'They're like a mortuary on Christmas Day. Both of them.'

'Try.'

Back with George Thomas, Herbie took a gulp of coffee and reflected that he would rather have brandy but it was too early.

'I'd like to hear about Angelle. First impressions. That's all very important, George.'

'I was just coming to her.'

Another cup of coffee and he was off again. Herbie thought he could see it in George's eyes, drifting back over the years to that austere apartment in Paris. 1941.

25

Angelle was a prattler, talking on and on, skipping over subjects like a stone across a still pond and making as many ripples. Nothing seemed still and quiet when she was about. Everything was punctuated by bouts of laughter, and it was only when George slipped in a question—if she had always lived in Paris?—that the smile went out of her eyes and seemed to be drained from her personality.

In a matter of seconds, the girl who had been all things happy, was crying. George made noises. ('I was still not very good at giving comfort to women. Particularly when I didn't understand the mainspring of the grief.')

Then, the sobs stopped almost as quickly as they had started. With a sniff, she pulled herself together and began to offer profuse apologies. 'You might as well know. Then you won't have to ask again.'

They stood in the small kitchen, the dishes washed and only half dried, some already piled on the bare table, while Angelle told George—in simple sentences, leaving out the minute detail —of how she came to be in Paris: and in Downay's apartment.

She was a teacher. Graduated from the Sorbonne in 1939. She had known Michel Downay only slightly then, though she did not attend any of his classes. 'He was a very romantic figure to us girls.'

The post she was after was that of junior *assistante* at the village school where she was born, near Reims. She had been there for less than a year when the Germans swooped into France.

At first it seemed better to stay put; where they were. But, as rumours and the sound of fighting all around them became worse, Angelle Tours decided to move. It was sometime during the first week of June that she spoke to the head of the school. He in turn talked to the parents and children.

Many of the families were already gathering their belongings in readiness. They decided to go together—parents, children, the head of the school and his three *assistantes*.

On the first day they were bombed and machine-gunned along the road. It was pitiful, horrible enough to drive a young woman insane. Out of seventy men, women and children from the village, only she was left with fourteen children. They had been together in a ditch. Nobody else made it, caught in the open as the waspish fighters came down over the trees and sprayed the road. George knew about that kind of thing: had experienced it on the long road back to Dunkirk.

'We had to give up using the main roads,' he told her.

'We also,' she nodded once, a brief downward motion. The head stayed down, eyes on the floor. 'I took the little ones and we went by devious routes.'

The children were frightened, some of them in acute mental agony, having seen their parents obliterated on the road. They were all tired, thirsty and hungry. Some of the time, Angelle carried the smaller ones. 'We made very bad going. In any case, by then I did not know where I was taking them.'

A couple of days after the strafing on the road, they turned up in a tiny hamlet—a church, farm and a few cottages. The curé was still there, bewildered but praying and going through his religious offices, measuring the days in prayer. He thought the end would come soon. Everyone had left, he said, except the farmer who was an old skinflint and went on running his farm almost oblivious to what was happening.

The curé took the children into the church where, he said, they could spend the night. It was about five in the afternoon, and Angelle crossed the road towards the farm hoping to beg milk, and possibly some vegetables, from the farmer. Skinflint though he was, she thought it would be possible. The curé did not want her to go, implying that the man was a lecher. Yet, if need be, she would sell herself for the sake of the children.

She almost reached the farm, stopping to look back as she heard the sound of engines. A small convoy of French lorries was winding down the narrow dusty track, only about half a kilometre from the hamlet. It was like you have in the cowboy movies—she smiled, wry and painful, lifting her head to look at George again—the Fifth Cavalry coming to the rescue.

Then, above the rumble of the trucks, came another noise.

Stukas. Six of them, peeling off and diving unmistakably towards the trucks. She saw the first bombs come away from under the aircraft, and threw herself to the ground. 'I clawed it with my fingers. I wanted to get right down inside the earth.'

The rest was as always: the ground shaking; explosions following one another, getting nearer and louder. The smell and heat. Screams. That particular thunder and wind of destruction. Then the terrible silence.

Six Stukas can do a great deal of damage to a small and concentrated area. The cottages were gone. All that was left of the trucks was a couple of burning frameworks. There were no cries: only the snarl of departing aircraft. Above all there was no church: only a pile of masonry and one wall with its window still intact.

She wandered for a couple of days, the most vivid memory of the aftermath being the farmer, still alive, with his farm buildings standing, driving some animals into the yard and calling out something obscene to her. He must have already been mad, or sane enough to split his mind from reality.

In the end, she decided to head for Paris. There were lifts from stray army trucks, and days of walking. She arrived one day ahead of the Germans to find Paris almost empty. Out of habit she wandered down to the Sorbonne and met Michel, who only vaguely remembered her. He brought her back to the apartment, put her to bed, fed and nursed her.

'I live here because there's nowhere else. I'll die for those children yet. I laugh as much as possible, because what else is there but to laugh?'

And Michel? George did not dare ask, but she must have seen the question in his eyes. 'He has a lot of women.' She laughed again, a little too loudly. 'That's the work he's on now. It's me when he feels like it. Or when I ask him. But he's a bastard with women.'

She stopped there, suddenly, as though realising she had been indiscreet, then launched into a story currently going the rounds. The Luftwaffe had built a dummy airfield, to the north, somewhere near the coast. There were canvas hangars and wooden aeroplanes. According to the tale, the RAF had bombed it during the previous week. Four planes, she said, planes with two engines, flying low. They had dropped sixty or seventy bombs. *Wooden* bombs. Her head went back, straining her small breasts against the grey dress, and she laughed as though this was a joke which should be enjoyed by everybody.

They sat and talked in the kitchen until Downay returned saying that George had only an hour before his rendezvous with Balthazar. He still seemed worried by George's apparent reluctance to tamper with the prophecies, because he made a long speech about the necessity of giving the Nazis what they wanted to hear. 'That's the trick. It's deception for the common cause. They must hear what they wish. They are like greedy children. We only give them cream. Understand?'

Sure, George understood. 'We'll talk when I get back from the Boul. Mich.'

'And tell Balthazar I want to send a message to London,' Downay snapped. Behind him, in the kitchen door, Angelle seemed to be signalling danger with her eyes.

*   *   *

Back in the present, in Herbie Kruger's flat, the telephone buzzed again. This time his office in the Annexe with some query.

'No calls,' Herbie growled. 'I want no more calls here today. Tell them I'll let the Duty Officer know when I'm free. Keep a list.'

He lumbered back. 'Sorry, George,' looking at his watch. 'Not time for lunch yet. Please go on. I'm sorry.'

26

Balthazar's real name was Bill Keefe and he originally hailed from Epsom. ('Where the salts come from. You've probably got it all on file.') For years he'd had deep cover in Switzerland. Like George he was a French and German speaker. The Rammer and Fenice had sung his praises loudly. After the 1938 fiasco at Munich, he had been brought back to London and given a radio course, though he'd done trade clandestines for years.

His cover was so deep he didn't really need it. He had managed to get himself put into Paris by his firm. All legit, except his name —Robert Moutray—and he'd been using that for aeons. He was, as far as everyone but the Rammer's team knew, a bona fide Swiss rep, selling to the new régime.

The bar was crowded: civilians and troops alike, and George recognised Balthazar immediately. He sat in a corner where there was an unrestricted view of all the exits—even the communal toilets. *Keep your sight-lines clear*, they taught at the Abbey. *Like when you're sixty days at sea—backs to the wall and every exit blocked.* (They still teach it.)

Balthazar was short and fat, sweated a lot and had his spectacles in a neat case on the table pointing directly towards his glass of Pernod.

George pushed his way over, paying no attention to anyone else, having gone through all the routines on the way over. ('But, then, I thought I knew it all within ten minutes of hitting the street. You do at that age. Amazing how quickly confidence comes: back-doubles, reverses, standing alone and palely loitering at the odd street corner.')

'You *are* Moutray, aren't you? Robert Moutray. We met at a conference once. Your firm was thinking of publishing something of mine. Astrology. Thomas. Georges Thomas.'

Slowly he picked up his spectacles, placed them on his nose, grinned and spoke low, in English. 'Thought you'd never get here. Haven't got long and don't want to hang about.'

'Have care,' George stuck to French.

'Have care my arse. Half are bloody Frogs, and the rest are Krauts. Don't give a bugger for either.' For a deep cover man he had the security instincts of an absent-minded explosives' expert. Or so George thought. Balthazar must have seen the expression in his colleague's eyes, for he grinned again and went into French, calling for the waiter. George said he'd have a Pernod, realising that Balthazar had already established himself as something of a regular in the bar. Living the cover.

'Downay—Melchior—says that you're just in. The Abbey gave me to understand you'd been around some time.'

'Abbey's right.' He wiped his face with a large handkerchief. 'Wanted to fix up a bolthole. Must say I don't want to use it. That Downay's set me up a treat. Only nineteen, she is, and does it in twelve languages. Likes little fat men like me. Says there's more to get hold of. You okay?' as though asking if Downay had attended to George's sex life also.

'I'm in and we're operating. Should have something for you in a couple of days, if not before.'

Very quickly ('I'm only going through it the once'), he gave George the contact procedures, signals and alternates. Just in case.

When he had finished, George told him that Downay wanted him to talk to London. He had a message.

The Pernod arrived. They still served lump sugar with it. Amazing. George dribbled water through two cubes balanced on a fork, drop by drop into the yellow murk, thinking involuntarily of Maman and himself one winter—the thaw and a snowman they'd christened Hiram sliding into a white blotch on the tiny lawn. The old, recurring dream passed through his head.

'You'll have to vet it,' Balthazar sounded almost stern. 'I've had a return about that. Said I wasn't happy about Downay's associates. London say that you have to see everything—without Downay's knowledge. If he's got a message I need comment from you.'

George asked which associates he wasn't happy with—thinking about the SS.

'That girl of his, for one. The tart that lives with him. She's a mystery. Don't like it; nor a couple of others.'

'Women?'

What other kind of trouble was there? he asked, and said, yes, of course women: one young, the other older. He was very unhappy about Downay's motives. He began to explain, when there was a hubbub at the bar entrance and the sound of cars stopping outside, with urgent brakes and a quick slamming of doors. A pair of customers at the bar made for the door, fast.

'Jesus Christ,' puffed Balthazar. 'No heroics, Sunny Jim, but this is where we find out how good your papers really are.'

There were four plainclothes men and two pairs of uniforms: police. Not a Nazi in sight. They told everybody to stay where they were. This was a routine check. It was like a Hollywood version of a prohibition raid, but done in French.

All four were tough, sharp men. A breed, George thought. Could be nasty in a cellar with rubber sticks. They worked in pairs with a uniformed man accompanying each pair, and a couple standing by the door for good measure.

They hardly paid any attention to Balthazar's papers, but huddled over George's for a long time. Too long.

'Thomas?' one of them asked.

'It's there. That's me.'

'Georges Thomas?' The other.

'Yes.' He had the feeling that people were edging away from him.

'He with you?' the first *flic* shot at Balthazar.

Balthazar made a noise which said nobody in their right mind would be with George. In real words he told them he'd never set eyes on George until he sat down a few minutes before.

'Just a formality.' The first *flic*, who was tall and had a mole on his left cheek, put a hand on George's arm.

'My papers are in order.' He drew away, trying to shake off the hand.

'A formality.' The *flic* dragged George out of the chair and his partner caught the other arm. 'We're collecting letter Ts tonight.' He laughed and they edged him out of the bar.

There was no time to be afraid until they got him into the back of the car. He tried to talk to them, but they spoke only to one another, across him, paying no heed. He asked where they were going, but the pair of *flics* had become suddenly deaf. Five minutes later, the frightflies in George's guts turned to fireflies.

They were heading for the Arc de Triomphe and turning into the Avenue Foch. Ramilies, Fenice, Marc—at the landing point—and Downay had told him about the Avenue Foch and the SS Headquarters there—and that part of the SS which was the Gestapo.

They pulled up outside the building, and a SS sergeant leaped forward to open the door. One of the *flics* muttered that he was sorry but they were only obeying orders. The weak cry of many murderers.

There was a small signing ceremony as they handed him over, and a pair of muscular SS boys in open-necked shirts led him upstairs and along several passages to a door.

'Herr Thomas, thank you for coming to see us.' Kuche lounged behind a desk. In the corner, peering out of the window and drinking from a long-stemmed glass, stood Wald, scar and all. They both looked relaxed. George was sweating: wishing he had never met or seen Ramilies.

*   *   *

Far in the future, Big Herbie Kruger shifted in his chair, turning his head and concentrating. This part had not been in the file. Not in detail anyway.

27

The brawny lads pushed him into a chair. Kuche nodded them away and George heard the door thud behind him. He looked into Kuche's eyes to see if there was any hint of what was to come.

'What is ... ?'

'A few questions, that's all.' Wald came over from the window. 'Nothing to be worried about, Herr Thomas. We are, how would you say it? protecting our investment?'

So the long quiz started. Nothing nasty. No threats. Smooth tongues and constant backtracking. To start with they asked the expected questions. Where was he born? What happened to his parents? How did he tie his shoelaces as a child? Who was Claud Grenoir?

'He owned a garage in the village. Died when I was about sixteen.' Thank God for the cover that had been constructed via the newly formed French Section. These two had been checking him out thoroughly, and George hoped that Downay had been briefed as well as himself.

When did you first come to Paris? Where did you live then? When did you first work with Michel Downay?

'When he started the book—*The Prophet of Salon*—in the summer of 1937.'

'Why did he choose you?'

'He said I had a natural aptitude for the whole spirit of the prophecies.'

'Did you do all the groundwork?'

'Yes.'

'Did you not feel cheated, doing all that work and then watching Downay construct it into a book and get all the applause?'

'Of course not. It wasn't like that.'

Break. Nods. Smiles. He could sleep. They gave him a bare room with a cot; fed him frugally. Still no threats. Tomorrow they would talk again. *Live it,* Fenice had constantly said about the cover. *Get inside it and be the man we're constructing in you.* The man, Georges Thomas, whom they had constructed, did not sleep well. There were sounds within that building not calculated to make one feel at ease. Laughter. Two German voices, raised as though in quarrel. A snatch of song sometime in the early hours and, twice, the tramp of feet, not marching, but walking with purpose along the corridor: then stopping outside the door. Pausing and continuing.

George took a couple of reverse courses on the cover, decided that he had got it right, felt the churning of his stomach and the sweat on brow and under armpits; dipped into sleep and then out of it again.

Downay kept coming back into his head, and Balthazar's words of warning; *not happy with Downay's associates.* Ramilies, and the long secret night at the Abbey—*If he is one of theirs they'll use you to a purpose, dear heart. They'll have method. They always have method.*

Then Angelle came to mind, her laugh and the long thighs under her dress: her tears; the bullets and bombs ripping over that road, metal carving up the kids and their families. Quite suddenly George wanted her. The raging fear turned into a different kind of fire.

In the morning they brought foul coffee and good croissants. Then, back to the same office, to the same smooth arrogant Kuche and Wald. Freshly-shaved, Wald's scar looked as though it had been sprinkled with powder because it still hurt to take a razor over it. He got drunk and fell downstairs, George thought.

They went through exactly the same questions as the previous night, only in a different wording and order. They stayed courteous, and, when it was over, a private soldier brought coffee.

'It's good,' Kuche pronounced, and George thought he meant the coffee which was certainly better than the slop they'd fed him for breakfast.

'He means,' Wald smiled, the weak sun slicing through the window to make his blond hair a halo. 'He means that we are satisfied. Now we get down to the talking. Doktor Downay has told you what is required?'

George said that he had spoken with Downay at great length, and the Germans repeated that they were protecting their interests. They were answerable to General Frühling and he was answerable to the Reichsminister. So, Herr Thomas would understand they were all under some pressure. Doktor Downay had made certain promises but, so far, there was nothing to show. It took a long time the way they told it.

They broke for lunch. Cheese, bread and a good Hock. Apples. All very healthy.

'We would like to take you into our confidence.' Kuche spoke slowly, a bad amateur actor bent on perfect articulation. 'We take a risk, certainly, but there is no other way. You see, we are not certain if we can trust the good Doktor Downay. We would like to trust you, Georges Thomas, and assure ourselves that you understand what it is we have to supply to the Reichsminister.'

Reichsminister Goebbels, they said, alternately like old women repeating the endings of each other's sentences. Reichsminister Goebbels needed some firm, solid interpretation of the prophecies. Interpretations that would be convincing. *You understand?* They punctuated each phrase.

'I'm certain Michel Downay will give you clear interpretations,' George placated. 'He knows far more about Nostradamus than I do. I can read some of ...'

Ah, they cut him short. Perhaps Herr Thomas did not fully comprehend their meaning. They realised the Doktor was brilliant—a brilliant occultist—but the Reichsminister already had a brilliant occultist in Berlin. They were quite concerned for that gentleman's future.

George reiterated that Michel Downay was a man of honour, a scholar of honour. He would give them the truth.

This last seemed to make both Kuche and Wald very nervous and Kuche laid a hand on George's shoulder.

'We can be of great assistance to you. Understand? We can smooth many paths. Whatever it is you desire—money, status, rank, women. Understand? It is not altogether a question of truth. Understand?' *Verstanden?*

Ramilies had spelled it out. So had Downay. *They must hear what they want to hear.* Now, thought George, he had the SS telling him the same thing.

Perched on the window-sill, his favourite position, Wald laughed, like Pagliacci at the end of *Vesti la giubba*, but without

124

the tears. 'What is truth?' he asked, knowing that it wasn't original.

'Truth has a different angle for most people.' George tried to be clever. 'One truth can have many viewpoints.'

'So?' Kuche got to his feet. 'So what is it really? Is the Führer truth? Or the oath we take—*I swear to thee, Adolf Hitler ... Loyalty and Bravery ... Obedience unto death. So help me God.* Is that truth? What is the truth about Nostradamus?'

'He possibly means many things to many people. It depends on where you are standing in time, in relation to the prophecies.' He was rather pleased with that.

They both came back fast. That is what we mean, they said. Nostradamus must mean only *one* thing for the Reichsminister— the destiny of the Führer as the greatest leader the world has seen; the outcome of the war, assured with victory; the National Socialist Party as the most formidable political system of all time; the Third Reich as the most powerful and dominating factor in world affairs for a thousand years.

'Does Nostradamus mean that to you?' Kuche threw George a smile, as a dealer might toss you a card. 'He'd better mean that to you, Herr Thomas.'

George did not need any prompting. One could make out a good case, he said, knowing it was time to start dealing the cards back. There were many quatrains which indicated just such matters.

They both looked very relieved and suggested that Georges Thomas made certain the good Doktor Downay read the prophecies in the same way.

'Stand at his shoulder. Whisper in his ear.' Wald sounded like an operatic Mephistopheles.

Kuche said they were glad to have had such a fruitful conversation, and asked how George would explain his absence to Downay. They suggested he should say it had all been a terrible error. That he had been taken in and questioned about his papers. 'Questioning over papers can often mean waiting for long periods.' But they, the gallant SS-Sturmbannführer Heinrich Kuche and Obersturmführer Joseph Wald, had been summoned. ('You would naturally mention our names.') They would have set things right.

George left with them, the same black Opel car, though they

were heading for the High Command Headquarters. They would leave him there. It would look good.

Eventually, with relief, George walked out of the lobby of the Crillon Hotel. A free man. It was almost six o'clock and he stood for a few moments in the Place de la Concorde. It had been a long, long day and this was one of Paris' most incredible vantage points. A staff car drew up, disgorging a pair of high-ranking officers who did not even look at him, let alone the view.

In the distance, shimmering in a slight haze, like thin smoke, was Notre Dame, down the Seine; he could also see the golden dome of Les Invalides. A massive swastika flag floated above the Eiffel Tower.

It was a long walk back to Downay's apartment, but George needed the exercise to clear his head. He needed to be in the open and on the streets. It was almost seven when he finally plodded up the stairs. The elevator was still not working.

Angelle opened to his ring and threw her arms around his neck, holding him tight, as though this was the most natural thing in the world.

'Thank God. Thank God. Michel's been trying to find out what they were doing with you. He's out now and may not be back until the morning.' Her eyes said that this had nothing to do with him. Probably the girls? His fiction at the Sorbonne?' There is someone here, though,' her voice dropped. 'She's a friend of Michel's. He arranged the meeting. Come.'

George followed her through the vestibule, and there, sitting upright in one of the padded chairs, was Maman, looking more the countess than ever. If the folks down Lockhill Terrace could see her now, George considered, they'd have a fit.

* * *

'We have lunch now, Herbie?' George asked, looking around him as though coming out of a dream.

Herbie Kruger consulted his watch. It was barely noon. Not yet, he said. Not quite yet. 'I want to hear more while you're into it. Quite a shock seeing your mother sitting there, eh, George?'

'Not as bad a shock as the one that was to come.' George nodded, signifying he was prepared to go on talking before they stopped for lunch.

28

'Georges. I knew it was you.' She had usually called him Georges as opposed to George. In Lockhill Terrace it had been *Georges; mon petit Georges; Georgie.* George was reserved for moments of petulance.

'Where have you been?' she demanded, as though they were back in Didcot and he was home late from school.

To George she had never changed: small, neat with a superb figure. She was in her late fifties but still exuded sex from fingers to blonde hair, natural blonde without a trace of grey. Looking at her smoothing her dress over he knees, George knew why men went crazy over her, but still could not fathom why she had married his father.

A stream of questions were sucked through his mind as he stood gaping. Did Angelle know? How much did Maman know, or guess? Her relationship with Michel Downay? Ramilies had made a point of asking how she was, the day he had gone to the War Office.

Angelle had her hand on his arm and was repeating Maman's query, asking what had happened. George said it was his papers. Nothing serious: just took a long time.

'You have been with the Boche.' Like an accusation, his Maman did not take her cool eyes from his face. Then a hand flipped up and back on to the silk dress. 'It's perfectly safe, Georges. Angelle is aware that I am your mother; and, of course, I know you've come from England.'

He went over and kissed her. She still had that expensive smell which he remembered so well from their last meeting—the weekend leave in Paris before the Blitzkrieg. So she should, married to the owner of three scent factories. Managing Director of an exclusive house. Madame Roubert. The Countess as they'd always called her down Lockhill Terrace.

He asked after his stepfather, Maurice Roubert, sixty years of age, looking fifty; bronzed, fit. They had played tennis on that last weekend, and George remembered that he would not talk politics—reticent about the war.

Madame Roubert said Maurice was well and looked forward to seeing him.

'He's in Paris?'

'Certainly.'

'And Michel ... ?'

'Won't be back tonight. Not now.' Angelle gave him a little sad smile which said for certain that Downay was about his extra work at the Sorbonne.

'And you're here, Maman. Why?'

'Because Michel told me you had arrived. I wished to see you. What was wrong with your papers? Do they suspect you?'

He said that nothing was wrong. It was a muddle. They were quite satisfied and had let him go. Then he repeated that it was good to see his mother again; and looking so well, but really there were things that had to be done. He couldn't discuss any of it until he had talked with Michel. 'You're sure he won't be back tonight?'

Angelle shook her head.

'Stop play-acting, Georges.' Madame Roubert's face softened into a dazzling smile. 'Always the play-actor, Angelle. Always in fantasy.'

Oh Christ, George thought, we're in for childhood reminiscences. All parents do it. Very forcefully he pointed out that there was no fantasy about the present circumstances.

'No, it is all very grave,' his mother still had the smile in her voice. 'Very serious. We know that. But it is men like you they choose to send into the lion's den. Men with great fantasies. Play-actors.'

The Rammer had said something similar; about him being a good actor.

'You know, Angelle,' the smile turned into a laugh, 'he was always making up great theatrical events as a child. We had many happy times, you remember, Georges?'

How could he ever forget? The dream came back at least twice a week—still; himself with a tasselled tablecloth around his shoulders, declaiming.

'One I always remember. A great fantasy about a king who

could not get his crown off. It was stuck there on his head for all time, by a spell. In the first scene, Georges was the wicked magician who cast the spell. He walked on and said: "It is I, Hiram the Wizard". Hiram the Wizard. Very dramatic. I shall never forget that.'

George went cold. His mother had caught the dream and brought it into this room in Paris. She had also captured the name he had given as a token to Ramilies.

The name was to be played back as a clear password by a third person. He was Caspar. He was also Hiram the Wizard, from the depths of childhood fantasy, conjured from memory in Ramilies' attic, shuttered and barred in the West wing of the Abbey.

There was a dilemma for him, of course. Was his mother dealing the name back, or was it mere accident? She went on talking. Angelle moved towards him, resting a hand on his arm.

In mid-flow he stopped his mother. 'Maman, there are things ... I must speak to Angelle. Alone.'

She was put out and began a small, very Gallic, tirade against sons in general and her own in particular.

'Wait, Maman. Just wait a few moments.'

Angelle, taking no sides but looking alarmed, allowed herself to be propelled into the kitchen where George placed her firmly against the wall, holding her shoulders. Then he began a fast interrogation.

'What happened after I left?'

'Nothing. What do you mean, what happened?'

'What did you do? Did you eat? Make love? Did anyone call? Did Michel go out again?'

To each of the questions she opened her mouth, as if to complain, and then closed it again. Like a goldfish. A pretty goldfish.

'He went out. Michel went out. About half-an-hour after you left, he went out; then came back again, very excited. He said you'd been picked up and he was going to see what he could do.'

Michel Downay was well informed. Western Union could not have done it faster. Certainly the GPO would not have managed it.

'Not back since?'

'Yes, of course. He came back later and stayed here. It *is* his apartment.' Slightly piqued.

'Today? What about today?'

'He went out this morning, for about an hour. When he returned he said they had you at the Avenue Foch ... Georges, is that ... ?'

'Never mind. Go on.'

'Nothing. He had lunch and went out. He told me he would not be back.'

'Was he concerned?'

'About you? Preoccupied.'

'Angelle, listen. Did a fat Swiss ever visit Michel here?'

'The man he got rooms for? The one you went to meet?'

If she knew about that ...

'You saw him? Know where he lives?'

'Certainly. He is with one of Michel's students,' but the way she said it you couldn't tell what 'student' meant. She gave George the address. Somewhere between St. Sulpice and the Luxembourg.

He patted her shoulders, gently now. She raised her hands, resting them on his shoulders, her eyes watery, like a puppy. 'He won't be back tonight,' she said again, and George told her that *he* would. First he had to see the fat man. The Swiss. Balthazar.

'It'll be curfew in an hour and a half. You'll have to hurry. Is it wise?'

No, it wasn't wise, but there were reasons. Silently George weighed the odds that he would be watched on the street, by Kuche's and Wald's men, waiting for a link. Or by others? Put them against the danger of not being certain whether Maman was dealing the name back to him, and the odds were evens. He thought about Balthazar's warning: *London say you have to see everything.* At the Abbey they had told him to trust nobody: check, and then even when you're sure, check again.

Madame Roubert was quiescent. No arguments. This made him wary. Maman was always a great one for getting her own way. She did not even grumble. Come back tomorrow, he told her: come back and talk with us when Michel is here. She kissed him affectionately and he sent his good wishes to Maurice Roubert. She laughed. 'You'll be seeing him soon. We are a full house. Boche officers billeted on us.' That was all he needed.

George watched her, from the window, as she walked spryly down the street, and felt concern. He felt it also for Angelle whose presence behind him was like static. During the night, at the Avenue Foch...

She had another go at persuading him not to leave and make the trip over to the street near the Luxembourg Gardens, where Balthazar was holed-up. The girl's name was apparently Lucie. Dark, like a gypsy, Angelle said, as if this was a cardinal sin.

There were only a few people in the streets which George chose. Later, he recalled it was like looking at an avant-garde film. The alleys slick with rain, and an occasional light breeze juggling with the torn edges of posters; old pieces of newspaper skimming into corners, or the gutter, to lie soggy.

He remembered the back-doubles which he had known once in the days before the war, on holiday with Maman, and rehearsed again at the Abbey where they'd had him sitting for hours at a bare table with a map, learning the city, testing him like a cab driver.

Use the back streets as much as possible. The ones they can't corner you in with a car. If they were using a car now, George made it unrealistic for them. Yet, he knew within five minutes that it was a penny to a pound they had a footpad on the go. At least one; probably two. Very expert; definitely professionals. George spotted one coming towards him on two occasions: the same sallow face, a peaked cap doing nothing to disguise the military haircut.

He doubled back, retraced streets, crossed abruptly, dodged into doorways, even roused the concierge of one apartment building, asking for a mythical M. Albert Camus. Mythical? By the time he entered the Boul. Mich.—somewhere near the Luxembourg Station—the sallow footpad had got himself lost, and George was left with the other probable: big, with a face like an inexpert boxer, the jaw out of alignment, bulbous nose and a nasty right ear. He was a standard heavy, flatfooted enough to have served with some police force for a long time, dogged of manner and with enough weight to cause a lot of pain if he took you by surprise.

George had been certain about the sallow one. The pugilist was an unknown quantity, so he took him for a run around the park: in this instance, the Luxembourg Gardens where people were thin on the ground because of the rain and lateness of the day. Less than an hour to curfew. The Palace, George thought, looked as ugly as ever; he'd never taken to it, though pondered now, for a second, on the irony that it had been built by a later de'Medici —Marie, mother of one of those eternal Louis. The thirteenth, he thought. Good luck.

There were several soldiers around, replete with cameras. One turn around the main sweep settled things. The pugilist was a leech.

George led him down out of the Boul. Mich. end of the gardens and, making sure there was a good view, took him into the nearest alley. It was narrow and there was a certain amount of noise coming from high up among the buildings, though few people were actually treading the cobbles. Six hundred yards down, the alley narrowed to a funnel into which two more dark streets emptied. It was all very Victor Hugo. George turned right and waited; nobody about. Then the soft shoe shuffle of the boxer's approach.

He turned the corner and George took him fast, from behind.

Never hesitate, the leathery little man at the Strength Through Joy Camp had said. He also advised against killing while teaching silent kills. (*Six of them in 'orspital, what with all the paperwork and manpower tied up, is of more value than six of 'em dead.*) George did not think he'd mind dispensing with the paperwork on this one. It is unwise to leave anybody to talk, particularly if they're loitering after you with intent.

As George hit him the first time it crossed his mind that the man might just be doing a spot of minding for Michel Downay. But there was no time for conversation. The edge of his palm caught the boxer on the right side of the neck. He arched his back, just as he was supposed to do under the circumstances. The knee came up, catching him square and hard in the spine. George heard it snap as it made contact. The boxer did not even cry out. Dead before he hit the deck. *You're a dirty fighter, sir. That's what we want: dirty fighters.*

Less than ten minutes later, he was outside the address Angelle had provided; panting a bit, but without company. She had said the fourth floor. Sure enough, after George had knocked and rung for five minutes, he found Balthazar by forcing the lock. He was there in the flat—what was left of him.

They had done it in his living room. The girl was in the bedroom. Not much of the gypsy about her now. A lot of blood.

Natural enough when throats are cut.

Oddly, the place had not been rifled. The Mark I transmitter was intact, crystals and all, under the bed.

He made it back to Downay's apartment very quickly, in spite of the case weighing like a ton of lead. The Rammer had told him that you should always calculate the risk and then add some. George added double and then some. It still did not come out right, but he figured that one message sent out on the memorised frequency, around nine that night, should bring a response by nine the following evening. Twenty-four hours, then he would have to ditch the wireless.

Angelle looked relieved and did not seem to notice the suitcase. George asked to be left alone. He had a lot of work to do, but could they, perhaps, eat together at about nine-thirty? She looked pleased and reminded him, yet again, that Michel would not be back that night. He nodded, then locked himself into his room and began to sort out the message, dredging what he could from the RT and cipher sessions. He remembered Maitland-Wood spending the day at the Strength Through Joy Camp and saying they would probably want him to do a bit of cipher and wireless. Good for them.

He prayed that nine o'clock was one of the times the Rammer had scheduled for transmission and listening out. He found the crystals, hung the aerial from the old wardrobe and went through the complicated RT procedure. Ham-fisted with the key, but he reckoned they would spot him quickly enough. In all, he repeated the message three times. Twenty-eight groups of letters. When they'd put it through the machine it should come out as—

STOP PRESS FOR MARS. BALTHAZAR WIPED. CASPAR'S MOTHER IDENTIFIED ON TOKEN. PLEASE ADVISE. UNCERTAIN MELCHIOR. WILCO ALL ORDERS. CASPAR.

Mars was Ramilies.

After three minutes came the 'message received' letters. Then silence.

Angelle looked radiant. She had put on a plain frock, blue, and a little make-up. Also silk stockings, her last pair, she said, implying it was a special occasion. From somewhere she had got ham and potatoes; and some beans and fruit. There was no bread.

'Your mother is a tough lady.' Munching an apple.

'Yes, tough as old boots.' He told her that Maman had been brought up in a hard school, then went on to make careful, and subtle, enquiries about Michel's habits and friends. Whether Maman had ever visited before. The answers were reasonable enough. Angelle knew some of it; but, if she told the truth, not all.

He went on to ask what Michel really thought about doing this work for the Boche, and the dazzle went out of her face.

'He says you will both be moved to Berlin before long.' She paused, but it was more of a shudder. 'Then I shall be alone again.' Like it was the end of the world; then a deep breath, the tears not far from the surface as she struggled to replace them with the laughing side of her personality.

George knew how she felt. Tough, cold George Thomas from Lockhill Terrace had been through it too many times himself. When you drag yourself up and work at being something you are not, there are times you feel so lonely and insecure that you might just as well be the last and only person in the world.

There had been moments at Oxford when it was hard for George to even walk into a room, let alone look people in the eyes. But you brace yourself and carry on, leading the double life and knowing where you've come from. Pretending. Living fantasies and not letting the truth about yourself intrude.

Insecurity was a good word, and George could have taken a first class honours degree in being insecure at that time. You learn to live with it. Ramilies knew that. Why else, George thought, would he have been picked? Maman was right. People like himself, good at living out their fantasies, were the best kind for jobs like this. The official view, he knew, was different.

He reached over the table and took her hand, saying she need never feel alone because there were plenty of people around just like them.

Michel, she replied, was cold and distant. For a long time she had felt that she was in the way; that he did not trust her. Yet he used her from time to time. She spat out the word 'used'.

It all happened then, of course.

The ways of love, for George, were all second-hand, learned from Hollywood movies. Yet he liked to think that it went beyond that as they lay naked in her bed afterwards.

It had not been like you read in books, nor the erotic imaginings of his own mind. Not lust nor craving, but giving and receiving. Pleasure : yes.

It went on and on. She was not a noisy lover, and lord knew if they were any good together, but George—young and inexperienced George Thomas—felt that first coupling was like a sacrament. If ever I am to love, he thought as dawn crept into the room, it is here and now; fast with this girl.

They were up and dressed by the time Michel got home. He looked tired and winced with pain a couple of times when he moved, as though his leg was playing him up.

George knew what Angelle meant about his coldness. He was distant and awesome now, sitting sipping coffee by the stove, going through everything : from the moment George had left the apartment for the meeting with Balthazar, until the time of his return. George kept up the fiction about being arrested in error, and how Kuche and Wald had bailed him out.

Michel had seen the SS officers, of course, and it seemed that they had kept to their side of the bargain, but he held something back which did not come out until Angelle retired to the kitchen with the empty cups and plates.

It was only then that Michel told George about Balthazar and the girl, Lucie. The police were there now, and all hell was breaking loose because some Gestapo man had been found dead. A plainclothes man. 'Expertly killed. His back broken.' He looked accusingly at George and asked if he had been to Balthazar's apartment.

George already had a pact with Angelle. He had not left the place after returning on the previous evening.

'Liar,' a fine spray covered George's cheek. 'Georges, you are a liar. I had a man watching out for you. The cretin lost you, but I suppose you were leading him a dance.'

'Okay, so I went out and there was a tail.' Thank Christ, George thought, he had got the right footpad. 'Better a donkey without a tail than dead meat with one.'

*   *   *

'Okay, George, we break for lunch now.' Herbie stretched and went into the kitchen, calling back over his shoulder, 'Have a drink. Help yourself.'

He had unfrozen a quiche, cooked last week, and only had to make a dressing for the salad. There was soup, once more out of a tin.

Strain-lines showed around George's eyes. As they ate, Herbie said that he found it very difficult to think of the man sitting opposite him as the younger man who went through the whole Nostradamus business in 1941. Yet the two were the same, distanced and intertwined. 'Are you the same man you were, thirty years ago?' George tilted an eyebrow.

As he said it, Big Herbie realised the major reason for his difficulty. It was hard to see George at all. True, he was tall, but even now he had about him a chameleon facility. He recalled that, when they were apart, he always thought of George as a thin, bald, angular man—which he certainly was not. He also remembered once seeing him at an official function, dressed smartly in a well-cut suit. He had not recognised him.

George Thomas had one of the greatest natural attributes of a field man: the ability to merge into his background. George was a different person sitting in his own office, than the George who sat eating Herbie's quiche here in Herbie's flat.

He did not have to try. The ability was natural and would probably have been even more acute when he was younger—in '41. If George did not want you to see him, he could be almost invisible.

As for the story he told, that was alive and vivid enough. Truth ran through every nuance.

'Is it what you want?' George asked, slowly coming back into the present.

'Exactly. You have a very good memory: very good.'

'Can't vouch for all the conversations. Not exactly, you know. But they're near enough. It's odd, Herbie, but now I've got going, it's like watching an old movie. You remember things. Little details; words; conversations; even people and places. You know. I've been back to that building where Michel Downay lived. Once. I didn't even recognise it. Yet I can see it plainly now. There were so many odd things about that whole business— mental things that I'll tell you about when we get to them: things not in the report.' He gave a deep sigh. 'Ah well, that's the job, isn't it? Memory.'

'Remembering,' Herbie nodded his big head. 'Or forgetting,

George. We all want to forget some things.'

George forked up a mouthful of quiche and chewed, slowly as if he was thinking it over. 'Just now, I was talking about what Angelle felt like then. About being alone and insecure.'

Herbie made an affirmative grunt. He was pleased with the quiche. There would be enough of it left for him to eat for supper. Supper and the Mahler Sixth.

George said that he did know how she felt then. 'I know it even more now.' Back in the Forties, he supposed, there were times when being a piece of fraudulent currency really hurt. He remembered thinking, during one episode, that if he ever came through to the other end of the war, he would probably end up as a con man.

Big Herbie laughed. 'And you did.'

'Yes,' George's face became troubled for a second. 'Yes, I've become just that. Like you, Herbie. After a lifetime in this trade it's what I've become : living a dozen different lives and each one of them as phoney as a lead silver dollar. Like T. S. Eliot says—I am a hollow man, a stuffed man. Know how old I am, Herbie?'

Herbie said he had seen the file. George looked fifty in the right light; he would have put him at around fifty-eight, knowing the background circumstances. He was fifty-nine, going on sixty.

'Stuffed and hollow. At my age? And if I had kids I couldn't tell them much about what I've done. It's a relief to talk it out with you. Stuffed and hollow. It's a great profession, Herbie. Let's get this stuff out of the way. I want to tell you how I conned Michel Downay : conned him into thinking I was a genuine seer. A prophet in my own right. Shook the bugger rigid.' He fiddled with his briefcase, set down within reach beside his chair, and pulled out a small, worn, leather-bound notebook. 'Chapter and verse for the difficult bits.' He brandished it in the air. 'Can't trust my own memory with the fake stuff. Funny, 'cause I can remember the real prophecies well enough.'

'I'll get coffee. Can't wait to hear it.'

In the kitchen, Herbie turned the tape reel on the machine, then took the coffee through, entering his own living room and, at the same moment, travelling back in time to Michel Downay's Paris apartment on that crucial morning in 1941.

29

Michel Downay eased himself into a chair, stretching his leg painfully. The Gestapo man, he explained, was killed not far from Balthazar's hole-up. He said that his man thought there had been someone else in the circuit when he lost touch with George.

George shrugged and said he had not killed anyone. He looked Downay straight in the eyes. (Another thing they taught at the Abbey: *If you're going to lie directly, look them straight in the eyes and do it without smiling.*) He did not smile. 'Yes, I went to Balthazar's place. I wanted to check out something about procedure. Found them there—him and the girl—with their throats cut. You got any ideas about who'd have done a thing like that?'

Downay shook his head. It wasn't the style of the occupying power. Maybe Lucie had a jealous bloke on the side. He didn't know. He also changed the subject smartly. There was work to do. Kuche and Wald had been on at him. Very soon now they would have to take some comments to their General Frühling. The General was shouting; so was the Reichsminister.

Box clever, George told himself.

They got into a huddle, side by side at the table, Michel bringing his books and papers from the desk. He had made a list of the most obvious quatrains, together with his own personal comments: all written out like a ledger, in columns, showing the various interpretations which could be made of individual quatrains. The ones which might most satisfy the Propaganda Ministry were done in red.

The obvious ones were things like—

The fortress on the Thames will surrender
And the king will be confined within:
Near the sea there will be seen one in great distress
Facing his mortal enemy, who will assume power.

That was quatrain number thirty-seven from the Eighth Century. There were others, many of which George had on his own 'good' list.

Downay talked a lot of technicalities, mainly about the horoscopes which had been cast for Hitler. In particular, one which was actually published in the early Twenties. *A man of action born on 20 April 1889 with the Sun in 29 degrees Aries at the time of birth.* It did not mention Hitler by name, but spoke of a destiny to play a *Führer-role*, giving an impulse to a German Freedom Movement.

Caution. Play him, Ramilies whispered. *Let him come to you.*

George mentioned that current horoscopes predicted disaster. 'London's got a man doing them full time.'

Downay smiled and gave him the eyebrow treatment. 'They won't want any of that,' he said.

'Depends.'

'On what?' As cautious as George. You could see it in those cool eyes which must have held such a fascination for women.

'Depends on the Seventh Century.' George said it with a deaddrop face. The Seventh Century in those shuffled prophecies was incomplete. Incomplete by over fifty quatrains. Nostradamus had only recorded forty-two instead of his normal ton.

Michel relaxed. Muscles sagged, and the taut lines on his face smoothed out; the eyes brightened and the mouth lifted into an attractive smile. 'For a while I thought the English had sent me a dedicated astrologer.'

'They have.' George thought he sounded just about as casual as a tart on the make, so he followed it up by pointing out that he had certain talents and was a confirmed practitioner. 'The people who sent me didn't want you lumbered with any old rubbish.'

Michel looked concerned again, his right hand going up to his throat and then running down the side of his face, a gesture of nervous distress.

George held out a hand, fingers splayed, to calm him.

Michel opened his mouth to speak, but George slipped in under his guard, quietly quoting the first quatrain of the First Century:

'Sitting alone at night in secret study;
It is placed on a brass tripod.
A slight flame comes out of the emptiness
And makes successful that which should not be believed
     in vain.'

Downay leaned forward. In the kitchen something clattered, and Angelle came through to say she had to go out. There may be bread down the road. Yesterday someone told her there might be bread and she was going to join the queue.

George and Michel waited, making polite, monosyllabic, conversation until she had put on a hat and coat and left the apartment. As she went, Angelle gave George a shy, almost conspiratorial, smile.

'You slept with her last night, yes?' Michel had lived in the place with her for some time, so was certainly tuned to her moods.

People read people like books when they share lives, so there was no point in George denying it.

Michel shrugged as if to imply that she was nobody's property, or anybody's. There was something unpleasant about it. Aloud he said there were plenty of women. Enough to go around.

A bastard with women, Angelle had said.

Cold silence for a moment while Michel looked down at his ledger of prophecies. Then he repeated that first quatrain, and added the one which followed it.

'The wand in the hand is placed in the middle of the
     tripod's legs.
With water he sprinkles both the hem of his garment
     and his foot.
A voice, fear; he trembles in his robes.
Divine splendour; the god sits nearby.'

Both of the quatrains referred to the ancient rites of divination, the ritual through which the seer got his pictures of the future.

'So,' Downay tensed again. 'So we have the methods of proprecy. The Egyptian mysteries. The tripod and the bowl of water. The forbidden books. Night. Fear. All the standard paraphernalia of the oracles. You propose we should sit here in this apartment and bring forth visions to fill up those empty spaces in Nostradamus's incomplete Seventh Century?'

George knew he hadn't played Michel for nearly long enough, but there was a time-squeeze, and the moment might never be bettered.

'I've already done it,' he said quietly, just as Ramilies had instructed; just as they had planned on that dark night behind the shuttered windows of the Abbey.

Michel did not laugh, though interest was mingled with predominant amazement on his face and, especially, in the eyes.

'When did you do this?'

George told him in England, and that was one of the main reasons he had been sent to Michel.

The way Michel sat, still and immobile, reminded George of a hunter waiting for his prey to approach a water-hole. You could see the scepticism and hear it in his voice as he spoke.

'Georges, I am a psychologist. I deal with the behaviour of human beings, what makes them work: the machinery of their thoughts and subconscious, and how that machinery is conditioned by society, politics, family backgrounds, tradition, religion—yes, and by their dreams and superstitions: by their strange conceptions of the occult in some cases; and by the stars. At least Communism is honest, Georges, it mistrusts religion as an enemy of the State and of the mind. These brigands we're dealing with are feudal in their outlook. The soul must be owned by the State, so the State has to provide a mysticism. They tolerate the Church, but would prefer the mumbo-jumbo of legends and astrology. That is one of my motivations for writing about astrology and prophecy. Its connection with human behaviour. But you *really* believe in mystic prophecy?'

'I believe in what I have accomplished.'

'And what, may I ask, does that really mean?' Deep beneath his trimmed beard, Michel's lips twisted: the arrogant leer of an academic about to meet a challenge.

George said he would show him, leaving the table and going to his room. Under the false lining of the suitcase he had brought from England, was the packet of papers they had prepared so carefully during the early sessions with Ramilies and Fenice. They had even been typed up on French paper using a French machine, with a ribbon made in Nîmes.

'Before you see these,' George stood in the doorway looking at Downay, half-turned at the table. 'Madame Roubert?' He clutched the little packet of quarto pages to him as though they were gold, or, better still, a child.

'Madame Maurice Roubert? Yes?'

'What's your connection with her? How much does she know? Can she be trusted?'

'You question if your own mother can be trusted?'

George told him, sharply, that he questioned everybody. Trusted nobody.

Michel nodded patiently, one hand already reaching out, the fingers moving irritably, for George's papers. 'You know we're not fully organised yet. But there is some structure. Madame Roubert's husband, Maurice, is the leader of a group. A cell. Resistance, Georges.'

'Your own cell?'

He nodded.

'She was here. She suggested that it was your idea for her to come here.'

He smirked. 'Didn't you think it a good idea? Or do you dislike your Maman, Georges?'

If the security was sound enough, George admitted, it had been good to see his mother and know she was safe. With a slow affirmative nod, he stepped forward and handed over the papers.

They were good. Very good. Michel began to shake his head with pleasure as he read the first few quatrains. They were the easy ones, like,

> The armies of the leader from the Rhine
> Will be encamped through all lands.
> Their strength comes from him
> He will command and be respected.

And:

> The Great One born near the Rhine of the
>   Nordic Alps
> Will bring about a complete change
> All countries will bow down
> The city on the Thames will be his.

It was excellent, and Michel said so. George knew well enough that they read just like the real thing. Michel's reaction, when he came to the tricky bits, was almost violent:

'Holy Mother, they'll not ... What in God's name? ...' He read aloud,

> 'In one stroke the black ones with skulls
> Will take command of all peoples
> To bring fear into the hearts of men
> While the Great One will be cast out—

They'll never ...'

'Go on reading and think about it.' George prayed that he would not get cold feet or prove difficult. He knew he hadn't played him long enough. The idea had been to introduce these concoctions slowly, a piece at a time. *Feed him up gradually.* So Fenice had cautioned.

Downnay went on reading. Mainly aloud.

> 'The standard-bearer's castle, fashioned
> After the manner of the Court of Arthur
> Will be a place of blood; not there
> But in the dark capital.'

His brow creased like crumpled paper at,

> The one who carried the flag
> Will unseat the great leader of Germany,
> In one blow, aided by those with the skulls
> Dressed in night black.

'The standard-bearer? The Castle? King Arthur's court?' Downay queried, knowing well enough what it meant.

'The abortive putsch of 1923,' George prompted, trying to look innocent.

Downnay inclined his head, allowing sudden light to dawn on his face, signifying that he was familiar with the story of how, on the November evening in 1923, Hitler had made his ill-fated attempt to seize power, and Himmler, then in Munich, had carried the war banner, the *Reichskriegsflagge*, in front of the War Ministry.

It was rumoured that this was still one of the greatest days, one of the best memories, of Himmler's life; though it initially led to failure, except with women who saw in the ardent young man who carried the flag, a champion of the New Order.

'The castle? King Arthur's Court?' Downay repeated; not a genuine query, for he added, 'Wewelsburg?'

'Of course Wewelsburg. That's Himmler's Court, isn't it? His Camelot?'

That's what Downay had heard. But the rumours, he said, were scratchy. Back at the Abbey, George had been told a lot about the castle at Wewelsburg—mysticism, monasticism, the weird and odd pretensions of the SS.

'The Reichminister ...' Downay began.

George smiled. 'The Reichsminister,' he repeated, 'will like the ones which seem to show that the Führer is to triumph. They will be the ones which friends Kuche and Wald send to Berlin. The others'll fascinate them; stir them into action, maybe. Give them hopes?' letting his voice rise in question.

Downay's eyes glittered, the corners of his mouth defying the beard, creaming into a smile of genuine pleasure. 'Brilliant,' he whispered; adding that, of course, it was also very simple. Which it was.

Any Party Member; any ranker of the SS, would recognise the standard-bearer as Reichsführer-SS Heinrich Himmler. 'The black ones with skulls" were manifestly the SS itself. There were many other references. Things like—*Those who stand shoulder to shoulder where the lightning strikes twice.* (A comment on the lightning flash runes, the distinctive SS markings.) There was even an obscure quatrain which mentioned *The ring and the dagger of silver; With the face of death thereon*—coveted SS accoutrements.

'Georges,' Michel hauled himself up, gripping the table. 'I hope you understand how very dangerous all this stuff is.' The smile turned into a laugh, throwing back his head as though taunting the danger.

George did not laugh. He said that nobody could be really certain how far Himmler was hooked on the occult. It was much more probable that his particular stimulation lay within the Norse legends, combined with the odd bits of sanctity left over from his Roman Catholic upbringing. 'What is certain, Michel, is that the SS have great ambition. These quatrains might give a little push to that ambition. If senior members of the SS could persuade Himmler that it is his destiny to overcome the Führer—well, anything might happen. The Wehrmacht and the SS are at loggerheads already. A split within the Party itself could add confusion on a grand scale.'

'Or lead us to a convenient wall,' Michel said soberly. He bent over the papers again and read aloud,

> 'Before the Thames runs with blood
> The Great Conqueror will be forced
> To give way to his own people who ride
> On clouds of death, and bury many slaves.'

It was a sombre piece and a fitting counterpoint to the sudden loud knocking at Downay's door.

They looked at one another, locking eyes. A minute flicker of fear? Fumbling for his ebony cane, Downay hobbled across the room and into the vestibule.

Kuche and Wald came back with him, together with a sergeant George had not seen before. They all looked grim, stiff and very businesslike, as well they might. The Reichsminister of Propaganda, they said, had given their General twenty-four hours to come up with the right quatrains: ones which he could use to bolster up the nation, and spread despondency among the enemy.

General Frühling, in turn, had given Kuche and Wald four hours only. The time-ratio seemed a shade severe, and George said so. They had no option. Downay spread a hand towards the papers which lay on the table. A gesture which appeared to convey great generosity.

Michel hesitated after handing over his own documents, as if he would have liked more time to study those George had brought from England. George would also have liked more time, if only to stuff away some of the prophecies to use as a reserve. But Kuche and Wald held all the aces; and the firepower.

They told George and Michel to stay put. 'You will be hearing from us. Soon.' George reflected that if either of the men had any intelligence they would be hearing pretty fast.

As they left, Kuche gave George a look which had question marks engraved on his retinas. George replied with a small nod.

Angelle came back with the bread. They ate. At one point Michel spoke of going down to the University, but a glance out of the window showed there was a pair of ratty-looking men watching the building without any pretence of hiding either their presence or intent.

*   *   *

'So there you were,' muttered Herbie. 'More coffee? I get some.'

There we were, George agreed. All his assets had gone; the SS were watching the place and he hoped for some kind of message from London that night. Not good for the nerves.

Herbie came back with the coffee, poured it and sat down. 'And the message came?'

'Much more than the message.' George swallowed and continued.

30

It was a tense afternoon, there in Downay's apartment. They did not talk much and, around late afternoon, Downay started to behave like a caged animal: stumping up and down, using his cane to lean upon and bang hard into the thin carpet.

They came back at about five o'clock: the car arriving noisily, with a squeal of brakes which must have cost the Third Reich a few marks in rubber. Then the sound of boots outside—and the knocking.

Kuche and Wald were both very correct, on their best behaviour, but pleased and unable to suppress an obvious excitement.

Did the Herr Doktor and Herr Thomas realise what they had provided?

'We were still working on the quatrains ...' Downay shrugged. 'The time ...'

George said there were a number of things they had found difficult: hard to understand.

Did they understand the reference to the castle; the standard-bearer and to Arthur's Court?

Those were difficult, George admitted.

Not easy to comprehend, agreed Michel Downay.

'Good.' Kuche slapped his polished boot with the military cane he carried. 'Good. The General has sent some of the material to Berlin. He has also had a long telephone conversation with the Reichsführer-SS: with Himmler. There are certain officers who wish to discuss these matters, these quatrains, with you—as experts.'

'Officers in Reichsminister Goebbels' Ministry of Propaganda?' Downay sounded as though the question was so obvious that it need not even be asked.

'No.' Wald's smile vanished and his voice became more clipped. 'No. Some high-ranking officers in the SS. We are all to travel into

Germany ...' The tone bordered on being aggressive.

'Berlin?' George feigned excitement.

Wald shook his head. 'We shall leave quietly in the morning. No fuss. Just the Herr Doktor; yourself, Herr Thomas; Major Kuche and I; together with a small detachment, a sergeant and four men. For protection, you understand. You will be going to meet the standard-bearer at Arthur's Court.' He thought it was a very good joke. No wonder they looked pleased, they had cracked the prophecies. The superior knowledge of the SS had triumphed. *Natürlich.* Only members of the SS knew the real ways of the SS.

'Tomorrow?' Downay made a show of sounding irritated. 'I don't know if I ...'

Kuche slapped his boot again. 'You will make yourselves ready to leave here at eight in the morning. We will provide the transport. The train leaves at nine o'clock sharp from the Gare du Nord.'

After the SS officers' car pulled away, Michel stood at the window for a long time, looking down into the street. After a while he relaxed and turned back into the room.

'They've called off the watchdogs.'

Angelle had come in from the kitchen and George took her to one side, quietly telling her the news she had dreaded.

Michel made some off-hand remark about her naturally being able to stay in the apartment. 'You'll be quite safe here. Besides it will keep the place aired.'

A bastard with women.

With Angelle, there were tears just under the surface. George sensed her shiver as they touched hands, and he whispered that it was all right. 'We'll be coming back. It won't be for long.'

As though making some sudden resolution, Michel turned towards them. There was much to be done before the morning. Only he could arrange it. The glint in his eyes should have warned George there and then, for he was like an officer who had made a decision and was full of enthusiasm about his strategy, right, wrong, or, as in this case, foolhardy. He would be out for some time, he said.

George warned him that Kuche and Wald seemed serious. 'They're picking us up at eight in the morning and it's only an hour or so to curfew now.'

He made pooh-poohing noices, saying something about the curfew presenting no problems for him. He would be back in the early hours. Maybe around three. George felt he was suggesting that they would have the place to themselves and could enjoy it during his absence.

For a second, hatred showed in Angelle's eyes as she watched Michel leave for his room. Her face was wiped clean of expression, and her shoulders sagged like an old boxer ready to move in and finish off a victim.

He returned, stuffing an automatic pistol into the pocket of his jacket, knuckles white on the head of the ebony cane. Yet he moved quickly, almost jaunty in his walk, as he went to the vestibule and shrugged into the theatrical topcoat. Then he grinned and raised a hand in mock blessing. 'Benedicte, my children.'

The door closed behind him, leaving only the faint echo of his halting walk, the stick clipping on the tiled floor, then the sound fading.

Angelle clung to George for a while, shaking but not crying, as he told her that on no account was she to stay in the apartment once they had gone.

She pulled back, panic on her face, the eyes seeking some order in the chaos, as though she was looking for hidden meanings in George's looks and words.

He floundered, searching for the best action. The most positive way of helping her.

'You can go to Maman's: to Madame Roubert's home ...' That could be a dreadful mistake, he realised, quickly correcting himself. Distraught, he held on to her: close so that she could not see his face as he weighed the odds. There was one possibility. He dismissed it as being too dangerous and compromising, remembering his own words to Michel. That he trusted nobody. Then he thought again.

One of the Rammer's last instructions concerned the place. One address. One safe house to be used only in unavoidable circumstances, in desperate emergency. To give Angelle access to it, he would have to reveal a great deal, like telling her that Hiram the Wizard had sent her and they should check with Mars.

He shelved it for the time being, needing to think the whole business through. It was already well after six and he still had to code-up tonight's message and stand by to receive at nine o'clock.

She wanted to stay with him, saying she couldn't bear to be alone, but eventually George persuaded her to leave him. 'There are things I have to do,' gently, as to a child. 'Things that will help you.'

Then he sat on the bed in his small room and worked out the groups. If he received their message, his own would be prefixed by a series of three letters, repeated three times. When decoded the rest would read—

PROPHET SWALLOWED. VENUS AND WARLOCK SHOULD USE ALL VERSES. CASPAR AND MELCHIOR EN ROUTE FOR ARTHUR'S COURT IN PEACE. FINAL TRANSMISSION. PIANO GOING OUT OF WINDOW. PLEASE REPLACE AND LISTEN OUT. CASPAR.

Venus and Warlock were, of course, the ginger Leaderer and his wireless man running *Soldatensender Calais*. With luck they would be broadcasting bits of the falsified Nostradamus quatrains within days.

He sat for a while looking at the groups of letters, thinking about Angelle. If the trip into Germany went wrong, very wrong, leaving Michel Downay and George Thomas in crumpled heaps, the SS would come looking for the third occupant of the apartment. He did not like to think of what that could mean. In the end, it seemed worth the risk. Struggling once more with the cipher, George added another series of groups. When unravelled they read—

COURIER GALAXY WORKING UNDER CASPAR. CLEAR FOR SPECIAL HOUSING.

The special housing was the apartment in the Rue Cambon, occupied by an elderly couple who had been purposely left behind during the debacle in 1940, and knew where a number of bodies were buried. Bodies like arms caches, and real living bodies who could help form a nucleus of saboteur organisations. There were precious few of these contacts left behind in France. Pure luck, and one man's foresight had caused any to be left at all. Galaxy was the arranged field name for any unknown quantity which George felt he could trust.

Dead on nine he sent out the call signal for Stellar; fingers slipping under the key, his palms damp, with sweat running down to his fingers. After one minute, he switched to listen-out.

They came on at nine-five. He gave the quick reception burst and then hunched over the set, pad on knee, pencil ready to take down their groups, left hand holding the side of the headphones.

There were twenty-eight groups, some of them very fuzzy, but George thought honestly that he had enough of the message to make sense. He did not fancy staying on the air for long, there in Downay's apartment, claustrophobic in the small room, with Angelle impatient in the kitchen not far away.

He sent out the prefix confirming reception of their message, then his own prefix. Three times. Four or five seconds later they gave George the go-ahead and he rattled off his own groups. London okayed, and he signed off; parking the gear, taking down the aerial, closing the case and pushing it under the bed. He would have to risk letting Angelle take the set to the Rue Cambon. He then started to decipher.

There had been a hopeless jumble around the middle of the reception. Any experienced operator would have insisted on a recount. It was not until George began working at it that he realised how bad the whole thing was. Whichever way he tried, it came out—

BALTHAZAR WILL RETURN NEXT MOON. DO NOT ACCEPT GHYEBNSH AMTETAN AND GLYXJY. DEEPLY CONCERNED REGARDING VIABILITY OF LEMINHJS FARHELMN AND MOTORBLADE. LISTEN OUT ON SCHEDULE.

It was signed MARS. Ramilies himself; and the muddle was indecipherable. He had no idea what MOTORBLADE was supposed to mean. Confusion.

The longer he looked at the scrambled message, the more depressed George became. DO NOT ACCEPT jumble. What was he not to accept? The Hiram the Wizard token from his mother? If so, how far could he go with Michel Downay, or even Angelle Tours? Or any of them? Were they DEEPLY CONCERNED REGARDING VIABILITY of the whole operation? If so, they were too late.

He thought again, was it Maman or Downay? Here I am being seduced by the SS, working for Ramilies, side by side with Michel Downay, and heavily attracted by the girl Downay had used and lived with.

To say that George was worried at that point was an under-statement in trumps.

He burned the sheaf of notes, and went back into the main room, head buzzing with thoughts about his worth as an agent in the field; a manipulator of great, if evil, men through the dreamings of a sixteenth-century occultist.

Angelle sat very still, her knees primly together, in one of the chairs by the stove. Her face was too tranquil for comfort. It was as though she had just painfully accepted the news of a terminal illness, or that a reprieve from a death sentence had not been granted. Acquiescence was written all over her, as though she knew there was a penalty for life—which there is—and she was about to be called to account.

George went over, bent down and kissed her. She clutched at him, and it was like being dragged down into a deep pool, so that in the end he had to slide his lips to one side to gain breath, gasping as though emerging into sunlight. It was like that often over the next few hours: a whirlpool which took both of them down with it.

They used her bed on that last night, and whispered close together in the darkness. It was hot and there was hardly any noise from the street below her window. Sometime, long after midnight, she held him to her and laughed. 'Hiram the Wizard. You have removed the crown instead of fixing it to my head for ever. That is how I shall think of you now—always—my Wizard.' As she spoke, her body stiffened, and she repeated it, 'Hiram the Wizard.'

He wondered, of course, if Angelle was not trying to play the token to him. But the situation had become so complex that he said nothing, except that was the name she should use when she went to the safe apartment on the Rue Cambon. All the details.

It seemed to calm her and they drifted into sleep, then woke, suddenly. She was sweating and said it was a nightmare. George realised he had also dreamed—dream full of cartoon characters: of Ramilies, Downay, Kuche and Wald, Himmler and the Chap-linesque Hitler, all emerging in grotesque shapes from a bubbling cauldron tended by the old Brueghel woman at the house where the original reception committee had taken him.

Again they fell into a shallow doze. Woke. Made love. Then woke again to the slam of the door. Michel Downay was back and calling their names loudly from the living room.

'It is all arranged,' he said. 'We have the bastards now.'

*   *   *

'Thank you for being so frank, George.' Herbie made a note on his pad. He made notes all the time: a small misdirection, lest George thought he was being taped.

'I think it's everything of importance.' George looked weary.

'I mean thank you for being so frank about Angelle.'

'Oh,' he smiled. ' "When I was a young man courting the girls". A lovely lady.'

'Lovely indeed, George. You feel up to going on?' It was not quite three-thirty.

'We have to go on, don't we? Only the rest of today, tomorrow, and a few hours on Thursday. Got to tell all. Orders.'

Herbie put out a huge hand, gently. 'I know you don't like it, George, but it just might be important.'

'Bloody Kraut. You're too bloody thorough by half.' He laughed. 'Well, there's a lot to tell, my old Deutsche buddy. Downay's mad plan; the hell on that train; the nightmare at Wewelsburg.'

'And what followed. Wermut.'

'Yes, Wermut. Wormwood . . .'

'Give me another half-hour then I'll get tea. Okay?'

'Right,' George leaned back in his chair. 'So, we woke up to find bloody bearded Michel Downay back home and as pleased as a ram with two cocks,' he grinned.

31

'It is all arranged.' Michel was still in his coat, leaning on the ebony cane, looking dishevelled and tired. Then he laughed, almost the laugh of a maniac, throwing back his head. For a second, his bearded face looked very young, the eyes extraordinarily bright. George wondered if he had been with a woman, the eyes had that particular sparkle which comes afterwards.

'I have interrupted,' he laughed again. 'I have become a sexual term, yes? Monsieur Coitus Interruptus.'

George put an arm around Angelle. She had wrapped herself in a flimsy robe. He had just managed to climb into his trousers. Angelle was shivering, but it was not possible to tell if it was with fear or rage.

'What is it you've arranged?' George tightened his grip around the girl's shoulders.

'The storming of the Bastille and the Winter Palace; the Siege of Troy. All is arranged, and I have a new quatrain for you, Georges.'

There was a real scent of danger in the air, blossoming between Michel and George. Angelle still shivered, and George quietly suggested she should get dressed. She gave a simple wag of the head and disappeared through the door and down the passage with Downay calling after her that coffee would be a good idea.

The apartment was cold, for they had let the stove die down, unbanked before bed. Dawn had not yet started to glimmer outside, and the taste in George's mouth was sour, his eyes sore and heavy. The whole feeling was of that waiting, quiet time, as though the apartment itself resented people in it being up and awake.

George's watch showed four-thirty. 'A new quatrain?'

Michel Downay's mouth dropped, the smile vanishing as he spoke—

'In his great castle, at the round table
The standard-bearer, surrounded by his knights
Will die, slain by those who come summoned
By him for the prophet's sake.'

It took a few seconds for the meaning to sink home, and in that time Angelle came up quickly behind George, whispering that she was going to get coffee.

'Michel?' There was an echo in George's voice. 'What nonsense have you arranged? The standard-bearer will die ...?'

'Simple, my dear Georges. Simple and complete.' He was taking off his coat, one hand resting on the top of a chair to steady himself. 'You would agree, from what our friends Kuche and Wald have said, that the SS have summoned us into the presence. "You are going to see the standard-bearer at Arthur's Court", that's what Wald said—right?'

'Yes.'

'We are being summoned into the presence of Himmler himself. The direct result of your Himmler quatrains is that we are to meet Himmler.'

George said that it looked that way.

Michel continued, 'We are to be taken to Himmler's sacred castle, his monastery at Wewelsburg where he holds court and passes some mystic hours with the high priests of the SS. We, George; you and I, are to be invited in : to explain ourselves. You realise that? Into the place where he keeps the Holy Grail. We go by train. Soon. With a very small guard.' The smile again, thin this time beneath the beard. 'On the journey—which, if you haven't yet worked it out, will be long and arduous—there is going to be a slight readjustment. A changing of the guard. Suddenly, our own people will be with us. That is what I have been arranging.'

'To what end?' Knowing already and appalled by it.

'Once inside that godforsaken castle we will be close enough to carry out a military coup. The one known attempt on Hitler's life—the Beergarden fiasco—failed, and was probably meant to fail. The assassination of his right-hand man, the Reichsführer-SS, will not fail, because we will be close enough to do it.'

'You're crazy.'

'Crazy. No. I am a realist.'

'To what end, though?' George went on to point out that he was, to all intents and purposes, an officer of the British Armed Forces, sent to collaborate with Downay on one specific mission. That mission had now virtually been accomplished. He had not been sent to assist in some crackbrained operation which included an attempt on the life of the Third Reich's second man.

Michel simply smiled, dropping into a chair; gently as a man will ease himself into a warm bath.

'Georges, it is an opportunity not to be missed. What do you really think they intend to do with us at Wewelsburg? Welcome us with open arms? It's the SS we're dealing with, not your Lord Baden-Powell's Boy Scouts. Idiots they may be, but they are not foolish enough to be taken in for long. We can only keep this Nostradamus game going for a short time.'

'The idea was to penetrate the Ministry of Propaganda ... Goebbels' bright lads...'

'And we've ended up with Himmler on a plate. Yes, we might have caused some unpleasantness for a while. They would have played with us. But in the end it would inevitably be the firing squad. Or worse. The way I see it, we can make a maximum effort. Kill off one of the most dangerous beasts and possibly, just possibly, get away with it.' He stopped short as Angelle appeared with steaming coffee.

She smiled at George as she placed his mug on the table near his arm. The smile clawed at his guts.

When she had gone, he asked what had actually been done, and Michel told of his visit to Maman and her husband, and of the meeting they had called during the night.

George thought of the Rouberts' smart apartment with the Rembrandt in the hall. He wondered if it had changed much now the SS were billeted there. Come to that, he wondered how Michel Downay had managed to hold his little party there with SS officers so close. When challenged on it, Downay gave a superior smile and said that they were being well-cared for at the time. Some of his 'students', George presumed. Then Downay outlined the plan which had been agreed and put into effect.

George listened, heart sinking. He thought about the wireless transmitter under his bed, and of Ramilies. Could he warn Ramilies of the madness taking place here? Warn him and then cut loose?

'You don't approve of the strategy?' Downay swallowed a mouthful of the scalding coffee.

George told him, in plain words, that he thought some people might call the plan brave, if foolhardy. Personally, he wanted nothing of it.

'You have a better suggestion?'

He had, but there was no way to do it: no hope of running for cover, or making some haphazard exit from France. The trap, thought George, was there, and he was caught in its claws; Ramilies' claws; the saw-toothed claws of the SS; Michel Downay's mad claws; and the velvet honeyed claws of Angelle Tours.

Light started to filter through the curtains, and Michel said he would go and pack; maybe get a little rest. As he reached the door—

'Georges, are you armed?'

'No.'

'I'll see to it then.'

'Not wise.'

'The object is to come through in one piece.'

'I have my hands. They can be lethal.'

'No doubt. They'll stop bullets also?'

Angrily he said that he would rather go unarmed. At least until the first part of the operation was completed safely. If it ran true, and there were no snags, it would take place sometime that night, around nine or ten o'clock; just inside Germany. At Aachen. Michel made some comment about always having regarded the English as being mad, and left.

Angelle was in her room, lying on her back, the dress discarded and replaced once more by the thin robe which barely covered her nakedness, the material clinging to her breasts and stuck to the curve of her thighs, as though they were damp.

She cried, repeating George's name again and again as he stretched out beside her, tears soaking his face. He soothed, and tried to convince her that, if she did as she was told, all would be well.

Once more he went through her instructions. To give them ten minutes after they had gone, then check that the building was not being watched. She had to go then, fast and with the suitcase wireless. The old couple in the Rue Cambon would know what to do. 'Just tell them you've come from Hiram the Wizard and they are to check with Mars.'

Yes, he told her, he was going to Germany; but if the plan worked—Michel's plan—he could be back in Paris inside a week. She must not worry. If possible, the people in the Rue Cambon must persuade London to get her out. 'If I don't see you back in Paris, I'll see you in London. Soon.'

'I don't trust Michel,' was all she said.

They made love once more, among tears and whispers. Only then did George tell her that he loved her.

The parting was brutal. The facts simple, the emotions indescribable, as though they were both being torn to pieces.

At five minutes past eight, Michel Downay and George Thomas sat in the back of the large Opel car with Wald and Kuche who seemed both excited and overawed at the prospect which lay ahead. Behind the Opel, a large truck bundled carrying baggage and the escort, Waffen-SS: a sergeant and four men, spruce and armed to the teeth. They also appeared happy in the knowledge that they were returning to the Fatherland.

In the Opel there was almost a party atmosphere. Wald talking about the honour of it all. Kuche proudly proclaiming that they were to travel in style.

For everybody's sake, George hoped the style was not one that would cramp the movements of his stepfather. If things were on schedule, Maurice Roubert and his merry men should already be boarding the train at the Gare du Nord.

The small convoy rounded the corner into the Boulevard de Denain. Ahead of them stood the façade of the Gare du Nord, hung with its red swastika drapes. Ahead of that, the rails and track which would bear them to Himmler's magic castle.

* * *

'Good. I get tea now, George.' Herbie made for the kitchen, but could not interrupt George's flow.

'Herbie, I remembered I had a churning sensation in my guts. It seemed a sense of déjà-vu I could not place. It all seemed so familiar: the smell of smoke and grit; stale air and engine oil; a sense of anxiety. Maybe it was memories of going up to Oxford for the first time? You know, leaving the old things behind. Lockhill Terrace. The cycle ride to the Grammar School. All that.'

158

'I understand.' Herbie switched on the kettle and fiddled in the cupboard for the cake tin. 'A good English custom, this. Afternoon tea. I always like afternoon tea.' He came back to look at George slumped in the chair. 'I know you got to Aachen; and I know what happened there.' One enormous hand on the door. 'You talked about strange mental things. Did anything of note take place before the operation at Aachen?'

'Oh yes.' George lifted his head and smiled. 'A whole bag of tricks happened before Aachen.'

The kettle boiled. Herbie made tea and carried the tray through, placing it on the table between them and saying that he would be mother: pouring and offering cake.

'So a whole lot of things happened? Such as?'

'Such as the arrival of my stepfather.'

'Good tea, this.' Herbie savoured. 'Go on. Your stepfather?'

32

A small metal destination board on the side of the coach announced that the train was going from Paris to Aachen. At least Michel had got that right. At Aachen, his information was that they would be transferred to a German train.

Kuche was also right. They were to travel in style. A whole special coach reserved for them: a converted Wagon-Lit with three sleeping compartments, a day coach, and a small dining car.

This coach, Kuche said, was used by high-ranking officers and had been obtained for them by General Frühling on Himmler's personal request. They were going the easy way. (George wondered which way they would return.) When they reached Germany there would be a similar coach to take them on the onward journey. The implication in the SS officer's voice was that German Railways would provide better accommodation than SNCF.

They sat together in the day coach. Wald and Downay in close conversation, Kuche leaning his head back on to the small antimacassar and looking at George as though trying to hypnotise him.

'We're not going to Berlin then?' George tried to be ingenuous. 'I really don't understand. I thought it was the Herr Doktor Goebbels who wanted our work; who wished to employ our specialist knowledge. Now you say we have this coach on the orders of Reichsführer Himmler.'

Kuche smiled and drew on his cigarette. A man who held four aces and knew you could not win. Then he began to speak with some elegance.

'You are a scholar, Herr Thomas. I understand that your historical knowledge has contributed much to the interpretation of these prophecies. However, you admit that some of those in the batch we had from you were difficult.' He leaned forward tapping George's knee. 'I can tell you that what you have found perplexing is more clear to us.' A hand flapped towards Wald. 'Some things are immediately recognisable to those of us who have a deep knowledge of our own history and the mystic order of our Society. By Society I mean the SS. We are not just an elite corps formed to wage war, you must understand. *We* are an Order, I suppose akin to the Jesuits of the Roman Catholic Church. We also have rites, ideals and a mysticism of which we are proud.'

He went on to say there were things in those quatrains which no Frenchman could be expected to recognise. 'It is a great honour, you must understand, for Reichsführer Himmler to send for you personally.'

While he talked, George caught part of the conversation going on between Wald and Downay. Wald was asking for chapter and verse on the batch of quatrains they had provided.

Michel was cool and lucid. There were things in the world of the occult not easily visible to those who did not fully understand the methods by which a seer, like Nostradamus, worked.

Like a man patiently explaining the facts of life to a seven-year-old, Michel talked of the methods of divination, in particular the way in which the whole pattern of Nostradamus' Ten Centuries was broken by the fact that more than half the quatrains were missing from the Seventh Century.

As he was getting into his stride, George glanced out of the window. It wasn't haphazard. There was a feeling of compulsion. Two familiar figures were passing the carriage window: one in the uniform of an SS Major; the other, a woman, clinging on to his arm. The man was Maurice Roubert, George's stepfather. The woman his wife, George's mother.

He felt fury building in his head. Downay's plan had enough danger in it as it was. True, Roubert was to board the train, but nobody had said anything about him coming on dolled up as an SS Major. George wanted to shout at Downay, strike him and scream. It was both stupid and dangerous. His mother's presence increased the anxiety. Surely they would not be foolish enough to allow her to come along for the ride: or as some kind of cover for Roubert?

'Herr Thomas?' Wald's voice cut through the detached anxiety. 'I'm sorry.'

'Someone just walked over your grave, yes?'

George pretended not to understand.

'It is an English saying.' Vulpine grin. 'You appeared pre-occupied. Concerned.' The grin did not seem to reach his eyes, and there were danger signs flicking from Downay.

'Not at all.' Pull yourself together, Thomas, he thought. 'I was merely thinking about the matters which the Sturmbannführer was discussing. Things are beginning to drop into shape.' He played it by ear, by instinct, hoping that he could manipulate the conversation.

'With us also, Herr Thomas. Doktor Downay has been explaining to me that you are by way of being a prophet also: a man of divination, a dreamer of inexplicable dreams.'

Oh Christ, George thought. Wald's voice was becoming unpleasant.

'Am I right ... ?' Plunging slightly, George still tried to manoeuvre the conversation his way. 'Am I right in saying that the prophecies we have given to you concerning the standard-bearer —the flag-carrier—have something to do with your own commander? With the Reichsführer? The Sturmbannführer here says ...' motioning towards Kuche.

'Heine, call me Heine,' Kuche, most affable, said that they were all friends, were they not? Heine and Joseph. Georges and Michel. 'A working team. We must present a united front to the Reichsführer, yes?'

George persistently asked again if he was right.

The Germans exchanged uncertain, covert glances followed by a studied indifference. Then Kuche coughed. When he spoke it was one of the salted quatrains that came out, which meant they had almost certainly swallowed the bait whole—hook, line, sinker and rod.

> 'From the Saxon dynasty, a German King
> Who conquered the peoples of Poland
> Shall rise again, a full ten decades later,
> To lead the New Nation into victory.'

Michel stepped in. 'Now *that* had us guessing. We think we've identified the king. There was a King Heinrich—Heinrich I—eight hundred and something to nine hundred and thirty-six. Are we right?'

A horn sounded on the platform and there was the usual bump and lurch. Then the steady forward pull, rocking slightly as the train slid from the station.

'We're off.' Wald brought his hands together.

George craned forward to see if he could catch sight of Madame Roubert, Maman; mentally breathing with relief as he saw her arm raised, waving farewell on the platform.

'Heinrich I,' Kuche said. 'A German king who conquered the peoples of Poland.'

'I think a more correct reading would be "the Slav people". If there was to be any probing, George was determined to lead the way through the labyrinth.

Kuche looked impressed.

George knew all about Himmler's hatred of the Poles.

Kuche hesitated. Then—'Reichsführer Himmler has special affinity with king Heinrich I. To start with they both have the same name. You would have no knowledge of this affinity though.'

George agreed: he had no knowledge of it. 'How could we know anything like that?' Ramilies knew, the Abbey knew. He knew all right.

Kuche explained that in 1936, on the thousandth anniversary of King Heinrich's death, the Reichsführer had made the king's tomb a sacred place: a place of homage.

Ramilies had spoken a great deal about the way in which Heinrich Himmler claimed to be able to speak with King Heinrich, as though he had a direct line to him. It was one of the few occult clues they had about the Reichsführer. The belief in himself as a second King Heinrich, and the strange mystical sense he had concerning his personal Camelot: the castle they were now almost certainly heading towards—Wewelsburg, where the Reichsführer held spiritual retreats with his senior officers; where he had his special court.

'You see now what this prophecy might imply?' Kuche snapped open a gold lighter, igniting a cigarette.

'That his destiny is to be the Führer? To take the place of ... ?'

Wald hissed something, telling George to keep his voice down. Kuche merely nodded, the smile still on his mouth.

'The Reichsführer can be identified as such in that quatrain. Just as he can be identified as the standard-bearer. Believe me. The castle fashioned after the Court of King Arthur is yet another indicator.'

There was silence, but for the rattle of the train. A Waffen-SS man stood in the corridor, a machinepistol in the crook of his arm : on guard.

Kuche spoke lower. 'The SS have always known their destiny. The Führer is the Führer. We are pledged to follow him to death. But if it is certain that he is to be replaced by the true man of destiny—Reichsführer Himmler—then there are those who feel, perhaps, the sooner this happens the better it will be for Germany. You will have to convince the Reichsführer that Nostradamus has so prophesied.'

George stared blankly out of the window as the outskirts of Paris rolled past and the train shifted easily through the complex mesh of lines and points. He found it difficult to believe his ears or his mind. These people were taking the whole thing seriously. He had never really believed they would. When he had put it to Ramilies, the old boy merely replied that the same kind of doubts must have passed through the minds of those hearing about Christianity for the first time. How can men take this nonsense as truth? As positive? Ramilies was right. There were those within the SS who would be only too happy to see their leader as the head of the Third Reich.

Himmler himself, the Rammer had counselled, *will be the stumbling block. He regards his Führer as God, even though the SS is his great obsession.* George remembered him musing, *Now if it was that arch-bastard Heydrich, we'd have no problems. Heydrich would sell his tainted soul for the top job.*

Soon after, they all went through to the small dining car and had coffee, which was better than the stuff Michel had supplied. Kuche said they should make the most of it, and Wald laughed. In Germany, even the big-wigs drank stuff that tasted like the floor of a forest. Pine cones : acorns. Kuche raised his eyebrows and said more like acorns that came from a cow's backside.

'Mückefuck,' using the rudest colloquialism. Gnat's something or other.

They all laughed.

* * *

164

Now. Forward almost four decades, George Thomas hesitated in his narrative.

'George? You okay?' Big Herbie Kruger switched on a table lamp. It was not yet time, but clouds had gathered bringing dusk to the late afternoon, even on this spring day.

'Yes.' George looked at him, biting a lip. 'You're not going to believe the next bit, and don't ask me to explain. I don't know the answers.'

'This one of the strange mental things you talked about?'

'Very strange. The first one. After we had drunk the coffee.'

33

'I began to feel drowsy. I'd finished the coffee.'

'Not surprising; you were tired. After the night, I mean ...' Herbie was suddenly embarrassed, confused at what he had said. 'Forgive me, George. No disrespect to the lady, but ... well ... ?'

George smiled, passing his hands, palm flat, to and fro in front of his body. 'No, Herbie. I know what you mean. Yes, anyone would be tired.'

'Another piece of cake, perhaps?'

George took his second piece, biting into it, letting it melt in his mouth. Herbie was excellent with sponges. 'Good,' he pronounced.

'*Danke.*'

George said he knew all the tricks and realised Herbie wanted him to get on. Using the German to rein him in. 'Okay. Yes, normally I would be tired. This was a particular kind of drowsiness, or so it's always seemed in retrospect. I was looking out of the window.' He went on to describe how he had recalled other journeys in France, and how the countryside did not seem to have changed much. The odd ruin, bomb-site, here and there. Occasionally there were troops moving along the road. A lot of aircraft. Sometimes quite close. They passed near an airfield with ME109s parked almost alongside the tracks, nestling under camouflage netting, tendrils of ammunition hanging in belts from under the wings as the armourers worked on them.

'I remember being conscious of the rhythm of the train, and of Kuche, Wald and Downay talking, but they seemed a long way off.'

He could see his reflection in the window and then, quite suddenly, he found himself looking at the reflection, not of his face, but that of Angelle, overlapping his own mirrored image.

'I even smiled at her and she seemed to smile back; sad, wistful, as though she was a long way off and trying to make contact. I was quite awake then, but sleep came soon after. Sleep and the strange dreams. Weird and very real.'

He was in a cave, or something like it. The walls were bare rock. Moisture dropping. Night. A fire, with flames casting huge shadows on the walls, glistening and dancing. The smoke from the fire burned his eyes, constricted his throat; but he had to bend over the fire to tend a brass pot which hung in the flames from a small metal tripod.

'There was this big book I was holding as well. I read from it. Aloud. An odd language: half-French and part-Latin. The voice wasn't mine and it echoed. Two voices maybe? Another over mine echoing in counterpoint. The mixture in the pot went milky and then cleared. Then the pictures came.'

Herbie sighed, no hint of irritation, just a simple exhaling of his breath, loudly.

'I know what you're thinking.' George's face became set and solemn: as though he had misinterpreted the sigh.

'I'm sorry. Just that dreams are ...'

'Obvious?'

'Perhaps too obvious?'

'In this case,' George seemed to have softened a little. 'In this case, yes, very obvious. Look, Herbie, apart from one psychiatrist, you're the only person to whom I've told this story. Even *I* didn't need the psychiatrist, or any analysis, for the first part of the dream. All that time cooped away in Ramilies' flat, then the work on Nostradamus at the Abbey. The strain of the moment. Yes, I was dreaming about going through the ritual of divination. That's easy, dreaming about being Nostradamus himself. The thing that's interesting is the pictures in the brass pot; and what followed.'

'Tell me,' Herbie quiet and concentrating. From far away a siren wailed—police or an ambulance.

The pictures, said George, were most vivid. ('I can still see them in all their detail.') A battle. Night. Flickering from weapons. A wall and a large room. The thunder of explosives ('or so I thought'). There was rain also. People, comrades of mine, being shot to pieces. Then silence. Laughter. The dead who lay around getting on to their feet, rising as though the last trump had just blasted off. They were laughing and brushing dirt from their clothes. One of them was limping, walking towards a small man who carried a huge flag. They shook hands.

'That was it. I was aware of the train rocking and that I was awake again. For some reason instinct stopped me from moving.' Stay dormant: pretend to go on sleeping, he thought. Ramilies in the room at the Abbey. Hiram the Wizard.

Kuche and Wald were talking, droning on. Kuche reflecting on life back home. Wald boasting about the girls he'd had in Paris.

'Yes, the pictures are odd. Prophetic in a way.' Herbie was more interested now.

'Wait. There's more. When you've heard it all, you'll see how I managed to carry things through later. Nobody has ever successfully explained those pictures, or what I said when I woke up.'

'Which was?'

George had finally stirred and turned. Ah, Wald said, so our Sleeping Beauty is awake. 'He offered me a cigarette. Kuche smiled: like you do at children you've been watching sleeping on a journey. Downay remained inscrutable, behind his beard. Then I spoke and to this day do not know where the words came from—

"At the castle, death will come
To those who shall rise again and mock.
The standard-bearer shall link hands
With one he trusts. The true one will not rise."'

Downay had immediately looked very puzzled and asked what George was quoting.

'I told him I didn't know. Yes, Herbie, I thought, quite consciously at the time, you've been reading too much Nostradamus, old lad.'

Herbie's chin rested on his chest and he remained immobile for some time. At last—'Interesting. I understand how you were able to motivate matters later, after having that kind of dream. Hard to understand, though.'

'There were other things, later. We'll come to them.'

They had served lunch soon after he woke, George continued, even recalling the food—bean soup and fish with potatoes. A pleasant wine. 'Downay was taking in everything: the way the guards were doubling up as waiters. How the sergeant treated them, giving them orders quietly: an efficient man, not a bully-boy drill sergeant. Tall, muscular, a fighting soldier.'

'The next thing that happened was outside Aachen, yes?'
Herbie appeared to be hurrying him on. After all, Herbie knew
the outline. He also knew that was not the next thing that happened.

'No.' George swallowed the last piece of cake. 'The next thing
that happened was Kuche.'

'So.'

At around two o'clock they had arrived at Liège. By the time
the train pulled out again they were settled over coffee and
brandy. Kuche, George remembered, said that they had about
another five hours to go before Aachen, and the change on to a
German train. 'It was Downay who suggested we should rest. I
don't remember who decided on splitting up. I think Downay and
Wald went off and took over two of the sleeping compartments.
Kuche said we could share the third. I was feeling tired again.
Company wouldn't bother me. I didn't know that I was in for
another shock.'

'Kuche?' Herbie asked knowingly as though George had not
already led him there.

'Yes. Heinrich Kuche.'

34

'What was all that about the castle?' Kuche asked almost as soon as they got into the sleeping compartment.

George said he did not know. 'A dream. I was only half awake.'

Kuche put on a look of disbelief. 'Michel Downay has told us you are a seer; that you have looked into the works of Nostradamus and seen more than is written down. Is this another of your own prophecies? The castle and death?'

George didn't respond. He really wanted to talk with Michel Downay. Nothing seemed real any more, what with the stupidity of Downay's plans and the dream: the quatrains in his head. He felt very lost and lonely: in the centre of a vortex with a voice calling to him not to panic. Great, suspended, disorientation.

'What castle?' Kuche pressed. 'The castle to which we are going?'

'Possibly.'

'You're saying there's danger at the castle?'

'I don't know.' Nor did he—except that there was danger everywhere.

'Danger because of Downay? You've noticed something? Heard him say something? Don't forget, Georges, that you're supposed to be keeping an eye on the Herr Doktor for us.'

There was no cause for concern from that quarter, George lied, then followed through with the fiction about his own supposed powers of divination. He finished by asking the SS man, point blank, what they meant when they talked about going to Arthur's Court.

For the first time, Kuche admitted their destination was Wewelsburg and went on to talk about the place.

It was Himmler's dream, he said. Officially a school for SS leaders: in reality it was more. There was a tradition that the castle at Wewelsburg was the castle mentioned in an old legend which said that a Westphalian bastion would be the sole survivor of the next assault from the East.

'There's going to be an assault from the East?' George had settled down full length on one of the bunks. Kuche sat on the other, smoking all the time.

One day, he replied, it was bound to happen. Two such strongly opposed ideologies could never go on existing side by side. 'In the end, if we fail—if the Führer fails—Russia will dominate Europe. That's what their brand of Communism is about. They're pledged to binding the whole of Europe. If we fail it must come. Maybe not for a hundred years. The weapon you hold—the weapon of prophecy—is very important if we are to win.'

'So Wewelsburg is to be the last stronghold?'

'Naturally, if things go wrong.'

They'd already gone wrong, George thought, knowing he was being parochial; going on to play at being ingenuous again by asking about the treaty which existed between Germany and Russia.

Kuche made a schoolboy noise and laughed. He then continued to talk about Wewelsburg. Himmler spent a lot of time there. The castle was a meeting place for his leaders, the SS-Obergruppenführer, each of whom had a coat of arms above his own personal chair—the chairs, like those of Arthur's Court, set around a huge circular table. He asked again what the odd prophecy was all about. George, trying to keep his cover as a seer, explained that one had visions, pictures that were often inexplicable.

'You see things in detail?' Kuche appeared to be taking the matter more seriously now.

'Yes,' pretending to think about it. 'I saw a castle; fighting; men getting up from death, like children playing a game of soldiers. A man limping towards the standard-bearer.'

'The castle?' Kuche asked. 'Did you see the castle? Could you describe it? Was it like a fairytale castle?'

George had never set eyes on Wewelsburg at that time. Maybe Ramilies had described it, though it was never, he thought sadly, on the operation's itinerary. He did not have to think about the description, however. 'It was triangular,' he said. 'Triangular, with big turrets. Three circular turrets. One very large.'

Kuche remained silent, looking worried for the best part of a minute. Then, even more quietly than before, he breathed, 'We shall have to take the greatest possible care, my friend. Watch out for Wald, he's vicious, a sadist at heart. Trust nobody. Only me. You have to trust me, my friend Hiram—my friend Hiram the Wizard.'

* * *

Big Herbie exhaled loudly again, as though trying to disperse tension.

'I started to shake,' George told him. 'I really started to shake, bones like ice, bowels turned to water. A cliché, I know, but that's how it was. Heinrich Kuche was very definitely playing back the token to me.'

Herbie simply said, could he go on? Just a little further, before they called it a day.

'Aachen. I'll tell you about Aachen.'

'Yes, finish with that, and tomorrow morning you can fill in the gaps about Wewelsburg.'

George started talking again, dragging them both back to that French train rocking its way towards the German border in 1941.

35

George had always been one for tags—Biblical, Latin, Greek. Tags, dates and lists stuck in his head like musical people carry tunes. As he lay, face turned towards Kuche, the list of instructions, discussed and detailed by Michel Downay during the early hours in Paris, filed through his head.

About half-an-hour before we get to Aachen ... That was when it would start, Downay had said.

Now, following Kuche's sudden revelation, Seneca was also breathing into George's mind, criss-crossed with the take-over plot. *It's a vice to trust all, and equally a vice to trust none.* Maman? Angelle? Now Kuche? Each, in their own way, had played back the Hiram the Wizard token. Trust all? Trust none? Trust one?

George raised his head from the pillow and assembled a puzzled expression on his face. Who the hell was Hiram the Wizard? Some unheard-of occultist?

Pictures slip through his mind. The Abbey. Ramilies. Trust all? No. Trust none. You're on your own, Thomas. Play it solo. Trust none and see what happens.

Kuche went tight-lipped and cocked an eyebrow. 'If you choose not to know about Hiram the Wizard, Georges, then it's your own stupid fault.' Rest now, he said. 'You, of all people, should know that it's going to get very difficult later on.'

Waiting for danger was not conducive to sleep. George lay there with his eyes closed. Eventually he found a mechanism to ward off fear. Angelle. Tall; the curve of her waist in his hand; her skin and its texture; her cries. ('Sounds a bit sentimental now, but, when you're young ...') In the end, even Angelle's memory was overcome by the need to concentrate on what was to happen.

Get the instructions clear, Thomas. Make sure you know what will take place. About half-an-hour before they reached Aachen.

That was the strike moment. Somewhere on the train, at this moment, Downay's men would be making their way along the corridors towards the special coach, sandwiched between an 'officers only' first-class coach on one side, and a baggage car on the other. The baggage car backed on to the dining car end of the special coach. If Downay's contacts with SNCF had done their job, the baggage car would contain the long wooden boxes which Michel Downay had carefully described.

George must have dropped into sleep while ticking off the plan in his mind, for the next thing he knew was Kuche shaking him and saying they were not far from the German border. 'Perhaps we should wash, and join the others.'

In the corridor, two of the Waffen-SS men played sentries; bored, glancing out of the window at the darkening landscape, swinging their Erma *machinenpistolen* like boys acting big in a schoolyard. They looked very young.

Wald and Michel Downay sat opposite one another in the dining car. They had been drinking, the bottle almost empty, standing between them. At the far end, towards the baggage car, the sergeant lounged with the other two men, playing cards. There was no sign of drink at their table.

Outside it was almost completely dark. No sign of lights. Wald said it was defeatist to speak of the blackout and the night bombing by the *Tommis*, but their aircraft did get through. Not many, but it was better to take care. There was bombing. Not just the Channel ports as the French were told. Cities were getting raids. Not much; certainly not like the Luftwaffe was giving to the English cities.

Wald said he had personal experience of it. After France had fallen, just after his posting to Paris he had been given leave to attend his sister's wedding in Mannheim. He had even taken food from Paris. The whole family had somehow managed to get there, except for one cousin who was in the U-boats. They clubbed together with their rations, and the womenfolk prepared a great spread of food. A cold buffet. Spectacular, all laid out on a long table with the wedding cake as the centrepiece. It was almost like pre-war days. 'Enough food to feed the whole of a Sonderkommando.'

They had gone to the wedding, and just as it was finishing there was an alert so they were forced to stay at the Town Hall. No bombs, and after about one hour the 'clear'. On the way home, another alert. This time the wedding party had to take shelter. A few bombs only; but uncomfortable. Almost Christmas as well, the bastards. When it was clear, they returned to the house, relieved to see that it was still intact. But a bomb had fallen nearby. On wasteland as it happened. No casualties. The bomb had shattered all the windows and the beautiful wedding feast was covered in glass. Some large splinters and millions of fragments.

'Ruined,' he said. 'We tried to pick the pieces of glass from the sandwiches and rolls, but too much was powdered. Hopeless. Swine. So near Christmas as well.'

George stayed silent, thinking of his own run back to Dunkirk; of Angelle and the children; the glow of burning buildings in London. Michel gave him a quick look and asked how long to Aachen. Wald said, half-an-hour, something like that. What would happen when they got there? Would there be a long wait? Kuche said no, if all went well they would be quickly passed through the control point. The train would be waiting. He touched his briefcase, which had not left his side during the whole journey: all the necessary documents were to hand.

A few minutes later, Michel yawned saying he had to relieve nature, pulling himself up and limping in the direction of the corridor and sleeping compartments.

The train was travelling quite fast and there was a fair amount of rolling and external noise. George became alert; it was time to take care; time to separate himself from Kuche and Wald, place himself in a position where he would not be involved in any crossfire if anything went wrong. He stretched, craning towards the left, over the gangway, as if trying to see out of the opposite window. Eventually, he even crossed the gap to sit away from the two SS officers. The corridor was behind him, Kuche and Wald to his right, with Wald facing towards the sleeping compartments. The card-players were at the far end so that George could see them over three sets of tables.

He heard nothing, and the first he knew of the action was a sudden startled expression on the sergeant's face, followed by a cry from Wald. The sergeant reached towards his machinepistol, propped near his seat. At the same moment, Wald rose, his right hand travelling towards his leather holster.

Michel's voice came from behind George: crisp and powerful, giving the order for everyone to stand still; snapping in German with great authority. The sergeant froze with arm outstretched, while the pair of Waffen-SS privates and Kuche remained quite still.

George turned, flattening his back against the window. Michel Downay stood at the end of the car, flanked by two men. He leaned heavily on his cane. The men, dressed in shabby suits, held Erma machinepistols, undoubtedly the ones which had been handled by the two corridor guards.

'No heroes, please.' Michel's eyes shifted back and forth, very alert. The men behind him had dead-drop faces which said that it did not matter one way or the other to them. If necessary they would blast everyone to pieces. One of them moved forward, walking the length of the car, his eyes never leaving the trio ahead. The other went right, to cover Kuche and Wald. Michel steadied himself and began to come closer to the SS officers, calling in French to George, telling him to relieve the two men of their weapons.

George had just started to ease his back from the window, relaxing now that the moment had come, when Wald's hand moved, the tips of his fingers ripped upwards on the leather holster.

His palm hardly touched the butt of the Luger. Everything after that seemed to change perspective: slow; almost stop; slow; very slow.

Michel Downay moved in one flowing motion, as though the pain and discomfort of his crippled leg had suddenly been suspended. One gloved hand curled around the ebony cane, the other twisted the knobbed end. It flashed through George's mind that he should have anticipated this—a sword stick. The right arm coming back, a smile behind the beard, concentration and sharpness deep in the eyes.

The right hand moved up, the left down; feet apart, balance perfect; the right arm progressing upwards as the long steel rapier slid away from its sheath, almost liquid, like a stream of thin silver spouting from the black wood, rising and then moving down, whipping into line, the crack audible as the steel cleaved air. The arm and steel, now one perfect line from the shoulder, the tip defying the eye: straight, like an arrow.

Wald gave a cry, a yelping screech, as the blade touched the back of his hand. Michel's wrist gave a small flick. Then blood appeared as the tip of the blade moved in a long cross on the back of Wald's hand. Blood flowing even more as the blade plunged, spearing, into the wrist and then away.

Wald's hand, so near the pistol, jerked upwards, towards his face, the other hand grasping the ruptured wrist, a look of shock and disbelief crossing his face as he dropped back into his seat, blood welling through the circle of fingers.

Kuche huddled to his right, like someone flinching from a bomb; crouching like a child in the dark, face turned towards George, a plea in his eyes and both hands raised as far as his shoulders.

Michel appeared unconcerned, except for a brief command for someone to give Wald a cloth to bind the wound. 'We don't want to leave too much mess; too much blood. Might not suit the next Boche brass who have to travel this way.' He grinned at George. 'Now, his pistol, and Kuche's. I'm going to open the other door. Cover them.' He stumped forward towards the far end of the dining coach.

George felt light-headed and a little sick. Wald cursed with the pain and offered no trouble as George removed the Luger from its holster. As he did so, he glanced back along the corridor, seeing the sprawled forms of the two young Waffen-SS guards whose machinepistols were now carried by Michel's men. The door at the far end had obviously been closed and locked again after Michel had let his people in.

Kuche, still crouching, gave George a look which seemed to say 'I-told-you-so', and moved his hands down slowly to the buckle on his belt. Wald still rocked to and fro, clutching the damaged hand and wrist. George shook his head at Kuche, leaning over to pluck his Luger from its holster. There was death in the corridor, and he wondered how Wald and Kuche would fare now under Michel. The man was obviously determined.

Hefting the pistol in his hand, George asked Kuche for the briefcase. By the time he had it, Michel was opening the far door leading to the baggage compartment. There were four men on the other side. The first to come into the coach was George's step-father, Maurice Roubert, decked out in the uniform of an SS major: the same rank as Kuche. He smiled and called out—

'Georges, nice to see you. How d'you like the fancy dress?'

'Very pretty,' he tried to sound natural and relaxed. 'I saw you at the station. Nearly gave me a heart attack.'

Roubert's men followed him through, the Waffen-SS sergeant and his group handing over their weapons with disconcerting meekness. They looked frightened and confused, the sergeant throwing little glances towards Kuche, who loudly asked what was to happen to them.

George shook his head and shrugged.

Oblivious of the moaning Wald, Kuche hissed, 'Remember what I told you, Hiram. Understand? *Verstanden?*'

George gave him a brief nod which meant nothing, and carried the pistols and briefcase over to the table where the other weapons were being stacked. The men who had come in with Roubert were covering the sergeant and his pair, while the two who had made the dramatic entrance with Michel Downay disappeared along the corridor from where they had originally come.

'Smooth as silk,' muttered Roubert.

Michel nodded, looking pleased, then turned to order Roubert's men to get on with it—to strip the sergeant and his two men.

'You are going to behave?' Michel limped up to Kuche who had remained in his seat and appeared to be more relaxed.

'It depends. You were a trusted man, Downay.'

'And now I am forced to trust you. He's no good to me,' nodding towards Wald, 'so you will take us through the control point without making any fuss.'

'What's the point in that?'

'We are all going to Wewelsburg.'

Kuche gave a short laugh. 'Yes? And what good will that do you?'

'You will take us through, or . . .'

'You'll kill me? Like those two in the corridor?'

'It can be arranged.'

Kuche laughed again. 'I am an officer of the SS. Death is my capbadge.'

'Very melodramatic, but I'm willing to take the risk of trusting you to get us through. If anything goes wrong we shoot ourselves out of it.'

'So I lose either way.'

The two men reappeared from the corridor, now dressed in the uniforms of the pair of young men they had killed. They dragged the corpses gently down the gangway, between the seats and tables, towards the door to the baggage compartment.

Kuche watched, showing neither surprise nor disgust. He asked if that was how they were all to be treated.

'It is necessary.' Michel spoke as though they were merely files. 'But your own people have a fair record of sudden death. You are soldiers aren't you. You expect to die?'

'By the hands of other soldiers. Not terrorists.'

'Terrorists? *Merde*. What's the difference? Your troops, were they not terrorists when they raped my country?'

Out of the corner of his eye, George saw the German sergeant and his men being pushed into the baggage car at gun point. His stepfather followed them through and carefully closed the door. George tried not to listen to the unmistakable sounds of death and violence.

'You'll take us through?' Michael asked of Kuche again.

'It might prove interesting. As an officer of the SS my duty is to take whatever action is available to see that you are stopped.'

'We shall have to risk that.'

George laid a hand on Downay's arm, pulling him to one side. One of Roubert's men, now wearing the sergeant's uniform, came back through the door to the baggage car and walked straight to where Wald was hunched, prodding him with a machinepistol.

'Your turn now,' he grunted, forcing the injured officer to his feet.

Wald looked briefly towards Michel and George, muttered some curse and allowed himself to be pushed towards the baggage car, bent double, clutching his still bleeding hand.

When they had disappeared through the door, George, raising his voice, as though he wished to drown any sounds that might float back into the dining car, asked Downay if it was really going to be safe with Kuche.

They moved a few paces away.

'Who knows?' The thin smile again, behind the beard. 'My training, Georges, tells me that Kuche is no fanatic. It would not have been safe with Wald,' he nodded in the direction of the baggage car, his tone giving the impression that Wald was already no more. 'Kuche, though, has a complicated makeup. I don't

179

think he's so keen to die for his beloved Führer. Not just yet, anyway.'

'Could I speak with him? Alone, I mean.'

'If you like.' He opened his mouth to say something else, but Roubert came up at that moment and said they should see the arrangements which had been made in the baggage car.

Leaving Kuche under guard they went forward and into the long, dirty car with its piles of cases, trunks and boxes. Standing apart, near the door to the special coach, was a pair of wooden crates, like those used for packing weapons, each with a thick rope handle at each end. They were covered with official stamps and insignia, and all were labelled in transit to Reichsführer Himmler, Schloss Wewelsburg, Paderborn.

Six of the boxes had been firmly secured; the lids nailed down. The seventh was open and empty. It was no coincidence that the boxes would, at a push, each take a human body.

Michel grimaced, muttering that they were all stowed away safely, 'All except Kuche.' Then, as if suddenly remembering, asked George why he wanted to speak alone with the German.

'I might just convince him not to do anything silly when we get to the control point at Aachen.' He did not mention that Kuche's talk of terrorists had made him nervous, for in his own way the SS man had spoken the truth. At the Abbey the Rammer said that part of the brief some had been given was to operate like guerilla forces. There were those who had specifically been ordered to organise like the Sinn Fein structured themselves against the English in Ireland. Does one fight terror with terror? he mused. There was that, and the Hiram token which—since Downay's display of complete ruthlessness—had begun to play on his mind.

Kuche still sat in his place, his face relaxed and devoid of expression: a map upon which nothing registered.

George sent the guard off to the baggage car and began by saying Downay meant exactly what he said. 'He is very determined.'

Kuche nodded. All fanatics are determined, he said, as though he knew about these things at close hand. He then asked what the final objective was to be.

'Himmler,' George told him. 'They're going to kill the Reichsführer.'

Kuche smiled broadly. 'So you are the stooge, Hiram.'

George began a denial, but Kuche's hand came up. 'Don't be foolish, Georges Thomas. Your orders, like mine, are specific. You have no real part in something as ludicrous as this.'

'I have no option.'

'You've done your part. You've planted what you were told to plant. The Nostradamus stuff. You've helped push a wedge deeper between the SS and the Wehrmacht. Right?'

He knew far too much for it to be just some casual mistake, but George remained noncommittal. He could not afford to let go yet. Still keep solo. Trust nobody even though it's a vice.

Behind them, the door to the baggage car slid closed with a thump which had a great deal of finality about it.

Kuche seemed to make a quick decision. 'All right,' he muttered. 'I shall do as they ask. I shall also do what I can to protect you—and myself—it's part of my duty. But for God's sake put your trust in me and not in Michel Downay. When I tell you to run, or lie down, you do it without question, my little Hiram. *Verstanden?*'

Downay's voice behind them asked if Kuche had made any decision about seeing them through Aachen.

The SS officer looked at him with an indifference which touched freezing point. 'I have little option, but I don't see you succeeding with this stupidity, Doktor Downay. Wewelsburg is a fortress. Himmler is protected. Besides, what's the point?'

'One bastard less to deal with.' Downay sounded buoyant.

'There are others, worse, to take his place. There must be more to it than that.'

'Himmler's death will cause a small chaos,' Downay snapped, starting to turn away, his face filled with fury.

Kuche shrugged. 'A little chaos, like learning, is a dangerous thing. I'll take you through though—God help me.'

'God help you if you don't.'

The train rocked more violently as it slowed down. They were nearly there. Kuche said he would need his briefcase, so they gathered the things together while George's stepfather, Roubert, organised the men—all now dressed as members of the Waffen-SS.

There was a fine drizzle falling as they pulled into Aachen station.

36

'And of course there was more to it than just a little chaos. There had to be.' Big Herbie got up and walked to the window which led to his small balcony. Below, people scurried home from work. Insects, Herbie thought.

George smirked and said as Herbie knew the story, that was unfair. 'Of course there was more to it.'

'You got through the checkpoint, though.'

'Oh yes. Like clockwork. High precision Swiss stuff. Straight through and no questions asked. Our party had the right number of officers, non-commissioned officers and men. Kuche had matching papers. We went through and on to the German train quite quickly. I remember shivering a bit as I saw a working party loading the boxes into another baggage car—the boxes for Himmler.'

'And it was a better special coach?' Herbie grunted, humour dodging around the corners of his large mouth.

'About the same.'

'The ride uneventful?'

'More or less. We ate. The others cleaned their weapons. We slept.'

'And you talked again with Kuche?'

George gave a patient nod. He had been very confused, he said. The dreams; the operation; death. 'It was all a grisly affair. I think I had decided none of us had a chance of coming out alive. Of course, I should have known there was more to it than just a bunch of resistance people hitching a ride into Himmler's castle in order to kill him. As Kuche had said—what was the point?'

'You talked with Kuche again,' Herbie prompted.

Yes, George went on. They had eaten and Downay asked if he would mind acting as Kuche's guard. George agreed, and they had both been locked into one of the sleeping compartments. 'They had double bunks as opposed to the French train where they were more like the couchettes you get nowadays, only a shade more

182

luxurious. Have we time for me to go on—take you as far as Paderborn?'

Herbie consulted his watch, a big Russian Polyot, a relic from the days in East Germany. It was barely six, so he suggested a drink. 'Get me as far as Paderborn tonight and you've really earned your keep. Send you home to Mrs. George with a good report.' He poured two liberal helpings of Gordon's gin, opened a large tonic and set them on the table. 'So, you were locked in with Heinrich Kuche.'

'Yes, if I'm right we both sat on the bottom bunk ...'

... 'How's Ramilies, the old rogue?' Kuche asked ...

For almost the first time since George had been telling the story, filling in the gaps, something nasty and suspicious tweaked momentarily in Herbie Kruger's head.

37

'Strange bedfellows,' Kuche smiled. 'How's Ramilies, the old rogue?'

'Who?' You're on your own, Thomas.

Kuche shook his head, almost sadly. Georges Thomas should not be so stupid. Ramilies had been in Hamburg during the summer of 1933, just when Hitler was in the ascendency. 'He was looking for likely material. He found me, and I've been on the payroll ever since. Joined the SS the following year, much to the old devil's delight, but unhappily I've never been given a key posting. In some ways, I've been a disappointment to Ramilies.'

He went on to say that when he was ordered on to General Frühling's staff, and became naturally mixed up with Michel Downay, Ramilies saw a way in which he could be used. 'I was briefed about you in the house on the Rue Cambon.'

That could be trouble, George thought. He had sent Angelle to the Rue Cambon. It must have shown in his face.

'Don't worry,' Kuche looked up, lighting another cigarette. 'Are you not satisfied, Hiram? Hiram the Wizard? I'm Ramilies' boy, I promise you; and, while you're at it, you should watch yourself with that imbecile Downay.'

George thought about it. 'Supposing I knew what you are talking about?' he said slowly. 'And supposing I admitted I was already seriously worried about Downay? Where would we go from there?'

Kuche spoke with equal care. They would try to find a way of averting what amounted to the mass suicide of everyone on the train. 'Our job is complete. You've placed the quatrains. I've put them into the correct pigeon-holes. The ones that will please the Reichsminister of Propaganda have gone to Docktor Goebbels. Those that will throw Himmler into a blue fit have gone to those of his aides who have ambition for the SS. As I saw it, the next logical move—if it was safe—would have been to get Downay and yourself into the Propaganda Ministry, close to the seat of power where you might have done a lot of harm. Downay, it should be obvious now, is unstable. He is launched into something that can only bring harm to any resistance movement.'

George asked if Downay had any idea of Kuche's real involvement.

'Georges, don't be stupid. Of course he's no idea. The man's a romantic. The question is, what do we do either before or after the arrival at Paderborn?'

Almost absently, George mentioned that the quatrains should now be well circulated through *Soldatensender Calais*. As he spoke, he realised Kuche had convinced him. Lord help them if he was wrong.

Kuche sounded mightily surprised. 'You got a message out?'

'We had a radio. I thought you knew that. Your people put our operator out of action. Cut his throat; and that of his girl friend. But you knew. You must have known.'

'The Swiss you mean? I didn't know there was any connection. It had nothing to do with us. A straight criminal job. When we left, they were investigating a number of lines—the girl's regular boyfriend. Christ, they had another description ...'

'And?'

'Never mind. It would fit someone I've seen recently. You got the radio?'

George told him, and how he had raised London.

'The little act you did for us earlier? On the other train. The quatrain about the castle and the dead rising. The limping man shaking hands with the standard-bearer?'

George told him about that as well. Kuche did not look happy.

'How far are you really involved in the occult?'

They had a lengthy conversation about that, with George filling in details of his training and the amount of time spent concentrating on the prophecies.

'Yet you had the dream and came out, involuntarily with the words?'

'Yes.'

'Interesting if you were the only one among us who had a genuine gift.'

'It was a dream. My bloody brain's chocked full of the rubbish.' Then, 'Paderborn?' he asked, meaning what were they going to do?

Kuche nodded and repeated, 'Paderborn, and Wewelsburg.'

They were left alone for the best part of two hours, before Roubert came to say that food was ready. In that time they had only formulated a rough plan which involved cutting themselves off from the main group, either when they arrived at Paderborn, or later, inside Wewelsburg castle itself.

During the meal—bean soup again, followed by some kind of sausage served hot with unchristenable vegetables—Michel Downay appeared to be preoccupied; Kuche remained outwardly calm, but George had the unpleasant feeling that his stepfather Roubert had been detailed to watch him. The man's eyes rarely left him, and once, when he made an excuse to go to the lavatory, George found Roubert waiting outside as he emerged.

The train stopped several times, including a long wait in a siding at Cologne. At around eleven o'clock it again slowed and came to a standstill.

They were drinking: all of them including Kuche. A bottle of raw brandy which Michel seemed to be swilling down like water. He cursed as the train came to a jolting standstill, then left the table and walked up the carriage towards the baggage car—in the same position it had been on the French train.

Stepfather Roubert was distracted, in conversation with Kuche —an uneasy alliance—but George took his chance, left the table and followed Michel, pausing to pass the odd word with the other men who sat dotted around the dining car.

There was the usual concertina link between the carriages: a galley to the right and a lavatory on the left. Also stowage space for luggage, now occupied by the pile of weapons filched from the Germans.

Heinrich Kuche's Luger lay there with the Erma machinepistols. George casually picked it up and stuck it in his waistband. He already had Wald's Luger in his hip pocket.

Michel had not returned from the baggage car, though the door was pulled back slightly. George glanced through, but could see nothing, so went back the way he had come. Half-way down the carriage, Roubert turned from the table where he was talking to Kuche. It was as though he had only just realised George was missing and he asked, abruptly and loudly, what his stepson had been doing.

'Sniffing out Michel. He's been gone a while.'

'Don't worry about Michel. He'll take care of himself,' and, as though on cue, Downay appeared at the baggage car door, limping down towards them. They were holed-up in a siding outside Essen, he said. Looked as if they would be there for a while. There was talk of not arriving at Paderborn until the early hours. Perhaps, it was suggested, they should rest.

By this time, George was seated again: next to Kuche, and sliding the Luger over towards him under cover of the table. There was a slight pressure on his hand, a silent message of thanks, and the Luger was taken.

George felt Michel's eyes on him and looked up. The Frenchman was smiling, eyebrows raised quizzically, as though he held the key to some riddle. George asked if he still wanted him to act as Kuche's watchdog. He did not reply at once, taking another glass of the raw brandy. Then—

'We'll just rest here. In the open where we can all keep our eyes on him. Rota system. The chef de train is amiable enough. Says he'll inform us about what's happening.'

They stayed at a standstill for around three-quarters of an hour. At one point, George leaned across Kuche and tried to peer through the corner of the blackout blind. Nothing but pitch darkness outside. Roubert told him to leave it alone.

'We don't want some officious pig reporting us for not observing regulations, eh?'

Michel's head lolled against the back of his seat, but he stayed awake, still casting his odd smile at George from time to time and talking in bursts to Kuche.

For the second time, George began to feel drowsy, the same thing he had experienced on the French train. The others seemed to be a long way off. He was sweating, as though knowing what was to come: the same strange hallucinatory business. The cave and its damp walls, the cold and the fact that it was night. There was fear all around as though he was cut off from all human contact, surrounded by wild beasts.

It did not last long, nor were there any real hallucinations like the imagined nightmare pictures before. This time, he was pulled out of it by one of Michel's people bringing a tray of coffee to the table. He shook his head and looked down at the coffee, reaching out and sipping the vile muck, then resting his head on the back of the seat, closing his eyes.

At once, the image of the coffee cup came into his mind, transformed straightaway into the cauldron, the coffee swirling and going milky. Then the images taking hold. First it was Madame Roubert, Maman, who appeared to be crying and raising her arms in anguish. She was flanked by two figures who seemed to be dragging her away. Behind, there were houses and streets. Paris. Then, Angelle, running and in great danger, as though something terrible was at her heels. Lastly, and most horrible, came a whole montage of pictures which included Michel laughing as Joseph Wald walked towards him, the blood still dripping from his hand, his lips moving until he joined Michel in laughter.

'Georges. Georges.' Someone was calling his name and he opened his eyes to see Michel leaning across the table. The train was moving faster now, picking up speed.

'You've been asleep.'

George looked around. Roubert and Kuche were not in the carriage and Michel's people were asleep, except for one young man who stood at the far end of the coach with a machinepistol.

George spoke ('It just came. Like the previous time.')—

'The kingdom stripped of its forces by fraud,
The fleet blockaded, passages for the spy;
Two false friends will come to rally
To awaken hatred a long time dormant.'

He recognised immediately that it was not original. The words belonged to Michel de Nostradame himself.

'So?' Downay queried.

'So, I don't know. What I do know is that Angelle is in danger : she's running from something. Also, your friend Roubert's wife— my mother—has been arrested.'

'How do you know?' He did not seem impressed.

For a second, George wondered if he was going crazy, or that, somehow, the coffee had been drugged. (He remembered the last one happened just after drinking coffee.) 'I saw it.' His speech was firm, no slurring. Also he found himself believing in the dream or whatever it was. 'I saw it. She's been arrested in Paris. Where's my stepfather now?'

He was looking after Kuche. 'You're not trying to convince me that you're a genuine seer, Georges?'

'I don't know what I am.' Then, with a final plunge of concern, George asked him if what they were doing was really necessary.

'You mean Himmler? What we are going to do to him?'

'The whole thing. To me it has become pointless.'

'Too late for second thoughts now, Georges Thomas. I said before, London's little plot had only a limited life anyway. An act like this will be more useful.'

At that moment, Roubert returned with Kuche, who flicked a look of warning at George.

Ten minutes later, the train stopped again and Michel went off to investigate. They were just down the line from Paderborn, but would not be taken in until first light.

First light was a long time coming. In the meantime, Downay gave orders. Everyone was to behave as they had done at Aachen. There would be people meeting the train to take them to the castle at Wewelsburg. In the event of any trouble, Kuche would die: quickly: the rest would cover and make it look like sudden illness. Michel tapped his cane. The main object, he kept repeating, was the castle. Once there, they would carry out the orders he had already given.

He wished everyone *bonne chance*. Weapons were checked, and George joined in, heaving Wald's Luger from his pocket and making certain it was cocked and on safety. He even offered to stay close to Kuche, but Michel said that Roubert would be doing that from now on.

They came into Paderborn station just after six in the morning, tired and nervous, the tension crawling from man to man like obscene lice.

There was a group of Waffen-SS on the platform, and a slim officer wearing a greatcoat, with its collar turned up, paced to and fro, trying to gauge where the carriage would stop. Behind the pretty little station buildings, there was a line of transport: two large Mercs and a pair of Opel trucks.

38

'George, the dreams,' Herbie Kruger swallowed the last of his gin and placed the glass firmly down, as if to indicate there would be no more. 'The hallucinations?' He was thinking mainly that the Nostradamus quatrain which George had, involuntarily, quoted, was the one Claus Fenderman had scrawled on the final letter to his wife.

'I don't know.' George gave a sheepish smile. 'I still don't know. The memory plays false on some things but I do remember the dreams most vividly—if dreams they were.'

'Since then?'

George gave a negative wag. 'There was more at Wewelsburg. Got me through all that.' He looked at his watch. Just gone seven. 'You want ... ?'

'No. No. No.' Fast, rattling like a gun. 'You've done enough for one day. Fascinating, George. I'm just sorry to bother you with it.'

George said that confession was good for the soul, and asked if Herbie could give him any clues yet.

'I'm afraid not. If we go through Wewelsburg tomorrow morning and, maybe, get a start on—what was it called? Wermut.'

Wormwood, yes, George looked him straight in the eyes.

'Home to your good wife, then, George. Tomorrow a little later. Say, ten-thirty?'

'Wonderful.' At the door he asked if Herbie ever got lonely, living alone.

Didn't we all, Herbie countered. In this business loneliness was part of the game. Deep down he felt a stirring. There were always counter-ploys to loneliness. Drink, yes. Women? If you knew what you were doing. They said goodnight and Herbie watched George Thomas walk towards the lift. He turned back into the flat for a second and then glanced out again. George was gone, the machinery of the lift whirring. Yet the man's shadow seemed to be still there in the fully lit hall. An illusion; an optical trick of the light.

Closing the door, Herbie moved quickly into the kitchen, wound the spool of tape forward, marked and removed it, then fitted a fresh spool. He turned off the machine and carried the used spool into his living room, opened up the sideboard cupboard and delved around among the bottles for the lock to his private safe. Spool in; files out.

He dumped the files on the table and put the telephone within reach. There was more than one reason he wanted to be rid of George Thomas at this point. Odd, he thought, leafing through the files. For a day, the room had become, most clearly, so many places—Downay's flat in Paris; the rooms in the SS HQ, Avenue Foch; the streets of Paris; the trains. Yet nothing that yet linked into Hildegarde Fenderman or her sister Gretchen Weiss. Or was there? Did he have the first stirrings? There was that one quatrain, of course.

He found the file he wanted and quickly ran through its pages. The man was dead, yet somehow one vital piece of evidence was missing. The thing appeared to be intact, yet there was no doubt in Herbie's mind that the very first page of the file had been juggled.

He picked up the telephone and called the Duty Officer to ask if Registry was still open. It was, and old Ambrose would be only too pleased to wait for him. He transferred the call to Pix. Bob Perry was also working late. Herbie said he would be over in half-an-hour.

'I'll be here half the night anyway,' Perry told him. 'Rush job for Downing Street.'

'Doing social functions now, are we?' growled Herbie, adding that they would be providing snaps for the Royals before long.

'Take their own,' Perry signed off.

Ambrose Hill was waiting patiently in Registry. The first cross-reference Herbie required was easy. He took it to the end of the long polished table where the researchers spent most of their working lives, and read it through—cover-to-cover. He then asked if he could see Harold Ramilies' personal file.

'Christ,' Ambrose scratched his head. 'What years? He had a long innings.'

Herbie said he knew. From the Twenties until he died in 1948.

'I want to see his mid-Thirties stuff.'

It was a fat wad of paper which took Herbie a good half-an-hour to go through, identifying years and dates, times and people. He kept a pad near his right hand to jot down other cross-refs. What he read disturbed him enough to go straight to his own office in the Annexe and make two calls before taking the lift down to Pix.

The first was to Schnabeln, but it was Girren who was on duty. All was quiet on the Bayswater front. Frau Fenderman had been on a shopping expedition and was now eating dinner.

Secondly he telephoned the Director's right hand, Tubby Fincher, at his private number. When, he asked, could he speak with the Director?

'Not back until next month. I told you.' Tubby was in the middle of dinner and not at all pleased.

'I said, "speak", not necessarily see.'

'Ah.' Tubby became covert, dropping his voice. 'You want him briefed?'

'No. I want to talk with him on an unencumbered line. I want to make sure he is alone and that nobody else knows I'm speaking with him.'

'A quick jet would be easier.'

Herbie sighed. 'There is no time. It's the Fenderman thing. I'm uncovering dirt. It might just splatter when it hits the fan. I need to speak.'

'I fix,' said Tubby. 'Late tomorrow? Or do you want sooner?'

Herbie said sometime after seven tomorrow would be fine. 'Keep it a twosome, though,' a warning note as he signed off.

The DO had passed all messages up to Herbie's office as soon as he had been logged into the building. Nothing of importance. A call from 'Vermin' Vernon-Smith had been fielded by one of the twin-set and pearls brigade; Rachendorf had called twice from the West German Embassy. Would he please return the call soonest? Maybe. Maybe, after he had seen Bob Perry, Mr. Pix himself.

Perry had kept the prints under wraps. So far under that he could not immediately remember where he'd put them. There were two. Two out of the five Herbie had taken from the Registry files and cross-references. Ten-by-eight blow-ups from originals which were small ID size, *circa* 1940/1.

One was immediately recognisable in spite of the youthful appearance. The other, Herbie had never seen, but knew in spite of that. Perhaps it was the uniform; or the background.

Perry placed both prints under a high-powered illuminated magnifying screen, muttering that it was interesting to come across old juiced-up photographs done with this kind of skill. 'Wouldn't show in the small prints.'

He stepped back and switched on the magnifier. '*Look upon this picture and on this,*' he quoted.

'So? Brush up your *Hamlet.*'

'The Bard knew about the trade, Herbie.'

'So did Goethe—*Im übrigen ist es zuletzt die grösste Kunst, sich zu beschränken und zu isolieren.* For the rest of it, the last and greatest art is to limit and isolate oneself.'

Perry nodded, then started to point out certain things which showed up under the lens—a lack of shadow here, a ragged edge there—which made Big Herbie Kruger's heart beat a shade faster. Someone was not whom he seemed. Someone from the past. That very fact might just account for Frau Hildegarde Fenderman's presence in London.

39

Herbie's mind buzzed with possibilities and permutations. There were no irregularities on the other three prints he had given Pix, so he asked Perry to mark up the pair of doctored photographs and had all five put into an envelope.

Time was short. Work and man hours would be long. Forty-eight hours only before he was to dine with Frau Fenderman. The perspective was badly blurred. Really he should have pulled old Harold Ramilies' PF in the first place. Try now.

But, on returning to Registry, Herbie discovered that Ambrose Hill had locked up for the night and gone home. Even the security gate was closed; the time-lock in operation. He would have to make do with his notes.

Going back into his office, a whole pack of thoughts, doubts, theories and ideas started a merry-go-round in Herbie's head. The centrepiece of this mental carousel was, naturally, Hildegarde Fenderman. Around her, like the images George claimed to have conjured in the past, were a host of supporting characters. George himself, Kuche, Wald, Downay, Ramilies, Maitland-Wood. Maitland-Wood: he should have tried to pull his PF as well. He had a couple of abstracts from it among the Nostradamus files, now split between his office and St. John's Wood, but not the whole sweep of the Deputy Director's career.

Somewhat absently, Herbie unlocked his office safe and took out the balance of the files which he pushed, together with the envelope from Pix, into his briefcase.

It was too late now to ask Rachendorf, the BND man, out to dinner, but he might still manage to make contact. Amazingly, the German was still at his Embassy. 'There is a function here,' he told Herbie guardedly.

'I'm only returning your calls. Just got around to them.'

'Ah, yes. It is simply a small point.'

'Small so it shouldn't be talked about on the telephone?'

'No. Easy. A tiny piece of information. The lady who died. The one who worked for the Americans.'

'Yes.' He was talking about Gretchen Weiss.

'There was, apparently, trouble about her passport.'

'There is always trouble about passports.'

It was missing, Rachendorf said. Even though she did much work for the Americans ('You know what I'm speaking about?'), she held a Bundesrepublik passport. After her death there had been a delay. 'It happens in all bureaucracies.'

Herbie agreed and asked how badly this had happened.

'Six months.'

How six months?

'What I am telling you is that six months elapsed before any block was put on her passport. Our control people visited Frau Fenderman, who now occupies the Weiss apartment. She had not seen the passport. Knew nothing. Does it help?'

Herbie wanted to be sarcastic, but did not know if Wolfgang Alberich Rachendorf would appreciate the finer nuances of that particular art. 'It helps,' he said plainly. 'It would also explain how Fräulein Gretchen Weiss managed to make a visit, of two months, to this country last autumn, some time after her death.'

Rachendorf used a German oath of extreme obscenity.

'Vermin' Vernon-Smith was not obscene. He was acid. 'Try to get you people during the day and I have you invading my privacy after office hours.'

Herbie said he thought policemen—like priests, doctors and members of the security organisations—did not have office hours.

Vernon-Smith only grunted.

'I'm only returning your call.' Herbie stayed exceptionally polite. He presumed Vernon-Smith was calling about friends Nachent and Billstein, both formerly of the West German Security Service.

'Who else?' echoed the Special Branch man. 'Thorns in my flesh those two; but you'll probably be pleased to learn that the Bundesrepublik want us to toss 'em back.'

So, the BND wanted words with their failures. Herbie asked if they had made a court appearance.

'Yes. Very helpful beak, when the facts were pointed out to him : irregularities in Herr Billstein's papers; carrying concealed weapons. The car was dodgy as well—not to mention the quiet request from your Deutsche caped crusaders. Not the brightest of lads, Nachent and Billstein. Okay?'

'Vermin, you're a brick, as we English say.' At his end of the line, Herbie's face contorted into one of his massive grins.

'A what?' Vernon-Smith's voice rose an octave.

''Wiederhören, Vermin.'

He did not feel like lugging the heavy briefcase around Whitehall in search of a cab, so Herbie pulled rank on the Duty Officer and whistled up a car from the pool. It was outside in a matter of minutes with a small, handy-looking driver. Pole or Czech, Herbie thought. The department was lousy with East Europeans. 'Buy them by the boxed-set from the KGB,' Maitland-Wood had once joked. The *bon mot* had been considered to be in bad taste, particularly among the young trainee intellectuals from Oxford.

Big Herbie gave his address to the driver who said he already knew it. 'I stop on the corner, yes?'

The large head nodded twice. Routine was a killer. All ex-field men knew that—and most of the public, now that kidnapping and terrorism were so fashionable. Each day, Herbie varied routes to and from Whitehall. Official cars usually had to be instructed. Often he got them to drop him in the next street; sometimes he slipped from the car and did the last bit on the underground. Keep in trim, Herbie, he told himself. Become accustomed to the pace, make it second nature to you now, he hummed. This driver must have spent time in the field.

They stopped at the corner. Round the corner, but at a point where the driver could observe Herbie all the way down to the apartment block. Nearly two hundred yards, in old money, Herbie smiled. He thanked the driver who said, okay, not to worry. 'I see you in,' the motor running and lights switched off.

Herbie was half-way down to the building with its trim frontage—clipped lawns, shrubs and a low wall bordering on the pavement—when he suddenly felt very vulnerable. It was not unusual. His size did not help. He had always been conscious of his height and breadth, conquering any obsessions by making use of the physical attributes. Big Herbie. Big Dumb Herbie.

He glanced back, a casual flick of the head. Nothing. A car on the opposite side of the road starting up, the lights flaring. Nothing unusual, but ... then the sudden squeal of rubber upon road surface and the full-gunning of the engine. The car coming out at speed. A stoppo driver's take-off with ful revs, brakes off and the clutch let out fast. Expensive on tyres.

Herbie began to run. Instinct. Doesn't matter if you're wrong. Glance back. He was not wrong. The headlights were doused and one spotlight shattered the sodium-lit street, blinding him. He turned his head away and closed his eyes, running on memory. In the bright after-image he was conscious of his own car, around the corner, moving out with lights on.

Eyes open again. Almost at the low wall. After that a zigzag through the shrubs to the entrance. The oncoming spotlight blazed and dazzled the whole area ahead while the sound of the engine pulled him in, absorbed him as it closed fast.

A thousand images from the old days. Running. Streets at night with the rattle of feet following; narrow walled alleys; spotlights coming on suddenly at the Wall in Berlin. Shouts. Running.

The low wall. Herbie leaped and began the slalom through the shrubs. He heard the crash as the car fractured the wall. He could feel it now with its tyres biting the grass. He took a final dive, full length, rolling at speed towards the enclosed doorway, then balling his body hard into the entrance for protection.

The car slewed sideways on and hit the brickwork, less than a foot from where he had landed. He could see neither driver nor number plate—only conscious of the grind of metal on brick, and then the frenzy of the engine and the wheels trying to grip the damp grass as the machine slid past, out of control, then steadied and headed away, smashing through the low wall again and out into the road where Herbie's own car caught it broadside on, pushing it, skewed over the road.

He saw his own driver start to open the door, then close it, as the rogue vehicle gunned forward and took off down the road. A German car: Opel Kadett, souped, and probably reinforced, but the plates were obscured.

Herbie picked himself up, aware of people now—craning from windows, a couple of young men coming out from the lift— 'What in God's name's going on?' 'You drunk or something?' 'Christ, look at the wall and the front here.'

It was okay, Herbie told them. Car. A drunk probably. He had seen the whole thing. ('Get the law,' one of the young men ordered his companion.)

They waited with Herbie, as though guardians of public peace.

They were obviously highly suspicious of him. The law arrived in the shape of a panda car. One young constable. Both the burly men wanted to tell the story, but Herbie quietly stepped in to say he was the one who had seen it happen. If the officer would come up to his flat ...

Once inside and alone with the constable, Herbie flashed his ID and asked if Vernon-Smith from Special Branch could be alerted, and would he get his little panda car the hell out of it. The policeman started to say something about reporting to his superiors when the telephone rang.

'You've had trouble.' The Duty Officer. 'I'm afraid Zshlapka lost him.'

Who was Zshlapka? The driver. Did he need help? Just get the law out and 'Vermin' in. He would give a description of the car. The ball would be in 'Vermin's' court.

The young panda man took some persuading, but finally left to take radio instructions. His personal transceiver was not operating well in Herbie's flat which was not surprising when you considered the built-in deflectors.

His leg hurt. Bruised in the final roll, Herbie thought, building himself a large vodka. Down in one, then a trip to the bathroom. His leg was grazed, nothing bad. He combed his hair, sluiced his face, washed his hands and limped out again. The limp was odd. Two or three normal steps he could manage, then a couple of small steps. Mahler had a trick walk as well, he consoled himself, looking at the briefcase on the table then going over to unlock the long drawer in the sideboard. If things were hotting up, Herbie Kruger would take no more chances. The wicked dull black Sauer M38H felt snug and reassuring in his big paw. It was a long time since he had carried. But always the M38H. Little-known outside Germany and one of the best pistols of its time. Sensible now. Even an idiot could tell something stank from the past. Shots at Frau Fenderman. A car aimed at Herbie Kruger. He dialled the Duty Officer, asked after the driver, and said he wanted someone good to keep an eye out. Schnabeln and Girren were the only pair he could use from his own private army. (The others were off on short courses all over the place.) The DO said he could spare Worboys. Anyone could spare Worboys, but he was better than nothing. 'Tell him to watch it and give him a shooter,' Herbie ordered.

Vernon-Smith arrived; irritable but concerned. Was he sure it wasn't just an accident? Of course Herbie was bloody certain. 'And I hope I get the bastard before you do.'

'Vermin' went away puzzled, while Herbie took the last slice of quiche from the fridge, built himself a spectacular vodka, opened his briefcase and began to scatter the files over the floor. He took the remainder from his safe and added those to the pile, arranging and rearranging them into a kind of family tree. Nostradamus and his progeny of the 1940s.

So many were dead—the small abstracts on Ramilies, together with his own notes; Joseph Wald; Maurice Roubert; Cecille Roubert (George had been right. She had died in Ravensbruck); Emile and Michelle Sondier who had kept the house on Rue Cambon (blown and executed); Jean Fenice died in 1952—Ramilies had gone quickly with a heart attack in mid-1948; Sandy Leaderer was still alive, an old man in some home—*non compos* the note said; Angelle Tours ...

Herbie read through her file again, very carefully, then put on the Mahler Sixth. He had promised himself that treat tonight anyway. The strings strode through his large speakers, the orchestra taking up the gawky march theme which so suddenly ceases to be gauche and becomes lyrical.

Angelle Tours, thought Herbie. Then, on his knees he scrabbled around the documents again and retrieved the long file on Stellar, plus George's full PF. He checked name against name. Rechecked George's later work, mostly in the West, but he had done six or seven trips into the East in the late Fifties. Quick bring-'em-back-alive sorties. All smooth. Not a ripple.

He consulted his notes on Ramilies and the little he had on Maitland-Wood, then looked down the list again. Michel Downay; Frühling; Fenderman—but he was later: Fenderman and von Tupfel did not hit their marks until after Wewelsburg.

He had another vodka and repeated the names like a litany. So many dead. Old history. Hidden history. Now alive again. So alive that people were ready to kill for it.

Jesus, the thought striking him horribly. He grabbed at the telephone. The DO again. Even if you have to use the bloody Special Branch put somebody on George and his wife, for Chrissakes; and Maitland-Wood. 'I don't care if he objects. *Have someone there.*' At least he must cover those who were left from the ashes of Stellar and, later, Wermut.

Lastly he called Schnabeln. All was quiet. Any action at all? She had a visitor earlier. Male. No ID. Walked with a limp. Old. Used a stick, arrived in a taxi and left the same way. When? About an hour ago. Stayed fifteen minutes.

Herbie tidied up the files and dumped them into the safe with the photographs. He'd had one more look at those, all five, spread out on the floor, rearranging them in different orders.

He slept that night with the M38H under his pillow. At nine Tubby Fincher rang to say the call to the Director was on. Seven o'clock from his end in St. John's Wood.

George Thomas arrived on the dot. Herbie provided coffee. This was the last, long crucial part of the Stellar business.

'Straight on from where I left off?' George asked.

'You arrived at Paderborn. They were all waiting with transport.'

'Sitting comfortably?' George grinned. 'Then I'll begin.'

40

There were greetings. Heil Hitlers. Kuche produced the documents. The baggage—including the long boxes—were unloaded. The Waffen-SS at the station were put through the hoop.

Everyone was treated with great deference and taken out to the waiting cars. George was ushered into the first Merc, together with Michel Downay, Kuche and the SS Major who had been waiting at the station.

Maurice Roubert—looking worried because his charge, Kuche, had slipped his lead—got into the second car. The bodyguard of fake Waffen-SS were loaded into the first Opel truck. The baggage and the troops who had come down to meet the party, travelled in the second.

As the convoy moved off, Kuche introduced George and Downay to Major Flachs, Sturmbannführer Flachs, Second-in-Command to the Garrison of Wewelsburg. He smelled vaguely of eau de cologne and appeared to be a fastidious dandy. Colonel Streichman, the Garrison Commander, he said, was sorry he could not be there. 'You understand ... his duties at the castle ...' He made a motion meant to convey that the Colonel was occupied with things of greater importance. 'Which of you is the Frenchman Thomas?'

George signified that it was him, and Flachs nodded, looking pleased. He then turned to Michel and stated the obvious, that he must be the Herr Doktor Downay. The Reichsführer was looking forward to meeting them. George asked if the Reichsführer was waiting for them.

The pause was a shade long before Flachs quietly said they were expecting the Reichsführer a little later. He added that Himmler had been detained in Berlin with the Führer himself until very late on the previous night.

'The Reichsführer-SS is a very busy man,' Downay said, as though chiding George.

'There it is.' Kuche, sitting in front with Flachs on the outside, half-turned his head, his gloved right hand pointing forward. 'The Reichsführer's Camelot.'

Ahead of them loomed the great solid walls of Wewelsburg castle. Huge and triangular, with its high circular, almost phallic, tower eclipsing the two smaller towers which went to make up the massive three-sided fortification of stone and brick. It was little wonder that legend said this would be the last bastion of Westphalia. It had an indestructible look: impregnable, flagrant, brooding in the morning light.

Gazing at it in its haze of early marsh mist, George felt that unseen eyes watched them from the serrated battlements with concentrated malevolence.

As they drew closer, so the physical presence of the place grew more awesome in his imagination. Panic stirred in George's guts and sweat trickled down from his armpits, even in the cold of early morning. All the ancient fears stored in the collective memory of man seemed to be focused on his body, triggered by the castle.

As a child, George had hated fairytales, but loved the illustrations. This was no storybook illustration, except in the sense that it was the kind of place in which the giant lived, or one which brought restless dreams of unnamed horrors.

By the time the convoy passed through the gateway and into the large triangular cobbled courtyard, George felt physically sick, very tired and weary of the whole charade.

It was darker once they were through the ornate stone arch: the walls of the castle, the towers, rising on all sides, hemming them in and giving an immediate sense of claustrophobia.

Their driver turned sharp right, still going quite fast, taking the car in close to the base of the huge main tower. George glanced back. The rest of the convoy had followed, the other Merc stopping about ten feet behind them, and the Opel trucks fanning left and right so that the whole set of vehicles stood in the shape of a letter T, blocking them into the top of the triangle.

Flachs was out of the car first, and, as his door opened, they could hear the clatter of boots as the troops leaped from the trucks. The doors of the car directly behind them slammed shut.

At the base of the tower there was a small flight of stone steps leading to a heavy door. The door swung back to reveal a short, portly officer, his greatcoat collar turned up and the cap set square on a bull head. He came down the steps slowly, turning the toes of his boots slightly inwards, the long coat flapping, even in the shelter of the castle walls. He wore the insignia of a full General.

Kuche inhaled sharply. 'God. Frühling,' he said quietly, his hand reaching for the end of the seat just vacated by Flachs. 'My commander, General Frühling.'

The driver got out, holding the door on Downay's side. Michel Downay turned and smiled at George. 'Yes,' he muttered. 'The Herr General Frühling. SS-Oberstgruppenführer Frühling who, like all the Reichsführer's chosen ones, has his own coat of arms above his chair set at the round table in that incredible room up there in the tower.' He swung himself out of the car with surprising agility.

George opened the door on his side and stepped out next to Kuche, his right hand automatically moving towards his hip pocket and the Luger.

'Keep your back against the car,' Kuche murmured, low.

Several other officers had now appeared behind Frühling, following him down the steps. One in particular was pushing his way forward, a smile lifting the corner of his arrogant mouth, a wisp of blond hair showing under the angled cap, one hand placed carelessly on the buckle of his belt.

George thought, for a second, that he was in the grip of another hallucination.

'None the worse, then, Joseph,' Michel Downay spoke in German.

The officer touched the blood on his right sleeve and flexed his hand which showed no marks or wounds. 'Nothing that my bat-man cannot put right,' replied Obersturmführer Joseph Wald as he came towards the car.

Michel Downay chuckled and lifted his ebony cane, bringing it down with a thump on the cobbles. Like a thousand nightmare sounds, George heard the click-clack of weapons being cocked ready for use. He felt Kuche's shoulder against his.

They were surrounded. Not just by the troops who had met them at the station, but also by Michel's men in their purloined uniforms. The circle was unbreakable, a crescent of the evil eyes which were machinepistol muzzles; a break in the ranks, then

Roubert with a Luger; a Waffen-SS sergeant with another Luger to the right. In front of them the group of officers all looking at Kuche and George with the interest of scientists seeing some rare species for the first time.

Downay clumped his way over to General Frühling and raised his right arm in salute. 'Heil Hitler,' he said. 'I have brought them to you, just as I promised.'

They shook hands, and the tubby Frühling chuckled, 'And not a moment too soon.'

Kuche gave a sigh, followed by a curse.

'I am sorry, Sturmbannführer Kuche,' Michel Downay waved his cane towards them. 'And to you also, Georges Thomas. A slight deception; a little magic; a trick of the light here and there.'

Hands were already disarming them, pinioning their hands behind their backs. Roubert was among those doing the work.

'Perhaps,' General Frühling spoke. 'Perhaps you will both join us inside the tower so that we can offer you an explanation, and then give you the full details of what is going to happen here. What is to happen both to yourselves, and to the chief guest at our party—the owner of this magnificent castle. He should be putting in an appearance here, a brief appearance, within the next twenty-four hours.'

41

For a man of his bulk, General Frühling had a soft voice: the timbre of butter. 'Reichsführer Himmler,' he said with a smile of contempt that traced his lips like a breeze rippling a pond, 'bought this castle for one Reichsmark. He's spent millions on it—as you have seen, gentlemen.'

They had seen the steps which led down to the crypt under the huge north tower, and it had been explained that the crypt was of special significance to Himmler and the Order of the SS. They had also seen the huge dining room with its great circular oak table, around which the chairs, upholstered in pigskin, stood at intervals, each bearing the coat of arms designated to its owner: Himmler's chosen aides, his Oberstgruppenführer.

Frühling even proudly pointed out his own chair and, in passing, placed his palm on the back of another, saying that it belonged to Himmler's right hand—to Reinhard Heydrich—patting the chair and nodding as though conveying this was of special significance.

They were also shown through the massive library in Himmler's own quarters, and had seen the long gallery with its collection of weapons lining the walls. As they walked, Frühling explained the significance of the crypt. It was the Holy of Holies. When one of the chosen Oberstgruppenführer died, or was killed in battle, his coat of arms would be burned in the crypt. Specially constructed vents would carry the smoke up the tower and out of the roof, in a single plume. The dead warrior's ashes would be placed on a column in the crypt.

'As it happens, the chance is that the first shield, and the first ashes, will be those of our beloved Reichsführer-SS himself.' The laugh was like rancid fat.

So, General Frühling himself conducted Kuche and George around the building. He was backed up by Wald, the Garrison Commander, Streichman, and his second-in-command, Flachs, plus a pair of Waffen-SS sergeants, one of whom George identified as a Downay man from the French train. Michel Downay was with them, of course, as was George's stepfather, the sinister scent-maker, Roubert. They all appeared to be quite at home with one another.

Lastly they arrived in a room which overlooked the courtyard. George guessed they had left the fat north tower and were now situated within one of the battlemented adjoining blocks which ran from it.

The room was functional, with high doors, a large desk, some maps and chairs. Kuche and George were invited to be seated, and the remaining officers ranged themselves around the room. Frühling sat at the desk.

'I may as well tell you that the fact of Heinrich Kuche's treachery has been known to us for a long time,' the General continued, switching from his guide-book manner, back to a more military and businesslike brusqueness. Kuche, he added, had been marked almost since the first moment the British enticed him.

'It is only fair to say also that Herr Doktor Downay has been a loyal member of the Party, with an honorary SS rank, since,' he paused, 'since when, Michel?'

'I was recruited by agents of Oberstgruppenführer Heydrich himself in 1936, Herr General.'

George thought that Ramilies had said it all. *Now if it was that bastard Heydrich.* Heydrich, the blond beast, the cold and calculating right arm of Reichsführer Himmler; the intelligence behind the whole conception of the Police Forces of the Third Reich. More, the architect of the Nazi Espionage system, and the man whose logic inexorably led to the idea of a State purged of its enemies by death. Purged of bad blood by extermination. So, Michel Downay, psychologist, French traitor and expert on the occult and Nostradamus, had been recruited into Heydrich's intelligence services over four years ago. George loudly voiced his opinion that Roubert, his stepfather, was probably of the same breed.

Roubert nodded and smiled, benignly. 'Ah, even more so. My father was German. Your mother had no idea, by the way. I'm so sorry about that, Georges. I really did care for her. But one must think of one's country before . . .'

Downay interrupted him. 'The story is that the Reichsminister of Propaganda got his ideas about the Nostradamus quatrains from his wife. In fact it was a shade more complicated than that.' He smiled, the pride showing. 'I had quite a lot to do with it myself.'

Frühling tapped the desk, bringing everyone to order. 'I think we should make it clear that many things are double-edged. Downay, you see, was instructed to infiltrate the Communist elements in France—in Paris. He was also given orders to make contact with any possible subversive British elements. In some ways that is how Kuche was brought into play. We knew who had recruited him, so we merely placed Downay in his path. He hit the bait; and you arrived, Georges Thomas, complete with a new set of quatrains. Quite a clever move that. To set the Wehrmacht at odds with the SS. Clever, but not difficult. However ...' He looked around the room and explained that there were better games to be played than setting the SS against the Wehrmacht. For a long time, he told them, a faction of the SS had looked for change : drastic change. Now that change was coming. Thomas and Kuche should feel honoured. They were to be part of that change. Things were about to happen which even Nostradamus could not foresee.

There was no doubt concerning the allegiance of the SS, he went on. They were totally behind the Führer, Adolf Hitler. But what if something should happen to the Führer? What if his great and glorious plans did not mature? If something went wrong, Germany would be at the mercy of Hitler's beloved Heinrich Himmler. 'Our own Reichsführer-SS; our Chief of Police.' A large section of the senior SS officers were quite content at the thought. Happily, though, there were those gifted with a more far-sighted perception. Himmler had his mysticism ('You can feel it all around you here in this castle.'); what was really needed was someone with cold and concentrated logic.

A man like Reinhard Heydrich, George thought. The cashiered Naval officer whose driving force behind Himmler had played such a huge part in the personal success of the Reichsführer-SS.

As if reading his thoughts, Frühling said, 'We need at our head a man like Reinhard Heydrich. A man who has enthusiasm, vision and extraordinary organising ability.' He gave his buttery laugh. 'Not a bungling chicken farmer like Himmler. You—the traitor, Kuche, and the English spy Thomas—have been chosen to rid us of the chicken farmer, so that Oberstgruppenführer Heydrich can take what is truly his.'

He went on, but George was back thinking of Ramilies. The Rammer, in his little talks at the Abbey, had been at pains to lecture him about the in-fighting within the forces of the Third Reich. He was remarkably well-informed. *Reichsführer Himmler has blind faith in Hitler. Heydrich does not share that faith.* On another occasion he quoted Heydrich directly : *I shall be the first to do away with the old man if he makes a mess of things.*

'You are both marked for death, of course. At the moment.' Frühling's voice broke through the memories. 'Kuche will go quickly and soon. It is best. He has fulfilled his purpose, both for the British and ourselves. You, Thomas, will undergo a certain amount of interrogation. I suspect that the *new* Reichsführer might even tend towards leniency if you cooperate.' There was not a hint of sincerity in his voice. 'You must have some information at your disposal. The arrangements London is making about bringing agents into Fortress Europe. We shall see.'

He continued. Dabbling in the Nostradamus quatrains intrigued Himmler. They had intrigued Goebbels and Hitler as well, but the way in which they had been presented to the Reichsführer had led Himmler to ask for a special meeting here at Wewelsburg. The time and place were right. Also the dramatis personae.

'It is envisaged like a play, you see,' beaming broadly. 'If you are not spared, Georges Thomas. For instance, how were we to realise that an academic Frenchman like yourself, Georges Thomas, had designs on the Reichsführer's life? That is one way it can go. Also, what a shame that Sturmbannführer Kuche had to die at your hands trying to defend his chief. There is an irony about the fact that—if it is to be—Kuche will probably get a hero's funeral. It's the best we can think of at the moment. Heydrich will, naturally, rush to his Führer's side to comfort him on the loss of his most loyal friend and comrade. Heydrich will be the first to hear. Tomorrow morning: after it is done. By tomorrow night I should imagine his appointment as Himmler's natural successor will be ratified.'

Kuche spoke for the first time. 'You're really going to kill him? Assassinate Himmler, here in his castle?'

Frühling said of course. He sounded surprised that there should be doubt.

'Then,' Kuche rose, clicking his heels, 'I shall be very pleased to carry out that duty as my last act as an officer of the SS.'

'Now there's an idea.' Frühling slapped the table in good humour. 'Another piece of trickery. He's almost as good as you, Downay.'

In the pause that followed, George asked Downay ('I was amazed to find how casual I sounded.') how he had managed the incapacitation of Joseph Wald. After all, he had seen the blood pouring from the man's hand and wrist; saw him taken away to the baggage car where, he imagined, death awaited.

'We wanted you completely at ease with Kuche. It was clear he was unhappy about Joseph.' Downay went on to say he had always wanted to play the magician, but it really was quite easy : a device used for *Grande Guignol* in the theatre and cinema. As it happened the apparatus was an English device using what the British, with their macabre sense of humour, called Kensington Gore. Fake blood; a large shaped bottle, tubes and clips, and a trick swordstick.

'You magic my dreams in the same way?' George asked, bitter as aloes. 'With a little something in my coffee? Dulwich Dream pills or something?'

Downay looked disturbed. He knew nothing of George's dreams.

Wald, as it turned out, was on detachment to Frühling directly from Heydrich's staff. His job had been to mastermind the Paris end. 'Doing a little gentle pushing,' as he put it; and keeping one eye cocked on Kuche. It had been Downay's people who had cut the throats of Balthazar and his girl. 'We needed to separate you from anyone who might suspect what was going on. Balthazar, as I'm sure you know, was already suspicious of Downay.'

That left only George's mother and Angelle. Angelle, they said, had nothing to do with them. She was good cover, a girl like that in Downay's apartment. As for Maman—Roubert looked quite serious.

'I'm sorry. I've already said so. People do get hurt. Innocent people. She's in custody. In the end it will depend on her.'

George's dream had her being dragged away in Paris.

'So,' Frühling puffed out his cheeks. 'Here we sit. Conspirators and conspirators. A moment of great history. Yet it feels normal. Strange that we can make history under these conditions.'

'Do you accept my offer?' Kuche asked. 'I'm quite genuine. I'll do it for you. If I have to die now, then nothing would give me greater pleasure than to take the Reichsführer with me.'

Frühling made a small shaking motion with the whole of his body. 'The arrangements, the details, for the Reichsführer's disposal have yet to be concluded. We shall see. Himmler, the chicken farmer, arrives at eleven tomorrow. There will be two cars. However it is done, his entourage will also have to die. How we do it depends, to some extent, on the cooperation of your friend Thomas. We shall see.' He made a dismissive movement, the hand raised as if to indicate that the prisoner was coming under starter's orders. Flachs, accompanied by one of the sergeants, led Kuche from the room.

They all turned their attention on George.

'There will be questions,' Frühling's small eyes looked dead. 'I think you should be prepared for a long session. Some nourishment.'

He nodded and they took George away: down steps and along passages so that he lost all sense of direction. Naturally he expected a dungeon. Instead, he was shown into a pleasant large room, done out in white. With some horror he reflected that it smacked of a hospital ward. There was a small bed, a table, two chairs. The rest was bare boards and white paintwork. The two windows had sets of very durable metal bars. George thought they need not have worried because when he looked down it was a long drop to the cobbled courtyard.

They left a Waffen-SS private soldier with him. Then another brought black bread and lentil soup. The soup gave him wind.

42

'More coffee? A drink, perhaps?' At the back of Big Herbie's mind an uncanny sense of unease had started to flower.

George said that a drink would be nice, though it was barely eleven-thirty. 'I go switch on the oven as well,' Herbie said. There was steak and kidney pie. The meat was cooked, but the pastry, well...

The worry had been there yesterday and it was there, vividly, this morning. He fiddled about in the kitchen and built the drinks —gin again—while he thought about it. He had read the whole file on this operation and what followed. It was George's show. George was here now, in the present in his own apartment; yet, as he told the story, the man in France and at Wewelsburg was not George.

Naturally, he calmed himself. After so many years how could it be this George? Are you, Herbie Kruger, the same Herbie as you were thirty, forty, years ago? We alter. We change sides, positions, attitudes. Time and memory shift the balance of perspective. Maitland-Wood's warning came to mind—*remember that even he'll only recall that which he wants to be retained.*

'They gave you a bad time in the room with the white walls then, George?' Sliding a drink over the table.

At the Abbey, George said, they had told him how tough the SS and the Gestapo would be. 'The full bit: rubber hoses, tearing your fingernails out. It wasn't like that. Not the first time anyway.'

Wald and the thin Flachs had been the main protagonists, with Michel Downay sitting on the sidelines.

'They started by pointing out that, even though I was the obvious person on whom they could pin Himmler's assassination, it might just be possible to come to some arrangement.'

Herbie said the carrot on a stick technique.

George agreed. 'If I was cooperative, the new Reichsführer—

Heydrich, of course—might be lenient. Some sort of execution would have to be carried out, but there were plenty of people they could use as stand-ins. It was pretty cold-blooded.'

'What were they really after?'

'I wondered that, to start with. I wondered what they really wanted, because they seemed to know most of it already. They knew a lot about my parentage, a bit about childhood. I put all that down to pillow-talk between Maman and Roubert. They were also well-up on my academic qualifications and military service. Ramilies had recruited me. *The same old professor who turned Kuche into a traitor*. I think Wald said that. They talked about the Abbey as if they had been there; but their knowledge of *Soldatensender Calais* and its link with the operation was very sketchy. Non-existent really. Also they didn't seem to know how conversant I really was with the Nostradamus prophecies, or the occult in general.'

'No threats. Just promises and letting you know they had a lot of information.' Herbie sipped his gin. 'Advanced for those days.'

'They knew it all. Not fools those confessors; no. It was like, let's see? Like a friendly chat between the Commissioners of Inland Revenue and one who is suspected of not quite declaring all his assets.'

'And you remained dumb?'

'Of course. Stayed like the three wise monkeys. I wanted to see where they were leading me.'

Herbie laughed. 'You found out, I presume.'

'Oh yes. Oh, I found out all right.'

43

Obviously, at some point they were going to get technical and ask about the way George was prepared for the landing in France. Where he had gone from, and all that kind of thing. They began to throw in asides about the general organisation in England. Happily, George knew very little. Ramilies had seen to that.

Eventually the important line of questioning emerged. It concerned George's personal use in two different areas. They wanted to know if Ramilies had hired himself a genuine occultist, and, if so, would he be of use to them—maybe through Goebbels' Propaganda Ministry. The other possibility was whether George was suitable material to be turned and played back to London.

To start with they began to harp on the occult and the quatrains he had provided.

'We gather from Michel that you claim to have written these prophecies while in some kind of trance. You claim to be a genuine prophet?' Wald glanced towards Downay as if seeking confirmation.

'I claim nothing.' George thought that sounded pompous and Biblical.

'But Downay says ...'

'I can't help what Michel Downay says. He's the bloody expert on Nostradamus. He's even written a book about him, and unjumbled the prophecies. I'm surprised you can trust him; like I'm surprised he even told you that I had provided any of the prophecies at all. You know the French—steal the sweat off your balls.'

Wald and Flachs thought that was quite amusing.

'But you're half-French yourself?' Flachs grinned.

George spat. 'So I'd only steal the sweat off one of your balls. I'm half-English so I'd filch it off the most potent one.'

The truculence did not work, and that disappointed George. He would rather have them aggressive. Then Wald asked if he now denied having any occult powers.

George shrugged. Downay came limping over to the table and leaned against it.

'Explain to me,' he leered, 'the quatrain you quoted on the train.'

'Which one?'

He came back with it very accurately:

> 'At the castle death will come
> To those who shall rise again and mock.
> The standard-bearer shall link hands
> With one he trusts. The true one will not rise.'

'You're the great interpreter, Michel. Have a go,' George goaded.

He asked again.

Okay, George thought. He had no idea about where the dreams sprang from—except overwork on the quatrains—nor how he had come up with the words. But, as Master Shakespeare said, there are more things in heaven and earth. If he played along with them: took it all a stage further he might just do the impossible.

'You want my interpretation? Right.' Once more George felt he was pontificating, but it was part of the character now. 'I believe it means that whatever's being planned here against Reichsführer Himmler is doomed. It will fail.' Then, turning to Wald, 'You've read the quatrains about the Reichsführer. He is destined to rise. He *is* destined to lead the Party and the Reich.'

Wald hesitated, not exactly shaken. 'On the train you said the true one will *not* rise.'

'Maybe; then the one who is behind your present plan is the true one. But he will not rise. Everything points to it. How much, Joseph Wald, do you really know about astrology, horoscopes, the occult and the methods of divination?' George prayed that Wald knew very little, because he was now in a case of selling Tower Bridge to an idiot mark. The old con: the money game: alchemy.

He forced his mind back to the nights in London, and at the Abbey, when he had culled some knowledge of these things from the books Ramilies had provided. Using all the technical phrases he could muster, George talked about divination, without actually saying that he was a seer. As he spoke, the confidence came. He sounded both lucid and authoritative: Nostradamus; the prophecies which really mattered; astrology; the quatrains he was supposed to have divined. 'They are in exact keeping with Reichsführer Himmler's horoscope. Check it with your own court astrologers.' Nobody, he said, could tamper with these forces.

Wald tried to make light of it, but Flachs, who had a weak mouth and worried eyes, seemed edgy; disturbed.

'There is no stopping us, George Thomas,' blustered Wald. 'Here, we are a determined group, and we work under the direct orders of a very powerful officer ...'

'Heydrich's ambition ...' George began.

'His backing is of more importance than mere personal ambition.' Wald turned, furious, his face thrust close to George. Then, he whispered, 'We have the means; we also have the scapegoats—yourself and the traitor, Kuche. Nothing, you hear me, nothing, can stop what will happen tomorrow.'

'Except the stars and fate itself.' George shivered, tensing his muscles to control himself.

'I have no belief in that rubbish. The fact that others believe it ...'

George, still conquering the fear and shaking, forced a smile, as casual as he could manage, the facial muscles battling hard. 'Makes no difference. What is written in the stars will happen. There are courses which will not be changed because men believe or disbelieve. You may well kill Kuche and myself. You will *not* kill Reichsführer Himmler. Not yet. His destiny is quite plain.' He went on; a line of dogmatic obstinacy. When they finally left him alone, George was certain he had convinced them at least that he was a confirmed and devoted believer.

While Wald remained unmoved, you could not tell what Michel Downay thought. Flachs, however, was another matter. It was at this point that George thought Flachs started to waver.

It must have been late afternoon by the time the first session ended. They had taken away his watch, so George had no idea of the real hour.

He stretched out on the bed, trying to recall everything Ramilies had told him, both about Himmler and Heydrich. Not much in fact, they had concentrated more on Goebbels.

That the pair disliked one another was obvious knowledge.

215

Facts had come via the Berlin Embassy during the Thirties. It was thought, however, that the two men were mutually dependent one upon the other: Himmler being the faithful and close friend of Hitler; while Heydrich was the cold, calculating organiser.

Himmler, even in his great position of power, was unpredictable, while Heydrich could usually be predicted up to a point, being the logician of the pair. He was also the one with fine Nordic looks, a master-sportsman—riding, fencing and shooting. Himmler had none of these attributes.

There had already been at least one attempt to overthrow Heydrich. Some bureaucrat had suggested that this Nordic god had Jewish blood in him. There were also stories about his sexual excesses and drinking. One tale concerned a drunken bout, after which he had entered his mirrored bathroom, caught sight of his reflection and emptied his pistol at the mirrors, shouting, 'I've got you at last, you swine.'

Both men were to be feared. Heydrich was positively disliked by the bulk of his fellow SS officers, and the wives were at loggerheads. Frau Heydrich openly referred to Frau Himmler as 'Size 50 knickers'. Frau Himmler had even pressurised her husband into trying to order a divorce between Heydrich and his wife.

In the end, George felt the first pangs of despair. He had played a psychological game with Wald and Flachs, just as he had played it with Downay. There was little he could dredge from his memory about either Himmler or Heydrich that would help now. Lord knew what Kuche was doing, offering to carry out the assassination himself.

The light was going, greying inside the room. In spite of the swirl of nervous tension, George drifted off to sleep. It was a sleep that brought two dreams. ('They were not like the other experiences. Just vivid dreams. Though, as you'll see, they eventually brought words.')

First, there was the car. A long Merc. It could have been coming into the castle, but in the dream it seemed to be in a more open place. The car was halted by a figure carrying a machine-pistol, but he did not fire. Then an explosion ripped open the back of the car and a tall blond man staggered out of the wreckage. Shouts and shots. Then the tall figure fell to the ground, his uniform cap rolling away in a cloud of blood.

The cap went on spinning, like a coin on a bar counter, slowing and finally coming to rest. The man who had leaped from the wrecked car had been in uniform. Now, when George—in his dream—looked back, it was a different man. This one was in shabby civilian clothes, his jaws tightly clenched, his head close-cropped and the steel-rimmed glasses he had worn were askew.

Voices called out George's name. A hand shaking him.

Wald, Flachs and Oberstgruppenführer Frühling were in the room. There was light. For a second, George still thought he was asleep, moving like an automaton as they ordered him to stand up. He started to speak, but Wald told him to be silent. Then Frühling asked him to repeat what he had been trying to say. The words were there, clear in his head—a shape; familiar, yet strange, like a view you think you have seen before.

> 'He who leads the skull heads will die,
> But not as a military officer.
> The one who wishes to be leader will meet his end
> From a carriage.'

They listened and then ordered him to sit at the table. The words and the dream still rang loudly in his own head: a sense of disorientation. Frühling asked what it was supposed to mean. George told him to get his tame expert.

'You mean Michel Downay?'

'Tell us,' from Flachs.

George felt he was back among them now, playing the same con game. 'It means what it says. Himmler will not die in uniform.'

'So?'

'Presumably he will be in uniform tomorrow. So he will not die.'

Frühling laughed. 'Michel Downay says that you are a fraud.'

'Downay,' said George, 'is an historian and a psychologist. He is also a sceptic. He has never believed me.'

'No. He does not believe you now.' Very final.

George shrugged and said it made no difference. Somehow, the dreams had given him renewed confidence in the part he was trying to play. Maybe he was only doing it to cut himself off from the unpleasant prospects of his circumstances. He went on speaking directly to Frühling.

'I've already told these two. Now I'll tell you, Herr Oberst-gruppenführer. Your plan against Reichsführer Himmler cannot and will not work. For him there is another destiny.'

Frühling laughed, and George hoped that he detected the laugh of an uneasy man. Frühling muttered something about it being superstitious nonsense then, turning to Wald and Flachs, told them to 'Take him apart.'

George's stomach flipped. He clenched his fists, waiting for the first blow, thinking Frühling was speaking in physical terms. But Wald took out his cigarettes and offered one to George as the door softly closed behind Frühling.

'You see,' Wald sat on the edge of the table, 'even the highest-ranking officer here cannot believe you. Come, Thomas, let's talk properly. Don't you wish to save your skin? There are ways, you know. A few answers and then a word in the new Reichsführer's ear...'

'There will be no new Reichsführer.' He found himself believing it now, as a man will start believing a lie repeated again and again. 'Nothing will change me, because nothing can change the inevitable.'

'Then it is inevitable that you will die tomorrow. Like Reichsführer Himmler.'

'If I'm dead tomorrow, there is a strong possibility, Herr Wald, that you will also be dead—and Flachs here; and Frühling, Downay, Streichman, and anybody else embroiled in your maniac plan.'

'Then talking is pointless?'

'Completely. I've nothing to tell you. I am an historian and an occultist. I know a great deal about divination. Why else would the British send me to help Downay? They had regarded him as an expert and a man of honour willing to help his country against a common enemy. It must be obvious to you that they would never trust me with military information. I'm only an amateur soldier: at best an interpreter of dreams.'

Wald said it was a great pity. 'If you are such an expert, then you already know that you will die tomorrow, in the courtyard, when Himmler's car arrives.'

George licked his dry lips. 'I have no knowledge of what will happen. No details, except that Reichsführer Himmler will not be assassinated, either here or anywhere else.'

Flachs was genuinely disconcerted : nervous. He began to speak, then the door opened and Frühling came in followed by Michel Downay. They both looked angry.

'So,' Frühling barked. 'So, now we know.'

George opened his mouth to ask what it was that they knew, but Frühling cut across him—

'I have just received a message from France.' Fine globules of spittle spraying around his mouth. 'For some time now, we have known of an illicit and illegal radio transmitter which purports to be an official Wehrmacht station. It broadcasts under the name of *Soldatensender Calais*. This afternoon *Soldatensender Calais* broadcast a programme concerning the prophecies of Nostradamus. They admitted the prophecies showed that the Führer would inevitably rule the whole of the Western world. Then they added a quatrain which pointed to possible upsets in the chain of command. The prophecy—' He turned towards Downay who read slowly from a notebook.

> 'The one who carried the flag
> Will unseat the great King of Germany
> In one blow, aided by those with the skulls
> Who are dressed in black.'

'One of your amazing predictions, George Thomas. A quatrain now being beamed from an illegal radio station. Our troops are out. They will find this station.'

Well done, Leaderer, thought George. He's got them going—believing it's coming from inside France. 'Michel, as an expert, surely there's not much sense in that quatrain,' he tossed towards Downay. 'Would anyone dare think of the Führer as the great King of Germany? I wouldn't. He is the great Leader. The one Führer. So to whom could the great King refer? King Heinrich I?'

Frühling frowned and puffed out his cheeks. Mouth open, as he caught George's meaning. 'It's one of yours though,' he shot at George. 'It links you directly to them.'

'Yes, it's one of mine.' Now, the final card; the last ace. 'Who knows that you have received this message, Herr Oberstgruppenführer? Several people, I've no doubt. So how do you explain matters to those who come here after Himmler has been assassinated? How do you defend the fact that you allowed me complete freedom? Enough freedom to walk up to the Reichsführer and

murder him? You've read my quatrains. You've got Downay here
—an expert. I am here. Now that you have this evidence, I should
be suspect; detained. Your head will roll anyway, Frühling. It
will roll even sooner if one hair on Himmler's head is damaged.'
He paused, counting three to himself like he always did before
answering a question at school. 'But Himmler's head will not be
damaged. It is an impossibility, isn't it?'

* * *

'You want another drink, George?' Herbie was getting one for
himself and George said, just a small one and was it time to eat?

Half-an-hour or so before the meal would be ready. 'Those
dreams, George? I'm not disbelieving you, but are you sure it
went like that?'

He nodded. Yes. Vivid. The details had stayed with the years.
'They haven't been embellished—not purposely, but with hind-
sight, you understand?'

There was no embroidery, George assured him. 'I know what
you're thinking, Herbie, but I had those dreams; just like that.
Then, in the following year, Heydrich was assassinated in Prague.'

'Rather as you describe in the dream. We're speaking with hind-
sight now, George.'

He took no notice. 'And in 1945, a rather shabby civilian admitted to a British officer that he was Heinrich Himmler. He then
bit on his cyanide capsule and perished. I shouldn't expect you to
believe the dreams took place, there in Wewelsburg, in 1941. But
they were the dreams, and that's how it happened. I can't explain it. Those dreams were the last of the odd experiences.' He
accepted the second drink, pensive. 'However you account for
them—and one shrink has put forward a theory—they gave me
courage; confidence. I was able to play the role with more
panache. To the end that at least one person had faith in what I
was saying.'

Herbie did not smile. The worry was growing in his mind as
they entered the last phases of this, the first part of George
Thomas' story. 'Your ploy didn't work though, did it?'

George smiled thinly. He had not really expected to con them
out of having a go. 'No, they swept it aside like the garbage it
was. Swept it aside and then told me exactly how the job was to
be done.'

44

'You will be disposed of in the general carnage. In many ways it will be glorious. A classic ritual—the bullfight, or an uneven gladiatorial massacre.' Frühling was disconcertingly off-handed. George was reminded of some latter day Nero.

'What if your Gestapo wants to question me about this wireless station? Its location? What did you call it—*Soldatensender Calais?*'

'Then they will have to get a good medium and question you through him. One rap for yes; two for no.' It was not really a smile on his face. Nor particularly evil.

'Your Reichsminister of Propaganda? What of him?' George tried. 'Goebbels has an interest in me. Couldn't he get a little restive if I'm plunged into oblivion?'

Frühling sighed, hunching his shoulders. A mockery to show he was not interested. 'Possibly, but we have right on our side in the person of Oberstgruppenführer Heydrich. I really don't think there will be much trouble.'

Ramilies' voice again, into George's ears from the Abbey— *Most of Heydrich's colleagues, and the officer corps of the SS, don't just dislike him, they hate and fear him. He has a following, of course. Probably the most dangerous man in Germany if we did but know it.*

'No, Thomas,' Frühling still spoke. 'I do not think you have much real talent for the occult. If I'm wrong, then you are at liberty to return and haunt me. At the moment we are busy, preparing for the arrival of the little chicken farmer, Himmler, tomorrow morning. A drama in which you have a part to play. Unhappily, Kuche cannot be allowed to do the job by himself as he so generously offered. Even I am not that stupid.'

George felt his throat go dry. When he spoke there was a hoarse croak at first. He asked if he was allowed to know what would happen.

Frühling gave a small nod. He sat at the table, flanked by Wald and Flachs. Downay stood by the door. He still had his notebook in one hand, the ebony cane in the other.

Frühling performed a little parradiddle on the table with the ends of his fingers. They were beautifully manicured, and he spoke now with a voice so buttery that it reminded George of autumn afternoons, toasting crumpets in front of the gasfire in his rooms at Oxford. He had a great longing to be back in Oxford as he heard Frühling outline the plan.

It would be a classic ambush. The whole operation was entrusted to only a few faithful people, who could be relied upon to keep the faith when it was over. This meant the elimination of certain innocent soldiers. Not ideal, but necessary. The rest, the faithful, would be silent to the grave.

He ticked off the names of those concerned on his fingers. Himself, Streichman, Wald, Flachs, Downay, the two Unterscharführen—the sergeants—who had been present earlier, and George's stepfather, Roubert.

Those ranks who acted as orderlies and servants would be going about their usual duties in the castle. Afterwards, they may well have suspicions, but would be in no position to make trouble. This left the men who had come from Paris—both sets—and the Waffen-SS garrison, numbering some twenty-five men. They could not be allowed to survive and were already detailed to act as the guard of honour for Reichsführer Himmler's arrival.

Frühling sighed again: a man unhappy with the terrible decisions of command. He rose and walked to one of the windows, motioning George to follow him.

'Even from here,' he pointed down into the courtyard, 'you can see that this enclosed triangle of stone can be sealed off. One simply closes the main gate and locks all the doors leading to the yard. This will happen when the Reichsführer's cars enter the main gate. That gate will close. All doors will be locked, except for one. The one at the foot of the great north tower where we met you on your arrival this morning. The Reichsführer will expect to be greeted there.'

George could see the door and the tower to the right. To the left, the long angled buildings rose with one of the two smaller towers visible. It was really starting to get dark now, the light turning the grey walls into an unhealthy black, a brooding and cruel colour.

222

'Imagine,' Frühling gave a small cough as though about to recite an epic poem. 'The guard of honour drawn up just below us here. Standartenführer—Colonel—Streichman and myself standing in the doorway of the north tower waiting for the Reichsführer. The two cars drive in through the main gates. They close. As the cars come to a standstill, the guard of honour presents arms. That will be the signal. Now, can you see the door set in the centre of the west wall?'

George strained forward. He could just make out the entrance.

'That door will suddenly open and two men will appear to propel themselves into the courtyard towards the Reichsführer's car. One will be an SS officer, the other a bedraggled civilian. In fact, they will be pushed—hurled—through that small door which will be immediately closed and locked behind them. Both will be armed, though their weapons will not be loaded. Can you imagine the small consternation this will cause? Yes, well, in this moment of alarm and uncertainty, Streichman and myself will retreat inside the tower, and that door will be locked.' As an aside, dropping his voice, almost confidentially, he added, 'You realise, of course, that it will be Kuche and yourself who will arrive unexpectedly in the courtyard. You will be thrown into the arena by your old friend Michel Downay, and one of the sergeants. They have their orders.'

The courtyard would now contain all those who were to either eliminate one another or be eliminated.

'The killing ground,' George muttered.

'Quite. Who knows what will happen when you are precipitated into the yard? Some fool may try to seize you. Someone may even open fire. Within a few seconds we shall know—and we'll only leave it for a few seconds. You've come up against the MG 34? No doubt you have. An excellent weapon, with a high rate of fire. Most accurate.'

George had come up against the MG 34 all right. First during training—the lectures on enemy weapons: *The MG 34 is a clever weapon: too crafty by half. Treaty of Versailles stopped Jerry making heavy machineguns so they came up with this compromise all-purpose job. Very high rate of fire, six to eight-hundred rounds a minute. Too high for accuracy on the ground.* How they had deluded themselves in the days of the phoney war. During the battle of France the accuracy of the MG 34 had looked pretty good to George; and the heavy ripping noise it made was one of the most unwelcome he had ever known. 'Yes,' he said, 'I've come up against the *Maschinengewehr 34*.'

Frühling hardly paused for breath. There would be three MG 34s. One mounted on the battlements just below the north tower, and operated by Wald. He would deal with the first car, presumably the Reichsführer. He would also most probably deal with George and Kuche at the same time. Flachs would have the second gun, mounted on the battlements just below the tower they could see from the window—to the left. He would open up at the guard of honour and the second car. Roubert was to be situated below the other small tower, out of sight from the window at which they stood, but to their extreme left. He would have a roving commission. 'He is the general cleaner. Three MG 34s all pouring fire into the courtyard should deal with any living thing in a very short space of time.'

George asked how he was going to explain slaughter on that scale.

'We have a way, Thomas. It will not concern you, because you will be part of the debris.' He shrugged. 'Perhaps, when you opened fire at the car, or Kuche opened fire at you—or the car whichever way we tell it—some dunderhead gave the order to shoot. Panic does strange things. Causes accidents. Leads to tragedy. Panic breeds panic. Don't worry your head about it. Now,' his hand descended on George's shoulder in an almost fatherly fashion, 'there is still the last chance that only Kuche will emerge from that little door. It depends on you. Have a talk with Wald and Flachs. Cooperation sometimes works miracles. Talk.'

His grip tightened and then the hand was removed. He turned away and walked stiffly to the door, followed out by Michel Downay, knuckles white on the head of his ebony cane. Downay looked hard at George as he left, the eyes dead of any feeling, all sparkle gone and no trace of hatred in its place. Oddly they seemed almost defeated eyes.

Wald and Flachs started off lightly, as they had done before. Their questions were simple, some of them the same as they had been earlier. Operational organisation, names, training establishments, airfields from which agents might be dispatched. It was straight question and answer stuff now, as though they wanted confirmation about what they had already told George they knew. Added to all this, there were new queries—how a propaganda radio could be run from within occupied France? What were the lines of communication? What further arrangements were in the pipeline? Again they wanted names.

George said he did not know and, if he did, he would not tell them. In any case it could help neither his cause, nor theirs. Tomorrow was a good day for the Reichsführer Himmler. The stars and the prophecies were clear. Tomorrow would be a day of disaster for them.

'I suppose you can give us an accurate weather forecast as well?' gibed Wald at one point.

Cloud had been gathering. George had seen it in the gloom, standing by the window with Frühling. Tomorrow, he said, it would rain.

Then, he thought, one last try. One final gambit—this time entirely from his own imagination. George looked hard at Flachs, whom he now certainly considered the weakest link.

'In the triple castle where lurk the cunning ones,
A triangle becomes wet with rain following thunder.
The blood of the deceivers will mingle with the rain.
He, who was to be overthrown, will triumph.'

'Keep your predictions for the next world, Thomas.' As he said it, Wald struck George across the mouth with the back of his hand. It was the start of a painful night.

45

The steak and kidney pie was excellent. 'If you ever go private you could be a chef, Herbie,' George said.

'If I ever go private I won't need to do another day's work in my life,' Herbie grunted. Then, 'Bad that night at Wewelsburg, was it?'

George said that the memory does not carry pain with any clarity, but yes, it was bad. Herbie nodded, he had been on both sides of interrogations—soft and hard. It was a good job that the memory did not carry pain, though physical pain, he thought, was infinitely preferable to the mental variety. He had used it and seen it used. It held more terror than the ancient instruments of torture.

George remembered the night in retrospect as a horrible dream. 'The worst of Bosch put into action.' Some parts were more unpleasant than others. Wald beating him in the kidneys with his fist; Flachs doing indescribable things to his feet and hands; Wald telling Flachs to go easy because the patient had to be able to walk in the morning.

'If I allow myself to think about it, I can taste the blood and tears.'

'But you got through?'

Yes, said George, he got through with the help of Angelle. Through it all, he centred his mind on her. 'She cried all the time, and I tried to think it was for me and the anguish. The thought of another human being, the hope for them, the chance that you may see them again, can take away a great deal. Angelle got me through because she was there—miles away.'

Herbie became a little embarrassed as George continued. Talking about that night of physical torture seemed to unleash flood gates, things recalled, pent up inside him for years.

'They threw water over me at one point, and gave me raw spirit to drink, to revive me for another dose of the same questioning. Angelle's face was there all the time, floating above me. I found that my memory of her was tactile. I could feel her flesh on mine, the smoothness of her skin and the taste of her nipples mixed with the blood; the taste of her mouth on mine mingled with the salt of my tears. My cries became a joint cry. Herbie, I fashioned my loins on her; her cheek against mine, her hair in my eyes. The pain was her pain also.'

Herbie coughed. Some cheese; perhaps he would like some cheese. Yes, cheese would be good.

'You told them nothing?'

'I stuck with the part, the role. I knew nothing except the most important thing, and they wouldn't believe that. Tomorrow their plot would fail and they would all lie dead, with Himmler gloating at his victory. I think I did honestly believe it by then. Living the cover. I told them that failed assassins were not qualified for other work.'

He described how the thunder came; and the lightning. How he heard the rain hitting the windows, and how, finally, the two men left him alone. 'One great ache and throb on the bed. I felt like a bloody great carbuncle.'

'I get the coffee.' Herbie reflected that he seemed to be saying that all the time. But his job was to listen not comment. He had to listen very hard. 'You slept?' he asked.

George didn't know if it was sleep, or a loss of consciousness following the torture. 'It was a gentle shaking of my shoulder that brought me round. Then a voice calling my name, down the long, wrong end of a tunnel.'

'It was time?'

'No. It was Flachs.'

46

George blinked, narrowing his eyes against the light as he woke. The thin face of Sturmbannführer Flachs came into focus. He was looking down at George, kneeling by the bed, eyes constantly shifting between George and the door. He spoke quietly, almost a whisper—

'Thomas. Herr Thomas. There is one thing I must know. Please wake. We are alone. I must ask you ...'

George croaked something that was neither pleasant nor anatomically possible.

Flachs insisted. 'You have impressed me. Greatly, Herr Thomas. I swear before God this is not a trick. It is raining. Pouring with rain. I must speak with you.'

George turned his head towards the German, squinting at him painfully through swollen eyes.

'My mother,' he began. 'My mother was an occultist. She knew much about the stars, about astrology. I know a little. I learned a little from her. This is a bad period for me. My horoscope. This is a time during which I have to take great care. I must know. Are you really what you say?'

George fumbled with the pain which even invaded his mind. He told the Sturmbannführer, through broken teeth and with a tongue which felt too large for his mouth, that of course he was what he claimed. 'Don't be a fool. Would I have done what I have? Flachs, I have access to the keys: to the future.' Pain ballooned in his head now he was almost fully conscious. 'Himmler will not die. His assassins will. It is written ...' It was like a dream; Flachs seemed to be sliding away from him. He could hear the rain beating hard against the window, and then inside his head. Rain and darkness. Oblivion once more.

The next time they woke him was a much rougher business: a pair of men hauling him to his feet and pouring scalding coffee down his throat. He ached all over and had great difficulty mov-

228

ing. The two men were there to see that he could move, marching him slowly up and down the room, then faster until he could walk and move after a fashion. Then Wald was in the room with one of the sergeants. Of Flachs there was no sign: George recalled him in the night only as part of a dream. The two men who had been walking him, left the room.

'It will soon be time.' Wald unsmiling, correct, serious. 'And you were correct, it is raining. Hard. The rain followed the thunder.' He looked at his watch. Less than one hour to go. He told George to sit on the bed.

'If you have a God,' croaked George, 'I trust you've made your peace with him.'

Wald took no notice; instead, he went over it all again: painstakingly, slowly. Very soon he would be manning the machine-gun on the battlements below the north tower. Already Flachs and Roubert were preparing their weapons. He added small technical details, saying the weapons would be mounted on the big solid tripods, to make certain the firepower was spread evenly over the courtyard. 'It will be a wet business.'

George said yes, they would get wet. 'All of you will be soaked: in your own blood.'

Wald smiled, said something to the sergeant and left.

The sergeant pulled George to his feet and continued the therapy, walking him up and down, trying to ease the muscles. Any sense of time had long gone, though the facts and circumstances now began to eat their way into George's mind. The charade in which he had shrouded himself was beginning to crack, so he tried to push reality away, centring his thoughts on Angelle.

Then Downay came in. He did not carry his ebony cane, but a heavier stick with a bulbous knobbed end to it, and was dressed in drab overalls with SS insignia on the lapels. At his hip, on the left side, hung a leather holster, unclasped to reveal the butt of a Luger pistol. The eyes were as dead as they had been on the previous evening, and when he spoke there was none of the old charm.

'Time, George. I'm sorry.' He did not sound it.

For a second, George felt panic and wanted to scream. He did try a lame attempt at handing off Michel, but the sergeant stepped up and put an arm lock on, sending a blaze of pain through him. ('Like knives cutting all over my back.')

He went quietly after that, along deserted passages, down three flights of steps. Finally into a corridor where Heinrich Kuche stood meekly with the other sergeant. Both the NCOs had their Erma machinepistols in the crook of their arms, fingers on the triggers and with the business ends directed at George and Kuche. In front of them was the small door, pointed out on the previous night by Frühling. Outside the door lay the courtyard, the three-cornered killing ground.

Kuche tried to smile. There were bruises on his face, one eye completely closed; the lips were puffed and the nose seemed to have been squeezed into a monkey wrench and then twisted. One shoulder was higher than the other, as though out of joint.

'They have a wet morning for it,' he mumbled, and George said it didn't matter about the weather. Then, raising his voice as high as it would go, 'The poor buggers don't know what's going to hit them.'

Kuche gave him a look which said—if there's any chance, whatever, we'll have to take it.

They stood together, silent in the empty corridor which was so narrow that people had to turn sideways in order to pass one another. Inevitably, George wondered if this was the way the Christian slaves felt, waiting to go out into the ring against the lions or gladiators, to certain death in the sun and sand. For himself and Kuche, it would only be rain and cobbles.

There was a small, glazed Judas squint in the narrow door which was to be their exit. Downay moved towards it, peering through. 'The Reichsführer was reported to be on time.' He turned back. 'The guard of honour is moving into position now, so your time of waiting will soon be over.' He nodded towards the wall behind them. 'There are a couple of quite useless machinepistols. We shall put them into your hands before pushing you out. Don't struggle or I shall see you destroyed here, on the spot, and to hell with Frühling and his plans.' The left hand hovered over his holster. George saw the two Ermas, minus magazines, leaning against the wall.

Looking towards the door, Downay stood to the right with one of the sergeants beside him; Kuche was between them, turned slightly to the right so that his shoulder—the good one—almost touched the sergeant's chest. George stood next to him, facing the door. The other sergeant was on his left. They were all very tightly bunched together, and George could see that the sergeant on his left had been forced, by lack of space, to lower the muzzle of his machinepistol. He looked relaxed, as though trying to let his muscles go in order to relieve the tension.

George tried to nudge Kuche, signalling desperately with his eyes that if they were to do anything it had to be now—and fast. Psychologically it was the perfect moment. The only moment.

From the courtyard there came the sound of a military command, and Downay leaned forward, slightly off-balance, to look through the Judas squint.

'The guard of honour is preparing to welcome ...'

Kuche moved, with a speed and aggression almost unbelievable in a man so badly beaten. Downay did not even finish the sentence.

'The other one.' Kuche shouted at George, his good arm moving forward, and then back with great force, slamming the elbow low into the sergeant's stomach. At the same time, Kuche seemed to turn and move his feet, kicking hard, so that the sergeant—already doubling over in agony—had his legs pushed from under him.

With his other foot, Kuche must have hooked Downay off balance. The last picture George had, as he moved into action, was of the sergeant and Downay both going down, while Kuche's hand moved towards Downay's holster.

The sergeant on George's left, reacted slowly, the muzzle of his Erma coming up a fraction late. George turned, moving in close, trapping the barrel of the weapon between arm and right side, still turning in the enclosed space so that any shots the man might loose off would be well clear of the others.

For the few seconds it took, George forgot the aching muscles and stiffness, bringing his knee up in the classic blow. It felt most unpleasant and the sergeant screamed with pain. George brought the knee down and the heel of his shoe on to the sergeant's ankle, equally hard—then up again to the groin: the double whammie.

The sergeant's face contorted with pain. George repeated the action. By the time his foot caught the man's ankle for the second time, the sergeant was doubling forward, so that George's knee rose and connected with his face. At that point the sergeant dropped his Erma machinepistol.

The shot came from behind George.

Kuche's sergeant was dead. George could tell, because there was very little of the man's face left. Kuche had fired with Downay's Luger, then turned to cover the Frenchman who was still on the ground, half-propped against the wall, cursing.

Almost casually, Kuche leaned forward and hit him very hard with the side of the pistol. Downay gave a small grunt and rolled on to his back.

Behind George, the sergeant groaned. Taking his cue from Kuche, George hit the man on the back of the neck with the wooden butt of the Erma.

There was silence which seemed to go for a long time. Kuche disentangled the dead sergeant from his Erma, checked it and moved to the door. George checked the weapon he had taken. The magazine was in place, it was cocked and on safety. From outside came the sound of vehicles entering the courtyard.

They both leaned against the wall, one on either side of the door, breathing heavily. George asked Kuche if he knew the situation—if they had told him the plan? He nodded, panting.

George indicated the door. 'Himmler's two cars should be just ahead of us ... the guard of honour behind them ... Up to the left, Wald is on the battlements ...'

'MG ... 34 ...' gasped Kuche, nodding hard.

'And two more ... Flachs directly to our right ... then my bloody stepfather across the courtyard, slightly right, below the tower ... Frühling and Streichman at the north tower doorway ... but not for long ...'

Rain splattered against the outside of the door, making them both start. Then, floating with the rain, the command in German for the guard of honour to present arms.

Kuche's breath was under control. 'Keep in the angle of the doorway. I'll try to get to the Reichsführer's car. You cover me— have a go at the others. Keep their heads down. I'll give what fire I can.' He chuckled, a two-syllable laugh. 'Ironic, George. It's up to us to save Himmler's life in order to keep our own skins.'

Another laugh and he raised a foot against the door. George grasped the large ring of the latch. For a moment they hesitated. Then Kuche dropped his leg and whispered, 'Hold on.'

Outside came the sound of rifles being slapped, mingling with the rain like the sound of wet sheets flapping on a line. George thought—that's it; we've both lost our nerve and it's going to

232

end. The MG 34s will open up and it'll be blood and rain.

But Kuche had paused only to reach down and drag a pair of spare magazines from inside the dead sergeant's battle jacket. He tossed one to George, then nodded. George turned the ring on the door and Kuche hit it with his foot. The door banged open, rain spraying in on their faces as though they were being drenched with garden hoses.

The blur of rain; an overpowering sense of being hemmed in within the triangle of walls; the pair of Mercedes cars pulled up behind one another; a glimpse of the guard in two ranks, stolid with rifles at the present.

George crouched, turning to his left and lifting the machine-pistol towards the point where Wald should be, below the tower. As he did so, there was a slight movement in the doorway of the north tower—Frühling and Streichman, like little dummies in a weather-house. He was also conscious of a uniformed figure hurriedly opening the rear door of the first Merc, his head down and collar up against the driving rain.

'Go.' Kuche shouted. 'For Christ's sake, go.'

George squeezed the trigger, letting off two quick bursts. Chips of stone flew from the battlement, and, as he looked, there was movement—Wald further along the battlement than he had expected. He swivelled and fired another burst, peering through the rain to check accuracy.

Through the concentration, he was aware of Kuche's foot-steps as the German ran out towards the first car; and of his yelling—'Reichsführer, get down ... down, they're trying to kill you ... down ... Reichsführer ...'

George fired another burst and began to turn, ready to rake the other two firing points. But Kuche was ahead of him. As he ran towards the car, he fired twice, from the hip: fast, turning and weaving as he went—short bursts in the general direction of where the other machineguns should be.

Then there were other shots—twice from George's left. He saw Kuche spin like a top, wavering and then falling as he went. In the north tower doorway, Frühling had a pistol in his hand and did not just stop at two shots; he moved his arm towards George.

George dropped the muzzle of the Erma and held on to the trigger. It did not matter any more about Wald, Flachs and his bastard stepfather, Roubert. It did not matter about Kuche, Angelle, Maman or even himself. He just squeezed the trigger and went on squeezing, in a way horrified at what was happening in the doorway—the two figures of Frühling and Streichman floating off their feet, enveloped in a spray of blood. He thought of ping-pong balls on a fairground shooting gallery, and the fact that killing by bullets was a messy business because blood does not seep or spurt; it jets.

Finally, the breech of the Erma clicked upon nothing. He unclipped the empty magazine, replaced it with the one Kuche had tossed to him; recocked the weapon, and went forward into the rain.

Kuche had nearly reached the car. Now he lay sprawled in the wet—the classic pose, with one hand reaching forward as though trying to claw the Reichsführer out of the car.

The guard of honour had not even reacted. It all happened so quickly. The officer by the car door was dropping to his knees, as if to crawl under the vehicle. George could just glimpse a figure within the car, immediately recognisable, his face registering bewilderment, the cap askew, but the metal-framed spectacles firmly in place.

George shouted towards him, just as Kuche had done. Yelling and running, knowing that he probably would never make it; feet slipping on the soaked cobbles, giving one burst with the Erma, to the right; then two to the left.

At that moment, Wald opened up with his MG 34, the bullets cleaving down too low, first ripping at the cobbles, then, as he elevated the weapon, striking the bonnet of the Mercedes, tearing at the metal.

Still running, George pointed the Erma in the direction of Wald's emplacement and started firing. All he could feel and hear was the rain, but he must have hit Wald then, for the MG 34 stopped, the final burst scything the bonnet in front of the windshield.

A last dive, and George flung himself through the car door, landing on top of the Reichsführer, still shouting that this was a plot to kill him. He was shouting in French and German alternately. It was like landing on a sack of dough.

Just as he got into the car, George called to the driver, telling him to get the thing into the safety of the main gateway. Impossible, of course. The engine was wrecked and the driver had no chest left. Wald's handiwork had ricochetted from the engine and through the dashboard. It was a miracle that Himmler himself was still alive.

Then the other pair of MG 34s opened up.

*   *   *

Herbie Kruger was engrossed. George talked fast, animated by the memories. Go on, Herbie urged him—like Kuche in the doorway.

More coffee, George swallowed, saying his throat was as dry as it had been on that morning at Wewelsburg.

After two to three gulps, he continued—

The other pair of MG 34s opened fire.

47

It took a moment for George to realise that none of the fire from the machineguns was coming down into the courtyard. The rip of the weapons was unmistakable behind the still-present hiss of rain, but the hail of expected bullets did not follow.

There were other sounds now. Running feet, heavy boots on the cobbles, shouts and, close in George's ear, a cold quiet voice telling him to get away. As he spoke, Himmler pushed at George, one neatly-manicured hand grasping his shoulder. He raised his head and saw the face, a mixture of surprise and disgust. The cheeks were puffy and the grey-blue eyes behind the spectacles appeared to be full of loathing: as though George was some unpleasant piece of human dirt which had to be removed before it could contaminate.

It made George's flesh creep, and he rolled away quickly. Outside the car, some of the guard of honour had closed in, using the vehicle as cover, in a protective capacity. They were looking up and away, past the second car, to where the machinegun fire was constant.

It was now plain why no bullets were reaping the harvest in the courtyard. The two gunners—Roubert and Sturmbannführer Flachs were engaged in a duel of their own, between the serrated battlements, below the two smaller base towers.

The bursts of fire were irregular, short and long; alternately, then together; both men's concentration drawn away from what was happening below them by some necessity to deal with the personal threat they created to each other.

Himmler's entourage, from the second car, had come out into the rain. Two officers ran towards the Reichsführer's car, while a third made for the small knot of men kneeling and bending over Kuche.

From where George lay, beside the car, he could see Kuche's face, grey, the lips moving, like someone making a deathbed confession. The officer nodded and spoke to the men around him, who lifted Kuche gently, carrying him back towards the doorway. The officer then came, at the run, towards Himmler's car, almost kicking George out of the way, speaking rapidly as he leaned in.

The fire from the MG 34s was still constant. Burst after burst, discordant, a strange beat and counterbeat, heavy and lethal, reverberating down into the canyon of the courtyard.

George turned towards the car, thinking—everyone's soaking wet except bloody Himmler. Then he heard what the officer was telling the Reichsführer.

Himmler sat bolt upright in the wreck of his car. He did not look dazed, bewildered or frightened any more. He looked very angry, as a child might look if some treat had suddenly been pitched from its grasp, or a beloved toy broken wilfully.

The officer—a short, greying, elderly man who looked more like a schoolmaster than SS—was passing on what Kuche had said. With relief, George realised that the German had told the most obvious tale—that he had discovered a wholesale plot to assassinate the Reichsführer; that he had confided in Georges Thomas, the Frenchman, because Thomas' confederate from the Sorbonne—Michel Downay—was heavily involved in the intrigue. They had tried to stop the whole business. It was also plain that Kuche was not badly hurt.

Himmler remained impassive as he listened, his eyes cold and weak, jaw moving slightly, the eyes flicking between his aide and George; occasionally distracted by the duelling machineguns. At last, he gave two blunt orders, nodded a curt, 'Danke' to George, and began to get out of the car.

Over by the door of the north tower they were clearing up the remains of Frühling and Streichman. The Reichsführer turned towards the battlements as the machinegun fire became more concentrated, and then walked slowly in the direction of the north tower.

George glanced towards the doorway which had been marked out as his private pass-gate to the next world. They had put Kuche down on the cobbles in the relative shelter of the wall, and were seeing to his wounds. Just as he took a first step towards Kuche, George caught a sudden movement in the doorway. Michel Downay, propped up by the sergeant who George had knocked

237

cold, stood there, both hands grasping an Erma machinepistol. He had a clear field of fire towards Himmler and the weapon was pointed directly at the plodding figure.

It went through George's mind that nothing was going to happen. They had only left the two useless Ermas in the corridor. But he should take no chances. With the courage of one who knows he is quite safe, George made a final effort and ran, placing himself between Himmler and Downay, squeezing the trigger of his own Erma as he moved.

There could only have been a few rounds left in the magazine, so he was lucky. They sprayed directly across Downay and the sergeant, catching both in the chest. The sergeant slithered away, and Downay went over backwards as if someone had caught him full tilt with a lance. As his heels lifted from the ground, the muscles of his right hand must have tightened around the grip of the trigger. There must have been at least one more spare magazine lying around in the corridor. The muzzle was pointing too high for any damage to be done, except to brickwork and the upper part of the doorway. There was just the one long burst, arcing upwards, and then, as Downay landed on his back, spraying around the corridor until the magazine was empty and he stopped twitching.

As the echoes died away, George saw that people were running for cover. Even the Reichsführer had broken into a trot. Above them the two MG 34s kept up their clattering dialogue, but Downay's last attempt seemed to have injected a new urgency into the situation.

George ran towards the door and had to hold back as they carried Kuche through. Kuche smiled weakly. His leg appeared to have been mangled by Frühling's bullets, but they had put a dressing on it, and a tight bandage, already blood-soaked.

Pausing inside the doorway, George peered out to the right where the machinegun duel still continued. As he watched, there was a final rattle of fire, both weapons sounding as if they were hammering towards the end of a deadly symphonic orchestration. Then the gun on the far side of the courtyard—Roubert's—stopped. It was like a voice being cut off in mid-sentence, a line suddenly going dead. The other weapon continued to fire, a long long stream of bullets chipping away around the castellated stonework.

Through the rain, George could see a grey shape slumped sideways, a white splodge which could have been a face, lolling back, the whole thing caught on the tripod mounting of the gun. So George lost his stepfather.

He craned around the door to see if he could glimpse Flachs, and saw the man standing, leaning out between two of the great teeth-like battlements. He had spotted George and was waving, swaying and waving, his mouth moving as though shouting something which was carried away with the wind and rain.

For a good minute he stood there, against the dark, bruised and sponged sky, and his wave seemed to carry a message—*You were right, Herr Thomas. Today was the day of victory for the Reichsführer, and disaster for those who planned treason.*

Then, suddenly, his arm dropped and his lips stopped moving, his head drooping on to his chest. The whole body sagged, and slumped forward on to the space between the battlements, where it rocked twice before toppling over, turning full circle in the air before landing in a huddle of arms and legs on the cobbles. Blood immediately began to spread from it, gushing out to join the puddles of rain. The blood and water were now the only things that moved within the triangle of stone.

48

'You think you finally convinced Flachs, then?' Herbie shook himself from the mental picture, described so vividly by George.

Who knew? George spread his hands. Perhaps he had convinced him, as he had convinced himself at one point. Maybe Flachs went to his place that morning with the intention of knocking out Wald and Roubert. Maybe he got cold feet when things went wrong for them.

'And you were asked to explain yourself?'

Not for a while, George told him. He had collapsed and remained unconscious for a couple of days. They nursed him, and one of Himmler's people—Gestapo as well—came to do the interrogation: mainly to verify Kuche's story, and the names of those involved. 'Interesting, Heydrich was never mentioned.'

'You didn't see Himmler again?'

Not then, but George had received a message of thanks from him. He had returned to Berlin and felt that he had work for a man like George. Work of national importance. 'I said that I thought the Ministry of Propaganda wanted me, but they said the Reichsführer was putting in a special request. There was also talk of my being decorated.'

'And Kuche?'

'Eventually came to see me. Nasty flesh wound, in his thigh. Soon mended. We were both posted together; to the same organisation.'

'Yes,' Herbie tapped his nose. He had read the file and knew that both Georges Thomas—the French Georges—and Heinrich Kuche had, indeed, gone together. To Berlin where they were sent to the building in the Wilhelmstrasse: to the headquarters of Amp VI, the Ausland-SA: the SS Secret Service Abroad. 'You became a spy, George, Right?' Giving him a flash of the big stupid grin.

'Right.' George laughed. Yes, they had put Kuche and himself straight into the heart of things. The plan was to play George back into France with Kuche as his controller. 'It was splendid. Kuche said we'd have cover for life.'

'You got to Berlin, when?' Herbie was oddly serious: very concentrated now.

Around the middle of April, George said. The Ausland-SD was undergoing a transformation. Heinz Jost, who had directed the service since 1939, was in the process of handing over to Walter Schellenberg.

'Who did not take over until June,' Herbie interrupted him.

True, but he was there. 'Running himself in. Kuche and myself went with the Reichsführer's special blessing. We were small legends.'

Herbie said that George did not go back into France: saying it; not asking.

No, George agreed. That was the idea. He worked close to Kuche. They thought they had accomplished a first-class penetration.

'You worked with Kuche. Did you play together also?'

Drank together, yes.

'Whored together?' Herbie asked.

It was not a question of whoring. Reluctantly, George told him there were women, yes. Plenty of women—the grey mice, the uniformed secretaries. Everyone was making the best of things. They'd had it good until then. Only then, after Barbarossa—the invasion of Russia—did things get really bad, but the RAF had started bombing. Unpleasant.

'And you didn't go back into France,' Herbie repeated.

No. Something came up suddenly. 'But you know all about it, Herbie.'

Herbie said he knew the bare bones, like he had known about Stellar. 'Not all.'

George nodded and said there was not much more to tell. Really the main details were on file. Not much to add.

Herbie pushed. '*Wermut* came up, yes?'

'*Wermut*, yes. Operation Wormwood.'

'That was what we would now call an ad lib operation, yes?' Herbie moved his huge frame in the chair, which creaked under him. 'An operation mounted quickly because of sudden and unexpected circumstances.'

George said that was right. It was organised and put into effect very fast. 'It had to be. Three days.' For him it began suddenly on the morning of Monday, May 12th, 1941. They sent for him and said he was needed for special training.

'Who did you see?' Herbie had to do this as an interrogation routine.

'One of the adjutants. One of Jost's adjutants.'

'You didn't see Kuche?'

'Kuche? No. Not then. Later, when they had the team together.'

'It was early in the morning on Monday, May 12th?'

'They telephoned me. Early, yes. I went into the Wilhelmstrasse building and one of the adjutants gave me the orders. There was a car waiting. They took me to an airfield outside Berlin, gave me an hour's instruction on the ground, then took me up in a Ju 52 and made me do a parachute jump. Then we hung around until dark. Bit of weapon work. On the range. After dark I did another jump.'

'Then back to Berlin?'

'Yes.'

'To meet the others concerned in Wormwood?'

Agreed.

'You must remember it well. Name the others, George.'

'You know already. Myself and Kuche. A captain called Fenderman, and another major—von Tupfel. They were professionals, those two. Young ex-hoods who'd made a place for themselves in the SS. Tough as they come.'

'All English speakers?'

George said they had to be, and Herbie asked if there was anything special about them. 'Anything, however small.'

'They were fed up. Both called back from leave. I think one of them came back from his honeymoon.'

Herbie asked which one. Fenderman, George thought, but he couldn't be sure. 'It was a very busy time.'

'Before I get tea, George, tell me how they broke the news to you: told you the scope of the operation.'

They had been taken into one of the offices on the second floor. There was coffee. Sandwiches. Then Jost came in with Schellenberg and three or four staff officers. The four men were officially introduced to each other. 'Kuche and myself excluded, of course, having been together for so long.' Then they were cautioned that what they were to hear was of the utmost secrecy. George paused as though he had said enough.

'What was so secret, George? Come on. Pretend I know nothing.'

'It was a bombshell.' George appeared to have tightened up. Even he had been shaken by the news. Rudolf Hess, they were told, had flown off on a private peace initiative to England. Rudolf Hess, the Deputy Führer himself; an old Party member, trusted friend of Hitler, had got into a twin-engined Messerschmitt 110 on Saturday night and flown to England with no authority.

The briefing officers feared that Hess was mad. The orders came directly from Hitler himself. The four-man team was to be dropped by parachute as soon as they had proper information regarding Hess' whereabouts. Their job was to execute him.

'Why?' Herbie spoke quietly.

'Well, we all know now, don't we? Hess knew as much as anyone about the plans for the invasion of Russia—Barbarossa. He had tried to make the trip a couple of times before, but aborted. The official line was that he had a brainstorm. He was convinced that, if he could speak with the king, together they might persuade Churchill to turn against Russia and save Europe from Communism. You know it all, Herbie.'

'Were they shocked—the briefing people?' Herbie was not to be sidetracked.

'Shaken, yes. But determined. At all costs we were to get to Hess and kill him.'

'Before he talked.'

'I suppose so.'

'I get the tea,' Herbie rose, then paused. 'Why you, George? Why did they send you?'

'I suppose that I had worked with Kuche before; I was an English speaker as well as French. They still regarded me as a Frenchman.'

'That's no reason.'

George agreed. He knew that and had thought about it often. 'Perhaps because I was mixed up with the astrology. It was mentioned. There were those who believed that Hess was motivated by his horoscope and by the occult. Rubbish, of course, but I believe they thought I might come in useful if we could interrogate the Deputy Führer before burning him.'

'That was in the briefing?'

'The first object was to locate and kill. If circumstances permitted, we were to interrogate him before death. Find out if he had talked.'

Nobody knows, thought Herbie as he switched on the electric kettle. Poor strange Rudolf Hess who spent the rest of the war in prison, was tried with the other war criminals at Nuremberg and had remained a prisoner—at the insistence of the Russians—ever since. And nobody really knows. All that was on record were the outside facts—that the Deputy Führer had flown the nine hundred miles over the North Sea alone, parachuted from his aircraft over Renfrewshire and was first picked up by a ploughman. Hess gave his name as Horn and told the authorities that he wished to go to Dungavel House as he had an urgent message for the Duke of Hamilton.

When the red tape was unravelled he was later taken to England, on a special coach of the Glasgow-London night mail. Nobody knew if he had disclosed any details of the High Command's plans for the Russian invasion.

To the duke he said that he was on a mission of humanity; that Hitler wanted no war with Britain. Churchill did warn Stalin, several times, of the imminent threat to his country. Stalin appeared to take no notice, and the Russians were not prepared when the onslaught burst upon them. Whether Churchill's intelligence came directly from Hess or not was another matter.

'There were reprisals against the German occult community,' Herbie stated as he carried the tea tray from the kitchen.

George grunted an affirmative. '*Aktion Hess*,' he nodded. 'Happened a month later. Purge of the astrologers. Orders issued by Bormann. Astrologers, faith-healers, fortune-tellers, clairvoyants, graphologists. Even Christian Scientists. Face-saving action. Like the Jews, the astrologers became scapegoats, accused of having driven Hess out of his mind.'

Herbie paused as he poured the tea. 'Lucky they put you on *Wermut*.'

'Very. I've always been aware of that.'

Herbie said they already knew about Kuche, what did the other two look like? George was vague. He recalled Fenderman as tall, light-haired ('He seemed preoccupied: self-contained.'); the other one was a big bloke—'Cropped head, bullish sort of man. Didn't speak much.'

'Cover?' Herbie asked.

'Amazing cover. Plainclothes police. We had a series of warrant cards—Metropolitan Police, Special Branch; three or four sets of Scottish cards. They knew, then, on the Monday night, that Hess was in Scotland.'

'Contacts?'

'Telephone numbers. London, Carlisle, Manchester, Glasgow.'

'They briefed you completely, then and there?'

'More or less. We would be dropped, under cover of an air raid. Civilian clothes under flying suits. Weapons—pistols, two machinepistols, grenades, explosives. If we were spot on the DZ we could walk to a telephone and get the latest information. They said a car would be arranged. The rest we would play off the cuff.'

'You went from Berlin?'

'No. We went that night—well, the early hours—to France. I never knew the place. There wasn't time. Somewhere in the north. Bomber station—HE 111s. Got there on the Tuesday afternoon. Left the following night. The Wednesday. About seven-thirty. Christ, we were in Manchester by midnight.'

'You had a chance to speak with Kuche?'

George said yes and that they had formulated a plan. Kuche felt they should put a block on the operation very quickly. 'After all, we had the telephone contacts and the passwords. We felt they could be traced and picked up by the local constabularies.'

'That what happened?'

'Sort of. Bloody thing went wrong though, didn't it?'

'Kuche was in charge?'

'Very much so.'

'How then did it go wrong, George?'

49

They travelled in a stripped-down Heinkel 111. No armament and only a pilot and navigator for company. The DZ was just inland from Southport. A long trip, cutting across the Western toe of England and up the Irish sea. Information had not been confirmed. Some reports still had Hess in Scotland, others that he was already in the south. The final decision to drop near Southport had been a compromise. There were good contacts in the area.

The aircraft was boxed in to a stream which split for a pair of different targets, Liverpool and Manchester. George sat next to Kuche, bundled into flying gear, conscious of the amount of weaponry he carried, and even more conscious of the two other men—Fenderman and von Tupfel—sitting across the fuselage from them.

Occasionally the navigator came back to let them know where they were. There was half-an-hour's warning before they made the final landfall.

Kuche went forward and then called for George. Looking ahead through the big plexiglass nose, they could see the fairy-lights and fireworks which denoted death in the air and on the ground. George had a strange feeling of detachment, as though none of this could hurt him. After all, he was going home. He was not even afraid of the jump any more, though the two he had done at the airfield near Berlin had scared him witless, particularly the night jump.

When it came to it, the whole thing was simple. The sensation of diving into a cold bath, the aircraft noise disappearing, changing into the close thrum of unsynchronised engines, then the gentle pull of the harness followed by the drifting sensation. He glimpsed fires and saw flares, ahead and to his right. Then the blackness came and he craned his eyes downwards, trying to distinguish the ground from the darkness.

He only saw it at the last moment, bending his knees and

spilling the air out of his parachute by pulling on the webbing. Then the jolt as he hit, knocking the breath from him, the canopy collapsing around him.

He was on grass, and details slowly began to emerge from the blackness as his eyes adjusted. Another figure, moving within a hundred yards. George called softly and got an answering whistle.

It was Fenderman and they were in a field bordered by low stone walls and bushes. The parachutes they buried in the bushes, both keeping ears cocked for the other pair.

Fenderman took a compass bearing, shielding his torch with one hand as they examined the map which George carried. If they were correct it was barely half a mile to the rendezvous, across another field which would take them to the main Southport-Manchester road.

George loosened the warm flying gear and they both unzipped the suits, opened the cases, which had been hung by webbing from their legs, and took out their overcoats and hats. They redistributed the arms and George made certain his Luger pistol was cocked and on safety, stuck into the pocket of his overcoat. He kept his hand on the butt all the time, once they had buried the flying gear with the parachutes and started to trudge over the short grass. Fenderman was a walking bomb, carrying explosives and grenades strapped to his body.

There was the smell of sea not far away; of earth and damp grass. It was the smell of England again.

When they reached the road, the other two figures rose from the verge, like spectres, and came towards them. Passwords again, then Kuche motioning them to walk in pairs, taking the road that should bring them near to the village where they would connect with a telephone booth.

It was almost nine-forty-five on the night of Wednesday, May 14th. They made the telephone by quarter-past ten. Military and civilian traffic—mainly military—passed them without stopping, and Kuche made the call.

'There'll be a car waiting outside a public house, half a mile along the road. A Morris.' He gave them the number, and said they were to approach the driver and say they were the officers from Manchester CID. The driver would get out and give them the keys. 'The target's being held in Buchanan Castle: military hospital, eighteen miles the other side of Glasgow. Near Loch

Lomond. Long drive.' He motioned Fenderman and von Tupfel to go on ahead, and fell into step with George. 'Let them get drowsy,' he muttered. 'You volunteer to drive. Other side of Manchester we'll stop in some quiet spot and take them. I don't want them getting anywhere near Hess.'

George agreed. The sooner they got it over the better, but it had to be quick and a surprise. Between them, Fenderman and von Tupfel carried most of the explosives and both the machine-pistols.

It went like clockwork to start with. The car was there. The only one outside the darkened public house, and the driver asked no questions, just handed over the keys to the battered old Morris saloon and disappeared behind the building. There was a full tank of petrol, and nobody complained when George offered to drive. They checked the maps and Kuche suggested that they rest. 'When you get tired, wake one of us and we'll take over. And for God's sake remember the blackout restrictions and drive on the left side of the road.'

The matt black discs which covered the headlights of the car, threw only a minute, downward beam on the road, making George drive with care and great concentration. He had memorised the route. Even so, there were times when he had to stop and check their position. By midnight they were through the outskirts of Manchester. By half-past he had set the car to climb north, finding it easier now that his eyes were fully adjusted to the appalling lighting. Thank God it was a clear night with no rain or mist.

By just after one o'clock they were in open country, moorland on either side, just visible in the gloom. Kuche tapped him on the shoulder.

'You mind stopping. I've got to relieve myself.'

George pulled over and wound down the window, letting a cold blast of air into the car. Fenderman and von Tupfel stirred and Kuche opened his door, asking if anyone wanted to join him. George said no, but the other pair began to lumber out and stretch, Fenderman shaking his head as if to throw off the fatigue.

George leaned over and pushed the door on the passenger side open, at the same time slipping the Luger from his pocket, thumbing off the safety.

They were going to take them now. He had no doubt about that from the way Kuche had positioned himself—furthest away from the car, his back to them, legs set apart and head down in classic pose.

Fenderman and von Tupfel stood close to one another between Kuche and the car. They were finished first, von Tupfel turning and starting to walk back towards George, as Fenderman buttoned himself up before he also turned.

George slid his rump into the passenger seat and lifted the Luger, keeping it ready but out of sight. Then Kuche called loudly—

'Halt,' cracking it in German. 'Fenderman; von Tupfel; halt. Stand still and do not move, or I fire. Wormwood is over.'

The figures froze, and George brought the Luger up pointing it directly between the pair, who were now about a dozen paces from the car. He began to get out—preparatory to Kuche's expected order for him to disarm one of them—when Fenderman moved: dropping to a crouch, and whirling round towards Kuche, now strolling forward with his own Luger ready.

Kuche had the edge, being only about four paces from Fenderman. He fired twice from the hip. The first shot spinning Fenderman. The second bullet found an even more deadly target—either one of the packets of explosives, or a grenade. Fenderman disappeared in a sheet of orange flame which seemed to engulf him before the thunderclap of the explosion.

The blast knocked George sideways against the dashboard, his ears a prison of pain from the shock wave. He blinked and thought he heard a long drawn scream of pain which seemed to come from the centre of the explosion.

He was aware of von Tupfel, loping, crabwise, as if wounded, towards the car, fumbling for a weapon which came up, the arm waving like a branch as the man tried to direct the barrel towards the front seat of the car. George fired twice. Then again, as the man kept coming. But the wagging arm fell slack to his side, and von Tupfel tumbled against the bonnet in a sprawl, bouncing off the mudguard and finishing in a heap beside the wheel.

Shakily, George climbed out and kicked the man's Luger out of the way, but there was no need; the head lolled back, the eyes glazed and staring into darkness.

George placed a hand on the car to steady himself, and felt

the slimy wetness. It took a moment for him to realise that it could be a part of either Fenderman or Kuche. Both had been ripped apart in the explosion and there was nothing left except the sharp smell of the explosion and the reek of burned flesh.

He leaned against the side of the road and was sick.

*　　　*　　　*

'So Deputy Führer Rudolph Hess was taken to the Tower of London, safe and sound,' Herbie said as though addressing the ceiling.

'Two nights later. They took him down on the night of 16th. On the night mail. Poor bugger, he's been between four walls ever since.'

'And you lost a good friend.'

'Friend?' George sounded surprised. 'Oh, Kuche, yes. Yes, I suppose you could call him a friend. A brave colleague anyway. We talked a lot in Berlin. Before . . .'

Silently, Herbie thought about Fenderman being blown to pieces on moorland at dead of night on Wednesday, May 14th, 1941, and of his widow claiming that he died at the hands of a firing squad in the Tower of London on Friday, 16th. It made no sense. But, then, there were many things that made no sense, and certainly some nasty little discrepancies in George's story. The memory plays tricks. Always trust the contemporary files rather than the memory. 'George, thank you so much.' Herbie rose, as though he wanted to be quickly rid of his guest.

'Got what you wanted?'

Herbie gave his idiot smile saying he thought so, and George asked when he would be let into the secret.

'Probably tomorrow, George. I drop into your office and we can talk, okay?'

'Can't wait.'

Herbie said that was good, and did George still live in that charming house near Hampstead Heath. George did, and, as he got into his coat, remarked that Herbie ought to come and dine with them some time. 'It's been a shade traumatic, going through this, you know.'

As they got to the door, Herbie grinned again, 'You are a unique man for the history books, George. The one man who saved the lives of two Nazi leaders. You ever thought about that?'

250

George nodded and left, making no comment, as though he would rather forget it all.

On the dot of seven o'clock the screened call came in from Washington, and Herbie spoke for over half-an-hour with the Director. He did not smile once during the conversation.

At the other end, the Director looked anxious after hearing the first few minutes of what Herbie had to say.

At the end of the call, Herbie made two specific requests—that the Director flash an instruction for Tubby Fincher's eyes only, and that he speak personally with the Director of the West German BND. The Director promised both would be complied with immediately, and that what was required from Tubby would be ready for Herbie within the hour.

In fact, what Herbie needed was there within half-an-hour, Tubby himself bringing the bulky Personal Files of both the dead Harold Ramilies and the living Deputy Director, Willis Maitland-Wood.

'Nobody,' said Tubby, 'will know the files have gone.'

At about nine, Herbie telephoned George's private number.

'Sorry to bother you, George. Just one point. Who came up to get you from Manchester, after the blow out?'

'The Rammer himself. Ramilies came up.' He sounded in a hurry.

'And you were debriefed ... ?'

'At the Abbey.'

'Ramilies again?'

'The set—the Rammer, Fenice, Leaderer ...'

'Maitland-Wood?'

Pause, lasting for not more than three seconds. 'No. No, I don't think Willis was around. I don't remember it. Herbie ... ?'

'Yes.'

'Nothing. No, it doesn't matter. Keep until tomorrow.'

'Okay. What happened after the debriefing?'

'Min. of Ag. and Fish for a spell. Resting. You know how they did things then.'

'No. I don't, but I can read. See you tomorrow, George.'

He had hardly put down the telephone when it rang again. He might have known that it would be Wolfgang Alberich Rachendorf, West Germany's man in London. He was in a state.

50

'Rung to ask for your boys back?' For the first time in an hour or so, Herbie smiled.

'Okay, Herbie. Okay, so you pull rank on me. No names no pack drill, yes?' Rachendorf prided himself on his knowledge of colloquial English.

'Oh, names will be named, Wolfie. Nachent and Billstein are your playmates, aren't they?'

'Okay. So we've had trouble in Bonn. We are sensitive.'

'And Frau Fenderman?'

'Not ours.'

'Ah.'

'We just wish to keep sight of her.'

'But one of my people saw Nachent speaking to her in the hotel.'

'No. Just marking her. The casual remark. A close view to make certain. Those two took over from our Bonn people.'

'I think we should talk, Wolfie. Face to face stuff, and call in our brave American allies as well.'

Rachendorf sounded crestfallen. 'If you say so, Herbie. But I don't know the score.'

'There are those who will know it, Wolfie. You feel like a little night music on the teleprinter?'

'What you want?'

'Gretchen Weiss,' Herbie thought he could hear a slight intake of breath at the other end of the line. 'Gretchen Weiss who worked for the Americans. Sister to Hildegarde Fenderman, widow of this, our present, parish.'

'Okay.'

'Your people must have a complete record—even without her passport. Say you meet me here, at my place, ten-thirty tomorrow morning, and you bring with you information gleaned from Bonn during the night.'

'I don't know . . .'

'All things are possible, Wolfie. I want Gretchen Weiss' movements in and out of the Bundesrepublik throughout the Fifties and Sixties; until she was taken ill in the early Seventies. We know she went over to see her sister. I want to know how often she came over here as well. I've no doubt she did.'

'I'll try . . .'

'You owe me, Wolfie, after crossing me with your two leash hounds.'

'A precaution only.'

'Precaution my ass. Sisters associating between East and West. One left and still running, yes? Still running and trying to make contact over here. We've got a dreamer in London who's been at it for a very long time. We want him, Wolfie. I think the Americans want him as well. Probably you do. It's time for power-sharing. Tomorrow at ten-thirty.' He gave the address and then signed off.

After flashing Scotland Yard to page Vernon-Smith, Herbie made his next call. Hank, his man at the American Embassy, who was at home. The conversation was very similar to that which he had just had with Rachendorf. The American still seemed worried, punctuating the talk with a lot of 'Okay, okay, Herbie, so maybe we didn't give you everything.' In the end, he promised to be at the St. John's Wood flat at ten-thirty in the morning.

A final call. To Schnabeln still watching the hotel. 'I shall be making a call to her around nine in the morning,' Herbie told him. 'She might possibly try to run for it so keep your eyes glued. Don't let her get near a station, airport or Embassy. Lift her if you have to. Then drive her around and call me.'

He had just got back to the files again when Vernon-Smith came on. There was no doubt who was giving the orders. Herbie went through it twice, and 'Vermin' only queried one point, asking if he needed higher authority, 'Your Deputy Director for instance?'

Herbie maintained that if Willis Maitland-Wood even had a whisper, the whole of Whitehall would not only have Vernon-Smith pounding a beat, but would also see to it that the beat was six feet under some bog.

On the whole, Vernon-Smith appeared to take it seriously.

Big Herbie returned to the files. The first essential was easily checked. It concerned recruitment during the Thirties. Harold Ramilies—The Rammer—had spent most of his time laying down stock from his post at Oxford University. (George Thomas' name was actually mentioned eighteen months before the lad joined the Army in late 1939.) Willis Maitland-Wood did his drives further afield, in Europe: Austria, Czecho, Poland and Germany itself.

During the years 1932, '33 and '34, Ramilies took short holidays, mainly in the Lake District. In 1934 he did visit France for a month. He went nowhere near Germany. Maitland-Wood, on the other hand, spent the summer of those years roaming around Austria and Germany.

Pieces of the jigsaw began to fit. Herbie went back to George Thomas' file and looked at his movements in the field after the war, during the Fifties and early Sixties. More pieces fell into place, though it was still circumstantial, a fairy story from which Herbie knew he would only get reaction if he told the tale directly to his customers. Or, perhaps, led them into situations which put them at grave disadvantage.

Already someone had made an attempt to at least frighten Frau Hildergarde Fenderman, if not kill her. Was it the same person who had tried to put the mockers on himself outside the flat, by driving at him full tilt?

He built himself his fifth drink of the evening, deciding that it should be his last of the day. Tomorrow was going to be a full and ferocious period.

The gun, which he now kept close permanently, lay on the table near the telephone which rang at ten-thirty, as he had arranged with Tubby Fincher.

'You finished?' Fincher asked.

'Near as I'll ever be. You want to collect now?'

Tubby said the two Personal Files should be back that night, so Herbie told him to come over. He was there within minutes, which meant he had 'phoned from nearby and was edgy.

'You'd better have someone with you tomorrow.' Tubby held the case full of files as though it was covered with germs.

'I have my own boys, Schnabeln and Girren. 'Vermin's' looking after the law. Who is there?'

He knew before Tubby told him that Worboys was available,

and the masochist in the big man gave a small smile. He nodded. 'Okay, perhaps he'd better get a real lesson. Give him some glory.' Worboys would report to him at nine-thirty and take orders from him and him alone. 'No matter how senior anyone else may be. For Christ's sake make that clear, Tubby. I really don't know what we've got—a mare's nest; one villain; or two; or none.'

He had not eaten, and sleep did not come easy. Herbie's mind revolved around the strange story of George Thomas' operation with the Stellar network, the dramatics at Wewelsburg and the abortive mission to assassinate Hess in England. He kept coming back to the awful picture of Kuche firing at the shadowy figure of Fenderman, and the terrible explosion which wiped out two of the four protagonists. He thought about Ramilies being rushed north, picking up George and taking him back to the Abbey, the hurried debriefing and, if he was right, the fast decision concerning the future : the face-saving and the inter-departmental fighting.

Before the operation, George had been kept under wraps, so only a handful of people would know—Ramilies, Fenice, Leaderer, Maitland-Wood, George himself, and, possibly, George's wife, for he had married in the late Forties, just before the end of the war, though they had met in London constantly from the end of '42 onwards.

Tomorrow, he thought, falling into a nightmare sleep.

51

They had to page Frau Fenderman at the hotel. For a horrible moment, Herbie wondered if she had taken off on her toes in the night. But she was only having breakfast in the main dining room. He said he was sorry to bother her at this time in the morning, but wanted to check that their dinner was still on.

'You have news for me, Mr. Kruger?' She sounded stiff and cold on the line.

'I think I have incredible news, Frau Fenderman.'

'You have found out about my husband? About Claus?' Urgent now.

'I know how he died. I may even be able to introduce you to somebody who was actually there. Will that calm your mind?'

There was a long silence, during which Herbie wondered if this was what Hildegarde Fenderman had wanted: if this was the end of a long search or only the beginning of a new phase.

'Can you explain more? Can you ... ?'

'Better wait until this evening, Frau Fenderman. That's why I have telephoned. I wonder if we can make our appointment a little earlier. Say six o'clock? I shall book a good restaurant, but, maybe, there will be someone you should see first.'

She said six would be okay, and Herbie added the last piece of bait. 'I might not pick you up myself. These are delicate times. If one or two men come from me, they will tell you that they are friends of 'Vermin'. Can you remember that?'

'Friends of vermin? It is odd. Vermin? Are you a rat-catcher, Mr. Kruger?'

'It is not good to use that word here any more. They are called rodent operatives nowadays. Yes, Frau Fenderman, I am a rat-catcher in some ways. In other ways I am like the Pied Piper of Hamelin. See you at six, or shortly after.'

He called the pay 'phone in the house opposite Frau Fenderman's hotel and checked that Schnabeln was there with Girren.

'If I can't be found, try Mr. Fincher—if she bolts that is. Just lift her and drive around. Drive to Manchester if you have to, but have her in the London area around six o'clock.' He added that he did not expect her to make a run for it. Worboys was ringing the bell while he still spoke with Schnabeln.

He briefed Worboys over a cup of coffee. Tubby Fincher had armed the lad, which did not over-please the big German, but he managed to get everything said without actually telling Worboys any of the finer details.

Hank, the man from the American Embassy, arrived just before ten-thirty; Rachendorf was ten minutes late. It all gave Herbie time to collect stuff from his safe—some of the remaining files, and the five photographs he had abstracted : two of the five being the doctored pictures pointed out by Bob Perry of Pix. The tapes of George's conversations he left locked in his safe.

Rachendorf looked unhappy. The American was full of bluster. Worboys sat near the door, the others were ranged around the table, coffee near at hand. Herbie opened—

'This may be a fairy tale, gentlemen, but I want to talk, see what details you have brought me, and discuss the matter concerning the two sisters—Weiss, who worked for the Americans in the West; and her sister, Fenderman, who lived in the Eastern Zone. Until her illness, Weiss travelled for you a little, eh Hank?'

Hank said that she did a lot of things. He had told Herbie as much already. But she also travelled, Herbie persisted. 'My friend here from the BND has details—haven't you, Wolfie?'

Rachendorf nodded glumly and removed a small file of flimsies from his briefcase. 'All her outgoings and returns since she started to work for the American Secretariat in the late Forties.'

There were two sheets, the dates and places ranged in sequence, running down each page in two files. Until the clamp-down, and building of the Berlin Wall, in 1961, there were infrequent visits into East Berlin. After that, about two official visits a year, to see her sister. But there were also visits further afield. From 1954 onwards, Gretchen Weiss had come to London on an average of four times a year. She had even managed a trip during the six months before she was finally confined to her bed.

'Well?' Herbie raised his eyebrows, looking from Rachendorf to Hank and back again.

Hank nodded. 'Okay. I guess we should have come clean when you brought the matter up. Our people were running her. The sister was a contact. Late in the Fifties—the spring of '59—she became suspect of being a double.'

Rachendorf laughed and said aloud, 'Suspect? We told your people.'

'Okay, okay. We knew she was working both sides against the middle. I had all this from the archives, and head of Berlin station last night. We kept her active and watched. It was felt we still had a hold over her if the sister—Fenderman—was kept in the East.'

'And you got soft-hearted when the Big C struck, eh?' Herbie was not laughing, his eyes had gone very cold. 'You knew all this and nobody thought it right to tell us? Even though she was paying regular visits to London?'

'The London trips were strictly business. She came over as a guide for visiting firemen.'

'Companion,' Rachendorf said, meaning whore.

'She reported on them.' Hank was putting up a fight, dragging on a Camel. 'We checked her out and she was ninety-five per cent right every time. She was a good watcher; a good cleaner. Gave us the works. Okay, we knew she was a double, but all doubles have their favourites. She did more for us than them, and we planted a lot of stuff through her.' He made a grimace. 'Okay, we'd have closed her down, but the cancer struck first. There was no danger in her.'

'No?' Herbie raised his eyebrows, 'No danger? I wonder if Wolfie would agree with you.'

Rachendorf swallowed. 'It's why we had her sister watched,' he spoke grudgingly. 'Gretchen Weiss used to visit people in London. You should know, Herbie. They were your people. We thought you were running her as well. That's why we watched the Fenderman woman. We thought she was simply carrying on a family tradition.'

'You don't know how close you may be.' Herbie grinned for the first time. 'This is a classic case of the left hand not knowing what the right hand is doing. We all know the squabbles in Western security during the Cold War. You—' he nodded towards Rachendorf, '—had internecine strife between your people and the Gehlen Bureau. Neither trusted the other. None of you trusted our people or the Americans: with respect to Hank here.' He paused and looked at Hank. 'Your boys trusted nobody. After the big scandals and defections, you trusted us—the British—even less. As for my people, they were all at loggerheads. In the meantime, Gretchen Weiss had two allegiances...'

'To the West...' started Hank.

'And to the Russians...' completed Rachendorf.

Herbie shook his head. 'I see it differently. She had two overriding allegiances. To herself, and to her sister. I doubt if we'll ever know. Maybe. We shall see. I suspect that her little courier trips were all carried out for love of Hildegarde. Because I suspect Hildegarde has a husband in the West. It's love and politics. Fanaticism and the hope that, one day, the lovers will be together in their little grey home in the East. The problem is...' Herbie stretched, '...that her husband is deeply entrenched into Western security and has been for a long, long time. Since the war. Maybe before the war even. I suspect he's probably done more damage than all the British traitors we've uncovered since the war. More than Vassall, even more than Philby—king of the lot. Maybe he even ran Philby.'

'Jesus.' Hank put his head in his hands.

'Unlikely to be of help.' Herbie sat very still and quiet. 'It's exceptionally complicated—a comedy of errors. People keeping facts to themselves. Personally I am now only working by touch and instinct. Wolfie,' he smiled, 'have you any details about Gretchen Weiss' regular meetings in London?'

'Only places. Descriptions.'

'Was the Tower of London popular?'

'Very. Every time. She would meet a man near the White Tower.'

'She would speak to a Yeoman Warder first?'

Rachendorf shook his head. '*He* would speak to a Yeoman Warder and leave a message—"If a lady asks..." You know?'

Big Herbie knew—leave a message at the desk. Say you've been delayed and it means you're there. The innocent third party technique.

'Then she would ask and be directed, or told, that the gentleman could not wait,' Rachendorf continued.

Herbie banged the table with the flat of his hand. The coffee cups rattled. 'Nobody thought to mention it. God in heaven, nobody came to us and said ... Never mind. I'll have the bastard now.'

'There going to be trouble?' Hank's hand was shaking.

'Don't worry about your pensions,' Herbie rasped, his voice gruff, not the usual soft Herbie Kruger, but a tone raw with hatred. 'Good morning, gentlemen. Just remain silent, like you have done all these years: not you personally, of course, but the beast organisations for which you work. Good. Morning.'

When they had left, Herbie picked up the telephone. 'We go and do some stirring now, eh friend Worboys? Lunch and then a big stir.' He dialled, fast, and spoke to Vernon-Smith who said he had everything laid on. Herbie set their meeting at the Annexe for two-thirty. Then he dialled Tubby Fincher. 'Flash him now,' the voice gritty. 'I want a meet at two-thirty sharp and I don't care if he's got an appointment with God.' Tubby said he'd see all was ready.

'Okay, lunch then.' Herbie let out a bellow at Worboys. 'Set the table for two. I get the best cloth, you find the best place settings. In that drawer, there.'

Worboys was galvanised into action. Together they set the table. Four courses, Herbie told him; and glasses for two lots of wine.

'I don't eat large lunches,' Worboys grumbled.

'You're not going to eat a large lunch.' Again the bellow. 'This is for a dinner party that isn't going to happen.' He set silver candelabra in the centre of the table and went around drawing the curtains and switching on lamps.

Worboys just stood around and watched, as though Herbie had gone out of his mind.

When it was all finished, Big Herbie Kruger emptied the ash-trays, cleared away the cups, looked around and told Worboys to get his coat. 'We go out to lunch. I won't be back here until late. Others might come though.'

They drove into Kensington and parked in Abingdon Road. There were not many people lunching at the Trattoo and Carlo was pleased to see them. 'It's been a long time, Mr. Kruger.' Carlo was good with names. 'No film stars today?' Herbie asked. Carlo said only a writer, and they laughed.

At two o'clock they left and drove down to Whitehall. Herbie was at his desk, Worboys by the door when 'Vermin' Vernon-

Smith arrived. A quick call to Tubby Fincher and they were on their way into the main building.

Tubby had cleared the Deputy Director's ante-room and stood guard himself. Herbie did not bother to buzz through.

'Sorry about this, Willis, but we have to talk.'

Willis Maitland-Wood looked surprised and went a shade white. 'You're always welcome, Herbie, but why ... ?'

'Just to sit and listen. So we get it all right.' He indicated Vernon-Smith, Worboys and Tubby Fincher.

'Get what right?'

'You tell me, Willis.'

'George?'

'Maybe George. George, Ramilies, Fenice, poor old Leaderer, and yourself, Willis. Old history. That bloody stupid Nostradamus Operation, and the aborted attempt on Hess. Have you not put it together yet? Or are you part of it?'

'Can't hear you, Herbie.'

'Get your ears fixed, Willis. Let's start at the beginning. Who recruited George?'

Herbie knew all that, Maitland-Wood said, and Herbie replied that he wanted it from the horse's mouth, so Maitland-Wood told him again. Ramilies was set to recruit young George Thomas while he was still at Oxford, but the lad went off and joined up. He picked him out after Dunkirk.

'Okay, so Ramilies recruited George and set up the Nostradamus business, knowing it was bloody dangerous: knowing that friend Downay was probably a plant.'

Maitland-Wood agreed.

'Right. But you were quite relaxed about it, weren't you?'

'Well ...'

'What were you doing in the Thirties, Willis?'

'Recruiting mainly.'

'In Europe?'

'You know that.'

'Where did you look?'

'All over.'

'No, what sort of people?'

Worboys leaned against the door looking terrified. Vernon-Smith stood stock still, listening, or at least going through the motions. Fincher seemed worried, hovering.

Maitland-Wood said he had looked mainly among dissidents. In Germany, for instance, he sniffed around the local Communists. 'They were good fodder, the younger intelligent ones.'

'You reckoned you could sort out their politics later?'

'We did in many cases. Youth is rebellious. Communism has an attraction which wears off with time and experience.'

'You had a good war, Willis. It's on record. Your people in Austria did incredible work, but some of them went back to the Russians.'

'True. You can't win 'em all.'

'What about Germany?'

'What about it?'

'In the summer of 1933 you were on a recruiting drive in Hamburg. It's in your book, Willis.'

'Then that's where I was.'

'Who recruited Heinrich Kuche?'

'I ... I'm not sure, Herbie. Was it me?'

'You know bloody well it was you, Willis. Tell me about Kuche, the man you put into the SS; the man who saved George Thomas and then penetrated the Ausland SD. Heinrich Kuche, the man who was killed on that incredible day's outing to burn Rudolf Hess.'

He was from a good family. Perfect material, the Deputy Director said. Disenchanted with what was going on, but not too overt about his contacts with the Communist Party.

'But he was a Party member?' Herbie came close to the desk. 'He was a committed Party member, wasn't he, Willis?'

'Weren't they all? Yes, I suppose he was.'

'And you got him to burn his card, have his name expunged, and join the Nazi Party.'

'Something like that. He was the right kind of family. They bought it, didn't they—or at least we know some of them did. He was into the SS like a shot.'

'And you did it, Willis?'

'Yes.'

'Funny.' Herbie pushed some papers aside and placed his great bottom on the edge of the Deputy Director's desk. 'Strange. George clearly recalls Kuche telling him that he was recruited by their mutual friend Ramilies.'

'A trick of memory. A mistake.' Maitland-Wood gave a nervous laugh and smoothed back his pelt of grey hair.

Herbie slowly shook his head. 'He was most explicit about it. According to George, he talked a lot with Kuche. Talked a lot about Ramilies. I don't think you were mentioned much. Haven't you ever wondered, Willis? Haven't you ever really kept your eyes open? Sure you recruited Kuche. But why the rest of it? Can't you see what you all did? What you've done?'

Maitland-Wood looked at him, face frozen in shock. 'Oh Christ. Oh no. He couldn't. After all we did to ...'

'Tell us about it, Willis. Tell us about it; and why.'

Vernon-Smith had a notebook out, but Herbie laid a hand over it.

The telephone rang and Worboys stirred, but Herbie picked it up and muttered into the mouthpiece that the Deputy Director was not to be disturbed—only if there was a call for him; Kruger.

After that, Willis Maitland-Wood talked. He spoke for nearly an hour.

52

Tubby Fincher took charge of Willis Maitland-Wood. He would see him home and stay with him. The shock had been as great to Willis as any of them. The Director had been notified and was already on his way back. But even a RAF jet would not bring him home in time for the kill. In the space of an hour, the Deputy Director had filled in some of the gaps. The fairy story was not an imagined tale any longer. Though the final act had still to be played out.

Herbie went up to George Thomas' department on his own, carrying a pile of papers, smug with the knowledge that Frau Fenderman had not stirred from her room all day. There had been no word from Schnabeln and Girren. Vernon-Smith was back with his own people, probably on their way to one of the final destinations at this very moment: 'Vermin' with a couple of his heavies and at least one woman officer.

The fourth floor was as alive as ever. The watch-bitch eyed Herbie with distaste. 'Tell him I have news,' Herbie said, and, like magic, he was admitted to the office where George sat in his shirt sleeves.

'No more questions, Herbie, for heaven's sake,' rising, smiling and putting out a hand. Only a year or so to run for his retirement, Herbie thought. Maybe George had figured on taking the golden bowler a little earlier. It would make sense of the last days.

'No questions, George. Answers this time.'

George said thank God for that. 'You really mean you can tell me what all the burrowing's been about?'

Herbie nodded. 'You'll understand, I'm sure. Woman I want to use in the East. Prepare yourself for a surprise, George, because it's a voice from the past.'

'Yes,' uncertain, interested.

'Fenderman . . .' Herbie started.

264

'Was killed with Kuche on the moor. Wormwood. I told you.'

'Fenderman was called back from his honeymoon for that operation. You told me, George.'

'That's right,' almost surprised.

'His bride's turned up.'

'His ... ?'

'Frau Fenderman. Beloved wife of the late Claus Fenderman. Your old buddy from Operation *Wermut.*'

'Here? Here in London?'

Herbie said she had been in London for a while.

'Christ. You been keeping her under wraps, Herbie?'

'Very close to the chest, George. Think I can use her. I've had the dogs watching her night and day. Until now, of course. We've cleared her. The dogs are off. In fact I'm dining with her tonight.'

George sat, half slumped in his chair, a smile, unobtrusive, around the eyes, he asked what she was like.

'Still good looking. Over the hill, though, like all of us, George. You understand now why we had to go through it all?'

George said, of course. 'I suppose Fenderman's name showed up in the files?'

'I don't like doing jobs by half.' Herbie grunted and laughed. 'George, you might even have been involved in some skulduggery from the past. Had to be sure. You ever meet her in Berlin?'

He didn't think so. After all, he had only met Fenderman a couple of days before they went on the Wormwood Operation. 'May have shown me a photograph. I was thinking about it last night after we talked. I remember, Fenderman was in quite a state about his wife.'

'You like to meet her, George?'

He didn't think he had the time. Depended on how long she was staying. Maybe next week. It would be interesting. 'You'll be seeing a lot of her, then, Herbie?'

'She's dining with me tonight, as I said. My place. Seven o'clock, but I'd rather you met somewhere else. I've got to put the question to her, if you see what I mean?'

'The old initiation ceremony? Yes. Recruiting's a funny thing, Herbie.'

'Painless for you, George.'

A shadow crossed George Thomas' face. 'Yes,' he said after a short pause. 'Yes, the Rammer was bloody good.'

Herbie told him he'd ring next week, and perhaps they could all get together—Herbie, George and Frau Fenderman.

When he reached his own office in the Annexe, the telephone was ringing. Schnabeln and Girren had Frau Fenderman, protesting, in the car. They had picked her up after she had actually got to Heathrow. 'Bit of a chase once we realised where she was headed.'

'Bring her in,' Herbie snapped. 'I'll have her at our rendezvous at six-thirty. Keep her in the car until I call you in. Going over there with Worboys in about half-an-hour; and keep her safe, Schnabeln, she's evidence.'

Worboys still looked shaken. 'Never mind, boy,' Herbie grinned. 'Think of the time you'll have telling the juniors about all this when you're an old hand.'

Worboys said he only understood half of it, and Herbie promised to fill in all the details when it was over. He then checked his Sauer M38H, stuffed it into his pocket, and said they were off to Hampstead.

53

The house stood back from Hampstead Heath, a large Victorian building with iron gates and a short drive lined by small conifers. Worboys got out and opened the gates. Herbie told him to leave them open. 'The others'll be along in due course.'

When she opened the door to their ring, Herbie thought what a superb woman she must have been when George first met her. 'Angelle,' he said, smiling. 'Sorry to barge in like this, but we had to...'

'George isn't back yet.' Her hair had remained a golden red, though now flecked with grey; she had kept her figure. Only the face showed the signs of age, the crows' feet around the eyes and the deep crescents on either side of the mouth. Her accent still betrayed her French origin.

'I didn't really expect him to be, Angelle. Do you know young Worboys?—Mrs. Thomas. Angelle Thomas. Angelle Tours once upon a time, I believe.'

They shook hands, and she held the door open for them. 'George telephoned. Just a little while ago. Said he might be late.'

'Yes,' Herbie's voice had become grave. 'Yes, I imagined he would do that. We really want to talk with you first, Angelle.'

She looked puzzled at first, then worried, as she led the way through to a large, comfortable room—large enough to spread furniture, the walls hung with three or four originals: nothing fancy, local artists, Herbie thought. It was almost six o'clock, the light starting to go, but the curtains remained open in the two big alcove windows which looked out on a garden that, in summer, would be a pleasant and secluded place—shrubs, a long broad lawn, flowerbeds. Country in the middle of Hampstead.

'Nothing's happened to George, Herbie?' She sounded really worried now.

'Not that I know about. Angelle—er, Mrs. Thomas—was with us during the war, young Worboys. A heroine in her own right.'

Angelle made a dismissive sound and then laughed—the laugh just as George had described hearing it for the first time in Michel Downay's flat so long ago in Paris. 'More than you were, Herbie,' she said taking their coats. 'You sure there's nothing wrong with George?'

'Nothing new.' Herbie let it fall flatly between them, and she faltered on her way to the door, then pulled herself together and continued on her way.

'Can I offer you something?' she asked, coming back without the coats.

'You might not want to, not when you hear what I have to say.'

'Oh.' Flat, but as though she understood. 'What's it about, Herbie?'

'Depends how much you know.'

'This official?'

'Very.'

'Ask me then.'

'I've just had to go through George's file with him ...'

She nodded, cool, collected. 'He said you were raking at the past.'

'You met him first in Paris?'

'You know that.'

'When?'

'You know that also. When I was living in Downay's flat in '41.'

'He went off with Downay, to Germany?'

'Yes.'

'And you went to the safe house in the Rue Cambon. They got you out. To England.'

'You know that also. I came and worked for F Section.'

'You did two missions. Six months in '42, and three the following year. You met George again in London?'

'It was the romance of the Department. Everybody knows that.'

'You met George Thomas in London—in Baker Street?'

She nodded. Herbie asked when, and she said during her first spell back in 1942. 'Just before Christmas.'

'You recognised him instantly?'

And she said yes, of course.

'I know, Angelle.'

'Know what?'

'I know what happened. I know it wasn't George Thomas you met. Apart from old Sandy Leaderer, who's now senile, everyone else is dead—Ramilies, Fenice, everyone except you and Maitland-Wood. He told us about it this afternoon.'

'Well, there's nothing to worry about then.' She sounded sharp and clipped. 'He's been accepted as George Thomas ever since he came back from the Stellar run. He's been loyal. He's been with your people ever since. Jesus, he'll be retiring soon. Ramilies and Fenice thought it necessary. Only a few people had handled George. The inter-departmental jealousies were rife. He could be of use to them straight away. A change of identity solved so many problems.'

'Didn't you get a shock?' Herbie spoke very quietly now.

'Ramilies was very clever. He knew we would meet, and that I would recognise him. Our first meeting since Paris took place in Ramilies' own office.'

Herbie's great head bobbed up and down like a Buddha. 'And you could tell the truth of course. The last time you had seen Heinrich Kuche was in Paris. Were you upset about George? The real George?'

'Of course. But I fell in love with George—Heinrich, I can't call him that, he's been George Thomas for so long. I've been in love with him since 1943. It's a long time, Herbie. What are you delving for now? There was nothing wrong. There's been nothing wrong. Ramilies and Maitland-Wood were worried when they found out he was the only survivor.'

'I understand George—the real George—was killed in the shooting, on the moor after the landing. Operation *Wermut*.'

'They were concerned. They'd been running him very close to the chest. They wanted to use him again. They were afraid that other people might want him put through the mill. Interrogated, possibly distrusted. Ramilies and Maitland-Wood always trusted him.'

'So Willis has told me this afternoon.'

'Well then,' she shrugged.

'I'm sorry,' Herbie said gently. 'Our George Thomas is in reality an ex-SS officer called Heinrich Kuche. He tells a good story. The real George must have loved you a great deal, Angelle. Kuche gave me the lot, chapter and verse. The whole thing from recruitment—oh, even before recruitment—up to the end of Wormwood. He told it from George's viewpoint, and occasionally it showed. Only occasionally. I couldn't see him. Odd.'

She repeated, 'Well then,' shrugging again and adding, 'What's wrong?'

'Angelle, your George—Heinrich Kuche—I think had a work name on that operation, Wormwood. I think the name was Fenderman. If I'm right, he's got another wife, and she's here in London. I'm sorry, but if I'm right, he has never been quite what he seems. If I'm right, he's been the deepest penetration agent the Russians have had within the service since the war. I think he's wanted to get out—go private—for some time; but he's in trouble, Angelle.'

Her mouth opened and closed, a little bubble of sound coming from the back of her throat.

Outside, a car drew up in the drive, crunching on the gravel.

54

Woman Detective Sergeant Maureen Cooper had been attached
to Special Branch for less than a month, spending most of the
time at a desk, learning the kind of trade with which they dealt.
That morning she had been prepared for yet another somewhat
boring day. Now, in the early evening, she found herself enveloped in a mixture of fear, nervousness and excitement.

Vernon-Smith had chosen her because of her build. She was
only thirty years of age, but, with a little judicious rearrange-
ment of her figure, plus a severe grey suit and wig, she would
pass—in bad light or at a distance—for Hildegarde Fenderman.

She had not thought twice about accepting the job. You did not
turn things down in the Metropolitan Police, particularly if you
wanted to get on in the Branch to which she had been assigned.
In almost ten years of service she had been in dangerous situations
before : though never in one quite as sensitive as this.

Vernon-Smith had been honest with her. 'You'll be a target
from the moment you leave the hotel,' he said, explaining that he
would be waiting for her at the flat in St. John's Wood, and that
she would be watched all the way. 'Our people'll be around, but
we can't give you complete immunity. The idea is to draw him
to you—to the flat. He'll probably have a go either as you're
arriving, or after you're inside.' He added that the latter was more
probable, knowing in his heart that if Thomas was going to strike,
he would want both Herbie Kruger and the woman in the same
blow.

Maureen Cooper braced herself for the most dangerous few
minutes. The cab, in which she had ridden from the Devonshire
Hotel, was drawing up in front of Herbie Kruger's apartment
block. Vernon-Smith would be waiting.

It was, perhaps, a good thing that she did not know that
'Vermin' Vernon-Smith waited with extreme anxiety, for the
watchers he had put on George Thomas in Whitehall had lost

271

their mark within minutes of him leaving the office building. Kruger and Worboys were at the Thomas house in Hampstead now, and the pair of heavies employed by Kruger's people had Frau Fenderman in their car—probably arriving in Hampstead any time.

All that did not change the fact that the Special Branch leeches had lost Thomas, or Kuche, or whoever he was. Thomas under wraps was one thing; Thomas away on his toes was a threat of some proportion. 'Vermin' had markers out—armed and everything—but they could not be everywhere, or see everything. You had to do this one by the book and keep well back.

But Maureen Cooper was in happy ignorance of all this as she stepped from the taxi and paid off the driver. *Walk heavy,* 'Vermin' had told her. *The lady walks a bit flat and doesn't hurry.* In her mind, WDS Cooper had two pictures—the woman she represented, and the man they were after. From the photographs he didn't look his age. From the description he was spry and in excellent condition.

She took a deep breath and walked, heavy and flat, slowly up the path to the entrance. There was relief as she reached the shelter of the doorway, then her heart jumped, for somebody stood inside the foyer, pressing the button for the lift. She pushed the doors open and walked in.

For a moment, she thought that the figure might be one of her colleagues—she'd seen nobody, not even the two-car tail on the taxi. But the man standing waiting was no colleague, nor was he anyone to worry her—an elderly man, short-sighted, stooped, pebble spectacles and ill-fitting teeth which he ground in an abstract and irritating manner. He moved badly, slowly, using a black walking stick with a silver knobbed head. She noticed the gloves and shoes were good quality, and the coat had once been expensive—getting threadbare now, the velvet collar frayed.

He stood back, or rather shuffled, almost losing his balance, as the lift came down. He looked so fragile that she opened the gates for him and asked what floor. Third, he said, the voice old, short of breath. Really the fourth but he had made a habit of always walking up the final flight. 'Keeps me in trim,' he panted with a croaking laugh. 'Never know when you're going to need that bit of strength. When the lift mechanics' strike was on ...' he puffed and chattered. Obviously wanted to talk. Maureen

Cooper felt sorry for the poor old bugger. She said she wanted the third also.

They stopped at the third floor and she held the gates open for him; he wheezed badly as he limped through. Poor old sod, she thought again. He's got a game leg on top of it all. With great courtesy the man raised his drab, old-fashioned, homburg hat, and thanked her, nodding the bent head and staggering on his way towards the stairs like an elderly drunk. She was conscious of something, then realised that he made very little noise—rubber-soled shoes and a rubber tip on his stick.

There was nobody else on the landing, and Maureen Cooper went quickly to the door of flat eleven, pressing the bell—a fast three, then one long and another fast three. Infantile: morse for SB, but it was at least a signal.

The door opened quickly, Vernon-Smith stepping to one side, an automatic pistol in his right hand. 'No trouble?' he asked quietly. As she shook her head, he motioned her in and closed the door. 'He'll possibly try here, or as you're leaving. We'll give it an hour.'

On the stairs to the fourth floor, Heinrich Kuche, who now thought of himself completely as George Thomas, cursed and lifted his head, one gloved hand grasping the ebony cane which had once belonged to Michel Downay, the other hand curling around the butt of the Luger in the pocket of the old coat with its velvet collar.

He was really quite surprised about his ability to imitate an old and crippled man. But it worked: and so simple, just the stoop and shake, the wheeze, pebble spectacles made of clear glass, the clothes, the badly fitting dentures. The limp was easy enough. The wound from Wewelsburg played up in cold weather, and he could simulate without a problem. He had always been good with voices and walks, and the little cache of equipment was always kept within easy reach. The small suitcase in his office, and the spare umbrella which just took the cane inside the canopy, knob downwards, the ferule strapped on just below the curve of the handle.

He hefted the cane now, standing on the stairs. He was superstitious about it. George had laughed in Berlin all that time ago, but he had insisted on taking it with him when they'd prepared for *Wermut*. Well, this was his private escape kit: this and the three clean passports, collected over the years, together with one thousand pounds sterling in cash and the four diamond rings which would bring in another couple of grand if need be. The escape kit he never thought to use; never wanted to use; did not really want to use now. But they had him. Herbie Kruger was a clever bastard: even tried to pull a trap on him. Christ, he really had thought it was Hilde coming in through the doors of the building—but, then, he had expected her. Getting old, George, he thought to himself. Then stopped, wondering stupidly if he should now start thinking of himself as Heinrich again. Or Claus?

No point in hanging around here. They would be watching outside, but he'd probably make it, using the old man's walk and wheeze. If he was stopped he had a driving licence in the name of Cocks. Henry Cocks.

George turned and ran lightly up the stairs to the fourth floor. He pressed the elevator button and the noise seemed terrific as the cage rose from the floor below. Concentrate on the old man, he told himself. Then get round the corner to the car. Drive and think. The lift descended and he began his shuffle out.

There was an old empty van across the road. That would be the nearest they would get. He paused as if to catch his breath, and then took a few more paces forward; stopped again and repeated the procedure every few steps, leaving longer gaps between the stops.

In the back of the van, among the radio equipment, the two plainclothes men watched him go. 'Can't see him turning nasty,' one of them laughed. 'More a danger to himself. Watch him if anything happens though. Don't want an old-age pensioner becoming an innocent victim.'

'More a mugger's mark,' said the other, returning to the night glasses with which he was sweeping the building and streets.

George made the car without any trouble. He had rented it using his other spare licence and insurance, and a slightly younger age than his own. No trouble. Like there was no trouble giving the pair of Special Branch leeches the slip. The old Post Office trick—he knew all the public places with two entrances and exits within a couple of miles of Whitehall.

He locked the car door from the inside, switched on the engine and then the lights. Luger within reach on the passenger seat, into gear and away slowly. He supposed the best bet would be some small hotel out of London. Somewhere near a station to leave the car, then a short train ride after 'phoning the rental people. No trace. The thin air trick. The only problem was that he did not want to go. Oh sod Herbie Kruger. God save him from women also. Bloody Hilde. If she'd only listened. After all these years. He might have known from the start that she would cling. The frighteners didn't work, and heaven knew, he'd taken a risk with that—stealing the car, making certain he didn't hit her with any of the shots on Sunday morning.

He'd risked it trying to take out Herbie as well. That was a desperate act of panic if you like. Silly. Sudden loss of cool. Unlike him, after all these years.

Funny, he thought, how life turns out. Maitland-Wood had only been a boy when he'd come to him with the proposition. He was even younger than Maitland-Wood as well. A child, playing politics. *You must sever all your connections with the Communist Party. Become a Nazi. Not overnight, but quite quickly. You're ideal material for the SS and you'd be furthering your own political cause if you came in with us. We need you.*

Poor old MW. He wasn't to know, even then, that Heinrich Kuche was already severing relations on orders from the Communist Party itself: that he was already a member of the GRU—the Fourth Department, founded by Trotsky himself and kept intact with the military machine. The military eyes and ears of the USSR.

But, then, Maitland-Wood—and Ramilies come to that—had a lot to learn about long-term situations. He'd liked George Thomas, liked him very much : they had been both of a generation—Kuche three years older—and to some extent had enjoyed the whole thing. Whatever else could be said, the conception of planting the Nostradamus quatrains had been a brilliant idea. Suicide, of course, but brilliant, and who could have foreseen the repercussions? Heydrich's plot against Himmler. His own cover blown as well as George's. It was an ill wind, though. It took them both to Berlin, though, naturally, he had never revealed that Jost and his Ausland SD had insisted on changes of name before they went. George became Hans von Tupfel and he, Claus Fenderman. When they went on *Wermut* who, on this side of the Channel, was to know that they had a pair of men with them called Schmitt and Braun. Christ, Smith and Brown, the classic dirty weekend names.

He had bouts of remorse and guilt, for setting up George's death, for a long time after that.

The GRU had been on the ball then, as well, giving him a list of contact names in Berlin. Hilde had been the first. Love? What did he know of love? Yes, they had loved—each other, each other's political drive and ambition for the Party. Why, in the name of everything, had he married her? Sex? Companionship? A welding of the bond? All gone. He had tried to tell her that when he'd gone—in this very disguise—to her hotel: to reason with her. When? A couple of nights ago.

'You have one duty now,' she said. 'You must leave. Come quickly with me. We can be in Moscow in two days. I told you this when I came before. Your time of usefulness is almost over. Come home, Claus. Come home with me now.'

She wouldn't listen. He'd told her last year when she came— and he had not seen her for years until then: only on the odd visit to the East to be rebriefed. She wouldn't understand. Angelle he loved. His home was here. Hadn't he done enough? Surely the Party would allow him this last request? All the help he had given to so many Soviet agents. Christ, even Kim Philby and that debacle. Aloud, against the hum of the engine, he realised that he was speaking aloud. 'I suppose I was what the newspapers call the Fourth Man in the Philby business.'

But Hilde wouldn't take no for an answer. Not last year, and not now. Stirring up a mare's nest by talking to the Yeoman Warder at the Tower because he, George, would not speak on the 'phone, or make any of the meets she tried to set up.

The orderly German mind, he thought. Drop a hint to someone official (and what was more natural than doing it in the way he had done it with Gretchen, their go-between, for so long) and the facts would come to light. Normally not here in England. By all logic it would have remained unnoticed, unreported. Herbie Kruger. Bloody Big Herbie. Herbie's new team for the East would probably have been the last piece of good information that George could send behind the Curtain—except the big one, of course, the action taken to seal up the breaches in NATO defence which had been lifted over the years from the Bonn Ministry of Defence.

With horror, he realised that he had been driving automatically: driving towards Hampstead and Angelle. Herbie would be at least a leap ahead of him.

Depression swamped over George Thomas like water. He felt very tired and did not want to go on. What was it he had said to Herbie only a few hours ago? A day or so ago? *I've become a con man. After a lifetime in the trade it's what I've become—a hollow man, a stuffed man.*

He was driving up along Hampstead Heath now. Then, past his own house. Two cars in the drive. So they were there, and Angelle would know by now. Maybe even Hilde was there. He wouldn't put it past Herbie Kruger.

He stopped the car; checked the pistol, and got out with great dignity. George Thomas who was Heinrich Kuche, felt very tired and almost disgusted with himself.

Slowly he walked back along the road towards the house.

55

Big Herbie had finished telling what he called his fairy story. Angelle, still in shock, wept quietly, rocking her body to and fro like a child. She occasionally shook her head at Herbie in a gesture of disbelief.

'In the main I'm afraid I'm right,' Herbie could not pull punches. 'You knew about the switch of identity. Ramilies and Maitland-Wood went along with it. Most elaborate extremes—faking the dossier photographs: everything. A labyrinth of deceit that's gone on for so long.'

She went on shaking her head. 'He was always so good, so loyal. I can't ...'

Herbie thought she was going to say that she couldn't believe it. 'The other one. She's in the car you heard just now. The car outside.'

'She?'

'Frau Fenderman. The woman I think he married in Berlin in 1941. The woman who has been running him as a Soviet agent since the early Fifties.'

'I don't ...'

'No, Angelle. I know. Please try and relax.' Herbie tried to soothe.

'The bitch is outside?' Her lips parted, almost vulpine.

'In the car. We picked her up earlier. I think she's been trying to lure him back East. She ran him—I've told you—mainly through her sister in the West. I believe she came over last autumn to try to take him back then. Not just for political motives. I think he resisted being recalled.'

'Last autumn?'

He detected a sudden tweaking of her memory: antennae picking up something. 'You want to say ...'

'Last autumn,' she repeated. 'He was most nervous. I've seen him like it before, but never as bad. The strange telephone calls I'm used to. It's part of the business. But they were worse: September, October—sometime then.'

Herbie's large head nodded.

'What will you do with her—outside in the car?'

'Could you bear to see her? I'd like to get her inside, under cover.'

She began to sob again. 'Oh Christ. I don't know. Herbie, it's all so unreal. A man you've trusted for such a time . . .'

He knew all about that, for Herbie was also facing a crisis. He had never been on close terms with George, but they were colleagues—the man he could never remember accurately—and they had met socially many times. Angelle, red-eyed and sobbing grief, he had always liked: she had been fun, always laughing—in public.

A terrible hatred crushed into his bones and clawed his stomach. The game was always one of deceit, but George's deceit went further than anything he had known. At that moment he would happily have crushed the man with his bare hands.

'Bring her in if you like.' She sounded tired, living for a moment in a land where nothing made sense any more. It must be like the bereaved, Herbie thought. No; worse than being bereaved. He asked if he could make a telephone call first and she gave a small noise of acquiescence.

The 'phone was in the hall and Herbie dialled his own number. 'Vermin' answered and gave him the news. 'You think he'll do anything desperate?' the SB man asked.

Herbie said it was difficult to tell. Who knew what was in George's mind. The facts were plain. He had resisted the offers to run back over the Curtain with his bride from 1941. Resisted twice. Even been violent towards the Fenderman woman; and against Herbie also. Both Fenderman and George had broken all the rules of good field agents. They had allowed personal emotions to triumph. He suspected that George's one aim had been to keep his cover safe, retire early and disappear with Angelle who had given him so much support. Hildegarde Fenderman, on the other hand, had probably loved him during their very brief marriage, and loved him even more while she was running him from the East. She had probably literally lived for the day when they could be together, either in East Germany or Russia, her whole working life held together by the hope which George had shattered.

'I'll get her under cover. Suggest you get out of my place. He may be waiting there still. You'll lift him if he is. Otherwise? National alert?'

'Softly, softly,' muttered Vernon-Smith. 'Airports and all that. We may never get him. Those bloody people always have the damnedest way of slipping through. Come to think of it he could be out already.'

'Doubt it. His state of mind would urge him to hang on. He's banked on spending retirement with his wife. His wife here, I mean. He may not want to run.' He asked 'Vermin' where he would go? Which station?

'We'll come over to Hampstead. If nothing's shown by the time we get there, you'd better bring her over and we'll keep her there. Your people'll want to sweat her at Warminster, I suppose?'

Herbie said it was most likely, and cradled the receiver. Opening the front door, he motioned to Schnabeln and Girren.

Hildegarde Fenderman appeared quite calm now. She had been difficult to start with, Schnabeln said.

She peered at Herbie in the darkening hall and Girren switched on the light. 'Ah, Mr. Kruger,' she gave a little laugh. 'So you are also a wolf in sheep's clothing.' Another laugh. 'That's melodramatic, no? A cliché?'

'Apt,' said Herbie, looking around for a door other than the one to the main room in which Angelle Thomas still sat wrapped in her private misery. The one across the hall led, he presumed, to a dining room or study. His hand was on the knob when Angelle came out into the hall. She was shaking, her eyes fiercely red, lips trembling.

'My husband's wife?' she asked, the voice breaking.

'We'll take her through here. Just for a little while.' Herbie tried to step between them, but Angelle launched herself forward, nails clawing, her mouth twisted, pouring out a stream of obscenities in French. Herbie grabbed her wrists and Schnabeln, with Girren's help, bundled Hildegarde Fenderman through the other door.

'I know. I know ...' Herbie spoke, like a lover—or a father?—in Angelle's ear as he led her gently back into her sitting room.

'I kill her. I kill both of them ...' Angelle collapsed again.

'Yes,' Herbie agreed. He did not want to leave her alone, yet;

he wanted someone to stay with her; afraid of what she might do. 'Yes, I believe you would kill her—and George.'

She looked up at him, the eyes large, just as George had first described them. She must have been stunning then, in the Forties. 'George,' she whispered. 'My real George. There was so little time with him, yet—yet. I wish I could have died for him: instead of him. In some ways I suppose I have.'

Herbie poured her a drink. Brandy. Forcing the glass between the long trembling fingers. He went to the door and called for Girren who came through. 'Just stay with her. Be kind,' he told him. 'Watch out for her while I have a quick word with the Fenderman woman.'

Girren nodded. 'I shan't be a minute, Angelle,' Herbie called to her; but she did not reply.

'I don't have to say anything.' Hildegarde Fenderman sat at the polished oak table in the Thomas' dining room, with Schnabeln watching the windows. 'You want the curtains drawn?' Schnabeln asked, and Herbie said he thought that might be good.

Then he turned to Frau Fenderman, who looked older than before, when he had seen her at the hotel. 'There is nothing for you to say. We know it all—or most of it. That which we do not know, can be guessed. Like, I presume you used the Nostradamus quatrains as a basis for ciphers.'

She smiled, the secret smile familiar to the faces of most women.

'You've got him?' she asked.

'Not yet. But we shall get him as we got you.'

'And you will put us both in prison.'

'He will be in prison, Frau Fenderman. You, on the other hand, may well be returned to your masters.'

She was good. He had to give her that. Only the most minute twitch of her right hand and a flicker of panic in the eyes. Hardly visible before the coldness returned.

'They won't be pleased with you, Hilde. Not at all. They're never pleased with anyone who blows a colleague out of frustration, or pique . . .'

'Or love?' she queried. She looked pathetic.

'Love? Hate? What's the difference? He wanted to stay. You've lived your life waiting for him to come back. You've pulled his strings for so long that you thought it would be easy. It wasn't and your initiative went sour, Hilde. Moscow won't like that. The DDR won't like it. I wouldn't like it much if one of my people did it.'

She asked for a cigarette and he gave her one of his, bending over her to light it. As he did so, she whispered, 'What will you really do with me?'

Herbie straightened up, towering over her. 'People will talk to you; perhaps for quite a long time ...'

'You'll try to dry me out?'

'If that's how you want to put it. Maybe. Then there is a real possibility that you will be sent home. A lot depends on the authorities in Bonn : and the Americans. We all bear a little guilt, except, possibly your dead sister, Gretchen. Did she know what she was doing, or did she think she was being romantic—a go-between for lovers ripped apart because of the war?'

'In a way that's what she was doing. Love lasts, Mr. Kruger.'

'So does hate, Frau Fenderman.'

Herbie tried to gentle her into talking more, but she clammed up after that. Eventually he went back to Angelle and asked if she needed a doctor? If she had somewhere to go? Yes, maybe a sedative would be a good idea. Yes, she could go to a cousin. She would 'phone shortly. She kept asking if they had got him yet, and what they'd do with him.

Herbie circled around it, asking, seemingly innocuous, questions —Had he ever been violent with her? Did he ever suffer from acute depressions? How were his powers of concentration these days? She answered in a vague manner, as though they were talking about someone she did not know well—not now anyway.

Herbie waited, passing time with the questions, hoping that Vernon-Smith would call. He wanted Hildegarde Fenderman off his hands. At one point he suddenly realised that George—their George, who was really Kuche—was older than his dossier showed. There was an age difference of three or four years between the two men.

At last the call came. Vernon-Smith and the bait—the WDS— were at Hampstead Police Station. Would Herbie like them to come down and pick up the woman?

'I'd better bring her up to you.' Herbie bit his lower lip. 'Let me get someone here to look after Mrs. Thomas and we'll come straight over. I think there's enough for a circumstantial case, but I shouldn't think we'll get around to charging her. Once the Director's back it will probably be the Warminster house for her.'

'Your bloody confessors,' Vernon-Smith grumbled.

In the end it was going to take Angelle's cousin a couple of hours to get over. The doctor arrived, and Herbie explained the problems without filling in the picture. Girren would stay and sit in until the cousin turned up to take over. He then went back into the dining room and said they were ready to leave.

'Where do we go?' Hildegarde Fenderman was terribly calm. Herbie wondered, late in the day, if she had been searched, and Schnabeln said she had—it was the main cause of her protests at Heathrow. They'd got a WPC to do it thoroughly. There'd been problems there as the policewoman had wanted their IDs double-checked.

They went to the front door, and Herbie stopped them, always cautious about entering and leaving buildings. Schnabeln could drive. He was to go out first and start the engine; open the rear door. Herbie would have Frau Fenderman out and into the back of the car in a matter of seconds.

She nodded—a woman who seemed at last to have accepted what had happened. As Herbie reached forward for the handle of the front door, she asked if they had got him yet.

'George?'

She shook her head. 'Claus,' she said with a small wry smile. Herbie told her to worry about that later, then opened the door and allowed Schnabeln out into the drive. There was a light, done up like an old carriage lamp, lit outside the door, and Herbie fumbled around for the correct switch, keeping the woman out of the doorway. He turned off the exterior light at last. Then the light in the hall, just as Schnabeln switched on the car's head-lamps and started the motor.

A streetlamp still bathed the drive in a yellowish glow. 'Okay?' Herbie looked at her and she nodded. 'I would suggest we move quite quickly.' She nodded again and stepped in front of him, beginning to walk out towards the car.

Crouched low in the bushes by the gate, George Thomas, who was also Claus Fenderman and Heinrich Kuche, saw Schnabeln go to the car. He saw the porch light go out, and then the light in the hall. The black ebony cane was still in the car, parked at the corner, but the Luger pistol began to come up in his gloved right hand. Pretend it's a practice shoot, he told himself. Pretend, and remember how you hate her, and the idea of going into the East. Take it to its consummation now.

He straightened up, invisible against the bushes, raising the Luger in a two-hand grip, sighting towards the entrance as the plump figure of his first bride came through the door, clearly visible in her grey suit.

56

There were four shots. A pair of twos in quick succession. The technique and accuracy of a marksman.

Herbie was slightly to the right and behind Hildegarde Fenderman, and his reactions were fast, leaping forward and pushing with both hands to slam her into the gravel.

Not quick enough for the bullets though. On a target the grouping would have been perfect. The first two toppled Hildegarde Fenderman backwards, catching her in the chest. Herbie, heaving her down against her backwards motion, must have aligned her head with the trajectory of the second pair.

The head seemed to split open, shattering, showering Herbie with blood and brains. She made no sound except the awful dead crunch on the gravel.

The Sauer M38H was in Herbie's hand without him even knowing it: the reflex leaping through his brain and muscles from the past.

He saw Schnabeln scrambling from the car, and a figure flitting through the gates.

Schnabeln was heading back towards the body. Noise, a scream and shout, came from behind him, in the door, but Big Herbie was away, his feet slipping on the gravel, pelting down the drive.

He skidded slightly as he reached the gates, conscious of his thumb working the safety off the pistol. One big shoulder hit the iron and he was out on the ramped pavement, turning to the right in the direction he had seen the figure moving.

It was almost a hundred yards to the corner where the car was parked, lights off. The figure was running, hard, his feet making no sound on the paving stones.

Herbie parted his legs and lifted both arms, grasping the pistol, finger already taking up the pressure on the trigger.

'George,' he shouted. 'George, stop. For God's sake stop.'

But the figure kept on going, almost to the car now, one arm

285

reaching forward towards the door.

Herbie pressed the trigger and there was the answering hollow click of a misfire. He swore, looked down at the weapon and re-cocked, lifting it again.

The figure was half in and out of the car when he pulled the trigger for the second time. Not just a click but the whole wretched sound of a jam—the cartridge stuck in the breech: almost impossible, unheard of, with that weapon.

In rage, Herbie's huge arm came back and he flung the useless piece of metal towards the car which now had its engine running, the tyres screaming as it shook its tail and pulled away.

Herbie began to dash after it, his eyes blinded with fury. Breathless, and in a terrifying rage, he finally reached the corner, sick with the realisation that, what with the speed and the light, the surprise and action of it all, he could not have told anyone with accuracy either the make or colour of the car. Nor had he marked its licence plates.

Now it had disappeared into the traffic, and the big man stood, helpless, explosive with fury, his hands lifting and falling against his sides in a gesture of frustration.

Very slowly, with head bent, he turned and walked back towards the Thomas' house, his shadow incredibly immense across the road.

*   *   *

The hotel near Pangbourne was most comfortable and the staff seemed very considerate to the old man. They thought he was a sweet old boy, though the porter mentioned that he should really get those teeth seen to. Tipped well. Name of Henry Cocks. Said he would be staying a week or so. Doctor had recommended a rest. Peace and quiet. A taxi had brought him from Reading, though he had rung earlier to make a booking.

He had eaten well. Drunk some claret, and had a bottle of whisky sent up to his room. Whisky and hot milk.

Henry Cocks lay on the bed now, the door locked and a glass of neat whisky in his right hand. Two weeks here, he thought. Two weeks and then Henry Cocks would go, probably the soft route via Ireland.

It was no good brooding because there was only one place left to go—if he wanted to live. He would make up his mind about it later. All he really wanted now was sleep, but every time he closed his eyes he saw young George Thomas, walking with Schmitt, back towards the car on the moors. They were close together, and Braun a little to their left.

He had taken aim most carefully, around George's waist, because that was where he carried the grenades and explosives. It had been lucky. One shot. One shot had blown him and Schmitt to nothing. Braun took more; and Hilde ... well, he had to be certain about Hilde. But for her he would be in the comfort of his home now.

Angelle, he thought. Oh God, Angelle. He was going to be so lonely without her. At his age as well. Loneliness was the cross you bore when you were a stuffed man, a hollow man.

*　　　*　　　*

Herbie Kruger brooded. He had a vodka the size of the Empire State in front of him. It was late, and he thought everything was covered. The Director would be back later. He would write the report tomorrow.

George was away, and clever. He wondered if they would ever pick him up. He had grave doubts about that, but it would keep: someone else's problem now.

Before pouring the vodka he had called Angelle. She was sleeping the cousin had said, but then she had come on the line. Like so many people in shock she seemed almost too calm. Yes, she was all right. She would be fine. Yes, yes, it would be a good idea for them to have dinner sometime. She would probably be going back to stay with her cousin later that night, or first thing in the morning, but she would keep in touch. She supposed they had to have the policeman on guard at the gate. Herbie said it seemed a good idea.

*　　　*　　　*

In the house at Hampstead, Angelle Thomas put down the telephone and returned to packing her suitcase. It was the second call that evening. Downstairs, the cousin she had never seen before, sat quietly reading. She had kept his number ever since George gave it to her a year or so before. 'Just in case.'

The first telephone call had come through half-an-hour before Herbie.

'Are you okay?'
'Yes.'
'You forgive me?'
'I think so. I don't know.'
'You have rung the number?'
'Yes.'
'Do as he says. But only if you want to. Please. Please.' Then
the line had gone dead, the 'Please, Please' echoing in her head.
Of course she would go. He would need her. She would need
him. No matter what was in the past. She might even kill him
like she had told Herbie, in her rage.

*   *   *

Herbie went over to the tape machine and put on Mahler's
Kindertotenlieder—Songs on the Death of Children. As he slid
the tape into place he wondered if anybody had thought of putting a tap on the Thomas' telephone. Vernon-Smith hadn't mentioned it. Unlikely George would be foolish enough to call her.
No. Maybe, tomorrow, first thing, he'd see to it.

He pressed the Play button and went back to his drink. Chris-
tina Ludwig's voice filled the room, clear from the speakers:

> *Nun will die Sonn' so hell aufgehn—*
> The sun will rise as brightly now
> As though the night had brought no tragedy
> The tragedy is mine alone,
> The sun it shines for everyone.
> You must not let the night engulf you ...

Big Herbie Kruger took a long pull at his drink. He swallowed.
Then swallowed again and felt the lump come to his throat.